Moon Dweller

A Paranormal Gothic Romance

(

Kristina Schram

Mischief*Maker*Media

Published by Mischief Maker Media (USA)

First printing: September, 2015

Cover Design, Interior, and Technical Expertise: GorKee

Cover Photo: Young Woman in Graveyard from iStockPhoto

ISBN: 978-1-939397-23-2

Visit Kristina Schram on the World Wide Web at:
www.KristinaSchram.com

Acknowledgements

With every book, I feel that I grow as a writer and I have numerous people to thank for helping me along on that wondrous journey. I'd like to thank my beta readers: Elizabeth Schram, Gordon Unzen, Keegan Unzen, Dan Unzen, Ian More, and Heather Duane. As always, your input has been invaluable. I hope to always be able to make your job enjoyable.

I'd also like to thank my fans. I take into account any suggestions you make, knowing that you love reading as much as I do, and so I understand that you get what it takes to make a good book. I think this latest effort of mine reflects those suggestions. I hope you think so, too.

I can never write an acknowledgements page without saying an extra something about my kind and incredible husband, Dan. He supports me in everything I do, puts up with my creative dramas, and takes care of all my technical woes without complaint. Dan, you are my gothic hero...without all the drama. Thanks for being there...may we grow old together.

☾

To my mother, Elizabeth...
A fellow Moon Dweller

The young man on the divan lay still as a discarded doll. His pallor could be seen from across the room, as though a lamp were shining on his pale skin. He did not move, nor did he speak.

"I am most sorry for your loss, Sir. Madam." The doctor bowed to the grieving gentleman and his wife—she, sobbing, him, clasping his head in his shaking hands. There had been nothing the doctor could do to forestall the hand of death, but still he wished that he could have done something for the Sowles couple. He had heard that they had struggled to produce this one child, and there were no more after him. The doctor had been summoned to the manor house a few times, given the job when he was just starting out, and they had been nothing but respectful to him. More importantly, they had paid his bill on time. They were good people, so it was sad that for this young man, the pride of his parents, early death was an inevitable outcome.

"We will take care of matters from here," the master spoke, his heavily accented voice hoarse. He did not look up. "Thank you for your time, Doctor."

"I will see myself out," the doctor said quietly. "I am most sorry for your loss," he repeated, awkwardly. He had been through deaths before, too many, but none like this. It was best to go now and leave this sorrowful place behind. There was nothing more he could do.

☾

The doctor never returned to Chateau de Sowles. They didn't call for him, and as his practice was growing anyway, his time was not his own. The Sowles stayed at the chateau until their deaths five years later—alone, one within hours of the other.

According to the rumors, not long after their son's death, the couple dismissed their servants, stopped leaving the house, and ceased to live any normal sort of life. The doctor was not called in to write up their death certificates, a younger one being asked by the family solicitor instead. The doctor was a little worried that he hadn't been summoned, but as it turned out he'd been out on a call, and the young doctor who went so eagerly was never the same after his visit to the chateau. He had felt a malignant darkness in the house, or so he told anyone who asked, and would never forget what it had been like.

The doctor wondered what would happen to the Sowles' money, the couple having been quite wealthy. There were no other children to inherit, if one didn't listen to the stories hinting at a child hidden away, possibly a result of the master's infidelity, though the doctor didn't quite believe this of the gentleman he'd known. Then again, how does anyone know another's soul entirely? The stories also hinted at the reasons why no one saw this child—insanity, illegitimacy, deformities, whatever the townsfolk's imaginations could concoct. People delighted in inventing wild stories, especially after a few pints when the winter winds blew and the dark descended early.

The chateau sat empty for a few years—watched over by a reclusive caretaker living in the gatehouse—and the doctor considered buying it himself. He was becoming a wealthy man, his status rising, and the house was in a prime location—river-front property less than a mile from the ocean, privacy on either side, with a sweeping lawn and a beach scattered with massive gray boulders for his sons to climb. Built forty-some years prior, the chateau had been constructed to withstand the winds sweeping in off the Atlantic and the brutal New England winters. It was strangely beautiful, a giant Gothic beast designed to both protect and deter. Despite its forbidding façade, it inspired in the doctor romantic dreams of times long ago.

But there were rumors about the grand house—voices at night, groans and moans, sightings of a young man, sometimes a child, drifting past the windows. The usual foolishness, but still enough to give one pause. And so he dithered until it was too late. A young couple bought the house, and the doctor purchased a nice manor right in town, much closer to his patients and quite fitting for his elevated status. The couple stayed at the manor for only six months, then moved out. Over the years, this pattern repeated itself, continuing well after the doctor died.

After years of intermittent occupancy, the house stood empty for more than a decade. And then another decade passed, and another. Always, there was a caretaker, staying in the gatehouse, keeping the house from falling into ruin. But no one would live in that haunted place anymore; its chilling reputation was too strong.

Finally, well over a century after the Sowles couple died, the house was bought by a man as a present for his future wife. From whom he actually bought the house remains a mystery. No one had lived in Chateau de Sowles for fifty years, but perhaps there was a legacy, keeping the house from falling into the hands of the town or greedy land developers.

And so the chateau was opened up, spilling its darkness out onto the overgrown lawn and gardens, letting in fresh sea air and sunlight.

And stirring up the troubled spirit within...

Chapter One

☾

I was stuck. Literally. My cell phone, sitting on the coffee table I'd lovingly restored years ago, was ringing, and I couldn't reach it because a good amount of my nightgown was trapped in the couch. I wasn't sure how I'd managed that, but manage it I did. After a brief struggle, I jerked the skirt part out from under a cushion, just enough to allow me to move, and rolled toward my phone.

"Hello?"

"Vi, dear! It's Ry."

I mentally reminded myself to check who was calling before mindlessly answering. What if it had been Jason? Or my parents? I shuddered and propped myself up on one elbow.

"Hey, Ryan. What's up?"

"I'm guessing you're not," he bounced back.

"Ouch. Why am I friends with you again?"

"I'm right, aren't I?"

He was, damn him. "What do you want, Ryan?" Ryan and I had been friends since our college days. He was a designer, and very good, but he could be a bit of a snot sometimes. Like right now.

"Touchy, touchy! I'm calling to rescue you, so a little more gratitude and a little less attitude, please. You're going out with me tonight. I won't take no for an answer."

I crumpled up a greasy hamburger wrapper, one of many decorating the coffee table. "I can't go out tonight, Ryan. I'm not feeling my best. Besides, it's a Wednesday. Nobody goes out on a Wednesday."

"Where have you been? Hump Day is the new Friday."

"I must have missed that memo."

"Oh, Vi. Just this once?" The sound of tapping came through the line, which signaled that he was also on his computer, either playing a game on Facebook, posting a picture on Snapchat, or perusing Pinterest, or likely all three at once, in which case he'd probably tweet about it. Ryan was a social media whore.

"I'm broke, I'm not sleeping well, and I think I've gained ten pounds. Nothing fits but my yoga pants. I know restaurants only say, 'no shoes, no shirt, no service,' but I really think I'm going to need something to cover my lower half."

"Tell me again…" Ryan asked, his tone slightly disapproving. "Why do you own yoga pants? You don't do yoga."

I love Ryan, but he could be a real turd sometimes. "They're the trend right now." More importantly, yoga pants go with anything, which is good because I don't like making fashion decisions. I often end up looking like a cross between a bag lady and a hippie. Well, according to Ryan, anyway.

"They make you look like you're wearing an inner tube, darling. Ditch them."

"Well that's nice to know *now*, considering I've been wearing them for the last year and a half." I pulled my afghan around me and burrowed deeper into the soft cushions of my salvaged Chesterfield couch. It was my favorite piece of furniture, not just because I'd been spending the last month occupying it, getting up only to replace a DVD, order takeout, and go to the bathroom, but because it was the first piece of furniture I'd transformed from dump ready to practically brand new. It was like my first child.

Though I think it's starting to smell a little.

I sniffed my armpit. No, that was me.

"Which makes them *not* the trend," Ryan pointed out, thankfully oblivious to the inner workings of my mind, which had moved on to wishing bad things on him. "And don't you dare wear skinny jeans. Those make you look like a grape trying to squeeze through two straws."

"You're so sweet, Ryan. But I'm *really* not in the mood to socialize." I tried to sound stern.

"You?" He feigned shock. "Darling, you live for it!"

"No, *you* live for it, Ryan," I corrected. Which was true. Ryan actually liked being around other people. Having grown up with Beverly and Charles Alexander, my socialite parents, I knew how to handle people. But there's a big difference between liking people and handling them. "I go along because you hate going out alone."

He giggled. "Maybe. Do you think I'm the reason Jason ditched you?" Silence. "Oops. Was that too direct?"

"No, of course it wasn't, Ryan. You're as subtle as a Mac truck." I nibbled on a ragged fingernail, tearing it even worse. I briefly closed my eyes before opening them to assess the damage. "I'm just not ready to see other people right now."

"I hate Jason," he said vehemently, even though he had a crush on him. "You know I hate Jason."

"As do I," I sighed. "More than you know."

"It's been over a month, Vi. Can't you just try? For little ol' me?"

"Don't remind me." I groaned inwardly. A whole month of inactivity. I was being stupid, risking everything like this, but I couldn't seem to help myself. I'd been through break-ups before, but not like this. This was the worst. I was tempted to take up smoking and drinking heavily, but resisted only because I couldn't afford either right now.

"Have you even started looking for another job?"

"Maybe," I hedged. Which meant, *How could I when I'm still looking for the pieces of my broken heart?* Melodramatic, but true. I simply wasn't ready to face the world again. Hell, these days I couldn't even face leaving my apartment.

"That would be a no." A long, disappointed sigh blew through my cell phone's speaker, right into my ear. I could almost feel the wind from it. Ryan was very good at sighs and had several variations at his disposal. "Being a hermit isn't good for you, darling."

"You mean it isn't good for you."

"Okay, yes. But you know I'm completely self-centered, Vi. I have to be. I'm the youngest of eight, my parents are Catholic, I'm gay, and I live in Maine. It's survival."

I rubbed my forehead. "I know. I'm just being bitchy. I think I'm PMS-ing." I wasn't, but it sounded better than just being a bitch because I felt like it. "I have to go, Ryan. Call Anna. She likes gay bars. Says she feels like the only woman in the world when she's in one."

"Anna has to work late," he said grumpily. Working late for Anna was code for Anna going out on a date…again. Anna went out with a different guy at least twice a week. It was depressing being her friend. She scored more than, well, a sportsperson who scored a lot. Not that I wanted to score that often. I just wanted to find the love of my life, my forever soul mate. Was that so much to ask? "And I don't want to go to a gay bar this time," he went on, a pleading note in his voice. "I'm growing out my hair first before I hit *that* scene again. This is a wine and cheese tasting at the new winery—free. My favorite price. And bonus, it's right here in Camden!"

"Don't you know any other women who want to pretend to be your beard?"

"I'm going to *pretend* you did not just use that horrid word."

"Oh, Ryan. It's only offensive to you because you can't grow one!" I wasn't always this mean, but the world had sucker punched me one time too many and I was punching back. I was sick of falling in love, sick of being screwed over, sick of my crap life.

"Well, you probably could," Ryan sniped back. "A red, curly one to match that mess on your head." He *was* always this mean.

"Nice. I'm going to get off the phone so you can consult your little black book of back-ups."

"You know, you're right," he said, suddenly chipper. "You stay home and recover, hon. Indulge yourself."

"You thought of someone?"

"Clever girl. I just remembered the new hire at Daphne's. Her name's Georgie. Isn't that cute? She's young, and she doesn't wear yoga pants."

"Great," I replied grumpily. "Have fun with Georgie."

"I'll tell you all about it tomorrow!" He clicked off and I shut down my phone, not wanting to talk to anyone else, not that anyone especially wanted to talk to me, not lately anyway. I had my friends, but they were pretty flighty and self-focused, as we twenty-somethings can be. Although, in my case, the end of being a twenty-something was fast approaching—like a bullet train, actually. I was on the less appealing side of twenty-five, single, jobless, and now, overweight. In Victorian times, I would be considered a hopeless spinster. Thirty loomed as a dark cloud waiting to envelop me with wrinkles and depression and the beginning of the end of my time as a viable partner and begetter of offspring.

Oh, dear God, my life is a mess.

Sighing, I picked up a worn takeout menu, eyeing it dully. Ryan's phone call had made me feel worse than ever and I needed to eat something to make that bad feeling go away. Unfortunately, as soon as the food was gone, the depression would creep back, which is why eating never solves a person's problems. But it sure is fun to try.

At any rate, after Ryan's phone call I was starting to think maybe I was the type of person who's easily replaced—by Ryan, by Jason, and by my traitorous parents, who have taken Jason's side over mine. That's why I had to quit my job. That's why I'm broke and can't afford to pay rent.

Adding to my woes, my lease is coming to an end in a week and the landlord's been pestering me to be sure I'm out by then. The heartless brute already had someone else ready to move in. Though, to be fair, it wasn't the bastard's fault. I had told him I was moving. I'd *thought* I was going to be living with Jason by now. Stupid me.

So now I was stuck without a place to live. I was depressed. And fat. And old. And jobless. And soon I was going to have to live in my car, which was likely going to be taken from me when I stopped making payments, meager as they were, on it. Time to find myself a shopping cart. In one week, I'd officially be living under a bridge.

I was so pathetic. I was also hungry. Unfortunately, my credit card was close to being maxed out. I had student loans to pay off, too. In an attempt to establish my independence, I'd told my parents before starting college that I was determined to make it on my own, so I would pay my own way. But as they say, pride goeth before a fall, and I was about to take a big nosedive. My parents could certainly afford to pay off my loans and my credit card debt, find me a new apartment and pay for that, as well. They'd do it. But doing so would put me firmly back under their thumbs, where they'd work on me to fix things with Jason, and I wasn't having that. He'd dumped me, not the other way around. Besides, I truly did want to do it on my own.

Nick and Kat, my older brother and sister, were now the good children, even though neither had become an architect or designer like me. They did, however, work for Alexander Architecture & Design, the firm my parents owned, as an accountant and a lawyer, respectively. I come from a family where architecture, antiques, and good taste are essential, and while my siblings don't actually design anything, they keep us rich by doing our books and making sure we stayed up-to-date on all the latest legalities in the architectural world.

We are truly a family business. My mother is an interior designer, my father an architect. I do both—interior design and architecture. But not for them. Not anymore.

Not ever again.

Before the fiasco, Jason and I had both worked at AA&D. When he canceled our wedding, my father refused to fire him so I quit. I have no idea why Jason left me—he won't say. But the end result is that I'm not talking to my parents. Nick and Kat refuse to take sides, but we never really talked anyway, so not hearing from them is sad, but nothing new.

My siblings don't dislike me, but they don't particularly like me that much, either. You see, I'm the prodigy in the family, the heir apparent. Some might say spoiled, and they'd probably be right. But I want to change that.

Anyway, at age five, I accompanied my father on a site visit. He was consulting on a project that involved historic preservation—basically returning a house back to the way it looked when it was first built. Ripping up grubby old carpet, knocking down walls that don't belong, stripping awful wallpaper and replacing it with historically accurate prints and colors, tracking down proper period furniture. That sort of stuff.

Well, the first thing I did when I walked into this particular house was point at a wall in the foyer and say, "That's not supposed to be there." After a week of arguing between my father and the current architect on the job, someone finally dug up an old blueprint at the historical society, and it turns out I was right. After that, my career path was pretty well set in stone, which was fine with me. I love doing restoration and design work, and as a bonus, it made me a sort of favorite with my parents.

Throughout my childhood, I continued to tag along on jobs that my mother and father took. I particularly remember helping them on a project in Portland when I was ten, and later, when I was older I worked with them for a year at Victoria Mansion as part of my internship hours. They taught me everything they knew and I absorbed it all like a sponge.

I love old houses and making them come alive again, so you could say that I bring the dead back to life, that I'm a Resurrectionist. That's not my official job title, but I think it sounds much more interesting than my real one—Retromodeler & Preservationist Architect. Not to brag, but I'm pretty darn good at what I do, in my own muddled, abstracted way. I'm not the most organized person, but then, I've always had my parents to bail me out when needed, to set things up, get the licenses, find the jobs (though now, actually, jobs come to them). I didn't ever have to handle the tedious details involved in running a business. See? Spoiled.

Now that I'm on my own, it's all on me, and so far, I've failed miserably. Maybe because I haven't even tried to find a job. My situation is growing desperate—I needed to find work, move, and get my life back together, ASAP. I needed it for me, but a bigger part of me wanted to prove to my parents and Jason that I didn't need them. I was a big girl. An adult!

Snort. Yeah, right. I'm an adult who can't even untangle her own nightgown.

I set down the menu—I couldn't afford takeout anyway—and rolled off the couch, narrowly missing banging my head on the coffee table. After some wrestling, I finally managed to free myself from the cushions. Apparently my couch didn't want to let me go any more than I wanted to go.

The refrigerator, when I checked it, contained two items…a nearly empty carton of orange juice and a half-eaten yogurt. Half-eaten because I'd accidentally grabbed a peach-flavored one at the grocery store, which I don't like, meaning to get strawberry instead. Some schmuck had slipped a peach into the strawberry section, damn their eyes, and half out of it after a long day at work, I'd grabbed it. I was halfway through eating it before realizing I didn't like it. How's that for idiocy?

I closed the fridge and fell dramatically against the cool stainless steel door. Tears of self-pity welled up in my eyes. I was so hungry. Stupid Jason! This was all his fault. If only he'd gone ahead and married me like he'd promised instead of ending things a week before our wedding. If only my parents hadn't supported him instead of me, my father telling me I needed to "get my act together" and my mother going along with him because that's what she did.

I don't have an act. With me, what you see is what you get. So what the hell was he talking about? Sure I was a bit absentminded, forgetting to fill the order for the wedding cake. And yes, I'd neglected to put down a deposit at the hotel where we'd planned to hold our reception and we lost our reservation. Probably should have sent out those invitations, too.

But I ask you...why does the woman have to be the one to do all that crap? I was working. I was busy! Jason is the organized one, anyway. He should have done it. Besides, I'd have been happy with a small wedding in a tiny chapel out in the woods and a lovely, intimate dinner at our favorite restaurant.

But neither Jason nor my parents wanted that. My father had invited a long list of 'important' clients, people I barely knew, and was setting our wedding up to be the social event of the season. Of the *decade*. I can understand wanting to make contacts, but this was *my* wedding, not some opportunity to earn more money.

So I might inadvertently, unconsciously, have sabotaged things.

I sighed and nibbled on my broken fingernail. If only I was as good at bringing my old relationships back to life as I was at restoring houses, I'd be much happier.

I sat down at the table, a stack of mail in front of me, taunting me. I was sure there were numerous bills in the pile, demanding to be paid, and I didn't want to know about them.

"Stop looking at me!" I yelled at the pile. It didn't listen. "I mean it!" I swung my hand, knocking the letters off the table, and they scattered across the floor.

Oh, great. Just add to the chaos of your life, Vi. You're such a child! I slid off my chair to clean up the mess, feeling like a fool. Letting the tears spill down my cheeks, I promised myself I could watch my favorite movie,

Lost in Austen, once I picked everything up. Yes, I was treating myself like I would a little kid, but the method worked. Rewards do.

I set the last envelope back on the table and pulled myself up to loom over the stack of doom. On top sat a thin envelope, addressed to me: Vianne Alexander, Architect. Not to Alexander Architecture & Design. No. To me.

Weird.

With shaking fingers, I ripped open the envelope and pulled out a single sheet of paper. I began to read...

Dear Ms. Alexander,

My employer, Mr. Rachat, has seen your work and found your expertise adequate to serve his purposes. Please call the number at the bottom of this letter to set up an interview. If you meet his standards, he will hire you to complete a project already in progress. You will be compensated, of course, with a bonus if you are able to finish your work in a timely and responsible fashion.

Sincerely,

Ms. Brittany Clark
Personal Assistant

I re-read the letter several times to be sure I wasn't imagining things. A job offering! And it had landed right in my lap, like a dream come true. But how had this Mr. Rachat gotten hold of my home address? The letter should have gone to AA&D's offices, not to me directly.

Was this too good to be true? Did I care?

Not a fig. This was a way out of my current situation. The answer to my prayers. It was time I started acting like an adult, and here was the perfect way to do it. I raced over to my cell phone, turned it back on, and tapped in the number at the bottom of the letter, the fingers on my right hand crossed so tightly, they hurt.

It was only later that I realized that someone had to either quit or be fired to create this job opening.

But by then it was too late.

Chapter Two

☾

My first interview was a piece of cake. Ms. Clark, who, within moments of introducing herself, became Brittany, called me back early the next morning. Our conversation degenerated pretty quickly to discussing the finer points of Portsmouth, New Hampshire, the small port city where the job was to take place, and I enjoyed talking to her immensely. She was funny and gregarious and made me feel completely at ease. Whoever had hired her knew what he was doing, and that made me confident that this job would be a good one.

I was to call back that afternoon at one o'clock for a more formal interview with a Mr. Paddington, who was apparently an architect himself, but unable to take the job due to other obligations. I imagined that if I passed his test, I'd talk next to Mr. Rachat (pronounced ruh-SHOT, according to Brittany). But I was wrong about that.

Promptly at one, I made the call, and after a few rings Mr. Paddington answered. The sounds of construction work rang out behind him, and I imagined he was talking to me while on a job. After going over my credentials and making sure I was licensed to work in New Hampshire—Father always made sure everyone at AA&D had reciprocity licensure—Mr. Paddington asked when I could start.

The question threw me. "Um, when do I *start?*" This interview process was going really awesome. He wanted to hire me! But I didn't want to seem too eager and answer, *today*, so I played it cool, just like a proper adult. "When do you need me?"

"As soon as you can clear your schedule. Mr. Rachat leaves on his honeymoon soon and he and his wife will be gone for six months. When they return, he wants the house move-in ready."

I gulped. That was a tight schedule. "The letter said that this was a work in progress, so I gather all the proper permits have been attained."

"Naturally. You'll have to get the plans you make passed, but that should go quickly. Actually, work on the house has begun, but"—he cleared his throat—"the current architect had to leave."

"Oh, no!" I cooed sympathetically. "Was he sick?"

"Something like that," Mr. Paddington responded vaguely. I had a feeling something else was going on, but beggars can't be choosers, and frankly, I didn't want to hear anything bad about this job, so I let the question go and hoped for the best. "So what do you think, Ms. Alexander?" he asked. "Monday too soon?"

My, he was an eager beaver. But I suppose being left in the lurch and on a deadline made him a beggar, just like myself.

"Well, I just finished up a project," which was technically true, "and was looking for the right sort of work." I smiled a little to myself. Father had taught me to always sound as though I was choosy about the jobs I took on, like I was in such big demand that I could afford to be picky. "I gather this job involves historic preservation, since that is my specialty."

"It does. Mr. Rachat wants the house returned to the state it was, dating to approximately the early 1890s, give or take, although the house is about thirty-five years older than that. Some rooms were converted to bathrooms, which will remain as bathrooms, but are in dire need of updating to resemble that time period as much as possible. The kitchen needs work, too. Even though the house's electrical, plumbing, and heating systems have been modernized over the years, Mr. Rachat is fond of the Victorian era and wants the entire house's décor to match that time."

Oh, goody! I *loved* the Victorian era. There was something about that epoch, with all its dark, moody grandeur and repressed sensuality, that set my little heart aflutter. It was a challenge, too, since most clients think they want the house to be exactly how it was back then, unaware of how things could be a wee bit inconvenient, like having no electricity, and with indoor plumbing considered a luxury. But I was always able to convince them to incorporate a bit of modern sensibility to lighten things up and make life easier.

I hope the house has a conservatory, I thought distractedly. I love conservatories. "What sort of shape is the house in?" I asked, pulling myself back to the present. Translation: What exactly am I getting myself into, Mr. Paddington?

"It's actually in excellent shape, considering that no one has lived in it for decades. But there was a family, paid by a trust fund set up by the original owners, that took on the job of maintenance, passing it down from generation to generation. They kept the place up remarkably well, and actually still live on the property."

"Why did the house stand empty so long?"

"Oh," Mr. Paddington replied airily, "most people can't afford the upkeep on manor houses, and this one is quite grand. It's one of the finest examples of Gothic Revival architecture in New England, and it's made of New England granite, so it's solid. The house stands at 12,000 square feet on 19 acres."

I released a happy sigh. "A bit smaller than my summer cottage, then."

There was a moment's silence, then a brief chuckle. "Mine, too."

I liked this guy. Whoever this Mr. Rachat was, he hired good people. "When will I meet with Mr. Rachat?"

"Oh, that won't be necessary. I've worked with him before and he trusts my judgment." He sounded quite proud of this accomplishment.

"This does sound like an ideal job for me. Can we discuss compensation?" I asked, feeling ridiculously pleased with myself for sounding so professional.

"Of course!" Mr. Paddington named a figure that left me breathless for a moment. "Plus you'll be able to stay on the grounds in the guesthouse, free of charge, if that interests you. Mr. Rachat would prefer it, but it's not a requirement for taking the job."

I almost couldn't breathe for a few seconds. My life was going from hell to heaven in sixty seconds. "That would be nice," I said in as neutral a tone as I could manage. On the inside I was singing. Staying in a guesthouse on a 19-acre estate doing a job that I adore, in a fantastic little city, and getting paid very well to do it, sounded absolutely perfect. I knew just enough about Portsmouth, added to Brittany singing its praises, to know I would love staying there. Father often took consulting work at Strawbery Banke—a restored village in Portsmouth—and I had traveled with him numerous times to help out. I didn't remember much about the small, cozy city—we stuck to one area and I was pretty young when we went—but what I did recall was lovely. Brick sidewalks, numerous old houses, ancient graveyards, a pretty park with gardens and fountains, and the nearby Piscataqua River. This job was turning out to be just what I needed—a place to stay, money coming in, and located a few hours away from my parents and Jason. It was the perfect way to break free of their influence and become my own person. To finally grow up. This goal, I realized, was fast becoming very important to me.

"So you'll take the job?"

"I'll take it. But can I start Tuesday?"

"Tuesday would be great!" Mr. Paddington's enthusiasm was catching, even if it was fired mostly by relief. But then, who wouldn't be relieved? He'd just saved a project, derailed by the architect getting sick. *If he truly had gotten sick…*

There was that nagging, pessimistic voice again. Perhaps he or she had gotten a better offer elsewhere, I told myself heartily. Hard to imagine that, though, the pessimist persisted, after hearing what I'd be making. But then, I was young and used to getting only a cut of the profits. Maybe what I would be making at this job was a typical rate for going on my own.

Either way, I didn't care. I had a job, a place to stay, and motivation to start showering again.

Vi Alexander was back in business!

☾

Ryan, when I called him—which was as soon as I hung up with Mr. Paddington—was not happy for me. "You're leaving me on my own in Camden?" he cried, his voice alarmed.

"You make it sound like I'm abandoning you, but the job's only for six months. Besides, you're the one who told me I needed to get a life."

"But not without me," he moaned piteously.

"It's May, Ryan. The tourist season is about to start, bringing lots of fresh meat to Camden. You love summer in Camden. And what about Georgie? She can keep you company."

"She's not as fun as I thought she would be," he replied grumpily, meaning Georgie had figured out Ryan was not into her, or her sex, and never would be. Why she couldn't pick up on that just talking to him was beyond me. With his dramatic flair for fashion, slim figure, and extravagant gestures, Ryan gave whole new meaning to the term flamboyant. It's part of why I liked him. I liked that he was who he was and didn't care what the haters said. I also secretly envied his ability to always be himself. It was something I had to work on, since I tended to just do what made people happy.

"Well, I'm not doing this to hurt you."

Ryan sighed. "I know, darling. I'm just feeling bitchy because you're off on a great adventure and I'm stuck here in boring old Podunk, Maine, doing the same thing day after day, year after year."

"Come visit me, then. Guesthouses at these estates are usually pretty spacious—that's where I'll be staying. I'm sure there'll be an extra room for you. You can come weekends and we can hang out in Portsmouth."

I could almost hear him perking up. "That does sound fun."

"Good. So now are you happy for me?"

"Of course I am. I always was, darling, even though this does sound too good to be true…"

"It does, doesn't it?" I agreed happily. "But it's only for six months. Even if there are huge problems, it will be great experience for me. I need to break out on my own."

"What's the place called?"

I paused. "Actually, I have no idea. So it will all be new to me," I said perkily, though I wasn't sure if that was a good thing. I reminded myself to call Mr. Paddington and ask. Then I could google the place to my heart's content.

There was a skeptical snort. "Have you told Charles and Beverly yet?" Their names came out in a hushed, reverent tone. Ryan had a crush on my whole family, not just Jason, and at times it could be very trying.

"No, and I don't plan to. They've made their choice—keeping Jason on even though he dumped me—and now they have to live with it. And you can't say a word to them about this job, either. Not a word!" I knew this was asking a lot of Ryan. It was very easy to get information out of him; he was like a three-year-old that way.

"What if they ask me about where you went?" He sounded panicky.

"You change the subject. You're very good at that."

"I am," he gloated, and I repressed a sigh.

"Better yet, just avoid them." I glanced at the clock on my microwave. "I've gotta go. I have to pack and move out, all in four and a half days…" I let the sentence hang, waiting for his offer of help, which I knew wouldn't be coming. Ryan despised manual labor, though he had a thing for manual laborers, often joking about his pretend boyfriend, Mañuel La Bor.

"Well, good luck with that sweetie. Let me know when I can come visit!"

His phone clicked off before I even had a chance to say goodbye. The rat bastard. I glanced around at my messy apartment, feeling my shoulders sag. This was not going to be pretty.

☾

I'm what you would call a buxom gal. If I go above a certain weight, I start to resemble a fertility goddess, which means all my clothes are a bit on the tight side right now. Crap. It was a good thing I didn't have any food in the house. *You'd better get yourself back into shape, Vianne Marie*, I told myself sternly, *and no time like the present.* I started with a marathon cleaning session that went until midnight on Friday, during which I ate sparingly, having only a couple hundred dollars left in my checking account that I'd need to cover too many other expenses. I experienced a few dizzy spells, which I knew were bad for me, but I was on a deadline and kept at it. I didn't want to start my new job looking like I'd spent the last month eating and watching movies, which I had.

The weekend flew by as I packed up all my belongings, ruthlessly re-cycling or trashing as much as possible. Sunday I tracked down a 24/7 storage unit and guilted my next-door neighbor into helping me move the big pieces of furniture. After that, I hauled boxes until I could barely walk. Despite what my parents and Jason might think, I could get my act together. I just needed the right incentive.

And getting married isn't incentive enough?

I shoved that thought out of my mind as I sat that night in a hot bubble bath, with far too many bubbles, and soaked my aching mus-cles. The thought, like annoying thoughts do, promptly returned. Why hadn't I come up with the energy and time to organize my own wed-ding? It wasn't that I didn't want to marry Jason, I reasoned, I just didn't like my parents using our wedding as a way to move up in the world. They were at the top of their field anyway. Why did they need this? And why did Jason let them get away with it? It was enough to make a grown woman cry foul.

After dragging my pruney behind out of the bath, I perused the packet Brittany had sent Overnight Express, providing directions, a key to the guesthouse, and a list of nearby amenities. She would stock the fridge, she said, so there was no need to shop before I came. I si-lently blessed her. On Tuesday morning at eight, I was to meet Mr. Paddington to go over all the blueprints, plans, what had been done, what needed to be done, and do a house tour. I couldn't wait.

Tomorrow I would pack my car with all the stuff I was bringing with me, place my key in an envelope to be mailed to my landlord, and head off on my new adventure. I was so excited I was shaking. Or was that food deprivation? I promised myself that as soon as I lost another couple pounds, I would start eating sensibly again. Well, I would start eating again. I never did eat very sensibly.

I slipped the packet into my travel bag and grabbed my phone, which promptly rang in my hand. My heart thudded. Please don't be Mr. Paddington calling to tell me the job was off. If it was, I was screwed. When he'd told me on the phone that I could sign the contract when I saw him on Tuesday, I'd thought it was a good idea and one less thing to have to deal with before I left. And I'd meant to call him and get more information on the project, maybe do a quick Internet search, but had run out of time. Now I could kick myself. These were the types of mistakes I made—trusting people too much and forgetting to do important tasks. This was not how an adult would act. I had to do better.

I looked at the screen and my anxiety about Mr. Paddington disappeared, to be replaced by a new one. A picture of Jason in his blue swim trunks, standing on the beach, had popped up on the screen—gorgeous, perfect Jason, a virtual Viking god with his tall good looks, blond hair, and piercing blue eyes. He was so very tempting, and I wasn't the only one to think so. He was very persuasive, too, in a polite but firm way, and could get me to see his way pretty much most of the time. He was the type of person who took charge and made things happen, which is part of why I liked him so much. And did I mention that he was gorgeous?

Oh, yes.

I stared at his photo for a moment, then, with a shaking finger, hit the icon sending the call to voice mail. Jason didn't do text messages, claiming his fingers were too big to type on a phone. He was probably right, but texts really were so much easier and convenient, not to mention impossible to overhear. I think he just prefers calling because people have told him he has a beautiful voice, which he does, damn him.

No way was I going to let him ruin this job for me...because he could. If he were calling to apologize, I would likely go back to him, follow through on the wedding, sacrifice my principles. I was weak, so very weak, especially when it came to him. But not this time. This time I was taking charge.

But first I would listen to his voice mail...

I waited a minute for him to finish speaking, then listened to his message: "Vianne, it's Jason. Listen, we need to talk. I would've called earlier, but decided to give you some space. I know you're angry with me for canceling the wedding, but as you might have figured out by now, I did it for us. If we can't work as a team, how can we get married? But this isn't the end for us. I know this. I just need to see you hold up your end. Can you do that for me, hon? Just prove that you want this as much as I do, that's all I'm asking. So let's talk and work this out. All right?"

I hesitated. Was that an apology? Or even an explanation? I played the message twice more, desperate for a glass of wine to soothe my frazzled nerves. It didn't sound like either one, I finally decided, but I'd have to think more about it. In the meantime, I had an early start in the morning and needed to get some sleep. I had committed to this job and would not back out of it. I would show Jason and my parents that I wasn't a total screw-up.

For now it wouldn't hurt Jason to stew a little. He'd waited over a month to check in on me. I could have died during that time, been out on the street or drinking too much, and he wouldn't have known a thing. He could wait a little longer to hear back from me. Once I got settled in at my new job I'd call him.

Now to force myself to stick to that. To aid in my resolution, I turned off my phone and shoved it in my purse.

And that's why I missed it—the call from Mr. Paddington telling me not to come.

Chapter Three

☾

The trip to Portsmouth from Camden isn't long, about two and a half hours, and I made good time even though I was exhausted. I just couldn't sleep last night; I was simply too excited to start my new life. I was also nervous as hell and had caught myself chewing on my fingernails on three separate occasions while driving. Anyone starting a new job would be anxious, but this was the first time I'd be on my own at a site—one I was just now realizing I probably should have checked out in person before saying yes. I'd be completely alone, without one of my parents or a professor guiding me, or at the other end of the phone in case I found myself stuck. I would be in *charge*, the head honcho, the boss. I wasn't sure I was ready for that sort of responsibility and the thought made me want to throw up the green tea and last slice of stale bread I'd scarfed down before leaving.

It didn't help that I was starving. Normally I'd be making a Dunkin' Donuts run for my typical morning repast of a bagel with garlic and chives cream cheese and a medium mochachino. But I was close to the weight I'd been at before my whole wedding fiasco; I didn't want to ruin my progress. I knew I was thinking anorexic thoughts—my weight's the only thing I can control right now—but that didn't worry me too much since I also knew it wouldn't last. I liked eating way too much. In fact, just thinking about eating made me drool. I wiped at my mouth impatiently. I had to concentrate during this next part. Portsmouth was a typical New England town, full of one-ways and odd angles and confusing streets. I didn't want to get lost. I had a GPS—forced on me by Anna after I got us lost three different times in one day—but we all know GPS devices can be sadistic little creatures that delight in ordering you to turn when there isn't a road to turn onto.

But anyway, I had to keep myself on track, mentally and physically. One bad project can ruin an architect's career and I couldn't afford that, for numerous reasons, number one being that I loved my job and didn't want to do anything else. I had to handle this project carefully, and knowing that the previous architect had left for reasons unknown (still wasn't quite buying the 'sick' excuse) didn't help.

I crossed the blue-green Piscataqua River Bridge, which connects Maine to New Hampshire. I was getting close! My dashboard Jesus, a gag gift from Ryan as a means to help protect me and everyone around me as I drove, did a bouncing dance I call, 'Getting Jiggy with Jesus.'

You might laugh, or think I'm being irreverent, but I'm totally not. Let me tell you, Jesus has saved me countless times, though admittedly, mainly from speeding tickets. I'm not an advocate of speeding, but sometimes a song comes on and in my enthusiasm, my foot starts to press down on the gas. I once got stopped while listening to the lyrics, "Ain't nothin' gonna break my stride." That song basically *dares* you to speed up. But anyway, the officer let me go, saying he couldn't give me a ticket with Jesus right there looking at him.

"Welcome – Bienvenue" a sign read. New Hampshire welcomed me. I smiled. It was a good sign. No pun intended. Okay, maybe a little.

I took my exit, with only a slight screeching protest from my old car, and headed into downtown Portsmouth. I passed a grounded submarine, the USS Albacore, and on my left was a scrap iron business, followed by a cruise line that carried passengers out to the Isle of Shoals. I reminded myself to take a cruise before I left Portsmouth. My reason was kind of morbid, but I wanted to see the island where there'd been two ax murders, a la Lizzie Borden.

I headed past a beautiful old Georgian mansion called the Moffatt-Ladd House and had to make myself look away so I wouldn't sideswipe a parked car. After a stop sign, I passed a restaurant aptly named Fat Belly's, then drove down a narrow one-way street, nearly clocking a pedestrian trying to sneak across where there was no crosswalk. I shook my fist at him. Don't people realize there are drivers like me out there?

Finally I re-joined the traffic at a strange sort of three-way intersection, ending up in the middle lane. "Turn left here," my GPS told me in a toneless voice. There was no left *here*, not unless I wanted to smash into a building, not to mention another car one lane over. Yes, a left turn was fast approaching, however it was not the street I wanted. Crap. I was already lost. I wanted 1A, so why was I on Islington Street, still going one-way, with no 1A in sight?

As I neared the traffic light, I sped up, then swung over into the left lane, cutting off a Jeep full of teens. The driver honked in annoyance, and I flipped her a "Sorry!" wave before making my turn, hands shaking and sweat beading.

A little farther down I spotted the 1A sign posted on a telephone pole, indicating a left turn was necessary. Aha! This is what I wanted. I made my turn, cutting off another car as I went. Flipping another "Sorry!" wave I headed down 1A at a leisurely pace, the better to enjoy viewing the beautiful old buildings—one of which was a spectacular stone church—along with a bounty of flowering trees, stately old maples and oaks, and numerous brightly-colored window boxes. Spring was here and everything was transforming at an amazing speed, leaves unfurling, flowers budding, plants doubling in size overnight. The whole world was going through a rebirth, and I felt the same way. A new Vianne Alexander was about to take her place in the world! It was a wonderful feeling.

Relaxing my grip on the steering wheel, I turned up my music player as Kate Bush's *Wuthering Heights* came on, and I sang along. "Too long I roam in the night. I'm coming back to his side, to put it right. I'm coming home to Wuthering, Wuthering, Wuthering Heights..." The words were so fitting, it seemed like yet another good omen.

Still singing, I drove past a massive cemetery on my left—South Cemetery, if I remembered correctly from my map. Bordered by a solid stone wall, I followed the graveyard for quite some time, driving slowly so I could study all the statuary, mausoleums, and gravestones. The cemetery was quite large and rather impressive. I would have to return some time and do a walk-through. I grinned. There was so much to see and do here!

Eventually I made another left, leaving behind a line of impatient drivers, and my heart started thudding as I drove down a long, tree-lined drive, shadowy and cool, with a low, roughly made stone wall keeping pace with me. This would be my first introduction to the house I would be working on for the next six months and I wanted to savor the moment. I lowered the window and stuck my head out like a dog, enjoying the sensation of wind on my face as I looked around. Trees of all kinds stretched back as far as I could see, and in amongst them lurked a number of large boulders, likely granite. This was the Granite State, after all.

I was surprised at the lack of visible human occupation. Portsmouth is an old city, with limited space, so property is expensive. How was it that so much land could remain untouched? Mr. Rachat must be very rich. I grinned happily. Money wasn't hugely important to me, but I liked what it could get done—fabulous renovations for less hassle.

I rounded a corner and the whole landscape opened up, revealing an intricate wrought-iron gate and sturdy stone walls, much higher and more neatly constructed than the one that had accompanied me for the last mile of my drive. The house was hidden behind the walls, but off to the right I could see the Piscataqua River in the distance, its waters blue and green and dotted with golden flecks of reflected sunlight. There were several islands in the middle of the river, serving as an effective buffer from the worst of the Atlantic winds that were sure to blow in off the ocean. It was a beautiful setting, obviously chosen by an aesthete, and I couldn't wait to see the house and grounds.

I was surprised that the gate was shut, but thankfully, not latched. I managed to open the heavy thing myself, though the effort left me a little winded. Screw the diet. I needed to eat, and soon. I'd been stupid to go without for so long. A person simply cannot function without proper food. I promised myself that as soon as I got into the guest-house, I would make myself a great big lunch. If I wanted to lose weight, I'd just have to start moving a little more.

Feeling heartened and mature, I climbed back in the car and drove onto the grounds, first passing a quaint, small stone building sur-rounded by red and pink roses—the gatekeeper's house. As I drove further in, I was even more thrilled by what I saw. The landscaping was amazing, if a bit dark, and it was obvious that someone was kept busy maintaining it in all its glory. Massive old trees, stately oak, deli-cate maple, and pale birch, low stone walls and pathways, giant urns and flowers, everywhere flowers, filled the spacious yard. Paths led off from the gravel drive, disappearing amongst the plants and shrubs, the forsythia and lilac, reminding me of a maze. I couldn't wait to explore.

After a couple hundred yards, the way opened up, revealing a stretch of bright green lawn, and then suddenly, there was the house. Oh, the house! Really, though, I should call it a mansion. Mr. Paddington had said the building was 12,000 square feet and I'd worked in houses that size and even bigger, but still, this house seemed more magnificent in its grandiosity than any I'd ever seen.

I'd been worried that the wall would cut off the view of the river, but my worries dissipated as I drove along. The ground sloped downward, keeping the house high, while the wall facing the river was lower down the hill. Because of this, the view would remain magnificent and unim-peded.

The closer I grew to the mansion, the more immense and dominating it seemed. A regular Addams family habitat, it had three main stories and a tower that rose to four. There was a mansard roof, a type I espe-cially like since they not only look imposing, but also make the most of the upper story living space. All along the roof, chimneys of various heights and sizes reached for the sky. Granite balconies, where one might sit with a glass of Merlot or a cup of tea and survey one's king-dom, were plentiful. Even the *porte cochere,* the carriage porch where you would park your carriage or car to avoid getting wet in a rainstorm, had a balcony. A covered porch surrounded about a third of the house, but was empty of furniture.

A mermaid weather vane spun crazily in the brisk, but refreshing, breeze coming off the river. Dormer windows (the cute ones that have their own little roofs) stuck their necks out on all four levels. I saw a shadow cross the tower's top window, as though someone was passing by, and I shaded my eyes for a better look. Perhaps it was a construction worker, innocently going about his or her business. Or maybe it was just a cloud passing over the sun? Either way, a delicious shiver shook my frame. This was just the sort of house that invited mystery.

Nearing the manor, I parked my car and practically fell out, feeling slightly woozy from not eating, the long drive, and the splendor of my surroundings. I leaned against the car and took in everything once more, my eyes sweeping the grounds. I didn't see the guesthouse and figured I should probably look for it on foot. On a whim, I headed south. When I passed around the far side of the building, I spotted the guesthouse a short distance away, off to the right and cozying up to the stone wall. It was a charming cottage, painted white, with English ivy crawling up its sides, and probably around 1300 square feet. It would be more than adequate for my needs, with enough room to put Ryan up for the weekend. I loved it immediately.

Wanting to explore, I ran back to my car and grabbed the key Brittany had sent me and put it in my pocket. Then I scurried back around the house and down the slight slope to the cottage. The smell of ocean brine swept toward me on the breeze and I inhaled deeply, swayed a little, and paused to let my head settle. Once it stopped spinning, I marched toward the cottage, feeling more excited and hungry with each step. I'd eat something first, then explore the house, then start unpacking. Oh, it all sounded so lovely, and I trembled in anticipation as I stuck my key into the keyhole.

New beginnings, here I come!

"What are you doing?" came a stern voice from behind me. I spun around and black spots filled my vision. I blinked a few times to send them away and when I could see clearly again, I noticed a man striding toward me, looking like some sort of warrior come to oust the invading foreigner. "And how did you get past the gate?"

I resisted the urge to raise my hands in the air. He might look intimidating, his face scrunched up in a threatening scowl, his hands in fists, but I had every right to be here. I drew myself up and pretended I was my father. "I'm here for the job," I said in my haughtiest voice, "and the gate was unlatched, so I simply pushed it open."

He stopped suddenly, about five feet from me, and I was able to take in more of him. He wore a white t-shirt spotted with dirt and paint and khaki painter's pants with a similar pattern of colorful spots. Scuffed brown leather work boots and a grubby Red Sox cap completed his outfit. He must be a construction worker. "You aren't supposed to be here."

"But I'm the new architect." I placed my hands on my hips, pretending to be more in control than I was. Architects are often a very confident species, and at times the confidence borders on arrogance—I need look no further than my father and Jason to know that—and right about now I needed to channel some of that arrogance. "And I don't exactly appreciate being interrogated by the…well, whatever it is you do here. Construction?" I asked loftily, even though I felt like a fraud. "Groundskeeping?"

He stared at me and I noticed he had bluish-green eyes, very intense, almost piercing, and he was using them to their fullest intimidating extent. "Groundskeeping," he replied after a moment's hesitation.

"Exactly!" I cried triumphantly. "So you don't have any authority to tell me to leave!"

"I have every authority," he said brusquely. "I'm the groundskeeper and gatekeeper and whatever else I need to be while Mr. Rachat is gone. I'm in charge of all of Chateau de Sowles until he returns."

Chateau de Sowles…so that was the name of this place. "But Mr. Paddington hired me to do this job!" I cried in protest. "He and I are meeting tomorrow to discuss everything and—" I'd nearly added, "to sign the contract," but decided to keep that little nugget to myself. No need for Mr. Groundskeeper to have a weapon to use against me. "Is he available?"

Groundskeeper guy eyed me warily. "No."

"Well, then I'll call him."

"Didn't Paddington tell you?"

My heart started thudding. This didn't sound good. "Tell me what?" I pushed out, feeling suddenly faint…or more faint.

"That the job has been put on hold."

"How long?" I whispered, feeling as though my entire world was about to come crashing in on me.

"Indefinitely."

"Oh!" I gasped. "And how long is that?"

He looked at me as though I wasn't quite all there. "Possibly forever."

It suddenly occurred to me that for a place in the midst of construction, it was awfully quiet. "But why?" I cried. "I can do this job! And this place"—I swept my arm across the landscape—"deserves the very best!"

"I'm sure you can do the job, Miss, but your services are no longer required. So please, just get back in your car and return home." He looked on the verge of losing his patience with me, but I didn't care.

"Home?" I gave a mirthless laugh. "That's just it. I don't have anywhere to go. I had to move because, well, something happened, and my stuff is all in storage now." Luckily I stopped before telling the man I was broke, too. Remembering this, I started gasping a little as a feeling of panic rose up inside me, quick as the urge to vomit. If this was part of being an adult, I didn't like it.

If I'd eaten something, I might have been able to handle the news slightly better, but right now I could only see imminent disaster: myself living under a bridge in a cardboard box, a flea-ridden stray cat for a companion, and a rusted, wobbly shopping cart for my few belongings. I would change my name to Annie and I'd feed the squirrels and… I shook my head. I was starting to lose it.

"If you're good," he said firmly, taking my arm and steering me toward my car, "you'll find another job and a place to live. In the meantime, get a hotel room. There are plenty in Portsmouth."

"But I can't pay for a hotel—" I bit my tongue and stumbled along behind him, cursing myself for letting that part slip out.

"Just call your daddy," he said. "I'm sure he'll take care of everything for you."

"I can't just call him," I snapped. "I'm not speaking to him. Not after—" I shut my mouth. I'd already told him too much.

We crested the hill and he stopped suddenly. I crashed into him and he swiftly stepped away as though I were on fire. "That's really your car?"

The car he was referring to was an old beater, the best I could afford after paying my student loans and for rent and food and all that extra stuff, like electricity. My parents hated it, Ryan hated it, and Jason despised it. He never said so, but I could see it in his eyes whenever he looked at the Beast—as I lovingly called my junker. To him, it was like a giant booger marring his freshly painted wall. Jason liked his life to be pristine and immaculate, which made me wonder what he saw in me, the very opposite.

"Yes, it is," I panted, feeling nauseous from lack of food. "He's not handsome, but he's solid, if a bit temperamental. We go way back." I glanced at my car fondly, recalling all the scrapes we'd gotten ourselves into—literally—including nearly taking out one of those oversized blue mailboxes on a street corner, along with the postman emptying mail from it.

"To the nineteen seventies?" he questioned sardonically.

I yanked my arm from his grasp. It wasn't easy. His grip was like a vice, its strength likely from all the manual labor he had to do to keep this place up. "Don't mock the Beast. He doesn't like it." I straightened up and pulled down my shirt, which had ridden up during my forced march up the hill. "I'm not leaving until I can speak to Mr. Paddington. There must be some mistake."

I pulled out my cell phone and tried to turn it on. It didn't comply. Damn. I'd forgotten to charge it last night and it had died during the drive. Everything was going wrong. I bit my lip to stop the tears of self-pity threatening to overtake me. Behaving like a child wouldn't help.

"I'll call him," he offered.

"Thank you," I replied stiffly.

I watched him as he found the number, then placed the phone to his ear. This close, I could see he had sideburns, which ended where his jawline began. His hair was a reddish color, a bit like mine, but lighter. A few freckles spotted his face and arms, but unlike me, his skin was nicely tanned instead of richly pink, like mine gets in the sun. I was only slightly below average height yet could stand in his shadow, so he must be a good six inches taller than me, all of it housed in a wiry frame, muscled and lean. When he wasn't scowling, he was actually somewhat nice looking, if you like the officious type.

"Paddington? Corin, here. Listen, we've got a problem." He spoke without looking at me, his gaze settling on something off in the distance. "That architect you hired? She's here. I thought you said you called her and told her the job was off." He listened. "You left her several messages?" He looked at me and I shrugged. I hadn't gotten any, but then my phone had died. "Well, she obviously didn't get them."

"Let me talk to him," I mouthed, miming to him to give me the phone.

He turned his back on me. "Uh, huh. Yes. I see. Well, you know what Mr. Rachat wanted to do. He won't change his mind." Silence. "Yes, I'll tell her."

My pounding heart grew so loud, I could hear it in my head. I swallowed hard and walked around to face Groundskeeper guy, a.k.a. Corin. "Let me talk to him," I begged, holding my hand out for the phone. "I'll change his mind. I have to. I've already—" No, no, no.

Hunger and desperation were making me sound pitiful and needy and I didn't want that. Absolutely not.

"Just a moment, Paddington." Corin turned his attention in my direction, his sea-like eyes focusing completely on me. I found his forceful gaze rather disconcerting, but tried to remain calm. "You have to leave. I'm sorry, but it's not possible for you to stay here." For a moment I couldn't breathe. My head spun once, twice, and I swayed. He grabbed my arm. "Are you all right?"

I looked up into his face, so serious and intense, and suddenly it became Jason's, and he looked so disappointed in me. Then, for some bizarre reason, I was back at the precise moment he'd told me our wedding was off, and I was reliving it, as I had in my dreams for over a month now.

"Please don't, Jason," I half-sobbed, my voice shaking. "Don't cancel the wedding. I'll be better. I'll do what you say, and I won't screw up again! I promise…"

And then I fainted.

Chapter Four

☾

I awoke to a gentle clattering noise and cautiously opened one eye, then the other, to discover I was lying on a floral-patterned couch that faced a stone fireplace, with a crocheted throw flung over me. Two overstuffed armchairs flanked the couch and a coffee table sat in front of it. It was a cozy space, perfect for drinking hot chocolate and snuggling up with a good book.

The noise was coming from behind me and I struggled to sit up, trying to remember what had happened. Then the memory returned. I was out of a job and homeless, and I had fainted like an idiot. When I was sitting fully upright, I looked back to see the kitchen, and Corin, working at the breakfast bar.

"When's the last time you ate?" he asked, without looking up.

"I had a piece of bread for breakfast," I replied indignantly.

"You don't look like the sort who can live on a piece of bread for breakfast."

"I'm not! But I've, well, I'd gained a few pounds, and I wanted to lose it, so I could take this job looking my best." His pained wince told me once again I'd said too much, and I wished, not for the first time, that there was a pill to treat diarrhea of the mouth. "I was going to eat as soon as I got into the cottage. I realized I was being stupid," I defended myself before he could start lecturing me—he seemed the lecturing type. "But then you came, and well, I just sort of blacked out for a bit. It was only for a bit, right?"

I remembered how far it was from the car to the cottage—a good two hundred yards—and flushed a crimson pink. "And you had to carry me all that distance…"

"Good thing I've been working out," he replied dryly.

Was that an insult? I think it had been. "Oh, well. Yes. Good thing."

"Do you like salad dressing on your sandwich?"

"Oh, yes!" I cried, suddenly starving. "Glop it on. The more, the better. Well, within reason. I mean, no one wants it inches thick. That would be gross." I clamped my mouth shut. I was babbling. But I was *so* hungry.

He looked up at me, his expression bland. "Good. Because I put some on."

"Thank you," I said demurely, trying to regain some dignity.

He came around the island, holding a plate and a glass of milk before him. He saw me eyeing the milk with a frown. "You're drinking this."

"I'd prefer a diet coke."

"You'll drink the milk."

"What if I have a dairy allergy?" I protested.

"You would've mentioned it when I asked about the salad dressing. And you would've told me to leave off the cheese."

My fists clenched. Oooh! He was just so logical. I took the plate from him with as much solemnity as I could dredge up, knowing full well that my red curls were likely springing from my head like mad snakes, and that my eyes were wide with irritation. "You needn't have troubled yourself," I said in my best Victorian drawl.

He remained standing, looming over me. "And have you pass out again? I don't think so."

"I wasn't going to pass out again! It's just…well, I was in shock and I hadn't eaten and…" I trailed off and took a big bite out of the sandwich he'd made, then I closed my eyes and chewed. It tasted so delicious. Turkey and Swiss cheese, lettuce and tomato, on rye bread, with just the right amount of mayo. I kept my eyes shut for three more bites, then opened them to drink the milk. I wasn't a big fan of milk straight up, preferring it mixed heavily with chocolate or on cereal, but I was so hungry that it tasted wonderful. I drained half the glass.

"Better?" he inquired, still standing.

"I'd be better if you didn't stand there looming like that. You look like Frankenstein."

His brow furrowed. "It wasn't my intention to loom…or look like Frankenstein."

I sighed. "I am better, but you need to either sit down, or go away. It's an awful long way to look up."

He nodded brusquely, then sat down in a chair as far away from me as he could get. I tried to recall if I'd showered today. I think I had. Yes, I had! I remembered packing my shampoo, conditioner, razor, and the like. So it wasn't body odor that was driving him away. No, it was simply me.

I took another bite of sandwich and glanced around the room. Large windows looked out over the lawn and I could see sunlight as it flashed on the river flowing in the distance. The room itself was dark, but tastefully furnished with antiques and cozy furniture. Living here would be no hardship.

When I finished my meal, I delicately patted my lips with the linen napkin he'd provided and suppressed the burp building up in my chest.

My stomach was struggling to process this unexpected windfall, and apparently wanted to let me know, by embarrassing me in front of others, that I'd not been very nice depriving it.

"That was lovely," I said politely, laying the napkin across the speckled plate and setting it and my glass on the coffee table. I spent a few moments picking stray crumbs off the couch and myself.

"Do you need the name of a hotel?" Corin asked.

I started. I'd forgotten he was going to kick me out. In fact, I'd already been mentally rearranging furniture. "Oh, no. I'll just…" I'd been about to say, *sleep in my car*, but decided there was no need to add to my humiliation.

"You'll just…?"

"Um, I don't know. I, um, guess I'll…" I trailed off again.

"Why don't you just return home, Miss Alexander?"

I turned to stare at him. "You know my name?"

"Of course," he replied.

"My lease on my apartment ran out," I said vaguely, "so I'm between places at the moment."

His eyes narrowed. "I'm sure your parents will take you in until you get another apartment."

"Listen, um—" I'd forgotten his name.

"Corin," he said.

"Right. Corin. What I wanted to say…" I clasped my hands together. "I know it's up to Mr. Rachat, but could you please talk to him? By the time he's ready to continue the renovation, I'll undoubtedly be working elsewhere, and he'll miss out on my vast knowledge and expertise." That last part was a gamble, but hopefully he'd go for it.

One dark, reddish-brown eyebrow rose up. The rat actually looked amused. "I'm afraid we're going to have to take that risk."

"But I was offered the job!"

"And there was no contract. I'm sorry, Miss Alexander—"

"It's Vi."

"Yes, Vi." His fingers rubbed at a sideburn. "You see, something unforeseeable has happened"—his voice was heavy and dark as he said this and I wondered what this unforeseeable event had been—"and Mr. Rachat is not in a place to go ahead on this project."

"I'm sorry about that. I really am. But I've left everything—" Again, too much information, and too pathetic sounding, as well. I clamped my mouth shut. No more. I would not have him pitying me. He stared at me for several seconds and I started to wriggle under his scrutiny.

What was he thinking? What were those shrewd eyes seeing in me? Too much, likely.

Finally, he said, "I'm putting myself out on a limb here, but...well, you can stay the night. However, you must leave first thing in the morning."

Stay the night? Why, that was perfect! It would give me the time I needed to rally my defenses, gather my wits, and convince Mr. Paddington to convince Mr. Rachat that if I didn't do this job now, he would kick himself. I suppressed the urge to grin like a fool.

"I appreciate it." There. Nice and simple. Dignified. He didn't reply, only studied me as though I were a painting on a wall, and not a very good one, at that. "You won't regret it," I went on, unable to help myself. I never did well when people stared at me. "I won't steal anything, either!" I laughed; he didn't. "That was a joke, you know. I'm not a thief."

"If you were a thief, Miss Alexander, I would expect you'd own a nicer car." With that, he rose and went to the door.

The word 'car' triggered a memory, from just before I passed out. I had said something, but for the life of me I couldn't recall what it had been. "I was wondering..."

Corin paused with his hand on the doorknob and turned to look at me, his stare unwavering. He was very good at those unwavering stares, which made me feel like I was ten years old and in big trouble. "Yes?"

"Well, did I say something to you? You know, before I blacked out?"

He regarded me for a long moment. "Nothing sensical."

"Did you get any of it?" I persisted.

"As I said, it wasn't anything that I understood, and I don't quite recall anyway."

Don't *quite* recall... He was hiding something and judging by the look on his face, I wasn't going to get it out of him. Damn. "Oh, all right. I just...well, if I said something, please disregard it. I'm sure it was utter nonsense. I was a bit out of it, and I'm pretty positive it was something stupid. I tend to babble, you see, when I get nervous. Like I'm doing now..."

His eyes remained unblinking and I had the strange feeling I was talking to a Borg. "I do see. Please lock your door tonight, and be gone by eight o'clock tomorrow morning. Mr. Paddington is coming by to do a walk-through and close up the house."

"Oh, yes. Eight o'clock. Of course." I smiled prettily.

"I'll leave the gate open for you."

"Fabulous."

He frowned, then opened the door and left, closing the door behind him a bit too hard. My shoulders slumped. What was I going to do? I had only a short time to prove Mr. Rachat needed me to do this job. And it had to be a good argument, a flawless argument. Whatever it was that had made Mr. Rachat cancel the project had to be big. But maybe not bad or tragic, I hoped, for him and for myself. If there had been a death in the family, I felt fairly sure Corin would have provided that information. It made good ammo for his argument. But he hadn't.

So what had happened? And did it have anything to do with the previous architect leaving?

I shook my head and stood up. It didn't matter. I had limited time, and I needed to use every second of it. I quickly washed my dirty dishes, noting that Corin had left no sign that he'd even been there, all sandwich fixing implements washed, dried, and returned to their respective drawers. What he didn't realize was that I wouldn't be so easy to store away.

I left my dishes drying in the dish rack and decided I would bring my stuff into the cottage. Perhaps I could claim squatter's rights for a few days. I snickered, imagining the look on Corin's face—horrified. Why not? It was worth a try.

When I opened my door and marched outside, I discovered my car parked beneath a stand of trees, about twenty feet back from the cottage. I had almost missed it, shadowed as it was, but in looking around, eager to take everything in, I spotted a headlight caught in a sunbeam. Behind the Beast was a gravel drive likely leading from the main driveway down to the cottage.

I had left my keys in the car, and felt slightly impressed that Corin had managed to start it. The Beast was an ornery one. He shouldn't have driven it down for me, though. He had done me a kindness, and it showed weakness on his part. My lips curved into a wicked grin. The man wasn't so perfect or indifferent, after all.

But when I opened the driver's door to fetch my keys to unlock the trunk, I found a note written in bold print. "I took the liberty of moving your car because I couldn't stand looking at it a moment longer." He didn't sign it, but he didn't have to, the bastard. Apparently my car didn't fit the standards of Chateau de Sowles. Well, screw him. He wasn't worthy of the Beast.

Muttering curses upon his red, stuck-up head, I hauled my luggage into the cottage. When the Beast was empty, I gave it a loving pat, then headed inside. I knew I was being irrational, but I didn't care. Corin struck me as the type who didn't like scenes. I didn't particularly like them, either, but I also didn't like being offered a job and having it taken away after I'd come so far and given up so much. I refused to acknowledge that two and a half hours wasn't really very far at all, and I hadn't really, *truly* given up anything.

In the bedroom, small but comfortable, I opened the doors of the dark wardrobe, more to snoop than to use. I didn't seriously believe Corin would let me stay here, but it was fun to pretend that I was spunky enough to make the attempt. It was mainly empty inside, except for a two-foot long cylinder propped in one corner. I recognized what it was immediately and plucked it out. Sliding off one end of the cardboard tube, I shook it until its contents slid out.

Blueprints.

I unrolled the prints on the simple white duvet covering the bed and examined them. When I saw what they were for, my breath left my body in one big whoosh. I had found the blueprints for Chateau de Sowles. The previous architect must have left them here.

I leaned closer, studying the beautiful blue lines, slightly blurry, the angles, the perfect, upper case print labeling all the rooms and their dimensions. There was one sheet for each floor. I picked up the thin paper and held it at arm's length, taking it in, analyzing it, memorizing it, then proceeded to do the same for each page. In doing so, I came to three conclusions. The blueprints I was studying were not the originals, but copies made to include the re-worked bathrooms. Second, there were three hidden passages and a secret room, and third, there were a couple things *off* about this house, though I couldn't put my finger on what either one might be.

But if I could, I thought excitedly, I just might have my ticket to stay.

Chapter Five

☾

After another hour of studying the prints—there was a lot to them—I gently rolled them up and stored them in the tube, returning it to the wardrobe.

Feeling restless I decided I needed to do something active to take my mind off my current predicament. Corin probably wouldn't like it, but I was going to take a walk around the grounds. He hadn't specifically forbidden me to do that, so it wasn't like I was rebelling, but I did look both ways before stepping outside. Funny how he made me feel more like a child than I did before I'd decided to grow up.

The sloping lawn that led down to the river was a rich green color, the grass thick and luxurious. The budding trees and flowers looked healthy and full. Corin was obviously good at his job. I shaded my eyes and glanced up at the house, wondering if I could get away with peeking in the windows. Maybe. But not in full daylight. I'd have to do it later…when Corin was safely indoors, unsuspecting of the shenanigans going on right under his stuck-up nose. The thought made me giggle. Really, I couldn't act like an adult *all* the time. That was no fun.

I headed for a gated doorway at the bottom of the hill. When I reached it, I found the small, wrought iron door slightly ajar. I was expecting a creak when I pushed on it, but it slid open silently, which was strangely creepier than the expected creaking. I wrapped my arms around myself and stepped through. The river was only about fifty yards away, and it was low tide, revealing stretches of wet sand along the banks and a sandbar farther out.

To my left was an island, which resembled a giant turtle floating in mid-stream. Beyond it, about a half mile upriver, was another island, connected to the mainland by two small bridges. In the distance, a white water tower rose up like a capsule-shaped rocket, and a couple of cranes sat unmoving, their arms raised high. On the rock-littered beach a crude boat launch had been fashioned, flanked on either side by seawalls, seaweed sprouting from cracks between the stones. A white rowboat with a green stripe, which could be pulled to shore with a rope attached to the seawall, was moored about fifteen feet out from the river's edge. Off to the right, the river curved around before meeting up with yet another bridge. Judging by the water flow, I would guess that the Atlantic lay in that direction.

The closer I came to the river the stronger the smell of brine grew. I stopped at the river's edge and closed my eyes to the sound of seagulls crying in the distance. I imagined myself rowing the rowboat across to the island—thump went the oars, splash went the water. Once on shore, I would head into the trees, the air around me cooling with each step, and in there amongst their secretive presence I would find a little cabin, nestled between two giant oak trees standing watch, like sentries flanking a tomb.

A tomb? Where had that image come from? I shivered in the cool breeze and opened my eyes. It seemed this place brought out my most morbid fancies. I liked that.

I started to walk along the wet sand, the seaweed crunching like dry noodles under my red flats, and thought about what might be inside the hidden cabin. A fireplace, of course. Dark paneling, overstuffed chairs, tiny landscape paintings dotting the walls. It would be cozy, intimate, romantic. A meeting place. Yes. For lovers. Lovers from long ago, when women donned beautiful dresses and men wore tails and top hats.

A gusty sigh escaped my slightly parted lips. I did so love a Victorian romance scene. I loved anything Victorian, actually, which was why I had to keep this job. I was already finding myself growing attached to this wild place, so isolated from reality, yet pulsing with life. I could feel it all around me, in the wind, in the birdcalls, in the flowing river.

I turned, hands in my pockets, and looked up at the dark shadow of the chateau. It loomed so beautifully, all soaring towers and gruesome statuary—gargoyles perched at every corner. It was both a home and a fortress. A person could feel safe here. Staring at the building for so long, I felt myself drawn to it and soon my feet were taking me back through the gate and up to the house itself, as though it beckoned me. I approached the giant dwelling with reverence, thinking of myself as a bride on my way to the altar.

I shook my head and smiled at myself. I really did get carried away, didn't I? But this house was special. I could tell. I was going to have to risk getting caught by Corin. I had to peek. I just had to…

I climbed the stone steps, running my hand up the balustrade, enjoying its cool smoothness beneath my fingers. Then, no longer able to delay the moment, I hurried up the remaining steps, stumbling on the last one, before righting myself and rushing to the nearest window.

Cupping my eyes I peered into the dark interior. I could see very little, which was horribly frustrating, and seriously considered picking the lock to get in. But then I spotted something… Actually, it was more as though I *felt* something. My skin prickled. Someone was in the house. Now I had to get inside. I had to see for myself who it was.

If I was lucky, the nearby door would be unlocked. I could slip inside, take a quick look around, and slip back outside, no harm done. I'd be a ninja, I'd be James Bond, I'd be—

"What are you doing?"

Being that I was still peeking inside the house, there was very little I could say that would excuse my behavior. I spun around to see Corin glaring down at me. "I was just looking." I held up my hands. "But not touching!" Well, except the window where my forehead had pressed against the glass in an effort to get closer, and very likely leaving behind an oily patch. Damnit, he was very good at making me feel like an unruly child.

"I'd prefer it if you would stay away from the house. It's locked anyway, so you couldn't touch if you wanted to." I frowned. "What?" he demanded.

"It's locked?" He nodded, warily. "Well, I thought I saw something earlier today...when I first arrived. Someone, actually. In the front tower. It was a shadow, passing by, and I had the impression someone was in the house, and just now, it *felt* like someone was in there. Was it you, earlier? Or a worker? I'm not sure who it would be now, though."

He shook his head. "No one is in there."

He looked so surprisingly grim as he spoke that I wanted to give him logical reasons for what I'd seen. "Maybe it was just clouds passing over the sun."

He didn't answer, just stared thoughtfully at the door. For some reason that worried me. He could have accepted my excuse, and we'd move on, but he didn't. "That first time...you thought it was a person?" he said at last. "In the tower?"

"Yes."

"And the second time?"

"The second time was just an impression of someone being there, and it felt human, whatever that means."

"Did you see a face that first time?" he asked.

I shook my head. Was it just me, or was that a strange question? "It was more of a shadow passing by." I waited for him to say something and when he didn't, I blurted out, "Why did the other architect leave?"

"Illness," he said shortly.

"Really? Or was that just his excuse?"

His eyes turned on me, their focus sharpening as though he were returning from some other world. "I couldn't say."

Couldn't, or wouldn't? Was there some sort of scandal being covered up here? It seemed the only thing that made sense. "Well, he was a fool to leave this job."

"I think he was only doing what he needed to do."

"I can't think of any reason that would make me leave a job before it was finished."

He looked slightly amused, like I was a simple child he wanted to humor. "No reason?"

"This is what I do, Corin." I clasped my hands together, as though begging him to understand. "I love it so much."

He looked taken aback. "It's just a job."

"No, it's not! For me, it's a passion. Houses speak to me. They have stories to tell, and if you listen closely enough, you'll hear them." I took in his expression. "I'm not crazy."

He shook his head. "I didn't think you were. You do, however, remind me of a type of person my mother talked about."

"Really?"

"She would call someone like you a moon dweller."

Moon dweller? "Why does that not sound like a compliment?" He shrugged. "Okay, I'll bite. What's a moon dweller?"

He thought for a moment. "Well, moon dwellers are people who have a hard time seeing reality. They prefer to live in a world disconnected from the hardships of life."

"I see. So you think I'm a romantic sentimentalist."

"Exactly."

"Well, you nailed that one on the head." I clapped. "Well done. I'd much prefer to live in a world of beauty than dwell in this 'real' world of yours, one that's full of hate and pain."

"Your unwillingness to acknowledge the real world could very well be the death of you," he said sanctimoniously.

"Yes, well, your pessimism could very well be yours. You can't live your whole life missing the beauty of it. That's not living, Corin. That's a slow death." I marched up to the door. "Now, are you going to let me in?"

He shook his head, his eyes darkening. "I can't. You wouldn't know what hit you. You wouldn't even see it coming."

His words knocked the breath out of me and I rasped, "See *what*?"

He backed away. "Goodbye, Miss Alexander. I doubt we'll see each other again. It's been,"—pregnant pause—"um, interesting to meet you." Then the coward spun around and fled down the steps.

I watched him go, all legs and stiff back, and blinked uncertainly. What was he talking about? And had that been a challenge?

I think it had.

He thought that just because I was a romantic, because I liked focusing on the beauty of life, that made me some sort of weirdo 'moon dweller.' Well, I would just have to show him I could also be a kick-ass, fully mature, and responsible architect.

And I knew just what I had to do to make him eat his words.

Chapter Six

☾

I spent the rest of the day in the cottage, moping about. After I deleted Mr. Paddington's messages, which told me little, other than that the job was off and I was to call him *right away*, I tried reading a gossip magazine. But I simply couldn't focus, which wasn't like me at all. Reading about celebrities and their strange little lives was a bit of a hobby of mine—okay, obsession. It was also my dirty little secret since that sort of thing was quite beneath our family, as my father often lectured. But I didn't care. I needed my gossip 'fix.' Unfortunately, today my fix wasn't fixing anything.

So I gave up and texted Ryan. I told him I'd arrived safely, the place was grand, that it was called Chateau de Sowles, etc. The subject of Corin did not arise, nor did I tell Ryan that I'd been let go before I'd even started. I was hoping I'd never have to tell him that. If that little tidbit got back to my parents, or to Jason, I'd never live it down. They thought I was a big enough screw-up as it was.

Which wasn't entirely merited. Sure, I had garnered a few late notices, and yes, I admit that maybe I hadn't taken mine and Jason's wedding planning seriously, but was that enough to cut me off? After the wedding disaster, neither had tried very hard to reach out to me, and certainly not with the aim to console me. A few hours after Jason canceled, Mother called and left a message to the effect that I'd disappointed my father and let them both down and had likely cost them several jobs because if I couldn't be trusted to handle my own wedding, how could I handle a million dollar project?

They were being unfair. Doing my job was way different. I felt passion for my work. I did not feel passion about picking out a dress I'd never wear again. At least in Victorian times they'd wear their wedding gown quite often that first year afterwards. I also felt no desire to pick out china patterns and waffle makers. Did that make me a bad person? Did that mean I wasn't committed to the relationship? No, it did not!

I was well into high dudgeon when Ryan typed that he was ridiculously busy and would get back to me...oh, and Jason had left him a message. I texted back, *R u kidding me? What did he want?* But he didn't reply.

Damnit.

I slid off the couch and wandered around the cottage, checking out the two guest rooms, either of which would be suitable for Ryan, the

bathroom—clean and pretty in white and a dusky rose, and then I perused the reading selection in the living area. There was quite a variety,
but I soon realized I didn't want to read. I wanted to *do* something. I
considered going back to the house and snooping around outside of it,
then changed my mind. I was going to do something even more daring. I was going to unpack all my stuff. I was going to settle in, and if
Corin wanted me gone, he'd have to remove me via bodily force. I
thought briefly about that and came to the conclusion that it wouldn't
be a bad way to go—he struck me as the muscular type, with all that
ground keeping to keep him fit. I snickered. I wouldn't mind him using
that body against me.

Making my decision, I jumped into the task wholeheartedly, hanging
up shirts, tucking away undergarments and pants in the walnut dresser
pushed against one wall. More than once, I stopped and studied my
reflection in the mottled mirror attached to the back of the dresser. My
cheeks were flushed, my red curls riotous, my blue eyes glowing. I was
enjoying myself, I realized. I was enjoying doing something naughty
and maybe a bit illegal. Perhaps not a good step on my way to being
more mature, but that might be okay. Yes, I needed to work at being
more responsible. But did I have to be *respectable* while doing it?

Plain and simple, I was tired of being well-behaved. In fact, lately I'd
seriously begun to doubt that my parents' decorum and unnatural control over their emotions was part of my nature. There was a bit of Irish
in our background, and it appeared as though it had all come out in
me.

I defiantly tousled my hair and poked my tongue out at my reflection.
It was time to let my inner rebel loose. I'd never really rebelled as a
teenager, other than a poorly thought out decision to shave my head
when I was sixteen, and attempting to smoke a cigar later that year, but
rebelling is a natural part of growing up. Yes, I was about ten years behind, but so what? I hadn't gained anything being a good girl, so why
keep doing something that wasn't working?

I spent the evening alone, eating spaghetti, garlic bread, and a nice
garden salad, and nursing a glass of Chardonnay that was absolutely
perfect. Mr. Rachat had good taste. Or Brittany did, since she'd likely
picked out the wine. I was tempted to call her and thank her, then decided against it. Likely she already knew about the job debacle, no
sense pulling her into my drama.

That night, I crawled into bed with the window cracked. I could hear
the faint sounds of river life, an owl hooting somewhere in the trees,
the flow of water as the river drifted past. That last one was likely just

the wind, but I wanted it to be the river, so it became the river to me. I fell asleep quickly and dreamed the sleep of the innocent, which was funny, considering what I was planning on doing in the morning.

☾

I awoke and stretched in the sunlight that shone bright and warm through the two windows facing the river. It was going to be a glorious day. I slid out of bed feeling giddy and faintly nauseous. So much depended on me getting this right.

My clock said half past six. I took a quick shower, fixed my hair, applied a bit of make-up, just enough to make me look less like Raggedy Ann, and headed to the kitchen to fix breakfast. Despite feeling nauseous, I ate heartily, figuring I'd need my strength. No way was I going to faint again. I'd learned my lesson about the dangers of not eating. After cleaning up, I headed back to my room and found the blueprints, laying them out on the bed. I donned my glasses, then checked my reflection one last time.

Whenever I wanted to be taken more seriously I put on my glasses. I know...it's predictable, but today especially I needed all the help I could get. With my matching dimples, round face and figure, along with a smattering of freckles across my nose and big, blue eyes, men either viewed me as an angelic cherub in need of rescuing, or a fertility goddess in need of being made a wife and mother.

I was neither, thank you very much.

Well, that was not entirely true, although I wish it were. I'm not very good at being alone, and I tend to be rather destructive when I'm on my own for too long. I needed to have a best friend, someone who would support me no matter how many boneheaded, idiotic things I've done. And while I love Ryan, I wasn't sure he was that special someone.

Question was, was that special someone Jason? He really was lovely to look at and ambitious, too. Ashley Winterton had her eye on him, and she didn't go for any old loser. I didn't like the idea of Ashley having any part of her body on Jason, however. The very thought of it made my skin itch and my fingers curl into fists. But was that love, or possessiveness, and was there a difference?

I turned away with a growl. Once again I was thinking about Jason when I should be thinking about winning my job. Feeling unnerved, I scurried over to my purse and pulled out an article from a local architecture and design magazine doing a story about a discovery I'd made. They had even taken my photo—in it I looked a bit windblown, but very happy as I posed in front of my find. The article was something I read whenever I was feeling particularly needy, which was pretty often apparently, judging by the tiny tears where the paper folded in half, and its worn softness. I read some of the words out loud, needing the confidence booster.

No one can find the 'essence' of a house and resurrect it like Vianne Alexander of Alexander Architecture & Design. Co-workers and clients alike have called her 'The House Whisperer' because of her uncanny ability to sense changes and peculiarities in a house—added walls, covered up doorways, hidden rooms. Watching her work, they've said, verges on a mystical experience. "I've been doing this since I was a kid," Ms. Alexander told *The Architect Alliance*, "and have never once grown tired of it." Ms. Alexander is indeed good at her job, and in high demand at AA&D.

I sighed and returned the article to my purse. Yes, I was a hopeless romantic, I was messy and I bit my fingernails, and I couldn't seem to pay my bills on time, *ever*, but on the job, I was a professional. I was good. Now to just convince Mr. Rachat, via Mr. Paddington, that he needed me on this job, and that it had to be done now rather than later.

And since I knew Mr. Paddington would be coming some time soon—Corin had wanted me out by eight for a reason—I was going to take the bull by the horns and catch Paddington alone. It wasn't much in terms of dastardly schemes, but it was something I wouldn't have done a month ago.

I scanned the blueprints one last time, tucked them away, then, closing the door behind me, scurried outside. Stealthily, I slithered into the Beast, backing it up so that it was completely hidden by the trees. Then I waited…impatiently, tapping my fingers on the steering wheel with a window cracked so I could listen. Time passed. I poked at Jesus and he bobbled. More time passed. There was no sign of Mr. Paddington, but fortunately, no sign of Corin either.

And then I heard it…tires on gravel. He was here!

Taking a deep breath, I slid out of the car and made my way up to the house, glancing around like a commando. Still no Corin. Good.

"Mr. Paddington!" I cried, greeting him heartily as he stepped out of his car. He was average height, with graying black hair grown just long enough to create a small Afro. His brown skin glowed in the sunlight, a slight sheen of sweat already forming on his forehead even though it wasn't that warm yet. He had perfect posture, which made me think of military training, and I felt a shiver of worry.

But now was not the time to lose my nerve, so I straightened my shoulders and marched toward him. He looked a little startled to see me, and I relaxed. Ex-military would be ready for anything, and he looked like someone who'd just been ambushed. "Ms. Alexander! I thought you were gone."

I gave him a grim smile. "Nope. Still here. I wanted to plead my case with you in person."

He winced and began to head toward the chateau, his strides long. I hurried after him as he entered the shade of the *porte cochere*. "I'm sorry, Ms. Alexander, I truly am. I wanted to make this work, but circumstances have rallied against us."

"But can't we convince Mr. Rachat together that this work needs to be done now?"

He had reached the top of the steps and stopped. I caught up to him, panting. He turned to face me, his expression contrite. "I wish things were different. You strike me as a nice young lady, and very well qualified."

"I am, Mr. Paddington! Just give me a chance and I'll show you what I can do!"

"It's truly not up to me. I'm sorry." He did look sorry. He also looked nervous, glancing over my shoulder. "Um, maybe you should go now."

"What's going on?" a voice rang out before I could take a step. I spun around. "You were supposed to be gone by now," Corin accused, looking thunderous. I noticed he wasn't wearing his baseball cap today, revealing more of his wavy hair, the sunlight adding golden glints to its red hue, and his clothes looked a little less ratty than yesterday's ensemble.

"Okay, okay!" I held up my hands in surrender as he climbed the steps. "I know I can't have the job, but can I see inside the house? I wouldn't be able to sleep knowing I was this close to going inside such a magnificent structure and didn't at least try to see it." Corin, now standing next to me, looked pained by my request. "I'll look," I promised, "and then I'll leave and you won't be bothered by me ever again." For some reason this made him look even more pained and I thought I'd gone too far, that once again, I'd blown things. When would I learn to keep my big mouth shut? No wonder Father didn't trust me to make the deal with clients, or to work on my own. I was crap at—

"Fine. I'll grant you a tour," Corin said, surprising me.

"You'll grant me a tour? Like a wish!" I clapped my hands giddily, then stopped, realizing I wasn't presenting my most mature self. If I wanted to be taken seriously, I needed to act seriously. Besides, while I really did want to see inside the house, I needed to find those anomalies I'd sensed from the blueprints. If I saw them, I'd know them.

One corner of Corin's mouth quirked up. Was he smiling? "Yes. Like a wish."

Mr. Paddington looked taken aback. "Are you sure?" he asked Corin, then, seeing my face, quickly amended, "A tour can't do any harm, can it?"

Corin didn't answer, his expression doubtful as he stepped forward and unlocked the front door. He looked around, as though fearing he would be caught, before motioning me to go ahead. I stepped inside, softly and with reverence, as though entering a cathedral. Inside, the décor was dark, as was fitting for Victorian fashion, but not oppressively so. There was a hint of mustiness in the air, not uncommon in unoccupied houses, especially one this close to the water. Accompanying it was the inescapable smell of dust, of which, when I looked around, there appeared to be surprisingly little. Someone kept the place clean.

The foyer, which Corin called the grand entrance hall, rose up three stories, the landing on each floor like its own four-sided balcony. A stately staircase, with elaborately carved newel posts and spindles, and which would likely impress royalty, led up to each floor. Overhead an oval skylight added light to the hall, but not enough to take away from the chateau's gothic atmosphere.

As we made our way through the building, each room revealed a new wonder. Numerous rooms had carved wood ceilings, possibly walnut and very expensive, and built-in bookshelves packed with books. Heavy brocade or velvet curtains covered the floor to ceiling windows in nearly every room and colorful oriental rugs dotted the hardwood floors.

The dining room was especially ornate. Decorating the ceiling was a pastoral painting of a blue sky filled with robust baby angels. The wallpaper was a shiny gold color embellished by bright flowers and birds. Wall sconces, like white crystal balls topped by golden crowns, were spread about the room. I especially liked the wooden relief panels around the fireplace depicting earthly delights. Clusters of grapes surrounded a young person holding up a wine goblet as though toasting us.

The lightest room in the chateau was the ballroom, which was decorated in the French-style, with pale blue walls painted with gold gilt, and cream-colored curtains adorned by pink and red roses. There was a pianoforte, and lots of soft and comfortable chairs and divans, their fabric matching the curtains. It was the most feminine room in the otherwise masculine house, and a nice respite.

There wasn't nearly the furniture I thought there'd be, but then I remembered why I was here…renovation and updating. If any work needed to be done, you didn't want furniture getting in the way or getting damaged. The best and bulkiest pieces, hard to move from room to room, were likely in storage. I wished I could ask Corin if I could see them. I wanted to ascertain how well they fit the Victorian period. Judging by what I'd seen so far, only the bathrooms needed work. Everything else fit the Victorian era like a satin evening glove.

We took a brief glimpse at the cellar, where work had already been done to shore up the foundation. It was surprisingly clear of detritus— tarps, used sealant or paint cans, tools— meaning the work crew had done a good job cleaning up after themselves. Afterwards we visited the outdated kitchen, which also needed work, and several upstairs bedrooms furnished with four-poster beds and heavy brocade curtains that I could imagine pulling open every morning to greet the day. The northwest bedroom would need new wallpaper since it was too modern, and the sitting room floor had been replaced and would need to be changed out. Otherwise, everything looked to be in excellent condition, almost like a museum. Even the attic, where the servants had probably stayed, was nicer than most.

The house had obviously been built with great attention to detail and loads of money. I considered telling Corin and Mr. Paddington the place had dry rot, just so I would have a job, but figured they would know I was lying. I lied like a little kid, all shifting eyes and fidgety hands. Blushes, too. Probably because I don't like doing it. Unlike Father. He lies like a rug, even when he doesn't need to. But anyway, Corin and Mr. Paddington didn't strike me as rubes, so it would likely be a waste of breath.

Knowing I wasn't going to get the job didn't stop me from enjoying myself, even though with every step I felt an increasing sense of someone waiting for me. Like I'd round a corner and run into him, or enter a room and there he'd be, warming his hands by the fireplace as he waited for me.

This sensation likely came from what I thought of as old ghosts. In my mind, old ghosts present as either glimmers or impressions. Glimmers are like shadows on the wall, fleeting remnants of the souls that had lived and loved in the house, hardly noticeable. Impressions put out more energy, showing more form and substance, while still remaining enigmatic. Are old ghosts spirits of the dearly departed? Or are they merely the result of alternate dimensions in time slipping through? I don't know, but I have a strong belief that what we can see and what exists don't always coincide.

The old ghosts in this house... Well, there was something very strong here, more an impression than a glimmer...so much energy. But was it good energy? Or sinister? I couldn't quite place my finger on it. Houses and spirits are odd that way. Once, early in my training, I'd worked in a house where a murder had taken place. My first day, I was standing in the kitchen and I felt it, a sensation strong and thick, like melted tar. It sucked the air from my lungs, and all I wanted to do was get out of there. The funny thing was, the murder had happened out in the barn, which felt absolutely fine to me.

Here in Chateau de Sowles, while the atmosphere did not exactly feel fine to me, it also wasn't sinister to the point that I wanted to flee. On the contrary, I felt as though I could quite happily live here. So what was it, I wondered, that was lurking around corners, begging me to find it? *Who* was it?

As we passed from room to room, I realized we had yet to see the unusual room I'd found in the blueprints, the one shaped like the bow of a ship. The front, or bow part, jutted out from the rest of the building, and looked as though it actually met up with the river at high tide. It was the one 'atypical' room in the house, and I looked forward to seeing it.

We headed down the staircase, back into the foyer, and I thought our tour was over until Corin turned and marched purposefully down a hall we hadn't yet visited. At the end of it he stopped at an open doorway.

"This is the Ship Room," he said to me over his shoulder, indicating for me to go ahead of him. I felt my stomach clench up with excitement. This was it. "I saved it for last, as it's the most interesting room in the house." I stepped inside and looked around. Immediately I felt something different about this room. "Monsieur Sowles, the man who had the house built, made his fortune in shipping. This room was his favorite."

I could see why. The views were spectacular. I wanted to enjoy them, but curiosity drove me toward the curved bow, the part of the room that jutted out from the building. The wall on the right, which faced the river, held two round windows, like portholes. I peered out one of them and looked down. Judging by the wet sand and seaweed clinging to the stone foundation, the river did indeed come this far up. I stepped back and spun around, feeling strange. I squinted at the entire room, at the walls, at the windows, doing mental calculations. Then I focused on just the bow part. Something was wrong with it.

"That's odd," I said calmly, though I really wanted to shout.

Judging by the number of wrinkles in Corin's forehead, he was obviously displeased by my observation. "What is?"

"The dimensions are off." I spun around again, growing more excited. This was it. This was my anomaly. Well, one of them. Someone, at some time, and for some unfathomable reason, had brought the left wall of the 'bow' out a bit, into the room. Not much. Perhaps the width of a brick, or a little less. Maybe that's why it felt so odd in here.

"What do you mean?"

I hesitated—he looked almost angry—then I explained, pointing to show what I meant. "It comes out too far. Plus there aren't any windows on this side. There really should be two windows on the left, just like on the right. It only makes sense."

Corin and Mr. Paddington squinted. "I'm not sure I understand," Corin said. "Why would someone bring the wall out?"

I shrugged. "Who knows why people do anything? But in a place like this, which was built all at once—with no add-ons and with obviously a lot of thought and care put into its construction—well, it's just very odd. This room is an anomaly in itself, but there's more to it than being shaped like a ship."

"Do you see it?" he asked Paddington.

Paddington hedged his bets. "I agree that there should be two windows on the left side."

"Maybe." Corin turned back to me. "Prove it."

I whipped out my measuring tape. "Stand back." I proceeded to measure the room, comparing the measurements on both sides of the 'bow.' I spoke the numbers out loud as I worked and Paddington's expression slowly turned to wonder.

"She's right," he said as I practically shouted the last one.

"See?" I was on my knees and turned to find Corin kneeling right beside me, a cryptic look on his face. His knee nudged mine as he leaned forward to study the wall and I could smell *Old Spice*. Very old school, this guy. "The numbers don't match up," I went on, willing him to look at me. "The question is, why? It makes no architectural sense, and certainly no design sense. The rest of the house is perfect. This room is the exception."

Corin turned and stared at me hard, and I changed my mind about wanting him to look at me. "How do you know this?"

"I found the blueprints in the cottage when I was snooping around." I caught his disapproving expression. "What? You wouldn't let me go in the chateau, or do much of anything else, and I was bored." I pointed a finger at him. "And don't tell me you wouldn't have snooped."

He pulled back, affronted. "I wouldn't have."

"Well, aren't you the paragon." He frowned. I glanced back at Paddington. "Does he do teasing?"

Paddington again refused to commit one way or the other, giving me a helpless shrug. I'm not sure I entirely blamed him. I'd only known Corin for a day, but I'd already figured out he was not an easy person to read, or handle.

Corin stood quickly, nearly knocking me over. A strong hand caught my elbow before I toppled, then lifted me to my feet as though I were a ragdoll. I wasn't sure I entirely liked that. Who wants to be that lightweight? Even someone like me, who isn't that lightweight.

"Paddington, I need to talk to you."

Paddington glanced at me, then followed after Corin's retreating figure. Straightening my shirt, I tiptoed over to the doorway and listened. Lucky for me, they hadn't gone far.

"Why didn't you catch this?" Corin demanded.

"Well, it's a very small difference. Hardly noticeable."

"What about the windows?"

"There are shrubs growing up against the wall outside, and maybe they got out of control and broke a window or two, so someone covered the windows up."

"Maybe." There was a pause. "But not likely. Just cut the shrubs, or don't grow them in the first place. You know, James didn't notice anything strange either. He would've said. That man never misses a chance to blow his own horn."

"To be fair, he didn't spend much time in there."

"No. I suppose he didn't."

"So what do you suggest we do about this?" Mr. Paddington asked carefully.

"I believe it would be in our best interest to find out why that wall is there."

"You think we should start up the job again?" My heart started to pound in my ears and I had to lean forward to hear over it.

There was silence, then, "I think Mr. Rachat would want to know about that wall. It is rather a strange anomaly."

"Uh, yes, all right," Mr. Paddington agreed. "I'll contact him." He sounded as though the last thing he wanted to do was talk to Mr.

Rachat. A few seconds of silence passed, and I strained to hear anything. I stayed very still, since I didn't want Corin or Mr. Paddington to find me eavesdropping. That would be very unprofessional and a blow to my newly formed adult image, not to mention embarrassing. But I was not going to stop listening. I had to know how this was going to turn out.

"Mr. Rachat, sir. It's Peter." Peter Paddington? What perverse parents he had. "We've found something." His voice became muffled and I couldn't understand a thing he was saying until, "So we can start up again?" I clutched the doorframe and had to work very hard not to whoop out loud. "Just the wall for the moment. And you want Ms. Alexander to be present?" More clutching. "I'll tell her."

There was some quiet discussion between Paddington and Corin and I took the opportunity to shuffle backwards and try to erase what must certainly be a triumphant and smug expression on my face. I'd done it!

"I suppose you heard all that?" Corin said dryly as he entered the room a few moments later.

I tried to look affronted. "Are you accusing me of eavesdropping?"

"It's not so very far removed from snooping, is it?"

I laughed, willing to be generous. "I suppose not. So I have the job again?"

"You have a smaller job. For the moment. If you're willing to be flexible, we'll take this one step at a time. Paddington is calling in someone to take out a small bit of the wall after lunch."

I nodded. "I can be flexible. I'm a very flexible person, you know."

He eyed me steadily. "I hope so."

I had a job! "Can I explore the house a little more thoroughly?" I asked sweetly. It's so easy to be sweet when you're getting your way.

He paused for a moment, considering my request. "You'll be careful?"

"It's just a house! I'll be fine."

He looked doubtful. "Do you really believe that? That houses are just houses? Inanimate and non-sentient?"

I stared at him, considering what he'd said for a moment. "No, I guess I don't."

"So then you'll understand when I tell you to be careful, to watch out."

A foreboding shiver pulsed through me, from my toes to my chest, resting there like a piece of ice. Granted I didn't know Corin very well, but he seemed the last person in the world that I'd expect to be fanciful like this. "What should I be watching out for?" I managed to ask.

He shrugged. "I don't know. But..." he paused and looked around the room. "Well, you'll know it when you see it." With that and a serious nod, he walked out, leaving me to wonder what I'd gotten myself into.

Chapter Seven

☾

After Corin left, Mr. Paddington returned to the Ship Room and told me, with what looked like regret, that he had to get back to his other job. Likely he wanted to see what was behind that wall. Before leaving, he shook my hand and told me to call him Peter. "I was right to hire you," he said, nodding sagely. "You are good." He shook his head. "Though I can't believe I missed that anomaly. The window part is pretty obvious, now that you've pointed it out."

I laughed. "Funny how desperation can open a person's eyes." Oops. Too much information. "Besides," I added hastily, "you weren't hired to work on the house."

"No. I'm just helping Mr. Rachat out. I'm more of a modern builder. Historical houses were never my forte. Not enough imagination, I guess." He smiled, then his brown eyes darkened as he looked at me closely. "While you're here... Just, you know, be careful. Okay?"

"Okay," I said, thinking he was the second person to warn me to be careful. "But remind me what I'm being careful about?"

"Oh," he said airily, looking away, "you know how old houses can be." But he wasn't looking away exactly, he was looking around him, as though he expected the source of the danger to be listening in.

I did know how old houses could be, but I didn't think we were on the same page about the dangers—rotting steps, asbestos, lead paint. "I'll be careful," I promised. "I won't snoop too much."

He laughed and turned to go. "As you might have seen, Corin's pretty possessive of this place so—" He stopped talking abruptly, almost as though someone had stuffed a sock in his mouth, and I wondered what he'd meant to add.

"Go on," I urged.

His eyes shifted and I had a feeling he wasn't going to finish his sentence. Not in the way he'd originally intended, anyway. "Oh, well, it's just that his ancestors have been caretakers here since the late 1800s. They're the ones who've kept this place in such excellent condition."

"Wow!" I looked around, impressed. "I had no idea. I guess that does explain a few things."

He nodded, looking relieved, and while I was sure he hadn't said what he'd been going to say, it was good information so I took it. "Yes, he cares very much about this place."

"I can see why."

Peter glanced at his watch. "I really must be going. We're on a deadline and my work here has put me behind schedule. I won't be around much after this, but if you have any questions, feel free to call me. You have my number?"

"It's in my phone."

"I'll be sure to check my messages." He gave me a wink and left. Yes, I definitely liked Peter Paddington and was pretty sure I had an ally in him. But would he side with me against Corin? I rather doubted that. It didn't matter, though, because Corin was only the groundskeeper, after all. Mr. Rachat was the boss. He was the only one I had to impress. Funny, though, how I felt this urge to impress Corin as well, probably because he seemed the type not easily impressed. A person couldn't help but want to prove themselves to people like him. It was very annoying.

I spent over an hour wandering around the house, getting a feel for it, memorizing the layout, examining the carved details more closely, taking in the expensive mahogany and walnut, the crown molding, and the beautiful wallpaper, most of which looked original, judging by its color, design, and pale patches where artwork had hung. I stepped closer and peered at it; it was in amazing condition. Corin and his forebears had done a wonderful job preserving the house. My respect for him rose another notch and I promised myself not to give him a hard time when he got a little protective about the house. I'd be protective of this grand old place myself.

When I'd gone through the whole house, I spent an hour searching for the hidden passages and room I'd found in the blueprints. I found all three passages—one ran from the sitting room to the cellar, one climbed all the way from the kitchen to the attic, and one was in the library. I meant to follow that one, but there was still that remaining anomaly I wanted to hunt down.

I was on the third floor landing, slowly rotating, when I realized what it was. There was no entrance to the fourth story of the front tower, where I'd seen the shadow yesterday. The first floor tower area was a parlor, the second was a reading room, and the third had been made into a sort of observatory. A cursory inspection of the observatory revealed no obvious clues, but the blueprints hadn't revealed a hidden door anyway, so I wasn't absolutely sure there was one.

I thought briefly that the entrance to the top floor of the tower might be through the attic, then realized the two areas were too far apart. So how did one get to the fourth floor? I was quite sure that Corin hadn't shown it to me, and wondered if it had been an oversight on his part.

Or maybe he was hiding something up there, like a demented wife or a criminal on the run. I laughed. Yeah, right.

I mentally reviewed the blueprints. Had they really built a tower floor to which no one had access? Maybe it was just for looks, but basically useless, like a folly. That didn't fit, though. Everything else in the chateau was designed to make maximum use of space. Based on what I'd seen, there was no way the original owner would have built a tower that no one could access. This must be my second anomaly. I hadn't seen the entry to the tower on the blueprints because it was likely the prints had been altered to cover any sign that there was one. In fact, it was also very likely that the blueprints I was looking at were third-generation, changed once, then changed again to include the new bathrooms. So now the trick was to find the entrance, if it existed.

In the end, the door was very hard to find. The raised wood paneling design in the observatory tower room was very good at covering the crack for the door and if I hadn't been looking I wouldn't have had any idea it was there. Soon after I discovered the door, I found its release button, which was a small knob in the paneling. I pressed it, hard, having the distinct feeling it hadn't been used in a long time. There was a pause, then a click, signaling the release of the latch. I was in!

I pushed on the door, and for a few seconds, it stuck. Then suddenly it released, and a gust of air blew out, as though the room had sucked in a deep breath and let it go. The breeze felt unusually warm on my forehead, almost like a caress, and a fine sheen of sweat beaded my brow. Then the door pulled away from me, even though I hadn't pushed it. *Probably just suction*, I told myself, though I wasn't sure I quite believed that.

After fetching a chair to prop open the door for light, I hesitated a moment, then stepped into the passage. A dark passage snuck off to my left and I wondered where it led before turning back and facing a very narrow, curving stairway. As I climbed the steps, I remembered Corin's cryptic words from yesterday. *You wouldn't know what hit you. You wouldn't even see it coming.* I remembered them now because I felt something waiting for me, at the top of the steps, up in the tower, and with each passing second, I felt the sensation growing stronger. That old ghost I'd been sensing earlier? I had the slightly terrifying feeling that I was about to meet it.

But that was just a feeling, of course. Father said that too often I let my feelings and emotions make decisions for me. I needed to be more logical, more rational. Then, and only then, would I become a great architect. It was why he insisted I continue working with him on projects, even though I'd been out of school for years.

So, ignoring my restless intuition, I took a deep breath and stepped into the room, then immediately paused and looked around. Unlike the rest of the mansion, the space was dusty, as though someone had shaken a bag of flour all over it, and obviously hadn't been entered in a long time. My shoes left prints as I slowly crossed the floor. If Corin knew about this place, he avoided it.

Stopping in the middle of the room, I looked about in wonder. For furnishing, there was a bed covered in a thick, pine green velvet duvet, two wide, leather chairs in front of a fireplace, and a built-in bookshelf, loaded with books, along one wall. Half-melted candles squatted in reflective sconces, and a plain candle on the bedside table was fuzzy with dust, its charred wick burned halfway down. I sidled over to the bed and peeked under it, only slightly surprised to find a chamber pot, luckily empty. I straightened up again. This had been someone's bedroom, or a hideaway. It reminded me of the cabin I'd imagined out on the island, as a lair for lovers.

Was this the same thing?

Goosebumps prickled my arms. A big part of me wanted it to be so. I couldn't think of anything more romantic than two star-crossed lovers meeting up here, secretly, passionately, their hearts racing, their hands and mouths frantic for each other…

A sigh whispered in my ears and a breath of air tickled my eyelashes, making me blink. Someone was in the room. I could feel him. Yes, *him*. Definitely male.

"Who's there?" I called, my voice trembling like a child's. The windows were shut, latches fastened tight. It hadn't been a breeze. "I've seen you, you know. If you're hiding in the house, you'll be found. Corin will find you and you'll be in trouble. He's not very welcoming, I can tell you that."

I leaned forward. Had that been a chuckle?

I shook my head. No, just my imagination. Despite the dry warmth of the tower, I shivered. I wasn't sure what to make of this room, hidden away and forgotten. Someone had once lived here, perhaps loved here, someone long dead. And I had blundered into his sanctuary, marring it with my aliveness, my curiosity.

Or had I been led?

I began to seriously consider this idea, since now I felt as though I couldn't leave the room. I wasn't sure if something was holding me here, wanting desperately for me to stay, or if it was because *I* didn't want to leave. I felt safe here, wanted, like a real person worthy of love and respect.

I broke off. Was that really me thinking that? And if it was, what did I mean by it? Did I not feel like a worthy person? Shaking my head, I crossed my arms over my chest and peered about the room, waiting. Another breath of air stirred around me and I spun toward the fireplace. My feet seemed to take me there of their own accord, as though I were a puppet, and as I grew close, something caught my eye—letters carved into the mantel…white wells amidst the dark wood. I read them out loud. "AS and CR." I reached out and traced the pale letter C, and when I started on the R, the image of two figures rowing to the island under the cover of darkness popped into my head, before disappearing just as quickly.

The air stirred again. Or was that just my imagination? Perhaps someone was in the house, opening doors, causing suction. But still… I hugged myself tighter. How exciting to find the initials of someone who had lived in the house! I wondered if the S stood for Sowles. After all, the house was called Chateau de Sowles after the original owner, Monsieur Sowles.

I had to ask Corin more about the history of the house. I recalled Mr. Paddington—Peter—mentioning that the place had stood empty for many years. So when had the last occupants left? Who were they? Was it the Sowles family? Or someone else? And if it was someone else, why had the Sowles family left? Judging by the state of this room and the fact that no one had occupied it for a very long time, it was possible AS had been the last to use it. Was he also the last in the Sowles line? What was his story?

I was on the trail of a good mystery, I could just feel it!

The wind battered against the window, startling me out of my reverie. I truly didn't want to leave this room, this haven from the real world, but it was time to get back to work.

Stay.

I gave a nervous little laugh as I crept toward the doorway. When I reached it I turned around. "I'll be back," I whispered.

I'll be here, ma chérie.

I actually giggled out loud. Really, sometimes what my imagination conjured up was a bit too realistic. I could almost believe someone was talking to me. Almost.

Still smiling, I carefully made my way back down the narrow stairs. At the bottom, I decided to check out the dark passage, only to find five feet along that it dead-ended at another door, which was locked. I headed back to the observatory, making sure to close the secret door tightly behind me. I was being more careful than I would normally be, having the strange feeling that I had to keep this discovery secret. *Just for now*, I assured myself. I'd tell Corin about the room later. After I'd had a chance to explore it some more.

No one was in the house when I went downstairs, so I returned to the cellar and looked over the foundation, which likely had been weakened by the house's proximity to water. The work was professional, I was happy to find, and while the repairs were modern, they didn't take away from the 'old house foundation' look. The previous architect—James—and the work crew had done an excellent job. So I could only assume James hadn't been let go for incompetence. Could he really have been sick? He'd have to have been seriously ill to leave a plum job like this.

Because, no doubt about it, this was a plum job. Not a lot needed to be changed and what did was manageable. I'd been worried that after not insisting on seeing the site before accepting the job that I'd made a huge mistake. I'd gotten lucky, though. The house was in great shape. I made a mental note that next time, however, I needed to look before I leapt.

I left the chateau to go eat lunch, though I found it hard going, getting distracted by a carving in the grand entry, then pulled toward a mosaic design, then to a pattern in the flooring. My growling stomach finally dragged me out the door.

Stay, ma chérie… I thought I heard as I closed the door behind me.

I'll be back, I whispered.

Promise.

I promise.

I skipped down the stairs, feeling buoyant. This place was truly a romantic's dream, and if I played my cards right, soon I'd have it all to myself.

Chapter Eight

☾

There was another message from Jason on my phone and I listened to it as I ate my sandwich. "Vianne… Answer, please. I know you're there. Just answer. Did you get my first message?" Put out sigh. "You can't ignore me forever." *You ignored me for over a month*, I thought. *I think I can manage a couple days.* I *hoped* I could manage a couple days. "I miss you, honey," he said in a different tone of voice, perhaps realizing he'd catch more flies with honey. "This last month has been so hard on me. I feel like the bad guy in all this, but really, I didn't do anything wrong, did I?" Technically, no. Morally, yes. He could have quit AA&D when I did. The two of us could have found somewhere else to work. He could have *not* canceled the wedding in the first place! At the very least, he could have called me once or twice afterwards.

But he had done none of that.

"Yes, I should have quit," he went on, as though reading my mind, and I brightened a bit. "But, well, this was supposed to be a surprise… You see, I was saving up for a down payment on a house. I found a perfect place for us. So I couldn't have both of us being unemployed, could I?" I couldn't believe it. He was buying us a house? How sweet! How romantic! I was about to stop the message and call him right away when he had to ruin it. "I know just the house, too. It's near AA&D, a perfect showpiece of a place. I can't wait to show it to you, because, well, it's mine—ours—now. I know you'll be thrilled with it. So call me, hon. Let's start over, okay? Your mother offered to take care of all the tasks for the wedding that you didn't do. She made me realize that planning isn't your forte and"—he chuckled—"I had to admit that she was right. So we're back on track, Vianne." There was a pause. "Remember what you told me? That you're not good on your own? I heard how you spent this last month, letting yourself go. You really need someone to look after you, and that someone is me. Call me."

I nearly chucked the phone at the wall, but settled for slamming my empty Diet Coke can against the table. It wasn't nearly as satisfying, but much less expensive. "Bastard!"

How could he just go and buy a house? And I knew exactly which house he was referring to, adding to my anger. A perfect showpiece was right, but it was too perfect, having been remodeled a couple years ago. It had no real character anymore, no real projects to take on, no way to make it our own. Come to think of it, I had told Jason all this only a few months ago, when we'd taken a walk past it and he'd asked me what I thought of it. So it wasn't like I was expecting him to read my mind—he'd asked me and I'd told him the house was lovely, but I wouldn't want to live there. Then I'd told him all the reasons why. And yet he'd still gone ahead and bought it. Apparently he hadn't heard a word after I'd said, "It's lovely…"

To go ahead and buy a house, any house, without asking me? Did he seriously think I'd go for that? I've been imagining and thinking about my dream house for most of my life. To exclude me from the process was just plain arrogant! *This isn't the 1950s*, I fumed. Besides, if I were to buy a showpiece, it'd be one like Chateau de Sowles. It didn't need much work, but I could still personalize it. It was missing a conservatory, after all, and the kitchen and bathrooms needed serious updating.

Even more insulting was the fact that he had gone behind my back and brought in my mother, sharing their little joke about how I wasn't organized. Yes, I admit I'm not organized, and yes, he could tease me about it, but when he recruited her because of it… That was inexcusable.

But the worst? Throwing my insecurity about being alone in my face. And who had told him I'd been a wreck for a month? I suspected Ryan, but it could have been Mother. When I didn't return her call, she tried stopping by a couple weeks later. I could tell she wanted to lecture me, so I hadn't let her in, claiming I was sick. She hated germs, and I knew that and used it to my advantage. But in the end maybe she'd won because she'd guessed the real reason I wasn't letting her in…because I was a mess.

I turned off my phone and pocketed it. Really, I was beginning to think I was better off without Jason and my parents interfering in my life. It felt nearly sacrilegious to think this way, and I actually started shaking a little. What if I really couldn't do this job alone? What if I failed? What if Jason was right about me—that I couldn't go it alone?

Screw him. I was going to do this. And it would start with taking down that wall.

☾

I stepped onto the driveway just as a black truck, its bed stuffed with work tools, pulled up to the house. I hurried over as a young woman slid out of the driver's side. I was both thrilled to see she was a Hispanic woman, and sadly, a little surprised. There were still so few women in engineering and construction work, and even fewer were a minority. We were likely making history just working together.

She strode toward me, hand outstretched and a broad smile on her face. Her black hair was pulled back into a messy braid, and she wore a simple white t-shirt and faded blue jeans. Her scuffed work boots were solid and no-nonsense and no doubt steel-toed. I liked her already.

"Mía Bonita, at your service."

"It's nice to meet you, Mía," I said as we shook hands. "I take it you're the owner of Bonita Babes Construction Crew." I indicated the lettering on the side of her pick-up truck. 'You break it, we fix it, and look good while doing it.'

She laughed. "In the flesh." She looked down at her outfit. "Though I'm not sure I fit the 'look good while doing it' part."

"You look great," I told her. She did. Unblemished by make-up, her brown-hued skin was healthy and fresh. "I'm Vianne Alexander. I was brought in to take over where the previous architect left off."

She frowned. "So the job's back on?"

"If I'm able to prove a theory I have."

She looked a little confused, but I didn't feel now was the time to fill her in on my scheme to keep my job. "Are you ready to take down that wall?" I asked her, trying to sound like Ronald Reagan and failing miserably.

She reached into the back of her truck and pulled out a sledgehammer and two large white bundles that had to be tarp. "I'm as ready as I'm going to get."

I eyed the sledgehammer warily. I didn't want her to destroy anything. "You have something smaller, right?"

She laughed and patted the side of her pants. Tucked into a painter's loop was a small hammer. "And I have a stud finder, not that it's done me any good in the date department." She threw me a wink, then looked over my shoulder. "But it works really well. There's a stud now."

I spun around to see Corin approaching us. He nodded at Mía and she nodded back as curtly as he had, though she was blushing. "Ladies," he greeted us.

"Hello!" I replied cheerily. "Are we ready to do this?"

He turned and faced the chateau. "I hope so."

"Of course we are!" I cried, bounding toward the stairs. I was eager to see what we would find. "Come on!"

Mía laughed and followed after me. A glance over my shoulder told me Corin was coming along too, though more slowly, as though he was regretting his decision. I figured we'd better hurry before he changed his mind.

"It's in the Ship Room," I told Mía. "I think someone covered up the windows."

"Really? I haven't been in there yet. We only did work on the cellar before we were told the job was being put on hold."

"That was you? Awesome. You do great work."

She preened as she went ahead of me into the room. I didn't bother waiting for Corin, who, when I glanced back, was coming down the hall, his eyes shifting around as though looking for something. It was this house. It made you feel like it was alive…and watching.

"So do you know what happened to stop work?" I whispered, not wanting Corin to overhear.

Her face instantly shuttered. "This wall?" she pointed, completely ignoring my question. I didn't think she was being rude; she looked too disturbed for that.

"Yep, that one," I answered, deciding to let it go for now. "As you can see, it's unbalanced, window-wise, and comes out farther than the right side."

She angled her head, squinting a little. "I do see it, but it's not as obvious as it sounds like it would be. Did you discover it?"

"I did." Corin entered the room. "It's a strange anomaly and apparently Mr. Rachat wants to know why it's there."

She gave me a funny look, then glanced over my shoulder. I spun around in time to see Corin's eyes leap quickly away from her. I had the feeling a warning message had passed between them, probably something about what had happened to Mr. Rachat. What that was I'd give my eyeteeth to know, but I had a feeling they were two of a kind when it came to gossip, so my teeth were safe.

I pushed against a spot. "I think you should start here, but you'd better double-check with the stud finder." I expected her to make another joke about its abilities, but she was all business now. She bent down and pulled the tool horizontally along the wall, then up and down, listening for beeps and lightly marking spots on the wall with a piece of white chalk.

"Good eye," she told me when she'd finished. "Your mark is right below something…perhaps the frame of a window."

I glanced back at Corin, wanting to see how he was reacting to my genius. But he was staring at the wall, his eyes troubled, his stance tense. What did he think would happen? It's not like we were breaking into King Tut's tomb. Were we? "There isn't some kind of curse I should know about, is there?" I asked him.

His eyes widened. "Who told you about a curse?"

I perked up. "Nobody. Based on your strange behavior, I just had the impression we were about to enter forbidden territory."

"There is no curse," he said succinctly.

I glanced at Mía, who had partially laid out her tarps and now had her little hammer in hand. She was studiously avoiding my eyes. "Did something happen when you were doing work in the cellar?"

"Why do you ask?" she replied nervously and I knew I had her.

"There's a theory that construction work on an old house can stir up spirits. You know, ghosts. Did you sense something strange once work started, something that wasn't there before? Weird noises? Cold spots?" When she didn't respond, I turned to Corin. Speaking of ghosts, he rather resembled one right now, his skin as pale as Casper's. "I've worked in a lot of old houses, Corin. I've pretty much seen it all. We've stirred things up many times." Which is why I felt that some-times I was more of a Resurrectionist than a restorer.

"You have a good imagination," he said stiffly.

"You did have paranormal activity, didn't you?"

"Can we get going?" he asked Mía. "I'm sure you have other work to do."

She nodded and began to tap on the wall where one of her chalk marks was. With one good wallop, she broke through the wallpaper. White dust flew out as she worked, digging carefully and meticulously through the plaster. When she had a small hole, she took out her flashlight and peered into the opening, then angled her head to look up. She squinted, then frowned. "I'm seeing a windowsill, round, just like the ones on the other side."

Corin frowned. "So someone covered up the windows, planted shrubs to make it look like shrubs were supposed to be there, and built an extra interior wall. Why?"

I shrugged, paying more attention to the atmosphere around me. Something curious had happened as soon as Mía had broken through the wall. Unlike a typical paranormal event, where the air gets cold, I felt a perceptible warming of the atmosphere, as though we'd tapped into a heater. "Do you feel how warm it's gotten?" I asked.

"So?" Corin replied testily.

"But don't you think that's odd?"

"It's likely the heat just kicked on."

I didn't think that was it, but from the perturbed tone of his voice, I decided not to push the issue. For now. "Maybe."

Mía pushed away from the wall and stood, dusting off her hands. Her expression was nervous. She gave Corin a look. "Do you want me to do more?"

He gave her a crisp nod. "I want it all down."

I stared at him. "Do you think Mr. Rachat would want that?"

"Mr. Rachat has given me permission to make the decisions on this," he said coolly, as though I'd insulted his ego.

"Okay," I said happily. "Just wanted to be sure we weren't stepping on any toes."

One eyebrow rose. "Really? You've been stepping on toes since you arrived."

I laughed. "Guilty." I stepped toward Mía. "Would you like some help?"

She handed me the small hammer. "I marked all the spots we need to work around."

"What about me?" Corin asked.

She looked at him in surprise. "I thought you'd have other things to do." He shook his head stubbornly. Apparently, being in charge, there was no way he was going to just sit back and watch. "Well, then, you can help, too. There are more hammers out in the truck."

"I'll be right back," he said grimly.

When he was gone, I asked, "Is he always this pleasant to be around?"

She shrugged and turned her back on me. "I guess you could say he's just very conscientious."

"Conscientious, and a bit bossy. And when I say a bit, I mean a *lot*."

She started tapping on the wall, and I kneeled down and tackled the lower parts. "He cares for this place," she replied. "It means a lot to him."

"Oh, that's right. Because his family has been looking after the chateau for over a century, right?"

"Right. I guess you could say it's in his blood."

"I guess so." I turned to look at her, but her eyes were focused on the wall in front of her, her expression intent on doing her work. I wanted to get more out of her about Corin, but I had a feeling she was rather protective of him, very likely because she had a crush on him. I recognized the signs.

"So tell me what you found in the cellar, damage-wise, and how you fixed it. You did an amazing job."

Mía's shoulders visibly relaxed and she launched into a discourse on the work she'd done as we fully unrolled the tarps, then began our work on the wall. Corin silently joined us, obviously listening, but not contributing, as we talked. My respect for Mía and her crew grew as she talked about the water damage and how they managed to save the stone structure without sacrificing its historical integrity. I really hoped I'd be able to work with her and her crew. I had some grand plans for the kitchen and knew they'd do a great job with it. That is, if I was given the chance…

By the time we'd loosened all the plaster, the room had grown almost unbearably warm. We were all sweating profusely. Corin had shed his Strawbery Banke sweatshirt and I had peeled off the aqua cardigan I'd worn over a pink t-shirt. Corin's eyes had widened when I'd done my daring reveal and I preened a little. There were some downsides to being so busty, but the girls were certainly good at getting attention. He quickly turned away, but I sensed him glancing over at me once in a while. It was all quite silly of me—enjoying his attention for something I had nothing to do with—but a much-needed balm for my ego after Jason had dumped me.

Finally I stopped. "This is ridiculous. Is there some sort of heater behind here?"

"I guess we'll find out." Corin stood up and dusted off his pants, though his swipes did little to remove the white, chalky substance. "Shall we?" He'd brought some crowbars to help remove the plaster and we went to work taking down the wall.

He pulled a particularly large piece down and when it hit the floor, it shattered. At the same time, I heard the house groan, like a dog stretching. Thankfully, I wasn't the only one to hear it. Corin and Mía glanced at each other as the sound echoed through the room, but neither said a word…almost as though they weren't surprised by it.

The groans continued with each dropping piece. There were a few more sections to go and we could see the windows clearly now, which were positioned exactly like the ones on the opposite wall. The wallpaper on the wall behind the one we were taking out matched the other side. Someone truly had come along and covered up an entire wall.

Corin reached up and pulled down the last few pieces, which neither Mía or I could reach. When the last bit fell to the ground, a strange sort of rumbling sound started up around us, and the floor began to shake, the walls, too.

"Earthquake!" Corin shouted. "Get down!" He dashed over and pulled me to my knees, sheltering me with his body. The shaking got stronger and the rattling louder with each passing second, and then I heard it. A voice, like a delicious sigh. "Ahhhhhh!" Or what I thought was a voice, anyway. It was so loud in the room, I couldn't be sure.

A gust of wind blasted against us and it was so strong and wild, buffeting us from all sides, it seemed as though we had a tornado in the room with us.

"At last!" a voice cried out, and then all was still.

A few seconds passed with nothing happening, then Corin leaned his face into mine. "Are you all right?"

I nodded and he scooched away from me, toward Mía. "Are you okay?"

She sat up and looked around dazedly. "We did this."

I crawled toward her. "We're not that strong! It was an earthquake, I think. We can get them in New England, but it's very unusual."

She stared up at Corin, whose expression was scarily ominous. "An earthquake," she repeated numbly.

He nodded vigorously. "Yes, an earthquake, Mía."

I looked around the room, suddenly doubting my own assessment. Other than the broken wall pieces on the floor, the room looked fine. The windows—all of them—were intact, the floorboards normal, nothing warped or cracked. I wondered how the rest of the house had fared, but had the strange feeling that there would be no damage.

"Did you hear the voice?" I spoke into the eerie quiet of the room. Mía went pale and I knew she had heard it. "He said, 'at last,'" I pushed. "Like he'd been freed."

I have been freed, ma chérie, a voice whispered in my mind.

His voice.

Freed at last!

Chapter Nine

☾

As I pushed myself to my feet I wanted to blurt out that this hadn't been an earthquake, and I nearly did, because that's what I tend to do. Just blurt things out without thinking things through. But I was learning wisdom. I wanted this job and to get it I had to keep my mouth shut and assess the situation first, go along and pretend nothing strange was happening. Because I was quite certain that something supernatural, something outside the norm, had just occurred. And I was quite certain that Corin and Mía didn't want me to think that.

With the wind, the heat had dissipated, the temperature quickly dropping several degrees and returning to what was likely a more normal state. But how had that happened? Or maybe I should be asking, What had we set in motion? If we had released a ghost, then weren't we supposed to feel a drop in temperature? I'd never once heard, experienced, or read about a *spike* in temperature happening.

I shivered a little, my feverish imagination producing frightening images of horned demons and raging hellfire. But I dismissed the demon theory almost immediately. The voice—what I already thought of as *my* voice—was definitely not the voice of a demon. I felt sure of this. Mostly sure, anyway. But if it wasn't a ghost, or a demon, what was it? A human playing tricks on us? Or, more specifically, on me?

I looked around the room, trying surreptitiously to check for cameras. Maybe I was part of one of those reality TV shows and any moment now someone was going to step into the room and do the big reveal. I imagined I would gasp in surprise, my hand flying to my mouth as my eyes widened comically.

I waited, but no one came in, and there was no big reveal. Hm. So maybe it was someone in the house that Corin and the others knew nothing about. Maybe we had a vagrant living in Chateau de Sowles, one that liked practical jokes.

"So, um, an earthquake!" I said. "Wow! How exciting!" I swallowed and toned it down a notch before continuing. "Maybe I should search the house, look for damage."

Corin nodded as he stood up, then reached out to help Mía to her feet. They shared a look and I felt a spasm of jealousy flare up in my chest. Though what I was jealous of I couldn't fathom; Corin was definitely *not* my type. Wait. Strike that. Maybe he was. In some ways, he was an awful lot like Jason. Above reproach, a bit imperious, and maybe lacking a little in both humor and humanity. So basically I was attracted to guys like my father—people who would tell me what to do so I wouldn't have to take responsibility for my life. I swallowed hard, tasting the bitterness of my self-assessment. Was I really that helpless?

"I'll clean up here," Mía said faintly. "Corin, would you mind helping me?"

He looked back and forth between us. "I'll be fine," I told him. "I'll be careful."

He frowned, then glanced at Mía, who was visibly shaking. Coming to the same conclusion I had—that Mía wasn't the type who scared easily—he made his decision. "Sure. We'll get it done quicker that way."

I wondered if Mía was truly frightened, or if she just wanted to get Corin alone to discuss what had happened. Seeing her pallor, I figured it was both. "I'll be back," I said, briefly considering eavesdropping before deciding against it. It was a bad habit, and not a very likeable one, but one I'd picked up ages ago to keep on top of what my father and mother had planned for me. It was the best way to avoid making them mad at me, and maybe a lot of why I'd attained my Golden Child status. But I was an adult now. It was time to act like one.

As hard and boring as that might be.

I made my way through the house, checking all the rooms, the electricity and plumbing, and the cellar, as well. The rooms looked pristine, as though nothing had happened. The only difference I could detect was the feeling that I was being followed. Before, I had experienced someone passively waiting for me, like I had to go to them. Now I felt as though the presence was more active, tagging along after me like a hungry wolf.

I was walking down a long, windowless hallway when the dim light I'd turned on snapped off, plunging the space into darkness. The blackness was complete and I froze where I was. "Corin?" I whispered. "Is that you?" The floor creaked behind me and I spun around. "Mía?"

Someone was there, but they weren't answering. I slowly began to back up, one hand sliding along the wood paneling of the wall. The creaking followed me, matching me step for step. My stomach was heaving, and my heart was beating too hard, and I thought I was going to throw up, then faint.

The way was growing lighter as I approached the end of the hall. Thankfully, it led to the foyer, and nearing the opening, I threw caution to the wind and turned to flee. Looking back over my shoulder as I ran, I ended up plowing right into Corin.

"Whoa," he cautioned, catching me. "What's going on?"

I'm ashamed to admit I melted into him like a helpless female. His arms, long and strong, wrapped around me and held me tight. When my heart rate slowed a bit, I pointed back behind me. "Someone was in the hall. Th-they turned the light off."

He stepped back from me and I regretted speaking up and making him push me away, then scolded myself for thinking that. If the person was still there, we needed to catch him. "Show me."

Drawing in a deep breath, I followed him into the hall. The light was on and no one was there. My cheeks flushed with embarrassment. "I-I don't understand! Did the electricity go out?"

He looked at me. "Not that I noticed."

My fingers curled into fists. I was proving his point about me—that I was a moon dweller, fanciful and incapable of being responsible—and it rankled big-time. I drew my shoulders back. He was not going to win this one. "Ah, well. I'm not sure what happened, but maybe the light was affected by an aftershock. You know, from our little *earthquake*." I kept a close eye on his face, but his expression remained bland. "The house is fine. No damage at all. Strange, considering the tremors we experienced."

"Yes, strange," he agreed. "But lucky, right?" he added with an encouraging nod.

"Right," I mumbled, annoyed he'd diffused my very pointed attack.

"Mía left," he said, almost awkwardly.

"Oh. But I didn't get to say goodbye."

"I'm sure you'll see her again, when you begin work on the kitchen and bathrooms."

"But…" I paused. "Wait… Are you saying I have the job?"

"I just talked to Mr. Rachat and he agreed to let you do the work. But there's a catch," he added before I could start jumping up and down with undignified glee. "He wants you to figure out why that wall was built, and when. When is important."

My curiosity was aroused. "I can do that." Truthfully I wasn't sure if I could…well, I could figure out *when*, but the why would be much more elusive. There seemed to be no good reason to build that second wall, cover up the windows, and plant shrubs as a distraction. No good reason at all.

But I would worry about that later.

"I would need a contract."

His expression was mildly amused. "Of course."

"And I'd need photos of the house, if any exist. Plus, I'd like to see the furniture that's been moved. I'm assuming it's stored."

"We have an on-site storage area for the furniture—to keep the nicer pieces safe during construction and for some needed restoration work. As for photos, there are none here."

I eyed him with skepticism. "*None?* That's unusual. Someone with the wealth to build a house like this would have had plenty of money for photographs."

"True."

He didn't elaborate. I wasn't sure if I believed him, but I couldn't exactly accuse him of lying. It occurred to me that since Corin's family had been responsible for the upkeep of the house for over a century, they were the ones most likely to have access to that sort of thing. It also occurred to me that he had yet to mention that his family had been groundskeepers for the chateau for over a century. Why was he holding that back? Because he didn't think I needed to know? Or was it because he was embarrassed by his background? Also a possibility. He seemed a proud man. Though the position of groundskeeper, especially at such a grand house, was a respectable job, so it was an odd thing to feel embarrassed about. Maybe, simply, the topic just hadn't come up.

At any rate, he didn't seem the type to be forthcoming about much of anything, which meant I was on my own. Fortunately, I remembered a resource that might provide some photos. The local newspaper. A house like this didn't get built without someone writing a story about it.

"All right," I pretended to let it go. "I'll just have to do without." Yeah, right. I wasn't happy with my father, but he had taught me a few good business tips…if you want something done, you don't let anyone get in your way. You go after it, and you go after it hard.

Funny, though, whenever I'd tried to do that, he'd shut me down.

"Why don't you take the rest of the day off?" Corin suggested. "I'll have Mr. Rachat's lawyer draw up a new contract and get it to you tomorrow."

"I don't want to take the day off!" I cried, just barely refraining from stomping my foot like a child. I cleared my throat and went on in a more dignified manner. "I'd like to start working on some designs for the kitchen. I have some great ideas!"

"You'll stay in the kitchen? I mean, in case there are more tremors. It's on the ground floor, so it's quite solid."

"I'll try. I might have to look at the rooms around it, make sure that what I want to do won't cause any major problems. You're sure Mr. Rachat is okay with the remodel? I was under the impression that he wanted the house to fit the early 1890s as closely as possible. I plan to do that the best I can…there are appliances that can be made to look like cabinets and the like. But it won't be *exactly* period. Same goes for the bathrooms. The rest of the house…well, I'll double-check, but from my initial assessment, very little has changed since that time period—some wallpaper, some flooring. It's almost as though no one lived here since then."

Corin looked away. "Some people have, but no one stayed for long. Probably too isolated out here."

"Probably," I agreed, though I didn't mean it. A person didn't come to a place like this without knowing it was isolated. I would bet my firstborn that something else had been going on. I could only hope the newspapers at the time held some answers for me. I shivered with anticipation. My work often involved being part detective, and sometimes I think that's what I liked best about what I did. I loved solving historical mysteries, and this place was full of them.

"Cold?" he asked.

"Nope! Just excited."

One corner of his mouth tilted upward, which I could only guess was meant to be a smile. "You really do love your work."

I nodded eagerly. "I do."

I do. I do. The phrase echoed in my mind and suddenly it came back to me what I'd said before I'd passed out on him, and why he'd let me stay the night. He felt sorry for me. My cheeks grew hot. "I told you, didn't I? About Jason. Oh, Lord. I'm so embarrassed. Please don't tell me you pitied me because of that! I don't want that. I really don't. I wasn't thinking straight, that's why I said all that. Ugh!"

"I don't pity you."

I met his eyes. He didn't look like he pitied me, not at all. No, he looked like someone who merely thought I was a pathetic loser. "He broke it off, yes," I hurried on, desperate to fix this, "but now I'm thinking maybe I didn't want to get married after all. I'm a modern woman. I can stand on my own. So there's nothing to pity!" With each word, my voice rose higher and brighter and I was hitting some false notes with great skill.

"You don't want to be with him?"

"No! Well, maybe. I don't know! He bought us a house without asking me!" Well… I hadn't meant to share that.

"As a wedding gift?" His tone implied that I was being an ungrateful snot.

I groaned. "I'd told him months before that I didn't like the house, at least not enough to live in, so I'm not being a spoiled brat."

He ignored the last part. "So what kind of house would you live in?"

"Okay, this *is* going to sound like I'm a spoiled brat"—I spun around, my arms thrown out and a grin on my face—"but I'd live here. Chateau de Sowles is amazing." I turned back to face him. "Pipe dream, huh? Like I could afford a place like this!"

"Mansions are important to you?" His voice was cool.

I scowled at him. "You're missing the point entirely, Corin. This house is more than a mansion. It's a world unto itself. The carvings, the exquisite tapestries, the artistic details. The setting, here by the river. It's a romantic's dream."

This time, surprisingly, he made no comment about my dreamy delusions, saying instead, "I wouldn't mind living here myself."

I laughed. "So we're both dreamers! And here I thought you were just a stick in the mud."

He looked offended. "I'm *not* a dreamer. If I truly wanted to live here, I'd make a plan to achieve it."

"Seriously, Corin? You're offended that I called you a dreamer, but not a stick in the mud?"

He crossed his arms. "Sticks in the mud are the ones who make sure things get done."

"Dreamers can get things done, too, it just takes us a little longer. And what we get done is often something that's never been done before."

He nodded slightly. "Touché."

"Exactly. So I can stay and work?"

"Fine. But be done at six sharp. I don't want you in here after dark. I'll close up the house. When you sign the contract I'll give you your own set of keys and you can do it yourself."

"Heaven forbid you give them to me before I sign on the dotted line," I teased.

He eyed me like I was a fly in his soup. "I simply don't have them on me at the moment."

"Oops!" I laughed. "I guess I'm determined to make you the bad guy in this."

"The bad guy?" he echoed, confusedly.

"You didn't want me to have this job, you know."

"You're right, I didn't," he admitted, and didn't look at all apologetic for it, damn his eyes. "And I'm still not sure you should do it."

"You don't? Why? It's because you don't think I could do it, isn't it?"

"On the contrary. I'm beginning to see just how talented you are." My eyes widened in surprise. "No, I'm more concerned about your welfare." Before I could respond, he turned and strode to the door. "I've work to do. I'll be back at six."

I nodded and after one last, speculative glance at me he left. When he was gone, I spun in circles, laughing delightedly. I'd done it! I'd gotten a job on my own, and one in a beautiful house that had a mystery to boot.

Take that, Charles Alexander! And you too, Jason Sanders!

Chapter Ten

☾

While fetching my work supplies from the guesthouse, I had to wonder why Corin would be concerned about my welfare, and why had he made a point of wanting me out of the house before dark? My sense that something was going on here, something odd, grew with each question. James, the previous architect, had left under mysterious circumstances, Mía was nervous, and both Corin and Peter Paddington had warned me to be careful.

To show I wasn't entirely stupid, I made sure to stay in the general area of the kitchen, a dark, dank space that I quickly determined could benefit from a few more windows. I worked steadily, reveling in sketching and planning and visualizing. In a relatively short time, I churned out a plan, utilizing every bit of space to its maximum potential. Later tonight, I planned to study the blueprints and assess the best placement for the windows and double-check the details of my plan to be sure I wouldn't run into electrical and plumbing problems. Tomorrow I planned to return to roughly map everything out. Then I would hit the four rooms that had been turned into bathrooms some time probably in the twenties. The job had not been well done, so I had my work cut out for me there.

My phone jingled, indicating I had a text, and I pulled it out. Almost six? Already? I sighed, and without reading the text, gathered up my work and headed for the foyer. Stifling a yawn, I flung open the door and headed out into the evening. The air was fresh on my face and I inhaled deeply. Letting my eyes flit over the landscape, I caught sight of Corin heading my way, and had the brief impression that I'd been hanging about a little, sort of waiting for him to show up.

"I'm still alive," I called out.

He approached the steps and bounded up them as though he hadn't been going all day. Though obviously he had. There was a light sheen of sweat on his skin and his forearms were speckled with bits of grass and leaves and a few light scratches.

"I can see that." He looked at the pile of papers in my arms. "Progress?"

"Lots." I was about to expound on what I'd come up with, then thought better of it. I had not signed a contract, after all. I suppressed a smug smile. I was getting good at this.

"Good." Corin was trying to look like he wasn't interested in what I'd produced, and he was doing an excellent job of it, his gaze on the house. "Any trouble?"

"None at all. No aftershocks, no lights going out on me. No strange sounds or spooky apparitions." The grin on my face faded when he swung around to face me.

"What do you mean?"

"I was kidding, Corin. Sheesh, you're strung tighter than a Stradivarius. Maybe you need a vacation. Mr. Rachat is working you too hard."

"I'm fine. Just needed to be sure we didn't have mice in the attic."

"Ah, yes. Mice." I wasn't buying it. "I assume you've had the house exterminated?"

"Yes. But they can come back."

"When's the last time you had it done?"

"A month ago," he replied, his eyes back on the house.

"So it's very likely not mice...or any kind of rodent."

"Probably not," he admitted.

I couldn't help myself. "So it could be a ghost?"

He shook his head fervently. "I don't believe in ghosts."

"They don't need you to believe in them to exist, you know," I pushed, even though the tense set of his shoulders told me to back off. It was a reaction I'd seen in my father often enough to know I needed to drop the subject, and *now*. But I hated dropping the subject, especially when I knew I was close to discovering something juicy. Still... Until I had that contract clutched tightly in my hot little hands, it was best to be safe and stay on everyone's good side. "Well, I'm going to go eat," I said. "See you tomorrow morning."

"Yeah, sure. Tomorrow morning," he replied absently. I took a moment to study his face, surprised to see a touch of unease in the slight furrowing of his brow and the quiet defensiveness of his stance. Even though he'd said he would want to live in the chateau and had spent most of his life living next to it, he was nervous about it.

I left him looking up at the tower room I'd been in earlier, his expression uncertain, as though someone had just told him to do something he didn't want to do. "Okay, bye." He didn't respond, and suppressing a shudder of foreboding, I scurried toward the safety of the guesthouse.

☾

After a glass of Merlot and a heaping plate of butter noodles, I felt much better. While eating I'd figured out what was going on, which helped drive away the quiver of anxiety that had been following me around since this morning. Corin was testing me. Being Mr. Rachat's emissary of sorts, he felt he had to know if I could handle working in a house that was, shall we say, a bit touchy. I say 'touchy' as opposed to haunted because, to be honest, I'm not entirely sure what ghosts actually are. What I'd felt and seen in other houses made me certain *some-thing* was there, however those experiences could simply have been an event that had inadvertently crossed the barrier of one time dimension and into another. What it came down to was that I didn't have enough proof to say definitively that what I'd seen were actual spirits of people who had once lived and were now dead.

But in my heart of hearts, I wanted to believe that's what ghosts are—the once living. It was an explanation that many would prefer to dismiss, but I liked it. Besides, who would want to live in a world where you could only believe what your rational mind allowed you to believe?

Not me.

Probably Corin would. I gave a little snort. He really was a stick in the mud. A good-looking one, sure, but I didn't need any more good-looking sticks in the mud in my life.

Speaking of sticks in the mud, I pulled out my phone and checked my texts and phone messages. I had one text from Ryan, but no messages from Jason. I felt slightly disappointed. Okay, a LOT disappointed. But I figured if I consumed enough wine I could send that foolish feeling far away. I was over Jason. I was not getting back together with him. Never, ever, ever.

"Text me," Ryan had written.

I quickly typed, "I'm here."

A few seconds later, "Jasons harassing me."

Ah. Mystery solved. Jason couldn't corner me, so he'd gone after Ryan. Smart move, and disturbing news. "U didn't tell him anything?"

"Might have said sumthing bout a job." Sometimes Ryan's texts are grammatically painful to read.

Crap. "Like what?"

"That u had taken one."

"U didn't say where?!"

"No."

Hmmm. "Really?"

"Might have mentioned NH."

Damn. "Anything specific?"

Long pause. "He showed up @ work. Client came, he left. Close one, Vi."

Too close. "Can't believe he came to Daphne's. Stay strong, Ry."

"Gotta go. Annas here. Goin hoppin."

"Have fun, u 2."

"Of course."

"BTW...u didn't tell Anna where I'm working?"

"Ta!"

He had. Double crap. Anna was a worse gossip than Ryan. At least Ryan would try to keep his mouth shut. Anna would not. She said it wasn't in her nature to keep quiet. Anna was an interesting friend to have, but I wouldn't trust her to do my laundry, much less keep my secrets.

I wondered how long I had before Jason showed up. A warped part of me couldn't wait to see him again. The rest wished he'd stay away for good.

I spent the next several hours poring over the blueprints, plotting out the details for the kitchen and studying the bathrooms, jotting down ideas as they came to me. As I worked, my eyes kept flitting to the tower in the blueprints, and I remembered my experience there with a shiver. Finally, eyes burning and focus shot, I put the blueprints away and grabbed a light jacket, thankful for my burst of rebellion that had encouraged me to unpack earlier. All I wanted to do now was return to the chateau. I couldn't go inside, but I could look at it. That would be enough. For the moment, anyway.

As I zipped up my jacket, I spotted something through the window above the bed. I climbed onto the bed and looked out, pleased to see that I could check on the house from my bedroom, especially as it looked as though there was a light on. Was Corin doing a walk-through? Checking that the doors and windows were locked? Was he concerned about burglars? The property was walled-in, so that particular worry couldn't be too realistic. Then again, teenagers have a knack for sneaking into the hardest of places.

Or was Corin only worried I would try to get back in?

Well, it wasn't me in there! I was being a good girl. I marched into the cool air coming in off the river, determined to set him straight. With each step, my indignation grew. I had every right to return to the house whenever I wanted! I was the architect! I was working here! I—Well, technically I was only a squatter at the moment, but still...

I had reached the house, but the light I'd seen failed to show itself again. In fact, it seemed very dark and still inside, as though no one was there. I tiptoed up the steps and tried the doorknob. It was locked. Hm. Did that mean Corin wasn't in there, or did it mean he was super-paranoid, locking the door so no one could sneak in while he was inside? Actually it was probably pretty smart to do that, but I was still feeling irrationally angry, so I swept my reasoning aside like dust on the floor. I wanted to be mad, and right now, Corin made a good target. The problem was, I wasn't exactly sure what I was so angry about, though I had a sneaking suspicion it had something to do with Jason.

With a sigh, I followed the wraparound porch around to the side facing the river. Arms crossed, I stood looking out at the water. A nearly full moon shone down on the black water, and the mirrored expanse reflected diamonds of light back up into the starry sky.

A breeze stirred the tendrils of hair around my neck and I shivered, wrapping my arms tighter around me. Long ago someone had likely stood here, in this very spot, and looked out at the river, just as I was doing. What had they been thinking? Were they happy? Sad? Was one of them AS or CR? *Who were they?* I wondered dreamily, the glittering water mesmerizing me. Lovers, childhood friends? What?

My eyes settled on the island's dark hump, splitting the river in two, and a sort of certainty filled me. Definitely lovers, and they often met on the island. It was the perfect hideout. It's where I would go, anyway.

Okay, so maybe I am a moon dweller. But was there anything wrong with that? I was pretty sure my father would say there was. He hated my dreaminess, my distractibility, even my use of intuition while working. He wanted me to be rational and scientific, which I could be and I was, but I figured, why not use both sides? So I did. Secretly.

It seemed a silly thing to care about, but it struck me that I'd always tried to hide that side of me. Father would question me about how I 'knew' certain things, and the first couple times I'd tell him that I just felt it. But after a few silent treatments, I quickly learned to come up with logical explanations for my discoveries. That appeased him, but now I wondered if maybe I shouldn't have subverted that part of me. I had a gift, and he'd made me ashamed of it.

Well, no longer! It was high time I learned to be the kind of architect I was meant to be, not just my parents' clone. I was Vianne Alexander and what made me good at my work wasn't just that I knew my subject thoroughly, it was because I could *sense* things.

Like right now. I could almost feel the house breathing around me, as though it had awakened from a long sleep. The house was returning to life, and I was pretty sure my arrival had something to do with it.

As I headed back to the guesthouse, none the wiser about the source of the light I'd seen, the troubling question occurred to me—was waking the house a good thing, or a harbinger of bad things to come?

Chapter Eleven

I slept well and awoke refreshed and raring to go. After breakfast and a shower, I pulled my curls into a bun and headed out into the fresh morning air, blueprints in one hand and my notes in the other. I hurried to catch up to Corin as he approached the chateau.

"You're awake already," he said, looking me up and down.

"You sound surprised."

"I simply took you for more of a night owl, that's all."

I squinted my eyes at him, searching for the insult. It was in there somewhere, I knew. Unfortunately, he was totally right. I tended to sleep in whenever I could. That's when I had my most vivid dreams. "I'm on a job, Corin," I replied primly. "It wouldn't be professional to sleep until noon."

He nodded distractedly. "Of course."

"Is that the contract?" I nodded at the large white envelope in his hand.

"It is. We can sign it inside, in the library."

"The library? Good choice!"

He held the door open for me, his eyes skeptical as I passed by him, into the foyer. "You like libraries?"

"I love libraries because of the books, of course—and yes, I do read, thank you very much—but I love libraries even more when they have secret rooms!"

The door slammed shut behind me and I spun around. To my surprise, Corin's expression was thunderous. I hadn't thought he could do thunderous. "What are you talking about?"

"The secret room off the library, duh! What other secret room would I be talking about?" Well, I could be talking about the fourth floor tower room, but I wasn't bringing that one up. He'd have to do it.

"There's a secret room off the library?"

I studied him, incredulous. "You don't know about it?"

He shrugged. "I was never told about it."

"But didn't your family serve as caretakers here?" I asked, finally putting it out there that I knew about his family and their strong connection to the chateau. "Wouldn't they have known?"

"Not necessarily," he replied stiffly, giving nothing away.

"There's no need to get all huffy, Mr. Huffenpuff. The passages and the room are on the blueprints, but it isn't obvious. There's a special mark for them, in code, but I've seen a variation of it before with other blueprints, so I was able to figure out what it meant."

"Special mark?" he echoed. "Code?"

I led the way to the library and he followed after me, obviously stunned. I took pity on him. "It's not common knowledge. Your average architect—one not trained in restoration—might miss the marks. Homeowners who didn't want hidden passages and rooms advertised to the whole world had the architect 'disguise' their presence."

He looked around the room. "Where is it?"

I led him over to a bookshelf. "It's a fairly common type. The lever is here." I pointed to a spot a couple inches to the right of the bookshelf. "Stand back." I pushed the button and the bookshelf swung halfway inward, the other half swinging out.

Corin's face lit up and for a moment I saw another side to him. "I never knew," he breathed.

But as he took a step forward to look more closely, there was a heavy gust of air and the bookshelf swung shut. "That was weird," I said, examining the shelf. "I know you shut the outside door because you *slammed* it, so it's not creating suction. Were you expecting someone?"

"Just Brittany, as a witness." He looked around. "Go check, will you?"

I nodded and hurried out of the room, feeling oddly shaken. I found the front door shut tight and no one answered my calls, so if someone had come in, they weren't admitting it to me. It hadn't been Brittany, I felt sure. She would have said something. I returned to the library to find Corin giving the button a frustrated punch.

"It probably needs oil," I assured him. "I'll work on it later."

He reluctantly stopped punching the button. "Yes. Okay. Though maybe I'll give it another try myself, this afternoon."

"Sure," I agreed. "Either way."

He pulled in a deep breath and his demeanor changed. Gone was the uncertain, frustrated normal guy and in his place was the other Corin, untouchable and unreadable. "Shall we sign the contract?"

"The sooner, the better," I agreed, setting my stuff on the massive desk, bare of paper or anything that made a desk someone's workplace. I was glad I wouldn't need to change out the flooring in here. Moving that desk would take some doing.

There was a knock on the partially closed library door, before it swung all the way open with a dramatic burst. "I'm here!" A lovely young woman with long black hair and a beautiful olive complexion announced as she bustled into the room. She had a large purse over one arm and a Dunkin Donuts beverage container clutched in her hand. The smell of coffee wafted toward me. I stared at the container enviously. "The traffic downtown is awful! The tourist invasion has begun." She spotted me. "You must be Vi! Come give me a hug!" She opened her arms and I obediently went to her. She somehow managed to give me a good squeeze, despite the bag and container. "I've been dying to meet you!" Her dark eyes flicked toward Corin. "Hello, Corin."

"Hello, Brittany," he greeted. Their polite exchange complete, Brittany gave a satisfied nod and turned back to me. "Everything all right at the guesthouse?"

"It's perfect!" I gushed. "You have excellent taste in food."

She grinned, her dark eyes sparkling. "Food is my forte." She looked me over. "You're not what I was expecting at all."

I sighed. "I know."

"Sorry!" she cried, laying a hand on my arm. "You must get that a lot."

I glanced at Corin, who was staring at me. "I do. But I can do the work."

"I don't doubt it, hon," she said. "Peter told me what you found." She laughed. "You showed that James creep. He really is high on himself, isn't he, Corin?"

"I don't think it's appropriate to talk about him with another architect."

"Oh, poo. She probably knows him." She turned to me expectantly.

"I don't know anyone named James, I'm afraid."

"That's his last name. His first is Mark."

"Mark James?" Oh, crud. I knew him, all right. When Corin had referred to him as James, I had assumed he was calling him by his first name. I'd worked with Mark a few times, when he'd served as a consultant at a few projects I'd been on. As soon as he found out who my parents were, whenever we crossed paths, he would harass me to go on a date with him. I always said no and he always pretended I hadn't. It was a bit irritating, but now I wondered if I could put his interest in me, or my parents, to good use.

"You know him?" Corin demanded, looking unsettled.

"I've worked with him," I admitted, then snapped my mouth shut. I was not saying anything more on the subject of Mark James. Corin, I hated to admit, was right. It wasn't professional to talk about other architects, especially when one has little good to say about them.

Brittany glanced back and forth between us, as though waiting to hear more dirt. When we failed to provide it, she sighed, then bustled over to the desk to set down her bag and the DD container. "I hope you like mocha lattes, Vi. I'm obsessed with them."

My eyes widened. "Oh, I do!" She opened the container and plucked out a large coffee cup and held it out to me, then grabbed another and gave it to Corin. "For Mr. Boring, plain black coffee." He took it with a grimace and Brittany held up her latte. "Welcome to Chateau de Sowles, Vi!" We clicked cups together and I felt suddenly very happy to be here. "Now let's get this party started. I've got loads to do today for Mr. Rachat. He's a regular taskmaster." Corin cleared his throat warningly. "Oh, you know he is, Corin. But I will add that he's also the best boss I've ever had, so you know I'm saying it with love." She gave him a wide smile and he shook his head before allowing one corner of his mouth to turn up into that sad excuse for a smile he had.

We took a sip of our coffee—it was delicious—then I signed the contract, with Brittany witnessing the procedure. Luckily the contract only had my name on it and not AA&D's. I wondered if that was standard, or if I'd just lucked out. When we were finished, she took the documents, her bag, and the empty container. "I'll leave you two to do what you do." Her grin was mischievous. "Later!"

"Thanks for the coffee," I called after her.

"No probs!" she yelled back.

"She's great," I said to Corin when she was gone. "Mr. Rachat hires good people."

"Including me?" he enquired, taking a sip from his cup, his eyes never leaving mine.

"Judging by the grounds, I'd say you were a pretty good hire, too."

"Pretty good?"

"Adequate?"

"That's worse."

I laughed. "So you're not going to try to find a way to get me to leave, are you?"

He frowned. "Why would I do that?"

"Um, because you told me to leave."

"I was only doing what Mr. Rachat wanted."

I thought about that. "Yes, I suppose that's true." I wondered if I dared ask what had happened to Mr. Rachat, then decided now was not the time. I was learning subtlety. I was also learning that if I wanted to keep this job, I had to step lightly. Which was a bummer. I really wanted to know.

"Now that you have a contract, I will support you through the process. Anything you need, you call me." He held out his hand. "Give me your cell phone."

I handed it over. He typed for a few seconds, then set it on the desk. Then he typed something on his own phone before pocketing it. "There. Now you can get a hold of me at any time."

"Even if it's just because someone turned the light off on me?"

"Even that."

"Excellent."

"That reminds me... You'll need these." He reached in his pocket and pulled out a set of keys. I took them with my free hand, delighting in their cold solidity. I now had access to the house whenever I wanted. "Please, always lock up after you're done with your work."

"Of course. Speaking of work, I should get cracking. I only have the six months to get a kitchen and four bathrooms updated, plus the other minor changes, *and* I have to do that research Mr. Rachat wanted." I held out my hand. Corin looked at it for a moment, then reached out and took it in his. His hand was warm and dry, calloused from hard work, but not rough. I felt a slight frisson run up my spine. "I look forward to working with you, Corin Groundskeeper."

"And I, you, Vianne Architect."

We smiled at each other, then his phone rang and our hands parted. Holding it up, he smiled at me, then left the room. I watched him go, then turned to the wall where the lever for the hidden room blended into the carved wood. I pressed it and the bookshelf slid open, easy as cutting through Key Lime pie. I pressed the lever again and the bookshelf slid back into place. How odd that it was opening so easily for me when it hadn't for Corin.

I decided not to tell him that.

☾

When I came downstairs to go to lunch, I didn't see Corin, nor did I see him the rest of the day, which was strangely disappointing. I did, however, make good progress on my work, putting together a detailed list of everything I had to do, then determining schemes for each of the bathrooms, one of which connected to the master bedroom and was large enough to add a powder room expressly for a woman's toilette. I was very excited about that. I've always wanted my own powder room and now here I could design one for Mr. Rachat's new bride. Hopefully she would love it.

While I would give my left arm to live in a house like this, and very likely envied her more than was healthy, I was also happy to be able to give her this gift, to be received after returning from a six-month honeymoon with her lover and best friend. I sighed wistfully. It sounded just like what a Victorian couple would do after getting married...go on a grand tour of the continent. My thoughts filled with hazy images of long lunches in Paris, a gondola ride in Venice, a hike across the English moors, jaunts through haunted castles.

That lucky, lucky lady!

Shaking my head with a smile, I returned my attention to preparing my thick grilled cheese sandwich and clam chowder for supper. After a filling meal, I did several hours of research on my laptop, figuring out the best materials and where I could find them, jotting down notes on various new ideas. Finally, pleasantly exhausted, I went to get ready for bed, surprised to see it was close to midnight already.

I was about to pull my nightgown off its hook when I spotted a light in the house out of the corner of my eye. Again? What was going on in there? I wasn't sure, but this time I could use my keys to get inside and track down the cause. Grabbing them off the breakfast bar, I sprinted outside, determined to end this mystery.

Like the previous night, the house was dark and quiet. I quickly unlocked the front door and hurried inside, not wanting to lose my culprit. Standing in the middle of the foyer, in the dark, I realized I'd stupidly forgotten to bring a light. But there was no way I was going to turn on the lights and alert Corin to my presence in the house. Despite what he'd said about supporting me, I had a feeling that if he caught me doing something he thought inappropriate, which could be a lot of things in his estimation, he'd report me to Mr. Rachat and I'd lose my job. So no light, even though I could barely see my hand in front of my face.

All this was going through my mind when I heard footsteps rushing past me and up the stairs. Without thinking, I raced after them, feeling warm air currents swirling about me. When I reached the second landing, I stopped in my tracks. What was I doing? It was dark and I was alone, with no light, not even a weapon to protect myself.

I began to retreat back down the stairs when I felt a hand grip my arm, hot and tight. I screamed loudly and tore away. As I rushed down the stairs, the house began to shake and I thought I heard a voice calling out, *Come to me…*

But that was not going to happen. Something was very wrong here.

I don't know how I made it down the stairs without breaking my neck, but soon I was outside, slamming the door behind me. I didn't stop running until I was back at the guesthouse, with the door firmly locked behind me.

Someone was definitely in that house, and that someone had grabbed my arm and tried to detain me.

If it was a ghost, it was a very solid one.

Chapter Twelve

☾

I did not sleep well, my thoughts cranking out an endless re-run of what had happened the night before. For a long time a part of me didn't really want to go to work in the morning, afraid of what I'd find when I got there. But damned if I was going to blow this opportunity simply because I thought someone had grabbed my arm.

It wasn't until I started to drift off that I figured out what had happened. Corin had been trying to get into the library's secret room, and I had caught him at it. So he'd fled, pulling my attention away from the library so I wouldn't know what he'd been up to. Damn him! He'd scared the crap out of me!

Armed with a mug of strong coffee, I marched resolutely toward the house. Corin was not going to ruin this for me simply because he couldn't stand that the secret door wouldn't open for him (though why it wouldn't was rather odd). He caught me as I trudged up the stairs and I rounded on him, thoroughly annoyed.

"You're looking tired." The jerk had the nerve to smirk. "Rough night?"

"I *am* tired, maybe because a certain someone likes to wander around the chateau at night."

The smirk faded. "The chateau? I wasn't in there last night."

"But I saw your light!"

His expression became skeptical. "Are you sure you saw something?"

"Positive, and this is the second night in a row."

"Well, it wasn't me. In fact, I wasn't even home last night until around one."

"One in the morning?" I almost couldn't believe it of the fuddy-duddy. "But I saw the light around midnight."

"Not me, then. I had a meeting with Mía."

Mía? At her name my mood soured even more. Crap. I'd been so sure it was him. Convincing myself of that was how I'd managed to sleep for a couple hours. And what was he doing with Mía until one in the morning? I didn't believe they'd discuss business for that long. More likely they were getting down to business. My frown deepened. "Then who was it?"

He studied me closely. "It wasn't me. It was probably just the reflection of the moon, along with that imagination of yours."

"I know what I saw, Corin. I can tell the difference between moonlight and a man-made light. Lights move up and down, the moon does not."

He took in my dignified stance. "It might have been one of the construction workers, forgot something probably."

"At midnight? I don't think so. The door was locked, too. I double-checked it when I left last night, as I'm sure you did. And isn't the gate locked?"

"All right, I believe you," he said brusquely. "I'll keep an eye out tonight."

I drew myself up. He was being annoyingly inconsistent. Before, he wouldn't accept my excuses for the shadow I'd seen in the tower, now he was making them up himself. "See that you do. I might be responsible for the project, but you're responsible for the chateau. I don't think Mr. Rachat would appreciate coming home from his honeymoon, the most romantic time of his life, to a burgled house."

"Mr. Rachat is not your concern," he said coldly, pulling back from me.

"Are you kidding me? He's my employer. He's of great concern to me. Now if you'll excuse me, I have a job to do." I swept past him, fuming. Arrogant jerk! My *imagination*, indeed! I'd show him my imagination, in the form of all the tortures I'd devise for him.

My hand on the knob, I realized how lucky it was that I'd gone ahead of Corin since I hadn't locked the door last night after my little visit. Crap. But Corin didn't seem to notice my mistake. He had retreated to the drive and was now looking up at the tower, an enigmatic expression on his face. Why did he keep looking up there? Maybe, after finding out about the library's secret room, he was realizing that there must be some way into the tower, too. A hidden way. And maybe he was thinking, as I was, that whoever was in the house could be hiding up there.

If someone was in the house.

Actually, in the bright light of day, I was starting to doubt myself. Had I really felt someone touch me? It had been dark; I'd been tired. I could have imagined it all.

But it was only as I opened the door to the chateau and stepped inside that I realized I didn't want to be imagining it. Yes, I'd been frightened, but what had really kept me up was reliving the memory of that sensual heat on my flesh. I closed my eyes for a moment and recalled the sensation—tingling sparks up my arm, bursting into my chest like fireworks, then gushing back down into my stomach, warm as honey. The experience had been intoxicating, with promises of more to come.

All that from a touch. I'd be insane *not* to want it again.

"Are you coming in?" I demanded of Corin.

He looked at me, surprised. His cheeks were flushed and his forehead was furrowed in thought. "Hm? Oh, no. I, um, have other work to do."

It was the first time I'd seen him flustered, and of course I knew why. "The door likely just needs some oil," I said gently.

"The door to the tower?"

I stared at him. "No! The secret door in the library."

"Oh." He started to say something, then stopped himself. "Have a good day." He spun abruptly about and marched away. I watched him go, not sure what to feel about him. He was an aggravating man, that was for sure, but sometimes I kind of felt sorry for him. Like right now. He was acting like a man being presented with a dilemma he had no idea how to resolve. I liked that sort of thing—mysteries and enigmas—but I had a feeling that for someone like Corin, the unexplainable was akin to torture.

My phone trilled and I looked down at it. Jason. I stared at the screen. Maybe I should just answer and get it over with. But I hesitated too long and the call went to voicemail. I debated whether or not to listen to his message now, then decided I should. I was already in a tetchy mood. Why not pile it on?

There was a strange pause at the beginning of the message, as though Jason was thinking of the words he wanted to say. I had never once seen or heard Jason at a loss for words, so maybe he was just taking a drink of coffee before starting.

"Vianne... Why are you doing this? What have I ever done to you that would make you do this to me? Yes, I put off our wedding, but that was because you hadn't done your part and it was no longer the perfect wedding. A perfect wedding is what you deserve, because you're perfect. Just the way you are. Yes, you're forgetful, but that's okay. I'm not. I'll take care of all that stuff. And yes, you're messy and I hate your car. I admit it. But I'm willing to overlook all your faults because I love you. I really do." There was another long pause, then Jason's tone changed, along with the theme of his message. "Ashley Winterton has been calling me lately. She's, well, she's been a good friend to me, and she's been offering her sympathy in my times of trouble. She said... Well, she said that you sabotaged our wedding, and that you couldn't really love me if you weren't willing to accept your mistake and move on. I hate to admit that she might have a point. But

I'm not giving up on you, Vianne. I won't! I'll find you and we'll get this wedding, and our relationship, back on track."

The message ended there, which was a good thing because I was about to explode. Never had I felt so angry with a person in my life!

"You dirty, rotten bastard!" I shouted at the phone. "How dare you use that tramp to manipulate me!" The first part of the message had been perfect. The second part—using Ashley—was not.

The problem was, Jason's ploy was working. I hated the idea of Ashley getting Jason, of getting her way in anything. Ever since I'd met her a few years ago at a fundraising gala event organized by her mother, she'd been a thorn in my side.

I wasn't the most competitive of people, but there was just something about Ashley that made me want to thwart her whenever possible. Maybe it's because she said things like, "You're lucky you're able to carry extra weight. There's no way I could do that. I guess my body just can't stand fat!" Or… "My housekeeper has that same dress! Isn't that the funniest thing?" And this gem, "You and Jason don't really look all that much alike." Um, should people who are dating resemble each other? Sounds a bit incestuous to me. The problem was, Ashley and Jason, with their similar lean torsos and blond good looks, would look amazing together, like models in a magazine. Damn them.

I turned off my phone and put it away. I was tired, and I was nervous about last night—because if that hadn't been Corin in the chateau, who had it been? Adding to my problems, I really needed to finish up the plans this week, by Sunday night at the latest, so I'd have time to get them approved. In a project like this, with such a short deadline, every hour was precious. That time wouldn't be wasted, of course, but the sooner I got the process going, the better.

I decided I needed to block out the rest of the world, so I inserted ear buds and got down to business, the morning flying by. After a quick lunch, I returned to work, making rough blueprints to re-copy later on the appropriate paper and with the exact dimensions. I made sure to triple-check all my measurements and be certain what I wanted to do could be done.

Before I knew it, it was six o'clock and my stomach was grumbling. This time I didn't see Corin when I locked up, which was just as well, because even though he wasn't the one who'd been in the house, I was still annoyed with him. Not sure why exactly, but maybe I just needed someone to be mad at right now.

I was worried, too, and my nature doesn't handle worry well. I tend to freak out at the littlest snag, probably because my father never put me in a position where I could make mistakes and then be the one responsible for fixing them. The stressful part was that this was my first real job on my own, so there couldn't be any mistakes. I had to shine. I wanted to shine! I wanted to show everyone what I could do all by myself.

After dinner, I worked on finishing the final blueprints for the kitchen. Having the previous blueprints made the job much easier. After copying those dimensions, I only had to fill in all the changes I planned to make. Tomorrow I would draw the final prints for at least two of the bathrooms, which I figured could be done in the chateau's library on that gloriously large desk.

It was half past midnight when I finished. Yawning, I put everything away, feeling absolutely done in. I'd never had to work so hard on a project and it was getting to me. Would the prints pass inspection? Had I thought of everything? I'd made sure to stay as close to maintaining period integrity as was physically possible. Luckily Father and I had done renovation work in the nearby town of Hampton, so I already had a list of reputable merchants who could provide the appropriate materials. That saved a lot of time.

I just had to make sure that Mía—for I was assuming she'd be the general contractor—knew how to do proper lead paint clean-up. Working in New England, I couldn't imagine her not knowing, but I had to be sure. I also had to ensure that Corin set up a written agreement with her for this next phase documenting all the important details, from beginning date to end, along with payment information and how labor and materials would be charged.

It was a lot to remember and my head felt like it was spinning. Before climbing into bed, I checked out the window. There was no light and I felt both relieved and disappointed at its absence. Then I felt nothing, because I was fast asleep, dreaming about blue lines and numbers and paint samples.

Chapter Thirteen

☾

Around three in the morning I was awakened by a sound. I sat up and looked around. Feeling a whisper of cool air sweep across the room, I realized that one of my windows had popped open, letting in the night air. I reluctantly slid out of bed and went to close it, the breeze being slightly more brisk than I was up to handling.

As I crossed the floor, I heard it. *Ma chérie...*

I shook my head to clear it and listened more closely, but nothing came. I scurried over to the window above my bed and looked out at the chateau. There was a light on in the tower. Someone was in there!

Grabbing my robe, a flashlight I'd found in a kitchen drawer, and the keys to the house, I hurried outside, expecting to be buffeted by the wind that had opened my window, but there was none to speak of. Pulling on my robe over my white, ankle length gown, I scurried across the lawn, its grass cool and wet beneath my feet. I was determined to catch my 'ghost,' whoever he may be, before Corin had a chance to interfere.

I have to admit that while a part of me wanted there to be a real ghost, another, cowardly part, wanted a logical explanation. Ghosts are fun to think about and imagine...from a distance. But in reality, would I be so calm if a real ghost approached me?

I sprinted up the front steps and had my key in the door before I could reconsider my actions. I needed to figure out what was going on once and for all. Whether it be a ghost, a stray cat, or a person, I had to know.

Once inside, I cursed my stupidity. I had not thought to check to see if the flashlight worked, which it didn't when I tried to flick it on. Once again I was stuck without a light. But I refused to retreat now. I shut the door behind me, turned the lock to keep anyone from fleeing, or coming in, and slid the keys into my robe pocket. Then I stood and listened in the cool foyer, my skin pimpled from cold and nerves, my hands trembling slightly as I tried to hear over my own labored breathing.

The sound came sooner than I'd expected. Footsteps. Pacing back and forth. Upstairs. Pulling in a deep breath for courage, I found my way to the staircase and half-blindly pulled myself up to the first landing. I tiptoed around the square to the next set of stairs and climbed them. When I reached the final floor, I was winded. My heart pounded wildly and my mouth was dry, as though I'd run a marathon. I was either terribly frightened, or dreadfully out of shape.

Very likely both.

I stopped before the secret entrance to the tower, having known all along that this is where I was heading. The footsteps sounded overhead, back and forth, as though whoever was up there was waiting impatiently for someone to come.

I triggered the lever and pushed the door open, then climbed the narrow steps as quietly as I could. Near the top, I paused, gathered my courage, then stepped into the room. What I saw made me catch my breath and I froze. The candle on the wall was burning, its flame glowing brightly and steadily. The light was real. But who had lit it?

In answer to my unspoken question, there was movement by the fireplace and I pulled backward, preparing to flee.

"Don't go." The words were solid, spoken out loud, not just some imagined voice in my head. Whoever had expressed them was as real as I was.

I tightened the belt on my robe, glad I'd brought along a weapon in the form of the flashlight. "Who are you?"

A figure rose from the chair on my left and I lifted the flashlight higher, preparing to strike if need be. It was a man, several inches taller than me, and dressed in a waistcoat vest over an open white shirt and dark pants. That's all I could make out in the candlelight, but it was enough to give the impression of a gentleman from the Victorian era.

What kind of joke was this?

"I think the more relevant question here is, who are *you*," he asked, his voice cultured and slightly accented, "and why are you in my house?"

I blinked, relaxing a bit. So it was the owner, not some crackpot. "*Your* house? You're Mr. Rachat? Aren't you supposed to be on your honeymoon?" I took a hesitant step closer. I wanted to see his face, which was in too much shadow to show his features well. The impression I gained as I'd moved closer, however, was of an attractive man.

"I do not know a Mr. Rachat," he replied, and took a matching step toward me, putting me back on alert. This move allowed the candlelight to strike his face and I gasped. He wasn't just attractive, he was stunning. His dark hair was a bit long, with loose curls that brushed against his strong jaw. Even in the candlelight I could make out long lashes framing deep-set eyes. His lips were full and glistened slightly, as though he'd just sipped from a glass of port, or maybe he'd just licked them. I found the image tantalizing.

"He owns this house," I managed to push out, trying not to stare and failing.

"I don't think so. *I* own this house."

Hm. Maybe he was a crackpot, after all. I tightened my grip on the flashlight. "But it's Mr. Rachat's name on the deed."

He paused to think that over and I couldn't help taking him in. Something about him caught at me, like hooks. "I am the owner in all ways that matter," he said after a moment.

"Okay," I replied carefully. "So what's your name?"

"Amenon Sowles."

My breath caught. Amenon. What a beautiful name. It sounded French, and being a devoted Francophile, I loved everything French. I had taken four years of French in high school, so I knew enough to get by.

"Amenon Sowles," I said aloud, then repeated it, Frenchified. Well, it made a strange sort of sense. This was Chateau de Sowles, after all. Maybe he was a relation looking to reclaim his ancestral home. "Your ancestors built the house."

He paused, then replied briefly, "Yes. My ancestors."

"But how come Mr. Rachat owns it now? Did someone sell the house without your permission? That's illegal!"

"I have returned to right many wrongs," he said.

"Returned from where?" I asked, once more suspicious. This was all very strange.

He took another step closer and his scent drifted with him. He smelled of wine and wood smoke and something deeper, more seductive. "You have not told me your name."

"I'm Vianne Alexander," I answered, trying to sound dignified. But it was hard when he was so close to me. He gave off a strong vibe, as certain people do—the ones who get their way because you simply can't think of a good enough reason to go against them.

"Vianne," he repeated, and his voice caressed the syllables of my name so that it sounded more like a prayer than a simple address.

"Yes, I'm here to do renovations on the house."

"You? A woman?" He looked genuinely surprised.

I drew myself up. "Just because I'm a woman doesn't mean I can't do the job."

"Well, it does not signify. The chateau does not need any work done." He peered around the tower room, his hypnotic eyes dark with memories. "I like it how it is."

For some inexplicable reason, I felt anxious to mollify him. "Mr. Rachat only wants the kitchen and bathrooms updated, but he plans to keep everything as close to how it is now as possible."

Amenon stepped back from me and I felt like I could breathe again. "You had them take down the wall in the Ship Room. Is that one of your changes?"

"Well, in a way, yes. I didn't plan that, but the room wasn't right the way it was. I'm pretty sure the original plan didn't look like that."

"No, it didn't," he said, his voice harsh with anger.

"When we clean it up and restore the original wall, the room will look better."

"You want to return things to the way they were?"

"I do," I replied eagerly, glad he was sounding more accepting. "The bathrooms and kitchen need to be changed, of course, because they're in awful shape right now. Plus I'll be making sure everything fits the same time period."

He looked back at the fire and the flames highlighted his beautiful profile. "Bath rooms. Those sound acceptable. All that work will take a while, I assume."

"I've been given six months."

He suddenly reached out and grasped my wrist. His hand felt hot, almost searing, but in a good way. "I need your help."

I swallowed hard. "With what?"

"Your Mr. Rachat is trying to take something that is not his."

"This house?" So I was right with my ancestral home theory.

He nodded and lowered his head to look me directly in the eyes. His own were dark, even in the candlelight. The intensity of his gaze made me feel breathless and unable to think straight. "I need you to not tell anyone that I am here."

"I could lose my job," I protested weakly. "And I know nothing about you."

"You have not told anyone about this room?" I shook my head. He reached up and with a long finger, traced a line down my jaw, stopping at my neck where my heart pulsed. He pressed the spot lightly. "Then you can simply pretend that you never saw me or this room."

"Yes, okay," I agreed readily, his touch making me reckless. "I won't tell anyone. But on one condition…"

The finger pressed a little harder, as though he were trying to reach my heart. "Yes?"

"That you answer one question."

"And that is?"

"Why are you trying to claim the house now? From what I've heard, the house has sat empty for years, decades even."

His finger dropped from my throat and he turned away, going to stand by the fire, his figure hunched and dark. "I was detained against my wishes."

"You were"—I licked my dry lips—"in prison?"

"Not the sort you're thinking. I am not a criminal. I did nothing wrong, and yet I was sent away for years on end, punished for a crime I did not commit. I have done everything in my power to return, and finally, now I have."

He didn't look very old. Early twenties, I guessed. I wondered if he'd been sent overseas for some petty misdemeanor as a young teen, maybe to some type of boarding school, and then had to earn money to get back. That would explain the accent, and perhaps his unusual dress style.

"So by the time you got back, the house had been sold. When did you arrive here?"

"Only a short time ago."

He must have been the man I'd seen in the tower window when I'd first arrived. "Who did this to you?" I was already imagining a scheming relative, hoping to inherit the house himself. What better way to do so than to get rid of the competition? Could the scheming uncle be Mr. Rachat?

"My parents," he rasped, and my heart seized in my chest.

"Your parents sent you away?" I whispered.

"I begged them not to, but they were determined. They blamed me for something I was not responsible for and would not listen to reason."

"Are they still alive?"

He shook his head. "I do not know."

"I'm sorry, Mr. Sowles."

"You must call me Amenon."

I nodded. "All right, Amenon. You've been done an injustice and I won't stand in the way of you trying to get your house back. I'm not sure how you'll do it. I get the feeling that Mr. Rachat has a lot of money and influence in this town. You'll need a lawyer, I suppose. But you have time. He's not due back for six months."

"That is good," he said, turning back to me. He smiled, the first bit of welcome I'd seen in him since I'd entered the room. I imagine he was suspicious of everyone, having been betrayed by his own parents. He came to me once more and took my hands in his; his uncanny heat and grateful smile felt like a benediction. He was the one who'd touched me on the stairs, not Corin. "You are an angel, Miss Alexander, and I thank you for your help."

"It's Vianne, and you're welcome. I'll make sure not to tell Corin—he's the groundskeeper. I won't tell anyone, for that matter. And I won't come back here, unless you need something."

He bowed his head, his delectable scent wafting toward me. Despite the heat he gave off, I shivered at his closeness. When he straightened, he said, his eyes sparkling mischievously in the candlelight, "You are welcome to visit me whenever you like, Miss Alexander... *Vianne*." He squeezed my hands. "Any time."

"Okay," I breathed. Then, not wanting to, but feeling I must flee before I did something I might regret, I pulled my hands from his. "I should go." I took a step backward, catching glimpses of candlelight reflecting off the window like a funhouse mirror. "And you should be careful with the light. It can be seen from down below. Curtains would fix that."

"I will see what I can do."

I took another step backward. "Goodbye, Amenon. It was nice meeting you."

"Au revoir, Vianne."

"Au revoir," I answered, trying very hard not to sound like an American as I said it.

I spun around and scurried out of the tower room and down the stairs, my feet flying like the wind, my pulse racing and my heart in my throat. What had I just done? Was I truly helping a victim of circumstance, or had I made a bargain with a madman?

As I raced across the lawn, it occurred to me that I could smell no smoke in the air from Amenon's fire.

It was as though it didn't exist.

Chapter Fourteen

☾

I awoke early Friday morning to the sound of my phone chirruping. Someone had sent me a text. I picked it up and blearily read a message from Ryan.

"Good news."

"Go on," I typed.

"Me and Anna r coming to visit u!"

I stared at the screen for a moment, suddenly realizing I wasn't sure I wanted them to come. Anna was just so predatory when it came to guys and— Wait, why did I care? It wasn't like I had anyone here I didn't want her getting her claws into.

Ma chérie…

Okay, scratch that. I simply had to keep her away from the tower, that was all. No problem. Anna wasn't really interested in old houses anyway. She was a thoroughly modern woman, all clean lines and white décor, like she wanted to live in a plastic container. Which was fitting considering how much plastic she had in *her* container. I'm not being catty here. Anna doesn't even try to pretend she isn't mostly fake, which is rather ironic, now that I think about it.

If the thought of being in a stuffy old house didn't put her off, all I had to do was start talking architecture and the tour would be over before it began. Actually, maybe Corin wouldn't want anyone inside the house anyway. I smiled. Yes. I'd use that excuse, because I was pretty sure it was the truth.

"Sounds great!" I replied, warming to the idea. Ryan and Anna would keep me grounded, and right now I needed to be grounded. The moon dweller in me was rearing its impetuous head a little too much, fantasizing all sorts of things about the mysterious Amenon. If I didn't rein in my imagination, I was afraid I would go a little too far, get a little too caught up.

"B there Sat after 4."

"OK. Will send directions via email."

"Thnx! Ta!"

I set my phone down and leaned back against my pillow. There was a lot to be done before Ryan and Anna arrived, including making up beds and getting my actual work done. I should also probably check with Corin to be sure it was okay if they stayed over, and what the rules were regarding the house and grounds.

But before rolling out of bed, I thought back to the night before…to Amenon. I closed my eyes and remembered the feel of his hands on mine, the touch of his finger on my pulsing throat, how he seemed to want to absorb my heartbeat. I shivered delightedly. Reliving the sensations was almost as tantalizing as the real thing. Should I return tonight? He said I could. I should. I had to ask him if he needed anything, like food.

Then again, I wasn't sure if going up there was such a good idea. It was one thing to look the other way regarding someone doing something potentially illegal. It was another to go out of my way to make his illicit stay a pleasant one.

Still, the idea of doing something 'naughty' was hard to let go. Just thinking about what I'd done last night—sneaking up to the tower, meeting a handsome and mysterious stranger, letting him touch me— sent courses of excitement through me. I was being bad, I was being rebellious, and I wasn't sure I wanted to stop. The secretiveness, the forbidden fruit aspect of it all, was just so alluring.

Ten minutes passed while I alternated between fantasizing about Amenon and struggling with how I should handle this, before I dragged myself out of bed and got ready for the day. Despite telling myself I likely wouldn't see Amenon during the day, I took extra care with my appearance, selecting a vivid blue shirt that emphasized my curves, then teasing and combing my hair until it behaved. A little mascara, and I was ready to go.

I spent the morning working in the library on the bathroom blueprints, disturbed only by my thoughts, which was slightly disappointing. After lunch at the guesthouse I returned to the chateau to find Corin in the library. When I entered, he was staring at the wall where the secret door was. It was closed tight as a tin can, and he looked rather annoyed.

"Still won't open for you?"

He spun around to face me. "It must be broken."

"No, it's not. I opened it after you couldn't. I think it's just you."

His eyes cooled. "Then you do it." He waved his hand to indicate I should give it a go.

I marched over and pressed the lever. The door swung open. "See?" I couldn't quite keep the triumphant tone out of my voice. Then I gave him a goofy grin. "Maybe if you believed a little more."

His expression turned wry. "You're saying that the door opened for you because you're a moon dweller?"

"That is exactly what I'm saying."

"I think it must be rusted and maybe changes in the moisture level affect it," he persisted, scratching his head perplexedly. "I should get some WD-40 for the hinges."

"I think what you should do, since the door is open, is find out where the passage leads."

He stared at me as though I'd just suggested a trip to the moon. "Go in there?"

"Scared of the dark?"

"Of course not. It's just that no one has likely gone in there for decades. The floors may not be stable and there might be rats, too." He sneaked a peek at me, like a little boy.

"Well, your greatest wish might be to become an old fogey, but it's not mine. I'm going in," I said determinedly. "It's my job to make sure the blueprints are accurate." Actually, I was making that up. I just wanted to see where the passage led, and for some odd reason, I wanted Corin with me when I went.

"Not alone."

"You can certainly come along," I offered him graciously, "but no fuddy-duddy attitude allowed."

"Fuddy-duddy attitude?" he echoed. "You think I'm a fuddy-duddy?"

"I do, and I'll think it even more if you start acting like one when we're in a *secret* passage! Now let's go. I have a lot to do today."

He pulled a flashlight from a loop on his waist and flicked it on. With a glance back at me, he stepped inside. I scurried after him, feeling excited. One of my favorite parts of my job is getting to do stuff like this, like something in a book or movie. It was an adventure most people never get to experience, and it was my job!

I must have giggled out loud because Corin asked, "What's so funny?"

"Nothing. I'm just really psyched about this. Aren't you?"

"I'm concerned for our safety, that's what I am."

"What did I say about the F-D attitude?"

He sighed. "And yes, I'm absolutely thrilled."

"Could you have said that in any more of a monotone?"

"Yes. Now pay attention to where you're walking." He flashed the light back and forth. "There might be debris or broken floorboards."

"Aye, aye, Cap'n Fuddy-Duddy!"

He didn't bother to respond so I followed after him, curious where this passage led. It wasn't clear on the blueprints, or even where the secret room was, just that it existed, so actually my excuse was legit. I really should record the passage more clearly and map out its dimensions, as well.

We shuffled along with bated breath, the strong flashlight beam lighting up the corridor like a beacon. It led us in a sort of rectangular pattern, and then we reached the end to find a flight of stairs. As we walked, something occurred to me—*what if this passage led to the tower where Amenon was hiding?*—and my enthusiasm soured. That would be bad. Very bad.

After following a number of passages and climbing a series of stairs, we at last met up with a door. As Corin put his hand on it I tried frantically to think of a way to stop him. Just as I was about to shriek over the presence of a non-existent mouse, he paused. "Do you hear something?" he asked in a whisper, leaning toward the door.

"No." Which was true. I hadn't heard a thing. Still didn't.

He waited a moment longer, then pushed. The door didn't budge. He looked around. "I suppose there's some lever for this, too?"

I joined him in his search, but it didn't turn up anything obvious, probably because I wasn't looking very hard. "I don't see anything."

He gave a frustrated sigh. "We'll have to look later. I need to get going."

"All right," I quickly agreed. "I have lots to do anyway."

We headed back to the library and into the light. Blinking, we brushed away cobwebs from our clothes. "Here," Corin said, eyeing my hair. He reached forward and plucked a glob from my tresses. "I don't imagine you wanted that in your hair?" He held it up, then threw it into the waste can by the desk.

I laughed. "I went through a Morticia Addams phase when I was sixteen and soon learned that deadly pale and black hair is not a good look for me. Not to mention that I'm just a bit too curvy to look truly Goth."

"Is there such a thing as too curvy?" He looked at me frankly, as though he truly wanted to know.

"There is when you're trying to find clothes that fit."

"Hm. I've always found clothes to be overrated."

I burst out laughing. "Why, Mr. Groundskeeper, you surprise me!"

He looked pained. "I didn't mean that. I just meant, well, fashion is so purposeless."

"Don't tell that to my friend, Ryan." I paused. "Speaking of Ryan, I was wondering if it would be okay to have guests this weekend? Two of my friends from back home want to visit me."

He looked dismayed. "*Already?*"

"They miss me," I replied dryly. "It's what friends do. But really, I think it's just that they want to get out of Camden and come visit the great metropolis of Portsmouth."

His cool reserve had returned as I was speaking—I could see it spreading across his face like frost on a window. "You are, of course, allowed to have friends visit. But I would rather they did not come inside the chateau."

"No problem!" I quickly agreed. "They wouldn't appreciate it anyway. Not like you and I do. No, we'll likely just hang out Saturday, then they'll be off again some time Sunday. Ryan never likes to stick around one place for too long."

"Is Ryan your boyfriend?"

I laughed. "I'm more likely to be Anna's type than Ryan's."

"Oh. He likes men and she likes women," he said matter-of-factly.

"That's true for Ryan, but as for Anna, well, let's just say she's open to all possibilities."

"Ah." He tapped his fingers on the desk where I'd been working, his eyes roving over the blueprints without seeming to take anything in. "Did you see the light again last night?"

"I was very tired and fell asleep right away." This technically wasn't a lie, but I was evading the whole truth, of course.

"Oh. That's good. I kept an eye out until about one or so, but nothing happened, so I went to bed."

"You must be tired," I said, glad that Amenon had waited until after Corin was asleep before making his presence known. The question was, how had he known to do that? Maybe he could see the gatehouse from the tower window, or maybe he'd simply gotten lucky.

"I'm used to going on little sleep," he replied.

"Not me. Sometimes I think I could sleep the day away. It's a bit of a waste, I know, but sometimes my dreams are just so lonely— I mean, lovely!"

"You just said lonely. Are you lonely?"

I smiled. "Of course not. Just a slip of the tongue."

"A Freudian slip?"

He was studying me, his expression something akin to concerned, even commiserative. I didn't like it. "What do you mean by that?"

He shrugged. "It's just that you've only been here a few days and your friends are already coming to visit you."

"They invited themselves."

"Ah. Well, I get the feeling that this is your first time on your own, so to speak. For a job, I mean."

I blushed, feeling caught out. "Am I that obvious?"

"Not really, no. I was wondering, though, when you'll be bringing in someone from AA&D to help. Mr. Rachat is still anxious to learn about that wall and you have a lot on your hands drawing up the blueprints for the kitchen and bathrooms." Ah, so he wasn't being concerned for my welfare; he simply wanted to know if I could handle the job. Bastard.

I drew myself up. "I'm nearly finished with the plans. You'll have them Monday morning, at the latest. Both you and Peter can look them over, see if they pass muster, then I'm sure Peter or Mr. Rachat's lawyer will submit them to the appropriate committee. We'll also need a detailed plan for Mía—you are hiring her?" Corin nodded. "And she does know how to deal with lead paint disposal?" He nodded again. "Once I submit the plans and the details for Mía's contract, I will start research on the wall. Is that fast enough for Mr. Rachat?"

"Uh, yes, I'm sure that will be fine."

"Now if you'll excuse me, Corin. As you can see, I have a lot to do." I turned and marched to the door, both annoyed with him and anxious to get him out of the library. Hopefully Amenon had heard us and knew enough to get out of the tower for the afternoon. Of course, with the secret door shut now, it was likely Corin wouldn't be able to get back in.

Still, maybe I should warn Amenon. I had something for him anyway. After I heard the outside door shut, I grabbed a bag I'd brought with me and headed up to the tower via the observatory. I had a feeling the library passage led to the locked door near the tower, but I didn't want to go that way in case Corin came back and caught me.

When I entered the tower room, I looked around, noting that it was now dust-free, as though Amenon had cleaned it from top to bottom. "Amenon?" I called. No one answered. The bed was neatly made, the fire out. No one was here. I spent a few precious moments taking in the room before closing my eyes and recalling with a shiver what had passed between Amenon and myself the night before…the heat of his touch, the whispers passing between us, the clandestine undercurrent coloring our every breath.

"Oh, Amenon!" I sighed softly.

When I opened my eyes and returned to the real world, I got to work, hanging the curtains I'd found in the guest cottage. They were a deep green and suited the room almost as though they'd been made for it. Finished hanging them, I stood back and admired my work. Perfect. Now Amenon would be safe.

It was rather strange though, I thought, as I grabbed my bag and left the room, that he wasn't here. Where had he gone? To see a lawyer? But how would he get there? He must have a car parked somewhere close by, probably outside the gates. But then he'd have to have a way to get out and back in again. He'd have to have a key or know a code for the gate, wouldn't he? I shook my head and laughed. The truth of the matter was more than likely very mundane and here I was, making it into some grand, illicit scheme.

Back downstairs, to ensure that Corin wouldn't use me to open up the secret passage to the tower, I decided to finish my work in the Ship Room and hope he wouldn't come looking for me. There was a coffee table in the room that would work for my blueprints. While I was in there I could gather a sample from the wall to send to a friend of mine, Katelyn, who did paint and wallpaper analyses for AA&D and owed me a favor.

I was determined to keep Amenon's presence a secret, at least until he could make a case for his rightful ownership of the chateau. If someone had cheated him out of his home, that someone needed to be brought to justice. I felt sorry for Mr. Rachat, but there was nothing I could do for him. Besides, he might be part of that injustice. Corin, too.

Gathering my work up in my arms, I realized I could trust no one.

Chapter Fifteen

☾

I spent the evening preparing the guest rooms for Anna and Ryan's arrival tomorrow afternoon, then started the blueprints for the last two bathrooms. I worked so late that I fell asleep face down on the breakfast bar. A sharp pain in my neck woke me around six and I groaned when I realized what I'd done. Rubbing my neck I went to shower. The warm water and a couple ibuprofens helped, but I knew my neck would be bothering me for the next couple days.

I was also annoyed that I'd slept through any chance of seeing Amenon's light, of seeing him. I'd meant to check on him, see if he needed anything, but I'd blown it, which put me in a foul mood.

Not wanting to deal with Corin, I decided to stay in the guesthouse and work my tail off to finish the prints. I knew Ryan and Anna would want to go to a bar tonight and there was a good chance I'd end up drinking too much, like I had a tendency to do in their company, so I needed to have the hard tasks completed and out of the way before they arrived.

The hours passed quickly. Before I knew it, the time had come for Ryan and Anna to be arriving. Earlier I'd texted Corin, asking him how to open the gate, and he'd told me I was to meet him there and he'd show me how, allowing me to come and go, as needed.

At a quarter to five, Anna texted that they were almost there, so I let Corin know, then headed out. The walk down the drive brought home just how sore my muscles were from leaning over blueprints, gripping my pencil feverishly, driving myself to finish, but I wasn't annoyed. The hard work had paid off—I was done with the blueprints! I just needed to write up the job details for the contractor, which I could do Sunday.

It was good to be outside now, breathing in the fresh air as I went to meet my friends. I hoped their company would help me shake off some of the anxiety I'd been feeling—trying to get the blueprints finished, knowing I was practically harboring a fugitive, wondering if I could really do this on my own, and dreading Mr. Rachat finding out that AA&D was not a part of the package.

Corin was sitting by the gate in a Mule, an olive green vehicle that looked like a cross between a tank and a golf cart. We had one at AA&D and I loved driving it. I waved to him and he gave me a little one in return, though his was distinctly less enthusiastic than mine, not that mine was all that pumped up. My arm was half-dead from working and my neck was stiffening up.

"They'll be here soon?" he questioned as he climbed out of the cart. He had a smear of dirt across his left cheek, but his shoulders were as straight and rigid as ever, like he hadn't just spent the day doing hard labor. I both admired and envied him his strength.

"For Ryan, soon is a relative term, as is time. He thinks he's well within his rights to show up whenever he damn well pleases."

Corin frowned. "And your friend, Anna?"

"She's worse, if you can believe it. But she did text to say they were close."

A minute of silence passed between us. For once I kept my mouth shut, opening it only to yawn. Corin broke the quiet at last, asking, "What are your plans for tonight?"

I shrugged. "Not sure. I'm not up to a big night out." I rubbed my shoulder and neck. "I slept funny and now my neck is killing me."

He stared at my neck for several long moments, then seemed to snap out of it. "Well, if you plan to leave the grounds, make sure you lock the gate. It's electronic." He walked toward the gate and pulled open a metal door in one of the gate's thick posts. "The code is 3872. Just punch it in and the gate will open." It occurred to me that to get in and out, Amenon would have to know the code. Of course, if this had once been his home, he should already know it. Unless Mr. Rachat had changed it when he bought the place, which was likely. "It will close automatically, but check to make sure it does. The day you came it didn't shut tightly. Not sure why, but I've been checking it ever since."

I gave him a salute. "Roger that. 3782 and double-check the gate to be sure it's closed."

"3872."

"Oops. 3872." I laughed. "Sometimes I can be a little dyslexic." Repeating the number in my mind, I made a note to write it down on my hand before I could forget it.

"And when do they plan to leave? Your *friends*?" Was I mistaken, or had he put an extra emphasis on the word, friends? No, I was not.

"My *friends* will likely leave Sunday afternoon."

A honk caught my attention and I looked to see Ryan in his red mini-Cooper, zipping up to the gate. He honked several times in a row to make a little tune.

"Give it a try," Corin invited and I punched in the numbers. The gate swung open and Ryan roared through the opening with yet another honk. After five seconds, the gate shut behind him, and like a good little girl, I checked to be sure it was closed. "Good job," Corin congratulated me, and instead of feeling patronized, I actually felt a little proud of myself. Which was entirely too pathetic.

I ran up to the driver's window. "Hey, Vi!" Ryan greeted. He peered over the top of his bright blue sunglasses, past me at Corin. "And who's this?"

"This is Corin. He's the groundskeeper. He was showing me how to work the gate. Corin, this is Ryan and Anna."

Ryan stuck out his hand and Corin paused for a moment, then leaned forward and shook it. Ryan tried to maintain his hold, but Corin found a way to escape. "Quite a grip you've got there, cowboy." Ryan winked at him.

I leaned down and peered in at Anna. She was wearing oversized sunglasses, but I could tell she was checking out Corin. "It's good to see you both."

"Good to see you both, too," she returned, licking her lips.

I shook my head at her. "Good trip?"

"We survived, *barely*," Ryan breathed. "But right now I really have to use the little boys room. I'm regretting that grande latte I inhaled on the drive."

"You should be regretting the two jelly donuts you also inhaled," Anna said snidely. "Your thighs are getting jiggly."

He smacked her shoulder. "So are your jowls."

"Pig!"

"Sow!"

"You can follow me," Corin said, sounding uncomfortable. "Come on, Vi."

I looked at him. "What?"

"I'll give you a ride. There isn't room in the car for you."

I looked at the back seat. It was filled with luggage. "You guys are only staying for a day!"

Ryan lifted one shoulder. "I couldn't make up my mind what to wear tonight."

"About that—" I started, but Ryan interrupted. "Seriously, Vi! I've got to wee!"

I hurriedly joined Corin and we puttered down the drive to the guesthouse. When we arrived, Ryan screeched to a halt behind us and hustled inside. I jumped out of the Mule and went in after him to give directions. "It's down the hall, on the left," I shouted at his fast retreating back.

I headed back outside to find that Anna had already recruited Corin to carry in her luggage. She watched him as a predator eyes its prey as he hefted her two bags and lugged them inside. "Well!" she murmured when he disappeared inside. "I'm surprised you let us come."

I turned to her. She was wearing her typical outfit of white and tight. White jeans, white blouse designed to show off her fake boobs, white sunglasses, white-blond hair. "What?"

"That Corin guy. He's totally hot. He available?"

"I don't know. Maybe."

"I'm going to find out." She sauntered inside, every step emphasizing her perfect butt, achieved through whatever the latest exercise trend was. She met up with him in the living room. Removing her sunglasses, she eyed him up and down. "I suppose there's a Mrs. Groundskeeper waiting for you back home. Several Groundskeeper kids, too?"

Corin shook his head, his jaw tight, and even though I'd only known him for a few days, I recognized that look. He didn't approve of Anna. "I'm not with anyone, and I'm not looking to be with anyone at the moment." He glanced at me. "Anything else?"

"Nope. Thank you for the ride and for bringing in Anna's luggage. You didn't have to do that."

He nodded. "I'll see you tomorrow."

He would? "Um, sure. Okay."

When he was gone, Anna gave me a desperate look. "I *must* have him, Vi!"

"Oh no you don't!" I said frantically, scrabbling for an excuse to keep her away from him. "I need this job, and I can't have anyone screwing it up. Or screwing the groundskeeper."

"But he's just so rough around the edges! So resistant. I must break him."

"This isn't *Rocky*, and you're not Drago." Strangely, Anna was a big fan of *Rocky*. "Leave him alone."

She pouted at me. "You just want him for yourself."

"What? No, I don't! He's a bit of a fuddy-duddy. Totally not my type."

"Jason is a fuddy-duddy, and you were going to *marry* him. Face it, you like fuddies."

Surprisingly, Anna was the one person who didn't think Jason was perfect. Maybe she'd tried something with him and he'd rejected her. "I like nice guys," I primly corrected her, "and Jason is a nice guy."

She gave me a look of pity. "So you two are still together?"

"No." I tugged on a wayward curl. "I mean, not really. He wants to get back together, though."

Anna leaned forward and did something entirely out of character for her...she touched me, gripping my arm, her French manicure a hair's breadth from biting into my skin. "Listen, Vi. You're better off without Jason."

"Why do you say that? What do you know?"

Her hand dropped from my arm and she returned to her typical pose of distant poise. "Let's just say I'm good at figuring out a person's character."

Ryan came into the room. "And you find *mine* irresistible, don't you, love?"

"Exactly, darling." She winked at him. For a brief moment I saw a softening around her eyes, as though she was quite fond of Ryan. Despite their sparring, or maybe because of it, I know she *is* fond of him, but she'll never admit to it.

She gave me a glance, then went into the kitchen. "What's to drink around here?"

"Not much," I said. "Just wine, I think."

"I'll take some of that."

"Me, too," Ryan sang, heading outside. A few seconds later, he returned, glaring at Anna. "He brought in your bags, but not mine! That's so sexist!"

She shrugged, expertly uncorking a bottle. I was amazed at how quickly she'd found a bottle, the corkscrew, and three glasses. "Just a little for me," I told her. "I slept funny last night and now my neck hurts."

"I thought you were looking a little crooked," Ryan commented, examining me with a tilted head. His bright blue sunglasses had transitioned to clear lens. He wore transition lenses because without glasses he was blind as a bat. He owned about fifteen pairs, coming in all the colors of the rainbow, and more. Today's glasses matched the color of his pants, but not the sunny yellow, button-up shirt with red polka dots he was wearing. He looked like a butterfly...on drugs.

"Alcohol cures all ills," Anna said, taking a drink. "Yum. This is the good stuff. Drink, Vi. You look like you need it."

"Yeah, Vi," Ryan concurred. "Your face looks like you slept on a rock."

"Oh nice, Ryan!" I took a sip of wine. "For your information, I fell asleep here." I pointed at the breakfast bar. "Because I was working. I'm on a tight deadline, and it's my first job on my own, so I want to impress my employer." I preened a little. It felt so grown-up to be talking like this.

"It's not Corin, is it? Didn't you say he was the groundskeeper?"

"No, it's not him. And yes, he is the groundskeeper."

"He would be perfect as my Mañuel La Bor!" Ryan clapped his hands.

I laughed and took another sip. "Yes, he would. Too bad for you he doesn't swing that way." I actually wasn't positive about that, but I had a feeling Corin was straight. My gay-dar was pretty good.

"I'm hoping to get him to swing my way," Anna said, holding up her glass as a sort of toast.

I groaned. "Can we stop talking about Corin?"

"Okay, fine," Ryan agreed. He ducked his head to peer out the front window. "That house is très creepy, Vi. How can you stand working there?"

Anna nodded. "You could film an Addams Family movie in that house."

"It's not creepy," I protested. "It's romantic!"

"Says the psychopath before luring us to our death in the House of Doom."

I punched Ryan on the arm. "Just for that I should murder you."

He pretended to shiver as he moved away from the window. I followed him and we both sat at the breakfast bar. "Well, don't think you're getting me in there."

"Fine," I said, pretending to be aggrieved. "You wouldn't like it anyway."

"We need to talk about Jason!" he cried, already moving on. "I don't know what to do, Vi! He's been continuing his ruthless attempts to get me to talk. I'm not sure how much longer I can hold out," he breathed, his hand on his chest.

Or how much longer you want to, I thought.

"I've steered clear of him," Anna said, looking proud of herself.

I gave her a fond look. Anna was not always an easy friend to have, but she did try to be good when it came to her besties, Ryan and me. "I appreciate it, Anna. I really do."

We clinked glasses and took a good, long sip. "So where are we going tonight?" Ryan asked.

I shrugged. "I have no idea. I don't really know Portsmouth at all."

"I know it," Anna claimed. "And I know just where we can go."

"I'm not sure I'm up to going out," I said. "My neck is really killing me."

"Oh, Vi!" Ryan cried. "You owe me this. I've been working really hard at not telling Jason everything. He's *so* persuasive."

"And remember that I've avoided him, too," Anna added, tipping her glass at me.

"We'll take a taxi," Ryan said triumphantly. "That way no one has to drive. Easy peasy!"

"I'm not sure I can afford a taxi," I tried again. "I haven't been paid yet."

Anna waved this aside. "I've got it. No worries." She meant it. Anna comes from money. Real money. My parents are wealthy, but Anna's parents are in the big league. They even own an island. But Ryan and I try very hard not to take advantage of Anna's wealth. We've always done our part when paying for things and I think that's why Anna has stayed friends with us, when normally she flits from acquaintance to acquaintance like a butterfly in a meadow.

I think part of her problem goes back to how her parents raised her—through a series of nannies. One night, when she'd had too much to drink, she confided that she didn't think she could ever truly love anyone because she just didn't know how, that it wasn't in her to feel anything real. Since then (even though I do think she's capable of loving someone, knowing how she is with Ryan), whenever she did something that drove me nuts I'd remind myself of her confession. It helped keep me from killing her.

I sighed. I really didn't want to go out, but they both looked so eager. "All right. I'll go. But I don't want to stay out too late. I still have some work to finish this weekend."

"Absolutely!" Ryan promised, and I suppressed another sigh. He meant it, at the moment, but a few hours in and he'd be back to cajoling me to stay out a *little* longer.

"I'm going to take a shower and change," Anna announced, though she looked absolutely perfect. I was the one who needed a shower and a change of clothes.

"Help me bring my stuff in," Ryan ordered, "and I'll tell you all about Jason."

I rubbed my neck. "I'm only carrying the light stuff."

"You can get my pillow."

I ended up carrying more than his pillow, and everything he had to say about Jason I already knew. When I told him that, he shrugged, unfazed. "He's not very imaginative, I guess." He looked down at himself and gasped in horror. "I'm going to go change, too. I'm all wrinkled."

He dashed inside, leaving me to close up his mini-Cooper and move it over by the Beast. As I emerged from his car, I spotted Corin approaching. I waved, then winced, my neck throbbing. "Couldn't get enough of us?" I asked him.

"I suppose you're going out tonight, even though your neck hurts."

"What makes you think that?"

"You seem the type."

"And what type is that?"

"I don't know. A fun girl."

That did not sound like a compliment. "I'll have you know I'm not a 'fun' girl, as you put it." That didn't come out quite like I'd meant it to. "I mean, I'm the type of girl who prefers getting takeout and staying in. But my friends like going out and they drove all this way, so even though I'm tired and my neck feels like it's broken, I'm going out!"

He stared at me for a long moment, something he seemed to like doing. "Okay, you're not a fun girl, then. But do you always do what everyone else wants?"

"No! I mean, well, that is…" Damn him. "I'm being a good friend here, Corin."

"Do they know you're tired, that your neck hurts?"

"Well, yes, but they've come all this way and I don't want to let them down."

"I see. So you're willing to make a sacrifice to make your friends happy."

"Exactly!" Now he was getting it.

"And they're willing to do the same for you."

I paused. He was not getting it.

But did he have a point? Because Ryan had simply done what Ryan always does…wheedled and whined and got his way. He was my friend, but did that mean I always had to be the one giving in? And should I always subjugate my needs to Anna simply because I felt sorry for her?

"Maybe not. But that doesn't mean I'm going to stop being their friend."

"Well, you know the saying… 'With friends like that, who needs enemies?'"

I scowled at him. "I'm a grown woman, Corin, and maybe I give in more than I should, but that's on me. Not them."

"All right."

I blinked at him. "All right?"

"You're loyal to your friends. But maybe someday you can be both loyal to them and to yourself."

Before I could answer that, he turned around and left. I stared after him, wondering why he'd returned in the first place. "Was there something you wanted?" I yelled after him.

He turned back around. "I just wanted to say that if you need me, just call."

"Oh. Okay. Thanks."

He left me, his stride long and no-nonsense, his back straight and so rigidly moral. I wondered what his plans were for tonight, and if they involved Mía. I hoped not, even though I had no good reason to hope for any such thing.

Chapter Sixteen

☾

The night started out fun. Despite my aching neck, I managed to enjoy chatting with Anna and Ryan about my job, then about their jobs, then about Portsmouth, then about all the good looking people in Portsmouth. We ate seafood for dinner, on Anna, because I was providing the digs and Ryan had driven his car to the chateau. Then we made our way to the trendy bar Anna knew about.

After a glass of wine, I really wanted to tell them about Amenon. I was also wondering how and when I could manage to see him again. Probably tomorrow night, at the earliest, which was depressing. Ryan ordered another round and when it came I prepared to tell all...wine has that effect on me. I'd make a terrible spy. But I knew I was getting in over my head and I needed advice.

As I opened my mouth to share, a young man approached the table, his hand pressed dramatically to his chest. "Ryan? Is that you?"

"Joey!" Ryan jumped up and gave him a hug. Joey was on the short side and boyishly handsome, with a smile that lit up the room. "What are you doing here?"

And just like that, our pleasant little get together turned into a noisy gathering of all the movers and shakers in Portsmouth. I hadn't planned to drink any more, but while sitting by myself, I sipped at the wine Ryan had ordered for me as he and Anna mingled. It wasn't until some time had passed that I realized that I could no longer see them anywhere. Actually, I had to go to the bathroom, and when I stood up, swaying a bit, *that's* when I figured it out. They'd left me!

More than a little tipsy, and without enough money for a cab, I consulted my phone to see what time it was. Midnight. Crap. What was I going to do? I looked around frantically. They had to still be here. They wouldn't have left me alone. That completely violated the friend code. *Completely!*

"Oh no," I moaned and sat back down, despite my near-bursting bladder. I sensed someone standing over me and blearily looked up. "Corin?"

He sat down beside me. "What gave me away?"

"That big, tremendous high horse you rode in on."

He frowned a little. "I thought I told him to stay outside."

I giggled. "So why are you here? Are you following me?"

His expression was bland, with nary a tic, giving nothing away. "I just wanted to get out for an hour or two so I came into town."

"To see Mía?" I slurred. "She's really pretty."

"She is," he said simply, and I hated him for it.

"Maybe you should go find her."

"I'll see her when she starts work on the chateau in a week or two."

"Oh. Well." I looked around the bar, which was spinning a little. "My friends abandoned me."

"Not exactly. When I came in here, they grabbed me and asked if I would look after you. You were sitting by yourself, staring off into space with a goofy grin on your face, so I left you alone for a bit."

I'd been fantasizing about Amenon, I realized with a blush. "Oh."

"Should I take you home?"

I realized all at once how tired I was, how much my head and neck hurt. "Yes, please."

"Wait here a moment."

"I have to go to the bathroom."

"Oh, well, by all means, go do that. Better here than in my car."

When I returned from a rather long time in the bathroom—I had to try to do some make-up repair—he held out a bottle of water to me. "Drink this," he ordered. "It will help for tomorrow."

I accepted it meekly, then hesitantly took the arm he offered. "Let's get you home."

"Okay," I murmured sleepily.

"Drink the water," he said as we strolled down a brick sidewalk.

I opened the bottle and tried to sip it as I walked, which was tricky business being that it felt like the sidewalk was rushing up to meet me. "You're nicer than you act," I said. "I mean, look. I mean... Oh, I don't know." I took a slug from the bottle and ended up pouring water down my shirt. The cold liquid woke me up a bit, but did little to help with my spinning head. "Crap."

"I would clean that up for you, but I don't think that's the kind of nice you're looking for."

"You bet your booby! I mean, booty!" I clapped a hand, luckily the one that wasn't holding the water bottle, over my mouth. I was just sober enough to realize I was doing a very good job of sounding like an idiot.

"Here we are," he indicated a red, open-topped Jeep. *Red Jeep?* I would have put him down as more of a black sedan sort of guy.

My head tilted to one side. "I'm not sure I can get in."

"I heard recently that I'm nicer than I look, so I guess I could give you a hand."

"Is that sarcasm, Groundskeeper?"

"It is, Architect. Now get ready, I'm giving you a boost."

Before I could say, "Holy Moly, Batman!" Corin's hands were on my waist and lifting me into the passenger seat. "Can you buckle your seatbelt?"

"Of course I can!" But I couldn't. After watching me struggle for several seconds, Corin reached over and buckled it for me. His arm brushed across my breasts and a hot, heady sensation spread through my body. My thoughts went immediately to Amenon—to the heat he radiated, to his obvious sensuality, and I gave a luxuriant sigh.

Apparently I slipped into a doze because the next thing I knew we were outside the guesthouse. Corin unbuckled me, but didn't have to reach over, so there was no inadvertent copping a feel this time. To my dismay I found I was rather disappointed, which is so feeble, it didn't even warrant further thought.

"Let's get you inside." Without asking, Corin lifted me out of the Jeep. I thought about protesting that I was a modern woman and did not need a man to help me, but by the time the words formed in my head, I was inside, sitting on the couch. "I'm getting you more water."

I fell back, my arms flung out dramatically. Damn, I was dizzy, and I was mad at myself for being in this state in front of Corin. More than likely he was going to report my little contretemps to Mr. Rachat. He returned at that moment and handed me a glass. I took a delicate sip, then, suddenly very thirsty, chugged it down.

"You aren't going to tell the big guy?" I asked, breathing hard as I wiped water from my chin. I knew I was looking all kinds of foolish, but it couldn't be helped.

"God?"

Despite myself, I snorted. "No! Mr. Rachat. He's going to think I'm an incompetent ninny. I didn't mean to drink so much, but it's been a hard week, after a hard month, and I was all stressed out and Ryan had bought me another glass of wine and I had nothing to do, but I'm almost done with—"

"What made it a hard month?" Corin interrupted, his tone gentle, but firm.

"Hm?" He handed me another glass of water, produced from God knows where. "Oh, nothing. I mean, it's stupid. I mean, well, it's stupid."

"You said that already."

"I know I did!" Crap, my head was spinning.

"I know it's been a hard week for you, but what made an entire month so hard? Was it Jason?" His voice was deceptively concerned and before I knew it I was telling him everything. I couldn't seem to stop myself and Corin was listening so attentively that I just jabbered on and on. Once in a while he'd remind me to drink my water, which I did, absently, before continuing. At one point, he handed me a couple red pills. "Ibuprofen," he told me when I gave them a questioning look. I shrugged and swallowed the pills, hoping they weren't roofies. Corin didn't seem the type, but one never knows.

Eventually, as all idiots do, I wound down, my story and energy spent. "Time for bed," he said, pulling me to my feet and half-pushing, half-dragging me toward my room. He gently pulled off my sandals and lifted my legs into bed, covering me with a blanket. I fell against my pillows and was out before the light turned off.

☾

I awoke to darkness and the feeling that someone had called my name. I blinked and ran a hand over my face, then glanced at the alarm clock on the nightstand. 3:33. I tumbled out of bed and used the bathroom, then checked Ryan and Anna's rooms. They were both in their beds, fast asleep. They had somehow gotten back inside the manor's grounds. Corin must have waited up for them. At the thought, I felt both grateful and embarrassed. The poor guy had lost sleep looking after my friends because I'd had too much to drink.

Remembering this, I returned to the bathroom and chugged down a glass of water, then stared at my bleary reflection in the mirror. Angry with myself, I scrubbed at my face with some soap and cold water and felt a little better. My head had cleared somewhat, the water and ibuprofen helping immensely. Another thing to be grateful to Corin for. I definitely owed that guy.

I was heading back to my room when I remembered what had awakened me. Someone had called my name. Amenon? My heart sped up and I hurried into my room to grab my robe. Maybe he needed me! But what if it was simply my imagination? Well, I could just sneak up to the tower, check on him—if he was there—and if not, sneak quietly away.

I made it outside without mishap; the grass was cold and wet on my feet. I liked the sensation. I felt like I was doing something completely out of character and entirely forbidden. It was a thrilling sensation, one that I was fast associating with Amenon.

I sighed and tried to remind myself that he was just another guy and I was probably building him into something he wasn't. I tend to do that in relationships, and it gets me into trouble. Look at Jason. I had put him up on a pedestal, and once there, let him dictate my life.

But maybe Amenon is different.

That's what you always tell yourself, I admonished. *And maybe that's why you will never have a real relationship.*

I stuck out my tongue and blew a raspberry at myself. I was sounding a bit too much like Corin, and that just wouldn't do.

The stairs to the tower creaked as I climbed them and I winced, hoping I wasn't making too much noise. I hadn't seen a light in the tower, so he might not be there. But I might not have seen the light because of the new curtains I'd hung.

At the top of the stairs, I peeked into the room. Once again a fire was blazing in the fireplace and I could see the profile of someone sitting in a chair in front of it.

"Amenon? Are you all right?"

His head turned toward me, slowly, lazily, as if he'd been expecting me all along. "Come sit by the fire," he answered.

I tiptoed across the floor and sat down. Even though I hadn't smelled smoke, the fire felt real enough, warm and welcoming. I wrapped my arms around myself and shivered, as one does when exposed to sudden heat. "I was worried about you," I said in a whisper.

"I am perfectly well," he replied. "As you would see if you looked at me, Vianne." There was amusement in his voice.

I looked up to meet his eyes, which reflected the flames like twin mirrors. His intense gaze, combined with leftover lightheadedness from too much wine, made me dizzy. "Sorry. It's just that I don't know you and it's the middle of the night and I really shouldn't be here."

"I'm glad you came. I was thinking about you." He leaned forward and the shadows about his face emphasized the hollows of his cheeks, the firm line of his jaw, his deep-set eyes.

"You were?"

"Perhaps that is why you came."

I nodded eagerly. "I wonder if we have some sort of connection. I feel sometimes that I can hear you calling me."

"Maybe we do." He paused. "Then you are not afraid to be here alone with me?"

"Afraid? Of course not." Which was a lie. I was a little afraid, as I should be. I knew nothing about him, after all. I was being a bit naïve, and yet I reveled in it. I was doing something dangerous, though not terribly so. Worse came to worst, I could break a window and scream my lungs out. "Should I be?" I added.

"You saved me," he said, not answering my question. "You freed me."

That's twice he'd done that—not answer me. Did he not hear me, or was he purposely evading me? I wasn't sure if I should be annoyed, or concerned. "What do you mean?"

"I have been trapped for so long..." he trailed off, his hands making a sweeping gesture that I did not understand.

"Trapped? You mean, when you were sent away?"

"I was banished, Vianne. You must understand this if you are to help me."

Something about all this niggled at me. "When were you banished, Amenon?"

"I think it must have been a very long time ago. These past few days I have seen things that are very strange to me."

I stared at him. "Are you...?" I stopped and pulled in a deep breath, which did nothing to halt the shiver running up my spine. "Are you a ghost?"

He leaned toward me. "I'm not a ghost. See?" He reached out and cupped my cheek with a strong hand. His fingertips traced my jawbone from my ear to my chin, making my skin tingle and my heart beat harder. "Could a ghost do that?"

"I don't know," I gasped, not sure how I got the words out since I felt barely able to breathe. "But if you're not a ghost, what are you?"

His hand dropped and he pulled away with a shrug. "That I do not know."

"Oh, Amenon. I'm sorry. I didn't mean to—"

His head jerked up. Then, before I could react, he was out of his chair and kneeling by my side, gripping my hand in his. "I am the one who should be sorry! You are my savior, and being clumsy with my words, I frightened you." His close proximity made me dizzy, as though he were a lover, undoing my shirt one button at a time.

I looked into his eyes and found myself spiraling down into their darkness. "You said I could help you. What is it you want me to do?"

"I want you to help me find a way back."

"A way back?"

His grip tightened. "Someone did something to me, Vianne. I'm not sure what. You released me, but I am not whole. Some part of me is missing."

"Amenon," I began cautiously. "You said you were banished a long time ago. How long?"

"I am not sure. I left this world in the year of our Lord, 1891."

"Amenon!" I cried, my hand flying to my mouth. "That was almost a hundred and twenty-five years ago!"

It was his turn to look stunned. "So long? But what of—" He stopped, then ran a broad hand over his face, as though to wipe away the truth of what I was telling him.

"When you say you were banished..." I paused, "Well, what does that mean exactly?"

He gazed at me, his eyes mournful. "I think I died, Vianne," he whispered sadly.

I knew deep down that he had died—it's why I'd asked if he was a ghost—but still the words shocked me. "And how did...?" I paused, then rallied. The question needed to be asked. "How did you die?"

His eyelashes fluttered and his jaw tightened. "I was murdered, Vianne. In cold blood."

Chapter Seventeen

"Murdered?" I echoed, feeling slightly sick. It was a powerful word, full of fury and ill intent, and my nausea grew. But was Amenon actually dead, or just crazy? I had to step carefully here. "But who did it? And why?"

"My story is age-old," Amenon said wearily. "I fell in love with a woman not of my class. My parents forbade us to see each other, but when I refused, they did something to me. Or had something done. Some sort of dark magic, it must have been, to take a part of my humanity from me." The words were bitter. "Then somehow they captured me in that wall, imprisoning me there for over a century. It has felt that long, and all of it a nightmare, one that seems never-ending."

"And the woman you loved?" The words came out in a half-whispered squeak.

"She...she must be dead." As he spoke, his head dropped and his body went rigid, as though the reality of his words had just reached his heart.

"I don't know how to fix this for you, Amenon, but whatever I can do to help, I will."

"Thank you, Vianne." His look was grateful, yet his jaw pulsed angrily. "But I am not sure that what was taken from me can be restored."

"What exactly was taken from you?" I pushed, sensing this was important to know.

His eyes shifted away from me. "I'm not sure."

I studied him, but he was looking down at our clasped hands. "So how do you know something is missing, or that they took it? And how did they take it?" The questions came tumbling out of me, one after the other. Everything he was saying seemed so unbelievable, so unreal.

He gave a defeated shrug. "I do not know the answers to your questions, but I know something's gone. I can feel it missing." He pressed a hand to his chest, just above his heart.

"But how can *I* help you get it back?"

His eyes lifted to meet mine. I expected to see great sadness in them, but there was only an emptiness, as if all his hopes had been drained from him. "Again, I do not know, but without it, I'm not sure I can ever really die. The woman I loved is gone and I have lost everything, even the right to escape this hell."

"You don't know what happened to her?"

"I do not. I was 'removed' from this world before I could warn her about my parents. I'm worried about what they might have done to her when I couldn't be there to protect her. I'm afraid to know, and yet I must. If only to put my mind at ease."

"I could try to track her down. I mean... You know, look for her descendants."

He brightened. "Could you?"

"She's long since died, of course," I said softly, carefully, "but at least you might be able to find out what happened to her after you died." All this was very hard to talk about. To him, her death would seem like it had happened only moments ago.

"That would be perfect." His warm breath fanned my cheek and his hot fingers squeezed mine tightly in gratitude. "Perfect."

"Then I'll do it." I pulled my hand from his grasp and laid it on top of his, patting it gently as though to help take away the blow of what I had to say next. "There's another issue, though. I'm sorry, Amenon, but if you died in 1891, there's likely no way you can claim ownership of this house. It's been way too long."

"That has occurred to me," he said forlornly. "I'm afraid I am unmoored, Vianne, with only you to turn to." I stared at him in wonder. No one had ever turned to me for help. I was the one who always ran to others, looking for reassurance, for guidance. It was a strange and powerful feeling to be the strong one for once, and I knew I couldn't mess this up.

"Of course you're feeling unmoored!" I cried sympathetically. "You've lost your love and your home all at once. Oh, Amenon!" I impetuously threw my arms around him, pulling him to me. Pressed against my chest, he felt warm and solid, his scent intoxicating and seductive. He was so very real, and when his arms closed about me, I knew I would do everything I could to help him.

"I don't know what to do," he said, his voice trembling with emotion. "I am lost."

I pulled back from him to look him in the eye. "I'm here for you, Amenon. I'll help you. We'll find your way again."

He nodded, his dark eyes staring into mine with such force that my mind spun as though caught in a tempest. "You are too good to me, Vianne. You are my angel."

"I can't do much until Monday," I said quickly, needing to get my feet back on firm ground—I was letting myself get carried away. "But I'll start my work then." He looked perplexed and I realized he likely had no idea what day it was. "Today is Saturday," I explained. "Well, technically, it's early Sunday morning. Speaking of which, I should get back to my room. It must be very late."

He let go of me and pushed himself to his feet. He reached down, his hand held out to me, and I stared at it for a moment before taking it. When our fingers touched, the contact was electric and I flinched.

"Are you not well?" he asked, his lips nearly touching my ear as I straightened up.

"I'm fine," I gasped. "Just a stiff neck."

"When will I see you again?" he asked, his voice wretched and hopeful at the same time.

"I'm not sure. Perhaps tomorrow night, but maybe not. I never know when I can get in here without being seen. But even if I can come tomorrow, I won't have any information for you yet."

"Your company would be all I ask."

I nodded. "I'll do my best."

He guided me toward the doorway, his steps matching mine as though we were dancing across a ballroom floor. "I shall count the seconds, Vianne."

The thrill I felt in response to his words came from something more than just being a helpful person, and I warned myself to pull back.

I had a feeling, though, that it was already too late for that.

☾

I could not get back to sleep, so I showered and got ready for the day. Cup of coffee in hand, I worked on the blueprints and had just finished up the design for the last bathroom when Ryan wandered out, stretching and yawning.

"There you are, Vi," he said through his yawn. "I was hoping your Prince Charming had rescued you."

"Um, yeah, thanks for abandoning me." I took a sip of coffee.

He stared at the mug in my hand and I sighed, then got up and poured him a cup while he flopped onto the couch. When I handed it to him, he said, "Thanks, hon, and we didn't abandon you. We made sure he found you before we headed to another bar. We knew you weren't up to it."

"I suppose this is where I say thank you?"

He waved that away. "Oh, please. You got to go home when you didn't really want to go out anyway, and with that tasty dish of yours."

"Tasty dish of *mine*? I don't think so."

He peered at me over the rim of his cup. "Darling, you should learn not to look a gift god in the mouth."

"I'm only saying that he has no interest in me. I'm not sure he even wants me here."

"Oh, Vi. Delusional as always."

"What do you mean?"

"I mean, when guys like you—the good ones—you have no clue. And when they aren't as into you, you seem to think they are and go after them like a butch lesbian after a good haircut."

"Is that sexist? It's certainly something-ist."

"Stop avoiding the topic. You have bad radar when it comes to men."

"Including Jason?"

"Jason is an exception to the rule. You really screwed this one up this time."

"I thought you were on my side!"

He shrugged. "I'm just saying you shouldn't give up so easily. You both made mistakes. Forgive and move on. That's my motto."

"That's not your motto. And you know," I pointed at him suspiciously, "this sounds like something Jason would say."

He hid his face behind his cup, pretending to be consumed by the process of drinking his coffee.

"He told you to say that, didn't he?"

"He's very persuasive, darling. You know I can't resist him. I've done my best, but he is so very persistent." He said this as though Jason were pursuing him, not me. "That's a wonderful quality in a lover, you know."

"Maybe, but not necessarily in a husband."

"You don't want to be pursued?"

"I'm not saying that, I'm just saying that I shouldn't have to be convinced to stay with someone." The words suddenly rang true in my mind.

"Whatever, hon. But I think you're making a mistake walking away from him."

"I haven't walked away from him yet. For the moment, I'm taking a break, trying to figure some things out."

"That's a relief!"

"I'm not saying I'm *not* going to walk away, either, so don't get your hopes up."

He pouted. "But I want to be your bridesmaid!"

"I didn't say I was never getting married." I grabbed my head. "Let's not talk about this anymore."

"Fine. I'm going to go shower." He stood up and stiffly left the room. I sighed. Ryan had no right to be upset. I was the one in the middle of a mess, not him. Though Jason was doing a fine job of dragging Ryan into it.

While he was gone, I went through my list of stuff left to do. Anna entered the room, blinking in the light, though it wasn't all that bright. "Where's the coffee?" she groaned, falling over the breakfast bar.

I poured her a cup and set it down in front of her. "Fun night?"

She grimaced. "The best."

"You don't look like it was the best."

"There was this ass named Clint at the last bar we went to who thought he knew me."

"Someone you've met before?"

"No, he just thought he knew my type."

"Ah. You mean he didn't instantly fall under your thrall?"

"Thrall? Are you seriously using that word? And no, he didn't." She grimaced. "He's probably gay."

"Oh nice, Anna. Just because a guy doesn't pant after you doesn't mean he's not into women."

"Of course it does."

"Corin didn't pant after you."

She hesitated. "That's because he's panting after you." She took a sip of coffee.

I suddenly felt rather hot. "Corin? Me? I don't think so." She shrugged knowingly and I hurried to steer the conversation back to her. "So this guy talked to you for a bit, then left?"

"Well, no. We argued for, like, two hours!"

"Two hours? What did you argue about?"

"Everything. Nothing."

"But you did it for two hours, and you think he's not into you?"

"He didn't compliment me or stare at my assets, if you know what I mean. He didn't do all the usual things."

"But isn't that good?" I asked, thinking of Jason. Did he do all the usual things?

She squinted up at me. "What are you saying?"

"I'm saying that I think you've finally met your match."

The squint faded and her expression turned thoughtful. "No. No way. Not him." But she said it without conviction, her gaze distant.

"So what are your plans today?"

"Hm? Oh. I need to eat."

"I can make us something."

She wrinkled her tiny, perfect nose. "I have a better idea. Let's go to The Friendly Toast, my treat. Their breakfast food is to die for and they have a cast molding of a bare butt on the wall."

I laughed. "Well, you've sold me."

Half an hour later, she and Ryan were dressed and ready to leave, going to show that miracles do happen. I loaded up the mini, managing to pack it efficiently so that I could fit in the back for the trip into town.

There was a long wait to get a table—Sunday breakfast crowd—but the day was sunny and bright and the breeze felt lovely. Anna spent the time waiting, furiously texting someone back and forth while Ryan and I chatted about Georgie, the new office manager at Daphne's Designs, and who was also very shy. Ryan was hoping to bring her out of her shell, and I warned him to leave the poor girl alone. He only grinned mischievously.

Once, when Anna gave a wicked chuckle, I whispered, "Is that the new guy, Clint?" and he nodded knowingly. "What do you think of him?"

He leaned toward me. "Those two totally deserve each other."

I wasn't sure if that was a compliment, but Anna was almost giddy over brunch as she complained about her new guy, Aaron, so I decided to take it as a good sign. Guys she dated typically bored her and she rarely discussed them. This one seemed different and I hoped she'd finally found someone who could make her happy.

I suppressed a sigh, wondering if I would ever find someone who could make me happy.

Not Jason? my sneaky little inner voice asked. I didn't answer.

Instead I enjoyed my Eggs Benedict and took in the charming atmosphere of the little diner. Decorated in a variety of styles and eras, it was meant to be kitschy and fun, and it was. I especially enjoyed viewing the horrid, oftentimes tacky, artwork on the walls. The food was hot and plentiful and tasted just right after imbibing a bit too much the night before.

After brunch, Ryan drove around downtown a little bit so I could get to know it better. I loved seeing all the people walking around, drinking coffee or eating ice cream. A row of motorcycles was parked outside a coffee shop, looking perilously close to tipping over, domino-style. Bright window boxes filled with cascading flowers were everywhere, as were old buildings and street musicians competing for tips. *I could really like living here*, I thought happily.

When I spotted the library, I made a mental note of its location. Monday, I would come back and start my research for Mr. Rachat and for Amenon. I could kill two birds with one stone, which was always a good thing for me, being that killing one bird was hard enough.

After an hour of touring, Anna said she had a headache and needed to sleep. She looked a little pale and drawn, but ultimately, smugly content. I told Ryan to drop me off at the gate, which he did.

"Come next weekend," I told him impetuously as Anna snored away, her tiny nostrils unable to handle her exhalations with any kind of delicacy. "We'll go out."

"I already have it in my calendar, hon." He gave me an affectionate pat on the hand, then honked as he drove away. When they were gone, I walked over to the panel and punched in the code. The gate swung silently open and I walked in, then turned to be sure it closed behind me. I double-checked it, suddenly grateful for its security. Jason would have to go through the gate to get to me. Now he was locked out and I was locked in.

When I turned to head back, I saw Corin driving toward me on his Mule. I waited for him to pull around me and stop. "Get in," he ordered.

"I'd really rather walk," I said, not liking his officious tone.

"We need to talk," he said coolly.

Frowning, I climbed into the cab and Corin hit the gas. He said nothing as we drove toward the guesthouse and I began to feel the dull throb of a headache coming on, not to mention that my neck was stiffening up again. Last night's debauchery was catching up to me.

Corin didn't speak until we were outside the chateau. He reached down and turned off the engine, then turned to me. "Do you want to explain why you keep going into the house in the middle of the night?"

Chapter Eighteen

☾

I hadn't expected the question and it hit me like a brick to the head. "W-what?" I stuttered, my mind frantically working to come up with an answer that didn't sound stupid or suspicious.

"I know you go in there late at night. I've seen you twice now."

"But how could you know?" I asked, then cursed myself. "It's so late, Corin. How are you possibly awake at that time?"

His eyes darkened to the color of stormy seas. "If you must know, something wakes me up...I don't know what it is. Now answer my question. Do you admit going in there?"

"I do. Something wakes me, too, and then I see a light in the chateau. Remember I told you about it? So I go and check it out. It worries me."

His expression mellowed a fraction. "Where do you actually see the light?"

"In the top floor of the tower," I admitted reluctantly. I should have lied, if only to protect Amenon, but I'm not good at it, and Corin had probably seen the light there, as well, and would know I was lying. Damn him.

"But there's no way to get to the top floor," he protested.

"How could you see me from the gatehouse?" I fired at him, figuring this was as good a time as any to deflect his attention from the tower.

"When I wake up, I go outside," he said, as if this was a perfectly rational thing to do. "I get this feeling that something is going on in the house."

"Oh." He was right. Something was going on in the house, but probably not what he was expecting. "You must have some sort of sixth sense, looking after it for so long."

"Maybe. But you haven't answered my question."

Of course I hadn't. Nor would I if I could help it. "You know, you've acted odd about this house since I first arrived, practically making it sound like there was a monster in there, that I wouldn't even know what hit me. And Peter Paddington and Mía both have acted strangely, too. Something's going on in there and I have this feeling that I've been pulled into it." It was the best I could do—make him go on the defensive. Besides, I wanted to know what they'd experienced, because I had a strong feeling it had been Amenon—his restlessness, his confusion and frustration, maybe even his anger.

"There were issues," he slowly admitted. "Noises, tools being moved around, strange changes in temperature. People have seen figures. I even once thought I saw someone in the tower window when no one was in the house. Have you noticed anything strange?"

"And you're just telling me this now?" I demanded, purposely dodging his question. I didn't want to commit to knowing anything. "Is that why Mark left?"

"It might have been. He only said he wasn't feeling well."

I gave him a squinty-eyed stare, chockfull of skepticism, but decided he was telling the truth, mainly because it sounded like Mark. He wouldn't admit to being scared. That was not a manly thing to do, and even though he was a raging hypochondriac, Mark also liked to pretend he was a macho stud, which was yet another reason why I tried to avoid him.

"So that wasn't an earthquake in the Ship Room, or something strange with the wiring when the light in the hallway went out on me?"

"I don't know for sure what was going on there," he answered, watching me carefully.

"Well, just so you know, I'm not leaving this job. If there are weird happenings going on, that doesn't bother me. I'm used to that sort of thing anyway. I've been working in old houses all my life. A person experiences things. It's no biggie."

He eyed me with a mix of doubt and reluctant admiration. "You're sure?"

"I'm sure."

"So you didn't find anything when you went in the house?"

"You said that part of the tower isn't accessible, so how could I?" I was walking a fine line here, and I didn't really feel very good about it. A part of me actually wanted to confide in Corin, tell him about Amenon. But I kept my mouth shut. One, I didn't absolutely know whose side Corin would be on, but I was pretty sure it would be Mr. Rachat's. Two, telling Corin that Amenon was some sort of spirit might be akin to career suicide, especially being that he didn't believe in ghosts. I couldn't take the risk. Besides, if he heard the truth, he might get Mr. Rachat to make me leave. That couldn't happen.

"Do you think the secret passage in the library leads to the tower?" the persistent little devil asked. "We did have to climb stairs."

I shrugged. "It's possible." I stifled a yawn. "Listen, I'm beat, and I still have to finish up some work. I want to get everything to you tomorrow morning, then I'll start researching the Ship Room. I thought I'd head to the library in Portsmouth to do that."

Corin looked momentarily thrown by the conversational curveball I'd tossed at him. "Oh. All right. That would be good. I can show you where it is if you like. The Athenaeum is a good source, as well."

"I know where the library is, but not the Athenaeum."

"Then I'd better take you there. I worked at the Athenaeum once as an intern and have a membership, so that will make things easier for you."

"Oh, um. Really?" Did I want to do that? "I don't want to take you away from your work."

"It's for the house, so I consider it part of my work."

"All right. Fine." And when I thought more about it, it was fine. I would have to find a way to research what had happened to Amenon's lover without Corin's awareness, but since Amenon's family had built the house, it really all tied together. Corin shouldn't suspect anything. Besides, I didn't especially want to drive in Portsmouth—the layout was a bit confusing—and Corin wasn't a bad companion. "Thanks for letting my friends in last night, by the way. I'm sorry you lost sleep because of me."

He nodded stiffly. "Sleep has eluded me as of late, so it was really no big deal."

"It was to me. I know my friends aren't exactly your favorite kind of people, but you took care of them anyway. Thank you."

"Actually, I don't mind your friends. They are different," he admitted, "and a bit self-centered, but who doesn't have some of that in them? And they do care for you…in their own way."

I considered his words. "Yes, they do. And I'm glad you were able to see that. Ryan and Anna aren't the easiest friends to have, but I imagine, neither am I." I laughed wryly. "But I'm glad we're friends all the same."

"I'm not so sure I can be as accepting of your ex-fiancé, Jason."

I gaped at him. "What?"

"You told me what happened. Last night?" he prompted.

"Oh." Had I? I tried to remember, then it came back to me in a rush and my stomach lurched. I made a fervent vow to never drink again. At least not in excess.

He must have seen something in my expression because he rushed on, "Don't worry, Vi. I won't tell anyone what you told me. I feel honored that you shared your story with me."

My stomach lurched again. "Actually, I'm surprised I talked to you about it. It was not a proud moment for me."

He looked away. "Well, I might have asked you about what happened between you and your fiancé."

What? "But how did you know about that?"

"That first day…when you passed out. You said something about it. About this guy, Jason. It's been bothering me ever since and I wanted to know what had happened between you two, what had gone wrong."

"So you were being nosy?" I asked indignantly.

"I just wanted to understand." He rubbed at his jaw. "How do relationships go bad? What's the turning point?"

He looked so earnest that my indignation died away. "I'm not sure if mine went bad," I clarified, "but I do know that things were happening in my life that felt like they were being directed by someone else. Mainly by my parents. They're very ambitious." It was something Amenon and I had in common.

"Well, their ambition has paid off. Their firm has a wonderful reputation. That's why Mr. Rachat contacted AA&D, actually. He'd read about you in an article and wanted to have all the expertise your firm has to offer for this project." As he spoke he was watching my face, a glint in his eyes as if trying to catch me out.

I swallowed and turned away, a trickle of unease wiggling its way down between my shoulder blades. "Yes, well, AA&D is much sought after. We know our stuff." I grabbed my purse and slid out of the Mule, eager to escape this conversation. I couldn't have him know that I was here on false pretenses, that I did not have the might of AA&D behind me.

"I'll let you get back to your work," Corin said when I turned to face him. "I'll stop by tomorrow around nine? You can give me everything and I can drop it off at the appropriate offices while you do your research. You can start at the library, then I'll pick you up and we'll go to the Athenaeum. Lunch on me, all right?"

"Hm? Oh, yes. That would be great. Nine o'clock," I repeated absently.

He smiled, almost mischievously I'd say if I didn't know better, then started up the Mule and motored back toward the gate. I watched him go, frowning slightly. Something he had said was bothering me, but I couldn't quite figure out what it was.

☾

I spent the rest of the day finishing up the necessary paperwork. It was good to have something to distract me from my worries, but when everything was finished and in crisp, white envelopes, ready to be submitted, the thoughts I'd been holding off came back to me.

My first concern, of course, was being found out. All Corin had to do was get a little suspicious, then place a call to AA&D and I'd be discovered in flagrante delicto, so to speak. Not only that, but they—

meaning my parents and Jason—would know where I was and track me down and ruin everything. I couldn't let that happen. But I also couldn't sign the papers with AA&D listed as the architects. I had to put my own name and hope Corin wouldn't notice.

I was also worried about Amenon, for a couple reasons. One, even though this had supposedly happened long ago, he had lost everything in the space of a few minutes. Was he safe being alone? I wasn't sure, but very likely not. When my wedding was canceled, I'd been knocked off my feet. So imagine realizing your parents had murdered you, the person you loved was long dead, and your home was no longer yours. Devastating didn't even begin to cover it. I would have to go to him tonight. Even though he was technically dead—something I was trying not to think too much about—I couldn't let him sink deeper into depression.

The problem was Corin, of course. I hadn't really answered any of his questions directly, so it wouldn't take long for him to realize that I knew something. Maybe if I snuck around to the back of the house when I was visiting Amenon, and made sure to keep low, I could go undetected. Having the curtains up now would help, too.

The fact that Amenon was a spirit made me feel a little easier about Corin finding his way to the tower. He should be able to fade in and out of existence, shouldn't he? But then, that led to another issue. Was I being a rube? Was Amenon really a spirit, a sort of ghost, or was I being suckered? To what end, though? How could Amenon, or any of them, possibly benefit from tricking me this way? Did it have to do with Mr. Rachat's sudden 'issue' that had stopped work on the chateau in the first place?

I groaned and dropped my head into my hands. I was exhausted. To add to my problems, Corin knew about Jason, knew about what had happened between us. It was rather humiliating, having someone know I'd been jilted. The only good thing was that he didn't seem to judge me for it.

Wanting only to drop into bed and sleep, I headed to the bathroom and washed my face in cold water to wake up a little. Then I donned my nightgown and robe. If Corin caught me as I headed to the house, I'd claim I'd seen something again. Or maybe I'd pretend to be sleep-walking. Whatever happened, I had to go now or risk falling asleep.

When I was ready, I glanced at the clock. A little after ten. Would Amenon be 'awake'? I hadn't heard him call to me this time, so maybe he was in another plane of existence. If he wasn't, then what did he do all day up in that tower? Brood on his misfortunes? It wasn't like he had distractions, such as television or the Internet, to take his mind off things. And he couldn't exactly seek revenge. His parents were long dead.

Really, he was a ticking time bomb.

This time, instead of dashing across the lawn for all the world to see, I slunk along the fence line. My goal was the back door, which was out of sight of the gatehouse and Corin. Considering I was trying to remain hidden, and that with each step, my heart pounded a little harder and a little faster, making it hard to breathe, I made it there in record-time.

Before I knew it, I was standing outside the tower room, gathering my strength to enter. Pulling in a deep breath and willing my hands to stop trembling, I climbed the last few stairs and stepped inside the room. The first thing I noticed was that no fire burned in the fireplace. The second was the lump on the bed.

"Amenon!" I cried as I rushed to his side, kneeling close to him. "Are you all right?" Without thinking I reached out to him, my hand pushing back the tendrils sticking damply to his cheek. He didn't move and I wondered if the dead could die again. "Amenon!" I cried again, shaking his shoulder.

"I have nothing left," he groaned, shifting slightly. Waves of heat emanated from him, another sign he was still alive.

"Oh, Amenon." I stroked his cheek, trying to comfort him, trying to remove his pain. "You've got me."

He stirred a little, his hand darting up to grab mine. "Yes, I do. You are my dear friend, Vianne. You're all I have."

Little flickers of warmth sparked in my chest as his hot fingers gripped mine. "Shhh…" I soothed. "You're going to be all right. Everything is going to be all right."

He squeezed my fingers. "I know this all occurred a long time ago, Vianne, but to me it feels as though it just happened."

"Of course it does," I crooned. "But we'll fix this. *I'll* fix this." It was a reckless promise, since I had no idea how to fix any of this. But if I could do anything to take away some of his pain, I would do it. Even in his agony, he was so beautiful and vulnerable; I longed to take his face in my hands and kiss it all over.

I froze and swallowed hard. What was wrong with me? I'd only just broken up with my fiancé and here I was, eager to jump into another relationship. Not to mention the fact that in Amenon's mind, he was still in love with someone else. I had serious issues if I thought this was going anywhere.

But then he gave a gut-wrenching sigh and all my doubts faded. He was a broken soul and I merely wanted to help him. That was all.

Liar.

I ignored the little voice. "I'm going to the library tomorrow," I whispered. "I'll find out what happened to your love. You didn't say before, Amenon. What was her name?"

"Camille," he breathed the name reverently.

"And her last name," I gently prompted.

"It is…" He paused. "Ah, yes. Renard." I avoided looking back at the fireplace, being pretty certain she was the CR carved into the mantel. Once more an image of the island—their hideaway—stole into my mind and I sent it away irritably, not liking that my intuition had been right. "While everything feels as though it happened yesterday," he went on, "I've been having trouble remembering things from that time. There is a growing darkness in my mind that hides my memories from me." His forehead wrinkled perplexedly. "Today I had trouble even recalling what my Camille looked like. It is as though she fades with every passing moment."

"Oh, Amenon. I'm so sorry."

He gave me a pained look. "With your help, this too shall pass, Vi-anne."

I gripped his hands in mine. "You're absolutely right. It will."

He made to sit up and I rocked back on my heels as his legs swung over the edge of the bed. His muscled thigh pressed firmly against my shoulder, and his hand found the top of my head to rest there, warm and solid as anyone alive. Slowly his fingers began to knead my scalp, sending electric jolts through my body. "I can't let them win," he said, his voice distant. "I can't, Vianne."

"They won't win, Amenon," I carelessly promised. At that moment I'd do anything for him. "I won't let them."

His eyes fluttered closed. "You are a true friend, Vianne."

Was I? Was I doing all this to help Amenon? Or was I doing it for myself?

It was an uncomfortable question and I sidestepped it, focusing instead on the hot, bewitching sensations spreading through my body, on the sound of our breathing, in and out in rhythm. In that moment, we seemed to have blended into one being.

I didn't want it to end.

Chapter Nineteen

☾

We sat like that for a long time, until finally Amenon gave a shudder of defeat and lay back down. "I shall be better tomorrow, Vianne… when you come with news of…" he paused.

"Camille," I provided. I couldn't help but feel a little smug that he had forgotten her name. But he remembered mine.

"Yes, Camille. Of course."

I left him sleeping heavily, as though drugged, but only after watching him for a few minutes as he slept. He really was beautiful. As I headed outside, I recalled what Ryan had said about how I only went after un-attainable guys, or at the very least, guys I wouldn't be able to hang onto. Was that true? Right now, my answer was 'maybe,' which helped me not in the least.

Back in bed, I wondered if it tired Amenon out, having to hold his presence in this plane as a solid being. He was doing something strange and wonderful, and I imagined that it must take something out of him. Perhaps with time, he'd become more adept at it, and hence, more real and strong with each passing day. He could go from being a spirit to being alive again. Could that happen? Was it happening right at this very moment? I didn't know, but I hoped so. I liked the idea of a world with Amenon in it, solid as any living, breathing person. If I could do anything to make that happen, I would. I was the Resurrectionist, after all.

I realized, right before I fell asleep, that this whole affair was probably more important to me than it should be. And yet when I awoke the next morning, excited to get to the library and start my research, I knew it didn't matter that I was caught in a fantasy. It felt good to be passionate again. After the canceled wedding debacle, I'd slipped into a funk that had felt like a living death.

Though maybe I'd been living in a sort of funk the whole time I'd been with Jason. The thought was nearly sacrilegious; at least it would be if I mentioned it to my parents, or Ryan, for that matter, so I pushed it out of my mind. I had more interesting and important things to think about…like how I was going to do research on both Camille and the Ship Room in the short time Corin would be gone delivering the application.

I'd figure it out. I'd done more challenging things in my life, like de-ciphering how to work all my phone apps. I could do this.

When Corin knocked on the door, I opened it with enthusiasm. "Hello!"

His expression went from his typical poker face to slightly stunned. "Hello, Vi. Are you ready to go?" he asked cautiously, as though trying to assess why I was so happy to see him.

I laughed. "Oh, lighten up, Corin! It's a beautiful day, and I finished the blueprints and now I get to spend time researching in a library. Three great things, don't you think?"

He nodded. "Oh, yes. Of course." I was surprised to see a look of disappointment cross his features before they settled into impassivity.

"Make that four," I added with a smile. Because really it was true. "I get to spend time with my favorite groundskeeper."

Corin's mouth split into a grin that lit up his face like sun on water and I felt suddenly even more happy. Inexplicably so, being that Corin was typically so serious. But he looked so joyful in this moment, that I couldn't help but feel touched. "And I get to spend the day with my favorite architect," he replied as he held out his arm and I linked mine with his. I liked the feel of it under my curled fingers, rather like the branch of an oak tree, solid and dependable. That was Corin, I realized. Solid and dependable, serious and sometimes stern, but you could count on him. He could end up being a good friend, and I found myself looking forward to that.

We headed out to his Jeep and Corin opened the door for me with a dramatic magician's flourish that I wouldn't have expected from him, but found myself smiling at. I deposited the paperwork in the backseat and climbed in the front, briefly recalling the night before when I'd made a bit of a fool of myself while in this very same seat.

Okay, more than a bit.

I decided to forget all that. Today was a new day. Today was a day of possibilities, and I was going to enjoy it.

"Merci, monsieur," I said as Corin climbed in beside me.

"Avec plaisir, mademoiselle." *My pleasure...*

"You speak French?"

"You sound surprised." He shifted into drive and we headed down the driveway.

"Well, I'd put you down more as someone who'd learn German."

"German?"

"It's very practical."

"And you think I'm very practical?" His didn't sound pleased.

"Isn't that what you strive to be?"

"Not in all things." The gate opened via a remote control he had clipped to his car's sun visor and he unexpectedly punched the gas, as though trying to prove a point. I flew back in my seat, my next words knocked out of my mouth.

"I guess not," I finally managed to say when I caught my breath.

He turned to me and smiled and I smiled back. He was acting rather strangely, and I found I liked it. When we reached the main road into Portsmouth, he slowed down, returning to normal. I didn't mind. It's easier to take in the sights when you're not hanging on for dear life.

I pointed at the cemetery off to our right. "Have you ever visited it?"

"Never really thought to."

"Hmm… I would love to see it some time. Maybe I'll go this week."

"I'll take you," he offered, a shade too casually.

"So you can keep an eye on me?" I joked.

He cast a sidelong glance at me, before returning his attention to the traffic light we were approaching. "Of course."

I laughed. "Well, I don't think I can get up to too much trouble around all those dead people."

"Strange. I think that's where you'd be most likely to get in trouble."

Before I could ask what he meant by that, he stepped on the gas and we passed through the intersection. Then I was distracted by a big, beautiful Victorian house on my right, and by the time I returned to reality, it seemed a bit late to ask him what he meant. But I did need to know something else.

"I collected samples from the Ship Room, so we can establish the when. But I need to send them to our analysis expert. Is there a post office on the way to the library?"

"I'll drop you off at the library, then I can mail it."

That would work and give me more time at the library. "All right, cool." An idea occurred to me…a way to buy even more time. "It's a long-shot, but maybe when you stop by the town office you could see if it has any records for the work done on the Ship Room."

"I doubt it. It's not the kind of remodel a person would want others to know about, is it?"

"No."

And I thought I might know why. If I took what Amenon had told me about his parents murdering him, then connected it to the building of the wall in the Ship Room, I had my answer. I was pretty sure the analysis would reveal the age of the wallpaper to be from the 1890s, the time when Amenon had died. What had they done to him? Sealed him in the wall? There hadn't been any bones, though, no skeleton found. It was all very odd.

"But I don't mind trying," he added.

"I just want to cover all the angles."

"Very sensible." Was he smirking?

"I don't always live on the moon," I said huffily.

"We're here," was his lame reply, turning into a parking lot.

The Portsmouth City Library was a large structure made of red brick, with a glass tower and lots of windows. "What a beautiful building!"

"The city deconstructed an old armory building," Corin explained, "and the materials were used to build the new library. It's very green and modern, while still maintaining the old-world charm of Portsmouth."

"They did a fantastic job. I can't wait to see inside."

"I'll come find you at noon and we'll do lunch. Then I can take you to the Athenaeum."

"That would be perfect," I replied, wondering what he was going to do with all that extra time.

"I have a few errands to run," he said, even though I hadn't asked the question out loud. Knowing my face, though, he'd probably just read my quizzical expression. "I called ahead and set things up so that you can use my code to access the databases or check out anything you might need." He passed me a slip of paper with his username and password on it.

I took it. "Thanks, Corin. That should make things easier. Everything's in the backseat," I told him as I slipped out of the Jeep. I waved as he drove off, thinking he was very thoughtful.

Inside, the building was full of light. While quite spacious, it felt cozy and welcoming. Judging by the number of people inside, it was a popular place to hang out. I took a few minutes to check out the antique bicycle display, along with all the amenities the library had to offer. Camden has an amazing library, but, being in a smaller town, would be hard pressed to compete with the funding the Portsmouth Library must have. If I lived here, I would likely spend a lot of time in this building.

When I asked about the reference department, the smiling woman at the main desk pointed me to the second floor, which could be reached by a spiral staircase. Filled with sunlight, the stairs circled around a majestic eagle hanging from the ceiling. As I climbed the steps, I admired the bird's splendor as light reflected off its golden wings.

Once upstairs, I introduced myself to Tom Reegan, the young man at the information desk, and he guided me to a computer. There he showed me where to find numerous resources to help me locate Camille.

"I could even search a database of local death notices and obituaries for you," he volunteered. "If whoever you're looking for falls in the right time frame, that is."

"That would be great! Her name is Camille Renard, and I'd say you'd better search from 1891 to..." I did a mental calculation. "Well, until 1990, I guess." That should cover the range, even accounting for an abnormally long life span.

He beamed. "You're in luck. We cover those dates."

"Perfect! Thank you, Tom." I gave him a big smile and he scurried off to start his search.

I began my search in the New England Historic Genealogical Society database but had no luck. I tried different variations on the spelling of Camille's name, but that didn't help, either. The other three databases yielded the same results. Sometimes I'd find someone with that name, but the birth date was too late to be the Camille I needed. Had she moved? Her name sounded very French, so she might have been an immigrant. Perhaps after Amenon's death she'd returned home, heart-broken and miserable.

Should I widen my search to France? It was a long shot and likely would yield numerous Camille Renards. I sighed and leaned back, rubbing my eyes tiredly. She was a veritable needle in a haystack. Perhaps Tom had had more luck. But when I approached the desk to find out, the despairing look on his face told me everything I needed to know.

"I'm sorry, Miss. I even tried spelling her name different ways, but as far as I can see, if there was a Camille Renard, she either didn't die around here, or, well, her death wasn't reported."

My expression must have reflected my surprise because he gulped nervously. "Portsmouth wasn't exactly the safest place during the Victorian era, all the way through the 1950s, give or take. Especially along the waterfront. That area was once known as Puddle Dock and it was where a lot of poor people lived. In the 50s and 60s, the area was 'cleaned' up, maybe not in the nicest way. It looks good now, though. It's where Prescott Park and Strawbery Banke are located."

Ah. I was familiar with both, having worked with my father at Strawbery Banke on a few projects. It did look nice now, though it was sad to hear about the families who'd once lived there losing their homes. "Well, thank you for your help, Tom." I looked around, frustrated. "Well, I guess that's that."

"Is there anything else I can help you with?"

I remembered the Ship Room. It was yet another long shot, but perhaps there was some information here about the Sowles family and their house. "There's another family I want to research, but I'm not as interested in their ancestry. Actually I'd like to see if they're mentioned in local newspapers."

His smile returned. "I could try looking in the Special Collections Room for you. It contains all sorts of information on the area, from obituaries to newspapers, photographs to tax records."

I brightened. "That sounds perfect."

"Just tell me what you're looking for and I'll track it down."

"Well, it has to be kept confidential…" He nodded encouragingly. "I'm looking for anything related to Chateau de Sowles."

He sucked in a deep breath. "I love that place."

"You do?" Here was a bit of luck.

"I've never been inside, but I came across an article on the house a few years ago and it's become a bit of an obsession with me since then."

I leaned toward him. "I work there."

His brown, bespectacled eyes widened. "You are so lucky!"

I grinned. "I feel like the luckiest girl in the world." I leaned even closer. "So you probably know all sorts of things about the place, with your obsession and all."

He shrugged. "I know everything there is to know that can be glossed from our files, which isn't much."

"Anything juicy?"

He gave me a boyish grin. "That's the stuff I like the best. I suppose that makes me a bit ghoulish, but it's not like it affects anyone alive today." *Little did he know,* I thought to myself.

"Go on," I encouraged.

"Well, there was a big mystery about the place. Back in the 1890s."

1891, I would bet. "What happened?"

"The heir to the Sowles fortune died. He was pretty young."

"What was his name?" I asked, a little breathless in anticipation.

"I'm not sure if I'm pronouncing it right… Amenon Sowles?"

"Sounds right to me," I said casually, though my heart was pounding. "Did they say how he died?"

"The rumors were that it was from dissipation…you know, drinking and carousing and the like."

"He partied too hard?" I could scarcely believe that.

"That's what it means, but I'm not sure it's truly what happened to him. Apparently he was quite the man about town, like a celebrity today, and yes, he had a penchant for getting into trouble, but nothing major, mainly what back then they would call hi-jinks or mischief making. He was everywhere and seemed to know everyone. He was featured in the papers on a regular basis."

"Was he well-liked?" I asked, mentally crossing my fingers.

"Oh yes," he breathed reverently. "The town loved him, as did the newspapers. His obituary said good things about him, too. Much-loved son, rising presence in the city, a gentleman of charm and affability, showed great promise, etc."

"Can I see an article on him?"

I thought he was going to dash off to the Special Collections Room, but he only reached under the counter. "I can do better than that." He pulled something out—a giant scrapbook, I could see now—and set it on the counter with a bang. He opened it and pointed to an old black and white photo. "This is the best one of him. There are a lot of photos of him, actually, but none really capture his face very well." He sounded disappointed.

I peered down at it. For being so old, and obviously taken outdoors, the quality was quite good. A young man, wearing a top hat and coat, leaned against a brick building. Even though the subject's face was slightly blurred, as Tom had mentioned, there was an unmistakable charm about him that communicated itself to the viewer. While it looked like Amenon, I couldn't be sure if this was him or not.

Well, to clarify, what I couldn't be sure about was if the man living in the chateau at this moment was the subject of this picture.

"What was the mystery you mentioned?" I asked, still studying the photo.

"Well, after Amenon died, the Sowles fired all their staff and lived alone in that big old house until their deaths five years later, pretty much at the exact same time. After that, people would drive out there to get a look at the place. Amenon was a bit of an idol, it seemed, and they came to pay their respects. More times than not, they reported back that they'd heard noises or had seen someone in the house. A man sometimes. Sometimes a child."

"A child?"

He shrugged. "Nobody knows who the child might have been. Perhaps one of the servant's? Folks less kind said it was the senior Mr. Sowles' child. Illegitimate, maybe, or possibly something was wrong with it and they hid it away."

"Wow. That's pretty sensational stuff."

"Oh yes." He grinned, his young face lighting up. "When they died, the house was sold, but no one ever stayed long. There was a codicil in the will that provided an allowance for a family to look after the house, so it stayed in good repair."

A family. That must have been Corin's ancestors. "An allowance to keep up a house that was going to be sold?" I wondered aloud. "Doesn't that seem strange to you?"

He frowned, catching my meaning. "Well, being that the house never stayed occupied for long, it does seem rather providential."

"Exactly. It's like the Sowles were expecting that no one would want to live there, yet they didn't like the idea of the house being left to rot."

He nodded. "Is it still in good shape?"

"Very good shape," I replied, and he looked relieved.

"So, in your research, did you ever get the sense that the Sowles were bad people?" It was a bit difficult asking such questions when I knew something Tom did not—that Amenon had been murdered by his parents.

"On the contrary. Before their son's death, they seemed to be upstanding citizens, donating to charity, getting involved in local politics. That sort of stuff. He was their only child—according to the records, anyway—and by *all* accounts they doted on him."

Doted on him? Well, maybe before Camille came on the scene. "So he might have been a bit spoiled, then, which is why he partied so much."

"I guess so. The thing is…" he paused. "Well, he never looks sick. Not once. And I have photos of him all the way up to a few days before he died. I know the quality isn't great, but he just didn't look like someone who was days from his death."

"Weird. Maybe he fell ill?"

He shook his head. "The doctor's report said nothing about an illness. In fact, the report was very vague regarding the cause of death."

I'll bet it was.

"Well, I guess if he did die from something like a drug overdose, they wouldn't state that."

"Yes, but you'd think the doctor would make something up. Like an illness. If only to protect the family name."

"You'd think." I rubbed my head, feeling like I was missing something important. "Tell me more about the family that took care of the house."

"Well—"

"Hello." Tom spun toward the voice at the same time I did. Corin. I glanced at the clock over Tom's head, dismayed to see it was noon already. Crap.

Tom slammed the scrapbook shut and slid it back under the desk. I had wanted to see more photos of Amenon, but now I wouldn't get the chance. At least not during this visit.

"Hello, sir," he greeted Corin, a little nervously. I couldn't blame him. Corin's serious demeanor made me feel a bit on edge, too, like I was constantly being watched for infractions and found a likely suspect.

"How did things go?" Corin asked me.

"I didn't find much," I replied. "Maybe I'll have better luck at the Athenaeum." I turned to Tom. "Thank you, Tom. You were very helpful."

He ducked his head shyly. "No problem, Miss Alexander." I'd told him a few times already to call me Vi, but he seemed to prefer the more formal moniker.

"Can I call you if I have any questions?" *And to set up a meeting to see more photos?*

"Yes, of course," he said, looking anxious again. "I'll search the Special Collections Room, too. If I find something, I'll let you know."

"Great. Just call or text me. Here's my number…" After he typed it into his phone, I said goodbye and thanked him again.

He bobbed his head at us, then turned to another patron with visible relief. To avoid further questions, I headed toward the stairs. Corin hesitated, then followed after me. It was only as I was leaving the library that something Tom had said earlier surfaced in my mind.

"…as far as I can see, if there was a Camille Renard, she either didn't die around here, or, well, her death wasn't reported." The whole sentence was a bit disturbing, but it was the first part that kept repeating itself in my mind. *If* there was a Camille Renard. What if she had never existed?

What if Amenon had made her up?

Chapter Twenty

☾

I headed out the main exit door and automatically turned right. Corin's hand clamped down on my shoulder. "I'm this way," he gently re-directed me.

"Oh. Oops! My mind must be somewhere else."

He came up alongside me, dropping his hand as we marched toward the parking lot. I rather liked it on my shoulder. It felt very steadying and solid and right now that's exactly what I needed. "So, did you find out anything about the Ship Room?" he asked.

"Nope." I didn't tell him, of course, that I hadn't even tried. Because I already knew why the wall had been erected. To trap Amenon's spirit somehow. And no newspaper article or official document was going to tell me that.

"Nothing?"

"Well, the sample will tell us when. But as for why, I'm not sure we're going to find that out through anything that exists in the public eye." It was the truth, but not all of it, of course. "How about you? Any luck?"

"Nothing. I think you're right. Whatever reason Henri Sowles had for putting up that wall will likely remain a secret."

"What makes you think he put it up?" I asked carefully.

His step hesitated, then I heard a little chirrup as he unlocked his Jeep. He opened my door for me. "I guess I don't."

I climbed into the passenger seat. "It's just that, well, there were other owners, right?"

"Yes," he replied. "Of course."

"We won't know for sure when it happened until we get the analysis back. So until we know the date, we can't say definitively who built the wall."

"Do *you* think it was Monsieur Sowles?" he asked, unexpectedly. We were driving out of the parking lot now, heading down a street lined with charming homes.

"Well, judging by the look of the work, I would say that whenever it was done, it was a long time ago."

He nodded absently and was silent until we found a parking spot on a familiar-looking one-way street with an array of quirky shops and restaurants. I soon realized this was the street I'd come in on when I'd first arrived in Portsmouth. Corin slid out of the Jeep and I did the same, though less gracefully. "I'll be back in a second." He paid for a ticket at the meter, stuck it in the dash, then locked the Jeep. When he was done, he indicated for me to go ahead of him. "It's this way." His hand settled on the small of my back and I felt a little shiver. Oh, dear. How could I be attracted to two men, while I still sort of had a fiancé? Maybe Corin was right. Maybe I was a moon dweller. Maybe I needed to pull my head out of the clouds and get my act together, just like Jason wanted me to. Perhaps this was part of growing up—learning to accept people as they are.

Corin escorted me to a corner café and we ordered sandwiches and iced coffees. "I've got this," Corin said, pulling out a twenty.

"What? No! I can't have you driving me all over town and then make you pay for my lunch, too."

"I insist." He wedged himself between me and the cash register and paid the bill.

"Fine. But then I'm going to have to pay you back."

"You can cook me dinner."

"You wouldn't suggest that if you knew how I cooked."

"I'll take my chances." I frowned, but inwardly I felt strangely light. I enjoyed a good banter.

When our food came, we headed outdoors. The day was lovely and warm with a slight breeze. I donned my sunglasses and tucked into my sandwich, a tasty ham and cheese concoction. Corin told me that he had simply dropped off the sample, since the office where Katelyn worked was right here in Portsmouth.

"I knew it was here, of course," I told him, "but I hadn't wanted to try to find it myself. I would've gotten lost," I confessed.

"This city is a bit convoluted," Corin sympathized, then proceeded to tell me about Portsmouth and some of its history, including the North Church, whose white steeple soared up toward the sky across the street from where we sat. Apparently George Washington had once worshipped there.

"The Athenaeum is over there." Corin pointed across the street, opposite the church, as he neatly folded his sandwich wrapper. He'd devoured every last scrap, leaving behind no sign that he'd eaten. My spot, on the other hand, resembled a 'cookie monster' scene. I'd never been a neat eater, a fact that plagued my mother and father throughout my childhood, and later, Jason, who joked, more often than necessary, that I should wear a bib.

I looked down at my mess, then quickly tried to clean it up. "Sorry. I just get so into eating."

Corin waved this away. "I don't mind at all. It's refreshing to see a female who likes to eat."

"Seriously?"

"Seriously."

I tilted my head sideways. "I feel like you know all this stuff about me, and my relationship issues, too, but I know nothing about you and yours." Corin stiffened, but I didn't regret my question. "Spill it, Groundskeeper. I can't stand it anymore. Why did you want to know what makes relationships go bad?"

His shoulders relaxed slightly, though the casual observer would be hard pressed to pick up on it. Even slightly relaxed, Corin's posture was perfect, like a soldier. "Are you asking me if I'm available?"

I scrunched up my wrapper. "Very funny. Throw me a bone on this one. I feel like a fool, being that I was practically left at the altar. I at least want to know something personal about you." I said this lightly, as though this were the entire real reason. But it wasn't. I was curious, too, if the perfect and serious Corin had a heart.

"Like you, I was engaged to be married."

My eyes widened as I slurped up the last of my coffee through a straw. "You were?"

"We ended it the day before the wedding."

"I'm so sorry." Unthinkingly I reached out and touched his hand; to my surprise, he didn't pull away. "That must have sucked."

He gave a dry chuckle. "Yes, it did."

"As much as it kills me, I won't ask you what happened."

"I appreciate that, but you're right. Tit for tat. You shared your secret with me and I want to share mine with you."

"Oh. Okay." I felt ridiculously flattered. Corin struck me as the type of person who kept his secrets and slights close to his chest.

His gaze drifted off toward the North Church. The clock struck one, a resounding gong that sent a little thrill through me. I'd always loved the sound of chimes. "Jessica and I had been dating for four years when I proposed to her. I thought we were going to grow old together." He paused, as though gathering himself. "And then, well, it's a cliché, actually. I found her with my best friend, John."

I squeezed his hand tightly. "That's awful, Corin! How could she? How could *he*?"

His jaw was rigid and he still hadn't looked at me. "I thought I knew her. John, too. But apparently I was a blind fool."

"When did this happen?"

"Not long before you came, actually."

I gasped. "So you and I are in the same boat right now?"

"I guess we are."

"Well, aren't we a pathetic pair?"

His eyes left the church and came to settle on me. A tiny smile lifted the corners of his mouth. "I think that title should go to Jessica and Jason."

I pulled my hand away from his, feeling suddenly strange. "But I'm the one who messed up the wedding, not Jason. And, well, he still wants to be with me."

I could actually feel Corin withdraw from me. "Yes. Of course. Entirely different stories." He abruptly stood. "They're expecting us at the Athenaeum."

A lump settled in my throat. I wanted to say, "But *you* didn't mess up, Corin. I did. I always mess up." But seeing his icy expression, I couldn't get the words out. He reached down and grabbed our wrappers, then marched toward the garbage can and ruthlessly slammed the papers into it.

He was obviously upset with me, and trying not to show it. But what had I done? I tried once more to explain myself, but the traffic was loud as we crossed the street and Corin was moving fast so I had to hurry to keep up with him. By the time we reached the Athenaeum, a narrow, red brick building, Corin's back was so rigid I knew there was no talking to him. I swallowed my words and followed him past twin cannons, set upright on their muzzles, one on each side of the door-way.

The small interior was dark and filled with books and antiques and old paintings. An elderly gentleman, sitting at a long table covered in magazines and lit warmly by a yellow glass lamp, looked up at us from the *Smithsonian* magazine he was reading. He was small and dressed as I imagine he imagined an English gentleman would dress...in a heather tweed coat and cap.

"Ah, Corin. You made it."

"Hello, George. Glad to see you're staying busy."

George chuckled and stood up. "I'm on a break."

"You're always on a break."

"Considering I'm a volunteer here, that would be about right."

"Did you have any luck with my request?"

George shook his head ruefully. "I found photographs, which you've seen, of course." What? So there were photographs! Corin hadn't been lying when he'd said 'there are none *here*,' but why hadn't he said, but there are some at the Athenaeum? "I didn't find anything on any changes made to the house. Did something happen?"

Corin hesitated. "Nothing major." Which was a major understatement, and yet the truth, too. "Just wanted to be sure I haven't missed something."

"I'm surprised your folk didn't keep record of that sort of thing."

I stared at Corin in surprise. He'd said nothing about any records. Of course, I hadn't asked about *records*, just photos. Sneaky bastard. "They did," he said, giving me a sidelong glance. "I just wanted to double-check."

George grinned. "You always were one for making sure all your i's are dotted and all your t's are crossed." He glanced at me. "I'm more one for getting it the other way round."

I laughed. "Me, too. Thank goodness for the Corins of the world."

"Amen to that," George heartily agreed. I'd actually meant it, but the scowl on Corin's face indicated he thought I was insulting him.

"So you've worked with Corin?"

George looked at Corin, who nodded. "Corin worked here as an intern for a summer. Right, Corin?" I thought it was odd that George had checked in with Corin before answering. What was so hush-hush about being an intern?

"I think I was more of a gopher than a historian, though."

"True. But you were a good gopher."

"Well, we won't take up any more of your time." Corin turned toward the door.

"Speak for yourself," I said. Yes, I had screwed up what I'd meant to say to him and he was angry with me for that, but that didn't mean I was going to waste this opportunity. "May I look around?"

"Certainly," George answered heartily. "A pretty lass like you? I'll give you the tour myself."

"I have something I need to do," Corin said curtly. "I'll return for you in an hour."

Before I could thank him, he was across the black and white checkered floor and out the door. I took a moment to admire the arched windows and doorway, all three with half-moon windows above them, then turned back to George. "I was wondering if you have any photos of Chateau de Sowles dating back to 1890, give or take."

"That we do, miss. Come up to the library. I keep records of the chateau up there, in their own separate area. Corin compiled them one summer."

"So you know Corin well?" I asked as we climbed the stairs.

"I'm not sure anyone knows Corin well," was his enigmatic response.

After that, we saved our energy for the climb, which I was glad we did because when we reached our destination, I couldn't help letting out a gasp of awe. "What a lovely room!" Numerous bookshelves lined the walls, and toward the back of the room, two additional bookshelves sat in the middle of the floor, each connected to the nearby wall with a wooden arch. Above us was a landing, which encircled the room, leaving the center area open. The landing was closed off with a sturdy railing, and filled with even more books. An elaborate chandelier hung from the ceiling and lit the room with a cozy light. I wondered if I could take the whole space and transplant it into my dream home.

"I can see why you volunteer here."

"Great place for a nap," George said with a wink. "Give me a moment and I'll go fetch the box."

He returned with a wood crate and plunked it down on a table. I headed straight for it. "I'm actually looking for someone in particular," I told him as I pulled out a photo album. "Her name is Camille Renard. She lived in Portsmouth around 1890. That's all I know about her."

"I can look through our records."

"Thanks, George. I'm Vi, by the way."

"Yes, I know. Corin mentioned you were coming."

Ah. I opened the photo album. "Do you want me to help?" I asked absently as I stared down at a large photo of the house, labeled at the bottom, *Chateau de Sowles, Summer, 1860*, which meant the house was practically brand new in this photo. George answered that he could handle it himself and I was grateful when he left me alone. Several more pictures of the house followed until I finally reached one with people in it. Scrawled in one corner: *Staff - 1890*. In front of the chateau's *porte cochere*, several people in formal, starched uniforms posed stiffly for the camera. I peered closer at one particular woman and a thought occurred to me. What if Camille had been a servant at Chateau de Sowles? If this was her, she was quite attractive. I had to suppress a sudden, hot flare of jealousy in my gut. I was being ridiculous. Camille was dead, long dead. *But not to Amenon*, a little voice whispered, and I told it to shut up.

I flipped through the rest of the book and was surprised not to find any photos of Amenon. There was a photo of Mr. and Mrs. Sowles, standing alone on the back porch. They looked quite young and carefree. They certainly didn't look like murderers. According to the date, the photo had very likely been taken before they had Amenon. More photos of the house appeared, labeled with the years, until finally the album ended with the date 1891. Still no photo of Amenon. Had they disowned him? Erased all signs of him after they had murdered him?

But *why* had they murdered him? According to what Tom had told me at the library, they'd doted on him. I couldn't imagine them getting so angry at his dating a woman of lower class that they'd kill him for it. Maybe they got into an argument and the father pushed Amenon and he fell and hit his head. That made sense. Even though it had been an accident, it had happened when they were fighting, so Amenon would feel his father had murdered him.

It all fit. I suddenly felt eager to get back to the chateau and tell Amenon what I'd figured out. Perhaps it would be enough to release him, or at least lighten the burden he carried of believing his parents had murdered him.

Of course, if this was what had really happened, then they had covered it up. And convinced the good doctor to go along, too. Then they had let go of all their servants and lived alone until their deaths. But why let go of their help? As punishment for their deed? Or to get rid of any potential witnesses?

I sighed. Just when I thought I had the answer, more questions emerged, making me doubt my theory. I closed the photo album just as George returned. "Find anything?" I asked him.

He shook his head. "Not a sign. That's not unusual. Back then, lots of people were overlooked for one reason or another."

"Well, thanks," I said, feeling disheartened. I'd been so certain I'd find her and learn what had happened to her after Amenon's death, maybe even track down her relatives. Amenon was going to be so disappointed.

"Are you sure you have the right name?"

"Yes. That's what I was given."

"And you're sure you were given the right name?"

"Ye—" I stopped myself. Was I sure? Hadn't I already wondered if Camille actually existed? "No, I guess not."

"People change their names all the time," he offered. "That's why I asked."

I nodded, slowly. That could be it. Maybe Camille had changed her name for a good reason. To avoid the same fate as her lover...

Chapter Twenty-One

☾

I went through the rest of the box, but found nothing useful. After I was done, I thanked George for his time, helped him put away the box, then went outside to wait for Corin. The breeze had picked up and carried with it a slight hint of the sea and a touch of coolness, too. As it whipped around the street corner and buffeted against me, I thought about what I'd learned. In some ways, I felt like I'd garnered a lot of information, and in some ways, I felt like I was farther from the truth than ever.

I would just have to ask Amenon if Camille might have changed her name and if he had any idea what that name might be. I would also share my theory about his parents, about the fight, and see what he thought. Hopefully my idea would make him feel a little less lost.

A honk interrupted my reverie and I looked up to see Corin's Jeep pulling up to the curb. He didn't look at me as I hopped in, and I'd barely had my seatbelt on before we took off. Corin maintained a cool distance and the ride was silent as we headed back to the chateau.

So I was surprised when, as we were passing the South Cemetery, Corin pulled over to the side of the road, parking near a wrought-iron gate.

"What are you doing?"

"I thought you wanted to see the cemetery."

"I do."

He slid out of the car. "Well, come on, then."

Intrigued, I followed after him, into the large graveyard that seemed to stretch on for miles. There were gravestones, of course, ranging from simple to elaborate, gorgeous angel statuary, and massive mausoleums, all markers of lost lives. I stood still, taking it all in. Corin noticed and stopped, then returned to stand by me.

"It's pretty overwhelming."

I nodded, biting my lip. All those lives, all those stories, each unique, but now forgotten. Someday that would be me and Corin and everyone I knew. Death was inevitable.

Except for Amenon…

Corin cleared his throat and I peered up at him. Was I imagining things or did he look nervous? "I wanted to apologize to you. I treated you rudely at the café, and I'm sorry for that."

"Oh. Well, thanks. I did have something more to say, but you weren't having it."

One side of his mouth turned up. "No, I was not having it. Please, say what you were going to say."

"Well, I wanted to say our stories are different because you weren't the one to mess things up. I was. I mess up all the relationships I'm in. I guess it's my thing." I shrugged, trying to look as though this didn't bother me, but my shoulders didn't want to cooperate and I ended up only looking slumped over.

"Oh. I—" He stopped and I stared at him. Corin at a loss for words? Would wonders never cease? "I'm sorry, Vi. I tend to be a bit quick to judge and some say I'm also pretty inflexible, both good reasons for why Jessica cheated on me."

"She could've just ended things with you!" I said heatedly. "I don't think there's any good reason to cheat. You just leave. It's that simple."

"I thought that once. But maybe things aren't as black and white as I see them. Maybe they shouldn't be."

"Maybe. But still…cheating. It's the ultimate betrayal, and it's not like you had kids together— You didn't have kids together, right?" He laughed a little and shook his head. "Right. So her ending your relationship would shatter no one else. She had no excuse." I paused and took a deep breath. "Did she say why she did it?"

"She texted me a few reasons."

"Dare I ask what they were?"

"She said I was cold, unfeeling, and boring."

"She said that? But she's the one who's all that stuff. Anyone with a conscience wouldn't hurt someone they supposedly love by cheating on them with their best friend. And talk about boring…she couldn't have picked a bigger cliché to follow." I touched his arm and he started, but didn't pull away. "Besides, you might be a little too serious, and maybe you follow rules a bit too rigidly, but I would never call you cold or unfeeling or boring. Quite the opposite." As I spoke the words, I realized how true they were. Corin was not the fuddy-duddy I'd led Anna to believe. I'd told her that, I think, because I didn't want her going after him, and well, because he had tried to get in the way of me taking this job. But he'd only been following his boss's orders. So his boss was the fuddy-duddy, not Corin.

"Thank you," he said, his voice rough.

He looked like he was about to say more, but I cut him off. "I'm not just saying that because I want to keep my job. I must admit you're growing on me, Groundskeeper."

He shot an amused glance at me. "You're not half bad yourself, Architect."

I looped my arm through his. "I'm going to need your support after that compliment. My heart's all a-flutter."

He laughed out loud and my heart really did flutter a little. It was nice to be able to make someone like Corin laugh like that. Very flattering for the ego, but also just a lovely surprise, like finding hidden treasure. Jason never laughed like that when I made a joke. In fact, I wasn't sure Jason had ever laughed like that in my presence. It was a chilling realization. Chilling, because I'd never noticed it before. How could I have been so blind to something so big?

"Shall we go see some graves?" he asked.

"You take me to the nicest places."

We spent the next hour reading epitaphs, some sad, some funny, some brief, some wordy. I felt like we were doing something for these people, taking notice of them, resurrecting them for a small moment. I liked resurrecting the forgotten, which was perhaps why I loved my job so much.

"You know," Corin said as he straightened up from studying a small gravestone, "I think the Sowles are buried somewhere around here. There's no family graveyard on the property, so it would make sense."

I perked up. "Do you have any idea where they might be?"

"Not a clue. But if I were to guess, I'd say they're over there, in the older section." He pointed off toward a part of the graveyard on the edge of the woods, shaded by a series of shrubs.

"Let's try it. Come on!" I took off down the gravel path.

I thought Corin would pass me quickly—speed has never been my superpower—but he stayed behind me. Still running, I glanced back. He was there, jogging. "You cannot be slower than me!"

"I'm not. Just enjoying the view." He cocked an eyebrow at me and if I didn't know better I'd say that he was flirting with me.

But of course he wasn't. Ryan's words came back to me and I scowled at the ground in front of me. *You have bad radar when it comes to men.* Was I really that clueless?

"Let's look around here," Corin said, catching up to me.

"Oh, thank goodness," I wheezed. "I don't think I can run anymore." I was glad to stop, and glad to have something else to focus on.

We were near the grove of trees, full of sumac and birch and even a mess of grapevines, when we stopped. We separated a little and started our search, hands behind our backs, heads rising and falling like hens pecking at the dirt. And then I found them...three gravestones sitting more in the woods than not. Two grand ones stood closer together, as though for comfort, and one smaller one was off to the side as though tossed away like a dirty sock.

Heart beating, I approached the two and crouched down to read the words etched in the stone. *SOWLES*, the tombstone proclaimed. Henri Sowles was on the left, and his wife, Julietta, was on the right. When I read the date of their death, July 23rd, 1896, I had to reach out and steady myself on the stone. They had died on the same day. Henri was 76, Julietta 69. They must have had Amenon late in life. As far as I knew, he was an only child, so maybe they'd had trouble having children, which would explain why they supposedly had doted on him.

It didn't explain why they'd murdered him, though. *If* they had…

Another explanation, beyond the accident, was forming in my mind. Maybe Amenon had it all wrong. Maybe he'd been delirious when he'd died and thought they'd done something to him, when in reality, they'd only been trying to help. It didn't explain the wall in the Ship Room, but perhaps the two incidents were unrelated. Amenon's spirit might have been restless and somehow got caught in the Ship Room when they'd put the wall up. Maybe the wall fixed some sort of flaw. It was something I would have to check out. I didn't want Mía doing something that might bring down a support wall.

"Corin," I called. "Over here."

He left his search and joined me, squatting close. My knees hurt and my calves ached and it was tempting to lean against him for support, but I didn't do it. Things were muddled enough in my life. I didn't need to get it wrong with Corin. Doing something like that could cost me my career and potentially a good friend. Corin was a good guy and I didn't want to do something stupid to hurt him, just like his fiancée had done.

"You found them."

"Can you believe they died the same day?"

"I knew they'd died close together, but not the same day. How strange."

"Not entirely. I've read stories where two people who love each other very much die within hours of each other."

"Do you believe that kind of love is possible?" He glanced over at me, one sardonic eyebrow raised. "Oops. I forgot who I was talking to. Moon dweller girl."

I punched his arm and the motion made me fall against him. He didn't move away and neither did I. I should have, but his solid mass felt quite nice and sturdy and I didn't want that feeling to end. "That's not fair!" I cried. "I know your mother told you about that sort of person, but I bet if she met me, she'd say I wasn't one of them."

"My mother passed away a couple years ago." His voice was calm, as though he'd just announced the weather forecast.

"Oh, Corin! I'm sorry." I immediately pulled away from him and stood, completely embarrassed. "I didn't know."

"Why should you?"

"I don't know. It's a stupid thing to say, actually, since there's no way I could know. But still…"

He pushed himself to his feet. "It's all right, Vi. She died of cancer. She'd been in pain for a long time, so it was a welcome release for her."

Was he really so calm about it? "And your father?"

His jaw clenched slightly. Not so calm about that. "I don't know who my father is. My mother never said, and after a while I stopped asking."

"Wow. That had to be hard."

He shrugged. "My mother and I were happy together."

"I'm sure you were." But I wasn't sure they were. Based on her seemingly negative opinion of anyone who had an ounce of sentimentality in their body, she might have been a bit bitter about life. And her relationship with Corin's dad obviously hadn't been a success, so that had to have colored her view of life, too.

"I don't want your pity," he said with more feeling than I'd ever heard come from him.

"You won't get it." Dang, he was touchy.

"Good."

"Good." Slightly irritated, I moved away from him, toward the nearby tombstone, my breath growing short. This had to be Amenon's final resting place. Though I realized, with a shudder, that there might not be a body in the casket.

I kneeled down before the marker, which was very plain, and read out loud, "Amenon Sowles. 1867-1891. Our sorrow is not enough." No beloved son. No angels or other symbols of an afterlife to decorate the stone.

Maybe they hadn't loved him, after all.

"You found Amenon," Corin said behind me and I jumped.

"W-what?" I stuttered.

He frowned and pointed at the stone. "Amenon. The Sowles' son. He died young, as you can see."

It took a moment for me to reply, being that my heart had just tried to climb up my throat. "Ah, yes. I found his *gravestone*. Right." I pretended to look closer. "Twenty-four. He did die young. Do you know what he died of?"

"No, though I've heard he was quite the man about town."

I smiled. "The man about town? What a quaint way of putting it."

"Fine. He liked to party hardy. Is that better?"

"No!" I laughed, then brushed away a leaf perched on top of the stone. "So, do you believe that? That he died from partying too hard?"

"I'm not sure I really care one way or the other. It happened over a hundred years ago. Let the guy rest in peace."

If only I could…if only Amenon would.

A rumble of thunder sounded in the distance. I looked up at the sky, filled now with dark clouds and thrashing branches. A sudden breeze, cold as death, pushed against me, and once again I found myself leaning against Corin. He reached down and steadied me with his work-roughened hands, then pulled me to my feet.

"We should go. Looks like a storm's coming."

I glanced back at Amenon's stone one more time, standing alone, separated from his parents by something greater than a stretch of grass. *Our sorrow is not enough.* What did that mean?

"We have to hurry," Corin beckoned.

Reluctantly, I turned away. Corin urged me on, and laughing, I ran toward him. When I got close, he dashed off. The rain began pelting down, massive drops that smacked hard against my skin. We made it to the Jeep, neck and neck, just as the skies opened and poured.

The whole ride home we sat quietly, thoroughly wet and lost in our thoughts, but every once in a while we'd glance at each other and smile.

Chapter Twenty-Two

☾

Corin pulled up right outside the guesthouse door. I thought about inviting him to stay for supper, but I was suddenly feeling very tired. Besides that, my phone had buzzed at me several times while in Portsmouth and I had a bad feeling about it.

"Thanks for the ride and for lunch. I owe you dinner, okay? Some time this week."

"Sounds good. What are your plans for the rest of this week?" he asked, trying to look casual. I couldn't help wondering if he was asking out of interest, or checking on my progress to report back to the boss.

"I thought I'd get going on ordering materials. Some of the stuff is easy to get, but I have to make sure I follow certain standards with a house this age."

"Ah, right. Does AA&D have contacts around here?"

"Loads of them. We've been doing work in Portsmouth and the surrounding areas for years."

"That's good," he said distractedly.

"I'm right on track, schedule-wise," I said defensively. "All the work should be completed before Mr. Rachat and his bride return. It will get done if I have to pound nails myself."

Corin shook his head a little. "Oh, I have no doubt of that."

"I might be a moon dweller, Corin, but I'm also a professional."

"I know that, Vi. While waiting at the City Clerk's, I looked over your work. You covered everything. The application should go through quite easily."

I relaxed somewhat, even preened a little at his compliment. "Thank you. I'm glad you think so. You must know something about architecture and design yourself, based on what I've seen of the grounds. I've been meaning to look around, actually, but I haven't had the time."

"I know a thing or two," he said modestly. "I'm something of a Jack of all trades—I like to know something about everything. It took me a while to get the grounds back into shape, though. They sat untended for many years, while my mother was ill. She was the expert and she meant to pass along what she knew, but she got sick so I mainly tended just the house and her. After she died, I had to learn a lot to bring the grounds back to life. I could give you a tour of them some time, if you're interested. How about tomorrow?"

"That'd be great!" I said a little more enthusiastically than the situation warranted.

"Around four?"

"That's a little early for me to be cutting out of work."

"I'd like to have a bit of natural light so I can show off."

I laughed. "All right. Four it is." I opened my door, preparing myself to dash through the downpour. "Thanks again, Corin."

"And Vi?"

"Yes?"

"Be careful in the house. I meant to talk to you more about what's been happening, but I found I didn't want to spoil the day. For you," he quickly added.

"Thanks. I think. I guess we can talk tomorrow."

"I'd like to get into that tower," he said, his voice distant. He was looking over at the house, at the tower. "Maybe together we can figure out how."

"Maybe," I hedged. "Goodnight, Groundskeeper!" I slipped out the door and raced to the house. It took me a moment to unlock the door, and I was quickly soaked by the cold rain. Finally I got it open, waved to Corin who was waiting to see me safely in like the good little gentleman he was, and shut the door behind me. I hoped he made it back safely, too.

A lot had happened to me today and frankly I needed a break. My head was throbbing from my sore neck. I needed a hot shower, a hot meal, and a glass of wine. After that, I'd try to sort out everything I'd learned.

But by the time I'd done all that, I found I didn't want to think about anything. The wind was howling outside and every once in a while I heard something crash to the ground. It was quite a storm. Corin had better not venture out in it to check on anything.

I used my phone to see the weather forecast. While the site was loading, I contemplated listening to the messages I'd received. I really didn't want to, but finally decided it might be something important.

I'd received two of them, I discovered, one from Jason, one from my father. *From my father?* Had hell just frozen over? He never called me. Ever. Mother did that. But it was his name and his number. I felt a rumbling in my stomach and realized I was scared. It wasn't exactly a big insight. I was often scared of my father, of his criticism, anyway. Now that I thought about it, we never had an interaction that didn't include some sort of judgment on his part. Strange that I'd never realized that, at least not on an intellectual level, until now.

Stalling, I watched the WMUR videocast and discovered we were getting hit by a wicked Nor'easter that was going to stall out over us for the next couple days. High winds, lightning, potential downed lines, coastal flooding, and falling branches were in store for us. Great. They recommended people stay indoors, if at all possible, which meant I wouldn't be able to visit Amenon tonight. Tomorrow or the day after, either. Not if the storm kept up with this intensity. It appeared I was stuck inside and could only hope the guesthouse didn't lose electricity or get washed away.

With a sigh, I went to my messages. Wanting to get the worst out of the way, I listened to my father's first. I already had an idea what Jason was going to say anyway.

"Vianne Marie Alexander, what in the hell are you thinking?" he began. "You need to come home and marry that boy. It's time to grow up. You're acting like a child. So you had a disagreement. Get over it. You are marrying that boy. Everyone knows it. You know it. Your mother and I know it. Jason knows it. So stop it with the temper tantrum and get your ass back here. I'm spending a lot of money on this wedding and a lot of potential clients plan to attend. I told them you were sick, so we can still save face on this if you just get back here *now*! This shameful behavior ends this instant. And I'll tell you this," he growled, "if I have to track you down, you will not like it."

The message ended there and I stared down at my phone for several seconds, shaken. I knew my father could be tough on me, but I had always thought he did it for my sake. To make me stronger, to make me independent. But no. It seemed he did it so I wouldn't embarrass him or bring shame on the family.

I took a big gulp of wine and considered what I'd just concluded. It was a new idea...and seemed a bit late in coming. It was so obvious I was annoyed with myself for not seeing it sooner. My parents had run my life for far too long and it had turned me into a mindless marshmallow, effectively keeping me in the position of eternal child to my father's all-knowing adult role.

But it was hard to be anything else when the moment I'd say something at a job site my father would take over, silencing my voice. Come to think of it, while working together he'd not only put me down, often in front of others (Jason, included), he'd take my ideas and pass them off as his own. I'd always been flattered by that part. A genius in the field, and he found my ideas compelling enough to make them his own. What an honor!

Oh, I just wanted to kick him! And myself for being so naïve!

Well, not entirely naïve, at least not the whole time. Ever since the wedding fiasco, when my father hadn't taken my side over Jason's, I'd been feeling differently toward him. It wasn't until just this moment, that I finally acknowledged this new feeling. I was starting to see my father in a new light, and it was a harsh one.

I thought back to the Hanover House project, when I'd discovered a hidden door in the wall that wasn't in the original blueprints. Even though my intuition was always right about these things, Father hadn't paid any attention to what I kept trying to tell him. Or hadn't seemed to, that is. The next day, when he'd been giving the renovation committee a tour, he paused dramatically in the room with the hidden door, then began rapping on the wall. "Why, I think there's something here." And they had oohed and ahhed when it was revealed that there was a door.

It was only after our work on a renovation south of Portsmouth, when he'd gotten sick and had to leave early, that I finally got my due. Father had consigned me to the cellars and while down there I'd discovered an underground tunnel, which later turned out to be linked to the Underground Railroad. I'd called in the committee and they were delighted. Father barely spoke to me for a month after that. When I'd asked my mother what was wrong, she'd only shrugged helplessly and said, "Well, you know how your father is. He needs his strokes."

"But don't I need them, too?"

"Oh, you'll be getting plenty of attention now," she said coolly, effectively ending the conversation. I don't know why I tried. Mother always took Father's side.

After that I began to lose my Golden Child status. Well, in the eyes of my parents, anyway. The architecture and design community, on the other hand, was taking notice of me. It's not every day someone makes such a valuable historical find. That was how I'd gotten written up in the newspaper. People started coming to AA&D, asking for me. It was rather heady stuff. But still, my parents' lack of support was hard. When I began dating Jason, I got some of my Golden Child status back, but it was never quite the same.

I'd done nothing wrong, and I was the one being treated like a criminal. It wasn't fair, was it? No, it wasn't, damnit!

My heart started beating hard, and it took me a moment to realize what was happening. I was getting mad. No, I was getting furious! I had always just wanted my father's approval, had worked so hard to pull compliments from him, then I do one thing wrong, and he turns his back on me. Just like that.

Was that why I hadn't tried very hard to make a success of the wedding? To punish him? It seemed so childish, but didn't all kids want their parents' approval? For the first time in my life, I felt bad for Nick and Kat. They'd come second to me for most their lives. They could have absolutely hated my guts, but instead, they'd tolerated me. I would have hated me. I owed them an apology and some major ingratiating. As soon as this job was over, I would begin to make amends. It would all be a part of me growing up, and instead of feeling nervous about it, I felt good. I was making progress.

But not with everything. There was still my relationship with Jason and what I was going to do about it. Thinking about my dad in this new light made me wonder if maybe I'd sabotaged the wedding not because I didn't love Jason, but because I was mad at my dad. Poor Jason. He didn't deserve that. It was time to set things right with him. I had lost my way a bit, developing a crush on Amenon, and perhaps a tiny one on Corin, too, but I was going to get back on track. I needed to stop chasing after a love I was never going to find…that of a father. It was time to be an adult and have a real relationship unmarred by my daddy issues. That would be nice for once.

I thought about calling Jason right then and there to apologize and maybe start the ball rolling again on our wedding, but first I'd listen to his message.

"Hey, Vianne. I hope you get this message because you're going to be getting a call from your father and I thought you should know. I didn't mean to tell him anything, but he cornered me at the office this morning." There was a pause. "I'm giving you the heads up, Vianne, because I love you. I'm trying to be patient, to give you time. I think maybe I was a bit unfair to you, making you do all the wedding planning on your own. I really am the organized one, aren't I? I should've done it. I should've known it would be too much for that pretty little head of yours." Another pause. "Listen, I'm going to give you your space…for now. But I'll be coming for you soon, Vianne. I will find you. You know I will. I'm very persistent when I want to be. And when I come, be ready to return home with me."

I swallowed and hung up. The call had started out somewhat promising, but by the end of it, I was feeling rather sick. Jason had gone from, "I'll give you time…" to "your time is running out." In other words, he'd acted like he was on my side, then turned the tables on me with a threat. In fact, he did that a lot. How had I never seen that about him?

Was there something wrong with me? Was I the sort of person that invited abuse? Did I wear a sign on my back that said, "Kick Me"?

Judging by the number of people in my life—family, friends, boy-friends—that had used me or treated me like I was twelve, or had criti-cized me to make themselves feel better, maybe it *was* me. Maybe I had some sort of defect.

The wind battered at the house, making it creak and groan as though dying. It sounded like how I felt inside. I buried my face in my hands and thought about getting very drunk. Then my phone rang. I jumped and stared down at it like it was a snake. The last thing I needed was to talk to anyone. Then I saw Corin's name. He'd typed it in as Corin Groundskeeper.

Smart-ass.

"Hey!" I answered with a smile. "You made it home safely."

"I did. Just wanted to check on you, make sure you're all right."

"I'm fine. I saw the forecast. Looks like we're in for a doozy."

He chuckled. "Now who's being quaint?"

"Doozy is a very modern term I'll have you know, used only by the coolest of the cool."

"Right." There was a moment's silence. "I just wanted to let you know that there are candles in the drawer by the refrigerator, along with a couple of lighters. It's going to be a bit cold, but as long as there's electricity, there's heat. If we lose electricity, there's firewood stacked by the fireplace." I turned to look and there it was. "We'll have to cancel our tour."

"Postpone," I amended. "We'll do it when this passes."

"Postponed. Yes, that's better. Though it will probably take me a couple days to clean up the mess."

"Well, thanks for checking on me. I just got a couple phone calls and—" I hesitated. Did I really want to tell Corin about what my fa-ther and Jason had said? Did I want to share with a near stranger that the two most important men in my life were jerks? "Well, I was getting worried about you."

"You were?"

"You seem the melting type."

"Only when I watch *Bambi*."

"You're not going out in this, are you?"

"Why would I?"

"I don't know. You're so conscientious that I could imagine you check-ing on things."

"Hm. That does seem like me."

"Well, fight the urge. They're just things."

"And if a tree fell on the chateau…I should just leave it?"

My fingers curled up at the horror of it. "Yes," I pushed out through clenched teeth.

"You don't mean that."

"I do. We can always fix the house. We can't fix your broken skull."

"Well, lucky for you, there aren't any big trees near the house."

I breathed a sigh of relief. "Lucky for you, you mean."

"Right. Well, I'd better let you go. If you need anything, call me. Though I'm not sure what I can do because a certain someone forbid me to go outside."

I paused. "Well, I guess you can come rescue me. But that's it."

He laughed. "Goodnight, Vi. Stay safe."

"You too, Corin. Bye."

He said goodbye, then hung up.

I was glad I answered his call. Because right now, Corin was the only person in my life who didn't treat me like some sort of brainless, helpless female.

Though maybe that's because he didn't know me very well.

Chapter Twenty-Three

I spent the next two days making phone calls and orders over the phone and on the Internet. The whole process was a bit tedious, but in the end, quite satisfying. From a local antique dealer I ordered antique sconces perfect for one of the bathrooms, and scored an old butcher-block table and various implements that would fit into a Victorian kitchen. I would need to drive out there to check everything over before delivery, but the business had an excellent reputation, so I wasn't too worried I would get taken for a ride. I had to remember that not everyone on this planet wanted to screw me over.

During the storm, Corin called to check in on me several times, but neither my father nor Jason did. I tried not to let their lack of concern get me down. I didn't want to talk to them anyway. But still… You'd think someone in my family would have been worried about me. Of course, I didn't call and check on any of them either. But I was on the lam. Checking in with the people you're running away from goes against all fugitive protocol.

In the end, I broke down and called my mother. She didn't answer, thank goodness, so I left a message saying that I was doing well, had followed a job, and was set up there for a good while. I also mentioned that I was safe during the storm and hoped that she and my father stayed safe as well.

She didn't call back. This was how my parents punished me—they stopped talking to me. That's why I'd been surprised by my father's call. By all rights, we should still be incommunicado. Of course, if he had guessed that I had a job, he was likely getting worried it was for another firm and he'd lose my expertise. He wasn't worried about me. Oh, no. He was worried about his own skin.

To a symphony of rattling windows, growling thunder, and rain hitting glass, I tried to stay busy with my work, but it did little to alleviate my worry about Amenon. Obviously he couldn't be killed in the storm, but he might be expecting me to visit. He might not understand that the bad weather was keeping me from him. It was all very frustrating. I had to tell him what I'd learned before I burst, and after the phone calls from my father and Jason, I needed to be with someone who made me feel worthy and important.

By Wednesday night, the storm started loosening its grip. Around nine, there was a knock on my door and I cautiously opened it to see

Corin, voluminous in a heavy-duty black slicker, standing outside, smelling of fresh air and the outdoors. His hair was wet from the rain and the droplets glistened in the outdoor light. For a moment, he looked a bit otherworldly. Then he spoke and I was relieved to hear plain old Corin. Normal and very real.

"Good to see you're all right," he said, his focus on me intense, as though checking me over for wounds. "I wanted to stop by earlier, you know."

"And I told you that if you went out in the storm, I wouldn't speak to you again. I'm glad to see you took me seriously."

He looked back behind him. "The storm's moving out. See?" He waved his hand at the river behind him. I couldn't see much, being that it was dark. "The wind has died down," he explained. "And the rain has nearly stopped."

"Ah." So they had. "So what are you doing now?"

"I came to check on you and see what the damage is outside." He held up a flashlight.

"You couldn't wait to do that until tomorrow?"

"I'm going to need all of tomorrow for cleaning up."

"Would you like some help?"

He shook his head, letting loose several drops of water. One hit me on the cheek, then rolled coolly down my face until it fell to the ground. "I'll be fine."

"I have to take some measurements at the house tomorrow. Do you want me to check it for storm damage?"

He paused, his face grim. "I suppose you could do that."

I crossed my arms. "Don't faint from gratitude."

His fingers tapped the flashlight. "I don't like asking for help."

"Really? I wouldn't have guessed that about you."

He shook his head, a small smile on his wet face. "I can't believe I came all this way, risking life and limb, just to be harassed."

"Oh, you just missed my smiling face."

His expression suddenly became serious. "You know, I should've come anyway. To check on you."

"Why? I'm a grown woman. And anyway, you called, like, ten times a day."

He grimaced. "Was it that many?"

"That might be an exaggeration, but each time you called we talked for at least half an hour. Though you are responsible for me, I suppose. Our boss wouldn't like it if someone died on his property while he was gone."

Corin took a step back. "No, you're right. He wouldn't like that. I'll let you get to bed." He nodded at my nightgown.

The sensation that I'd once again said something to hurt his feelings pestered me. He really was too sensitive. Maybe he had good cause to be, especially after what had happened with his fiancée and best friend, but still… "Don't stay out too long."

"I won't."

"Promise."

"I promise."

"Good. Now go. Do your checking."

He smiled and ducked his head as he left to brave nature. I watched him go, then stuck my hand out. The air was cool and a fine mist was falling, but generally, it looked like the storm really had run its course. Thank goodness. I was going a bit stir crazy, and I really wanted to see Amenon. I was worried about him, plus I didn't want him to think I'd abandoned him.

I waited an hour, then pulled on a pair of Crocs and a yellow raincoat that I wished wasn't so dang yellow. But there was no help for it; the falling mist was light, but enough to soak me before I made it to the house. Hoping Corin had gone inside, I risked scurrying directly across the lawn. I didn't want to get too close to the woods and have a tree limb fall on me.

By the time I made it into the house, I was shaking with cold and anxiety. It hadn't bothered me before—sneaking into the house without Corin's knowledge—but now it did. He had been kind to me these past few days and I felt like we had become friends. I wasn't really doing anything wrong, but it was certainly not professional, plus I was keeping a secret from him. A big secret. If Amenon turned out to be some sort of con man, Corin would likely get into trouble. He could lose his job and it would be my fault. I didn't want that to happen.

It was probably best if I told Amenon that I couldn't come back. I wouldn't give him away, I'd assure him of that, but I also couldn't continue to abet him. It wouldn't be fair to Corin.

When I entered Amenon's room, full of determination to do the right thing, I found him sitting in front of the fire. He heard me and rose from his chair. "Vianne!" he cried, striding toward me. I hadn't expected his reaction, or this sort of reception, and he caught me in his arms and pulled me close before I could react. Wet and cold, his warmth felt wonderful, and despite my earlier promise to walk away, I clung to him, reveling in his heat, his solidity, his exotic scent.

"You're freezing!" He pulled back and reached down for my jacket, searching for buttons he wouldn't find. "I'm not sure how to work this," he admitted. "But you must take this off. I shall wrap you up in a blanket and you can warm yourself by the fire."

He left me and I regretted wearing the rain jacket as I struggled to pull down the zipper with cold fingers. Finally I got it, just in time for Amenon to slide it off my shoulders, sending a shiver through me. Seconds later, the wet jacket was replaced by the blanket from his bed. I pulled it tight around me and ducked my face into the soft wool. It smelled of Amenon, of sleep, of time. I inhaled deeply and a rush of warm delight flowed through me.

Amenon took my shoulders and led me toward the fire. He lowered me to the floor, then sat close by. I looked over at him. "I thought you weren't coming back," he said softly, his dark eyes shining in the fire-light.

"I'm sorry, Amenon. I wanted to come, but there was the storm. It kept me from you."

"Storm?"

"You didn't hear it? Or see it? It was a Nor'easter, and it was pretty wild out there."

He frowned. "I don't always see your world. It's because of what I am, I think. This in-between creature, neither here nor there."

I looked at him with pity. "I wish I could fix that for you. I wish I knew what to do."

"Perhaps there is nothing you can do." He stared into the fire, looking as lost and lonely as someone as beautiful and alive can look.

"I went to the library," I told him, hoping to cheer him up. "I've been waiting for the storm to die down so I could tell you what I found."

His eyes lit up. "You've found what I wanted to know?"

I swallowed, regretting my enthusiasm. "Well, no. I didn't. But I did come up with a few ideas about what might have happened between you and your parents."

"Not a clue of what happened to her? Of her ancestors?" he persisted, as though he hadn't heard what I'd said.

"Not a clue, which is strange. It's like she never existed. Is it possible that she changed her name after you died? For protection from your parents?"

"Anything is possible."

"Amenon." I slipped my hand out from under the blanket and touched his. "Did she work here? At the house?"

"I—" he faltered, then dropped his head. "I don't remember."

I wished I had asked George to make a copy of the staff photograph. "I saw a picture taken in front of the chateau. There was a very pretty girl in it…she wore a maid's uniform. Could that have been Camille?"

He shrugged. "I find my knowledge of her slipping, Vianne. Every day it gets worse. I can't seem to hang onto her, but I know she was important to me. Now I feel almost as though she didn't exist. How can that be?"

He looked so forlorn that I squeezed his hand in sympathy. "I'm so sorry, Amenon. I wish I had more to go on." I looked around his room, as though searching for answers within its walls. Camille and Amenon had likely met here. It was possible they'd made love in this very room, something I tried not to think about too much. It would have been a huge risk, though, and I doubted they would've taken it too often. So where would they have gone to be together? To be safe?

I smiled. The island, of course. From my very first night looking out at the island, to the images flashing in my mind when I traced the letters CR with my finger, I had thought of lovers, fleeing to the island to hide their love from the world.

And having gone there, they might have left behind clues, clues that could lead to Camille's fate. I felt hope surge up in me, and I nearly blurted out my idea, but bit my tongue. No way was I going to raise Amenon's hopes needlessly. If this didn't turn out, he'd be none the wiser.

"You won't stop searching?" he asked, his eyes on my face. There was such hunger in his gaze. Such need.

I gulped. "I won't."

He slipped his hand over mine, encompassing it, and I felt waves of warmth flow through me. "I knew I could count on you, Vianne. You are my savior."

I shuddered inwardly. I had to bring this back to Camille. Because all I wanted to do right now was kiss Amenon, pour all my love into him, heal him, and in doing so, escape my own problems. I did not want to talk about a dead woman. I wanted to talk about everything but a dead woman, someone who felt like my competition. But I had to do it. "Can you think of another name Camille might have taken?" I forced myself to ask.

He shook his head ruefully. "I cannot. I cannot even imagine her doing so. It's as though I never knew her at all."

"I'll keep trying," I said quickly, in an attempt to quash any hopes his words might engender. "I'll look for any Camilles at all. She might have kept her first name, or just her last name. Or her initials. I'll try all the variations I can think of."

He nodded hopefully. "I only want to know what happened to her. That's all."

"I'll find her," I promised, then promptly wished I hadn't. It was becoming a bad habit of mine—promising things I might not be able to come through on. Other than the island, I had no clue where else to look. I'd have to go back to the library and do another search, and it would likely be a long task. Tom might be willing to help me, though. He seemed very interested in the chateau. I hadn't yet heard back from him, though, so the Special Collections Room hadn't panned out, which was disappointing.

"I...I had a thought about your parents," I said hesitantly. "About what happened between you."

Amenon's head jerked up. He'd been staring down at our hands, his fingers stroking mine with an intensity that was driving me mad. "I don't want to discuss it."

"I know it's hard, Amenon, but I was wondering... Well, I thought maybe what happened to you had been an accident. That you were arguing and you fell and hit your head. Or maybe you got sick and were delirious—"

"That is not what happened, Vianne." His voice had an edge to it, and he pulled his hand from mine. My skin went instantly cold.

"I'm sorry, Amenon!" I cried, instantly contrite. "It's just that I learned your parents doted on you. They seemed to think the world of you, and on your—" I stopped. I could not mention the gravestone.

"On my what?" When I didn't reply, he persisted. "Vianne. You must tell me." His voice rang with authority, and I found I couldn't stop myself from saying it.

"Your gravestone. It said, 'Our sorrow is not enough.'"

"They were right about that. It is not enough." The anger in his voice snapped at me like electric shocks and I leaned back from him, suddenly afraid. "Don't you see, Vianne?" he pleaded, the flames of the fire reflected in his dark eyes. "They are torturing me, even from beyond the grave."

"Are you saying they abused you?"

"No." He gave a bitter laugh. "No. They treated me very well. I was an only child. They gave me everything, actually. Everything but what I really wanted." Camille. "So no, I cannot forgive them. Even if it was an accident, I couldn't. But it wasn't one. I *know* this." He pressed a fist to his chest. "They wanted me dead."

I had trouble reconciling this with what I'd heard from Tom, but Amenon would know best. He'd lived it. People could be very good at hiding their true selves. My parents, especially my father, were experts at it. Even I, their child, hadn't realized just how good they were at subterfuge until recently. It was a big wake-up call.

The fear left me and I leaned toward Amenon again. He was a lost soul. Of course he was angry. He had every right to be. His parents had taken everything from him. A long life, his love, his home. And now here he was, stuck, lost, confused, angry. I had to do everything I could to help him. I could save him, make things right for him. Then maybe, just like in the show *Ghost Whisperer*, I could help him find his way to the light so that he could be free. I didn't want to lose him, but I wasn't so selfish that I'd make him stick around just for me.

I hoped I wasn't, anyway.

"I believe you, Amenon," I said soothingly. "There's something else I learned." He stiffened and I grabbed both his hands. "Just listen."

He laughed a little and relaxed. "Sorry. I am not myself tonight, Vianne. I missed seeing you. I thought you'd left me alone, and now I am out of sorts, trying to find my way out of this trouble." His eyes peered into mine, willing me to understand.

"It's all right, Amenon. I do understand."

"You can tell me now. I can handle it." He drew himself up, as though to withstand an attack, and I had to smile.

"Well, when I was at the library, the person who was helping me do the research told me about Chateau de Sowles. He said that after your parents died, the house stood empty. Townspeople were curious and would come out to the house to see it. Apparently there were reports of a man being seen inside the house. I'm not sure if that was you, as a ghost, or maybe just the caretaker."

"I do not remember wandering the house, but maybe I did. It is possible."

"Okay. But there were also reports of a child inside the house."

He leaned forward, his eyes yearning. "A child? Who was it?"

"I don't know. It might have been vagrants, though I doubt that, since there was a caretaker who looked after the house when it was empty. Many people bought the house over the years, but it never stayed occupied for long. It might have been a neighbor child, or the caretaker's child."

"I was the only child I know who lived at Chateau de Sowles."

"The servants didn't have any children?"

His eyes grew distant. "I do not recall any. My memory is hazy—it seems to get worse every day—but I do not think there were any other children."

I shrugged to hide my disappointment. I needed leads, and I was frustrated I wasn't getting any from him. "It was probably nothing. People imagine all sorts of things, especially if they're expecting to see something."

"Why did the people who bought the house not stay?"

"I don't know. It's a beautiful house."

He looked proud, which made him seem endearingly young. "It is. Would you stay here?"

"Yes! In a heartbeat."

He grew melancholy. "Good, because I wouldn't want you to go, Vianne. You keep me hopeful. You help me look forward to the coming day. You keep me alive."

I felt strangely flattered. "Some day you'll be free, Amenon, and I won't leave until you're released from this nightmare."

He clenched my hands tightly. "Promise?"

"I promise."

"Oh, Vianne. My angel!" He leaned forward and brushed his lips against mine. "Ma chérie," he breathed, and a hot, tingling sensation flowed through my body, into my limbs, making them weak with longing. He kissed me, and I thought that at last this fire inside me would be quenched. But the touch of his lips only stoked the flames, igniting a ferocious desire I hadn't known I was capable of feeling.

He pulled me into his arms and kissed me again, harder, more passionately. "It has been so long," he murmured against my lips. "Too long."

Our kisses grew more intense and I felt myself falling into a sort of delirium, a dreamscape of dizzying sensations. His hands stroked my back and I could feel their heat through the thin material of my nightgown. His fingers ran through my hair.

As we kissed, I poured all my frustrations—my anger, my loneliness and anxiety, into him. And I felt him do the same. We were like pitchers for each other. It was exhilarating and enervating at the same time.

Too soon, he pulled away and I gasped, wanting more. "I must stop."

"Not yet!" I begged.

His smile was boyishly pleased. "You've drained me, Vianne. You had better leave or there will be nothing left of me."

Unable to speak, I could only give a single, stunned nod, though I was barraged by questions: What had he done to me? When could I get him to do it again?

But I didn't ask them, afraid of what he might say. It was only when I rose that I realized I was practically gasping for air.

"Come back tomorrow," he said, squeezing my hands, then letting go, almost pushing me away. "I shall be stronger then."

"I'll come," I told him, backing away.

Was it my imagination, or did he look a little less substantial? Had I really, *literally*, drained him? I wasn't sure whether to feel disturbed by the idea, or triumphant.

Chapter Twenty-Four

☾

I awoke the next morning feeling smug about what had happened between Amenon and myself. The idea that I, Vianne Alexander, had affected such a specimen of perfection so greatly was just too delicious.

But then, as I thought more about what I was doing, a feeling of tawdriness spread through me. I had literally panted after him like a dog in heat. It was not a flattering image of myself, and I vowed that next time we met I would be cool, calm, and collected. Not all wanton and panting.

To add to my shame was the niggling voice in my head that kept whispering, *What about Camille Renard?* If Amenon had truly loved her, how could he forget her so quickly? It seemed a bit fortuitous. But then, hadn't he admitted that his memory of the past seemed to be growing dimmer each day? If that were the case, I wasn't really doing anything bad. I wasn't cheating on anyone, or encouraging him to cheat on anyone. Still…it was hard not to feel guilty, like I was doing something wrong.

To distract myself, I called the library and left a message for Tom, asking him if he would do a search on Camilles, Renards, and anyone with the initials CR. I hinted that it had something to do with Chateau de Sowles, which should make his search feel more fruitful.

After getting ready for the day, I filled my coffee cup, adding a healthy dose of creamer. I was feeling a bit tired, likely due to my late night with Amenon. After gathering up my work materials, I headed to the house to do measurements and assess for damage. The day was beautiful, painted by blue skies and warm breezes, but it couldn't cover the fact that the storm had wreaked havoc. Even from this distance I could see a wide array of detritus washed up on the beach. The island had been hit, as well. Seeing it, I remembered my idea to search it for clues. Luckily the little rowboat was still moored in the same spot I'd last seen it. Likely it was full of water, but I could bring a bucket and empty it.

Broken branches littered the grass close to the wooded area and some of them had landed farther out on the lawn, flung there by Mother Nature's hand. Corin would have his work cut out for him.

Speak of the devil, the hum of his Mule caught my ear as I neared the front steps of the chateau. I lifted my cup to him and he waved and pulled up alongside me.

"Quite a mess, huh?" I greeted.

"I've seen worse, but not by much, and that was from Tropical Storm Irene. I found branches driven into the ground on that one. Anyway, I probably won't be able to give you a tour for a couple days."

"Of course." I felt strangely disappointed, even though I knew this would be the case. The yard was a mess. But ever since Corin had mentioned the tour, I found I really wanted to see his work.

"As soon as I get this mess cleaned up?" he pursued, ducking to look me in the eye.

I smiled. "Sure. That would be great."

"Oh, by the way, the gate isn't working properly so I've left it open. If you leave the grounds, be sure to close it the way I have it, with just a slight gap. If it's closed all the way, we'll be trapped in here. I'll let you know when it's fixed."

"Aye, aye, Cap'n." I gave him a salute.

His blue-green eyes sparkled merrily. "Smart aleck."

"You know everyone else would have just said smart-ass."

"I'm not everyone else."

I was starting to see that. "You're one of a kind, Groundskeeper. Now, anyplace you want me to check especially?"

"You can look over the upper rooms for leaks, and the cellar, too. I'm anxious to see if Mía's work did the job. If not, map out where the leaks are and we'll get her back here to patch things up." This time I clicked my heels together as I saluted. He laughed. "Smart-ass."

I grinned and headed toward the house. "Better a smart one than a dumb one."

"I'm not so sure about that!" he yelled after me.

I just flipped him a wave and ran up the front steps. As soon as I stepped inside the house I felt my heart start to beat a little harder, as though Amenon and I were now connected and the closer we grew to each other, the stronger the signal between us. I decided I would check the whole house over first before heading to the tower, saving the best for last.

The cellar was dry as a bone, a fact that I was oddly thrilled with. Probably because it meant Mía wouldn't have to come out. I liked her, but… But what? Well, obviously she liked Corin and would flirt with him and I'd have to watch. I groaned as I headed back up to the first floor. Why did I care? So what if she liked Corin? What did that have to do with me?

Instead of answering my question, I turned my mind over to doing my job. I found one leak in the kitchen and made note of it for when the renovation began. Otherwise, the house was in great shape. Just the tower to check, then I could get on with taking the measurements I needed for a few of the items I wanted to put in the kitchen.

I took the steps to the tower room two at a time, anxious to see if Amenon was around. I hadn't encountered him as a solid being during the daytime and wondered if it was even possible. I wasn't sure why not. Ghosts didn't just come out when it was dark. But then, why was it that ghosts were often only seen and heard at night? Maybe we're just more open to things at night, I thought, when we're tired and our defenses are down.

As I entered the room, I saw him right away, standing at the window, dark curtains parted to show a small gap to the outside world. "Amenon?"

He didn't turn. "Come here," he said in a stern voice.

I hurried to his side. "What is it?"

He pointed down at the grounds, where Corin was cutting up a downed tree with a chainsaw. "Who is that?"

"That's Corin, the groundskeeper."

"Are you sure?"

"Yes. Absolutely. He takes care of the grounds."

"He is familiar to me."

"I imagine he is. When you were in your previous state—whatever that was, exactly—well, you probably sensed him when he was doing work in the house."

"I suppose I must have." His expression was thoughtful, even pensive.

As I watched him, I realized that he looked worn out today, as though he hadn't slept, which was strange for a ghost. I touched his arm, and even through his sleeve, found it warm, almost hot on my fingertips. "Are you okay, Amenon?"

He shook his head. "I do not know."

I remembered last night, about him looking drained, and I didn't feel nearly so smug now. "I'm sorry if I hurt you last night."

He swiftly turned toward me and grabbed my arms, his eyes wild. "Do not apologize for that, Vianne. You gave me back my taste for life! You made me realize how much I want to live, to feel again! You've given me hope at a time when I thought I'd never feel hope again."

I beamed up at him, thrilled to have been so helpful. "I'm so glad! I was worried about you."

His grip tightened and he pulled me toward him. My body melted into his and I laid my head against his chest. "You are an angel, Vianne. My angel."

Funny, I didn't feel like an angel. Quite the opposite, being that all I wanted was for him to take me to his bed and have his way with me. I blushed, but luckily my face was buried in his chest, so he wouldn't see me acting like a teenager with a crush.

"Do you like this man, Corin?" he whispered in my ear.

I started nervously. It was an odd question. "I do," I replied cautiously, wondering where this was going. "He's a good guy."

His hand stroked my hair. "Do you find him attractive?"

"I know other women think he's good looking."

"Would you be with him if he asked?"

I pulled away and searched Amenon's face. In the daytime, he was even more handsome, the sunlight filtering through the gap in the curtains accentuating his strong bone structure, the dark gloss of his hair, the heat in his eyes. He looked so real. So solid and full of life. "*Be* with him?"

I was surprised by the grim expression that darkened his features like storm clouds. He glanced out the window, then returned his gaze to mine. "I see I'm going to have to be more direct with you, Vianne. Would you be his lover?"

"His lover?" It seemed all I could do was parrot Amenon's words. In truth, I was shocked that he was asking something like this. It didn't seem to fit my idea of a Victorian gentleman, and his bold behavior both worried and intrigued me. "He's never asked, and I work with him, so I highly doubt that would happen."

"But if it could…" Amenon persisted, his eyes gazing into mine with the intensity of a hypnotist. I wanted to look away, wanted time to think, to form the right answer, but I couldn't.

"I, well, I don't think so." I wasn't sure this was true, but I had a feeling that if I said yes, Amenon would not like that at all.

His whole body relaxed. "Good. But you find him attractive?"

"I'm not the only one." I'm not sure why I couldn't answer Amenon's question directly, but it seemed important not to commit.

He smiled and his whole face lit up. "Good."

I wasn't sure why that was good, but I didn't feel up to asking, afraid of what Amenon would say in response. If I had it correct, he wanted me to find Corin attractive, yet he didn't want me to sleep with him. Had I just passed some sort of strange test? It seemed I had, since Amenon looked quite pleased.

He hugged me to him and I embraced his warmth and strength once more. It seemed I had imagined his fragility last night. He felt very real and substantial now, and I was glad for it. The question was, could he stay like this? Could he maintain his being in this world? Could he leave the house? The grounds? If so, how?

"Amenon?" I spoke into his shirt. "Have you tried to leave the house?"

He stiffened, but didn't pull away. "I have tried, Vianne, but I cannot."

"Oh." It was disappointing news. Even if something did happen between us, it would be limited to this place. We wouldn't be able to have a real relationship. And children? That was likely not going to happen.

I bit my lip, the pain forcing me back to reality. Once again I was jumping way ahead. We had hugged and kissed, but that could merely be Amenon's gratitude. Or he could simply be looking for comfort, being surrounded by the misery of his circumstances. He needed a friend, and I resolved right then and there to be his friend and not push for anything more.

But it was awfully hard with his hand caressing my back, up and down, up and down, driving me wild with a yearning for more.

"I think," he said into the silence surrounding us, "that if I were to find out what happened to..."

"Camille," I supplied, once again stupidly thrilled he couldn't remember her name.

"If I were to find out what happened to Camille, I think that I would know the answer to my dilemma."

"But how would that fix things?"

"I do not know. But I sense it."

"I called someone at the library," I told him. "I asked him to look for Camilles and variations on her name, and he's very likely doing the research as we speak. We'll find her, Amenon. I know we will."

"We will," he breathed into my ear, then he kissed me. The kiss was long and sensuous, and throughout it all, my mind whirled endlessly and my body throbbed like a drumbeat.

At last, I broke away and tried to push Amenon from me, but he refused to budge, hanging onto me tightly. "I'm going to drain you again!"

But this time, he didn't look drained. He looked stronger, and I felt triumphant. I was the reason for his recovery. I was giving him life. "I feel better than ever, Vianne. I told you that you were good for me." He smiled and it was full of the devil.

"All right. But let's not push our luck, okay?"

He laughed. "All right. Not today. But soon. *Soon.*" I all but swooned when he said this, knowing he was suggesting something more. Amenon made me feel so lightheaded, so sexy, so wanted. I didn't think I'd ever felt this good with any man. But then, had I ever met a man like Amenon?

Moon dweller.

Corin's words came back to me and I frowned. Was I really so out of touch with reality that I was considering having a relationship with a ghost? Apparently I was. Did that make me crazy? I didn't know. I was falling for the most unique lover anyone on this planet could have, and one that couldn't ever leave me. How could that be bad?

"I should go," I said, reluctantly disengaging myself. "I still have work to do, and I don't want Corin getting suspicious...or finding this place."

Amenon let me go with a sigh. "I shall very impatiently await your return."

"I'll try to come tonight," I promised.

"I'll be here," he said with a wry smile.

He gave me a light kiss on the forehead and I turned to go. I looked back at him one last time, but he was peering out the window again, his expression wistful.

It took me longer to do the measurements than it should have, being that my mind kept wandering back to my last two encounters with Amenon...our kisses, his dizzying heat, the idea of him being mine forever and forever. It was lovely.

But then I remembered something that I shouldn't have forgotten, and my good mood plummeted. Neither Amenon nor I owned this house. Mr. Rachat did, and he and his new wife were coming back in less than six months to reclaim it.

Not if I can help it, I suddenly resolved. This was Amenon's house, and it was up to me to make sure it stayed his.

So that I could stay his.

Chapter Twenty-Five

☾

The next day, still feeling a bit tired from my late night, I took a long break for lunch, then returned to check out the house more thoroughly to be sure everything conformed to the time period that Mr. Rachat wanted. I was under a dresser, looking for an indicator of its provenance, when my phone rang.

Without thinking, I pulled it out of my pocket and answered. "Hello?" It was crunched and dark under there, and dusty, too. I smothered a cough.

"Hey, Vi-Vi. What's up?" Oh, crud. It was Mark James, and yes, he insisted on calling me Vi-Vi. Yet another reason why we never dated. His voice was raspy, as though he had a cold, but I recognized it easily enough.

"How'd you get my number, Mark?"

He coughed several times, then said, "Word on the street is that you took over my job at Chateau de Sowles." Struggling with the French pronunciation, he said the name strangely, making it sound like so-less.

"You didn't answer my question," I said carefully, feeling suddenly hot. I scooched out from under the dresser and sat up, rubbing my temples and the back of my neck, which was still a little stiff. A headache had started about an hour ago, and hearing Mark's voice was making it worse.

"How do you think?"

"Ryan," I guessed. Mark had met him one evening after we'd finished work for the day on a job in Portland. Ryan had driven down from Camden to go out on the town with me.

"No. I had it from before. Remember? Ryan only told me about your new job."

"He did, did he?"

Mark hesitated before answering. "Actually, I might have seen something about it on Twitter." I vaguely remembered Ryan telling me Mark was following him. "He tweeted about visiting a friend who had a new job in Portsmouth, so I messaged him and told him I'd worked in Portsmouth and maybe I knew his friend. He didn't answer," he added, his tone a little miffed, "so I guessed you were the friend he was talking about and the one who'd taken the job at the chateau."

I relaxed a little, glad Ryan hadn't completely given me away. "So what can I do for you, Mark?" I asked, pleased that I sounded both calm and professional when actually I was seething inside.

"I was wondering how it was going for you."

"You were?" My heart skipped a beat. For some reason this otherwise innocuous question set off warning bells for me. "Why? What do you know?"

"Well, I… Actually, Vi-Vi, if I'd known they were going to hire you, I'd have stopped you from taking the job. Why didn't you tell me?"

"Why would I have told you, Mark? We haven't talked for months. And why would you have stopped me?"

"I thought we were friends," he said in a hurt tone.

"We are friends," I consoled him, but only because I needed information from him. In Mark's eyes any sign of friendliness from me was akin to a marriage proposal. Working for AA&D was his ultimate goal in life, and he thought the only way to get in was through me. Little did he know I was now non persona grata at AA&D… "You see, I didn't really tell anyone I was taking this job. I only told Ryan because someone needed to know where I was."

"Wait…" Mark said, and I groaned inwardly. He might be clueless when it came to women, but he was otherwise quite clever. "Why didn't you tell Jason?"

I sighed and rubbed my temples again. "You don't know?"

"I've been a bit out of the loop lately." His voice sounded a little cagey as he said this.

"Because you've been sick?" I supplied.

"Um, something like that," he hedged. "So what's this about Jason?"

"He broke off our wedding."

Mark inhaled a lungful of stunned air. "He did *what?* You've got to be kidding me. What's wrong with him?" I have to admit this was rather gratifying to hear, even though it was coming from Mark.

"You mean, what's wrong with *me*. Jason thought I wasn't doing my part and called off the wedding."

"So you're single now?" He sounded thrilled.

"I guess. Jason wants to try again, but I'm not sure…"

"Don't do it, Vi-Vi. If that jerk can't see how amazing you are, then he doesn't deserve you!" He gave an angry sigh. "I can't believe no one told me you didn't get married. I thought it was a done deal. Why didn't anyone tell me?"

I decided it was time to change the subject. "Why would you have stopped me from taking this job, Mark?"

"Well," he paused, then blurted, "because there's something wrong with that house, Vi-Vi. I felt it, and I tried to keep working there, but then one day, something happened and I just couldn't take it anymore."

My fingers curled tightly around the phone. "What happened?"

"I felt like something was in the house. Something evil."

"*What?*"

He gave a shaky laugh. "I know. Crazy, huh? But after all the weird noises and stuff getting moved, or disappearing, well, it was the last straw. So I left. And I really did feel sick. Still do, so I wasn't lying about that." He coughed again and I noticed it sounded phlegmy and thick. He truly was sick.

"You think the house is haunted? That it caused you to get sick?"

"Haven't you felt anything strange?"

"Not a thing," I lied. "Maybe you were just staying up too late and drinking too many energy drinks. Like you did on that one rush job in Boston. Remember that time you were seeing clowns in every closet?" I laughed.

"As a matter of fact, I don't remember that. I had mono, you know. And it's not funny, Vi-Vi. Something strange happened to me in that house. I can't believe you haven't felt anything."

"I'm sorry, Mark. I forgot about that." Probably because it had been strep throat, not mono, but strep wasn't dramatic enough for Mark, so he had decided mono sounded better. "So what do you think it was? The evil thing you felt?" I realized I was clenching my phone so tightly my fingers were starting to hurt. I tried to relax, but it was hard. The only strange thing I'd felt was Amenon, though there hadn't been anything sinister in it. Maybe there were two spirits in the house. Amenon and some other, more malevolent one…Monsieur Sowles, perhaps.

"I don't know, but it always seemed to happen when Mr. Rachat was in the house."

"Mr. Rachat?" Not Amenon, then. What a relief. But still…my boss? "You met him, then?"

"Of course I did. Who do you think hired me?"

My phone beeped at me and I glanced briefly at the screen. "Damn. My phone's going to die."

"Vi-Vi, you need to leave that place. I'd come get you, but I'm still not feeling well. I think I caught a virus. I wasn't sleeping well, and every day I just felt more tired and drained, so I'm sure my immune system was compromised—"

"Mark," I cut him off. As I'd mentioned, he could be quite the hypochondriac, and I didn't have that kind of time. "What do you know about Mr. Rachat?"

"Well, he's rich as Croesus, you know. Rumors are he made his money in real estate, but I've also heard he dabbles in the stock market, among other things. I didn't think he was a bad guy, but every time I felt the evil presence, he was there. It ended up that I just couldn't be around him anymore. I had to quit. I didn't want to—he's a pretty powerful figure in Portsmouth—but he didn't seem to hold my wanting to leave against me. I'm glad, because if he *is* evil, he'd find me and come after me. What Rachat wants, Rachat gets." His voice started to shake a little. "I'm thinking of moving south when I feel better. I think that would be good for me. Do you like warm climates, Vi-Vi?" he asked plaintively. "Lately I feel like I'll never be warm again."

"I'm not moving, Mark."

"Okay, fine. Neither am I. But I still think you should leave that job."

"I'm not doing that, either." My phone beeped at me again. "Listen, my phone's going to quit any second, and I want to ask you—"

"Vi-Vi, I'm not making this stuff up," he interrupted. "You have to leave that job."

"I'll be fine, Mark. Just please, don't tell anyone I'm here, okay?"

"I can't believe I'm saying this"—Mark stopped, as if reconsidering—"but, well, you should at least tell Jason where you are."

"I don't need Jason. Thanks for your concern, though. You should go see a doctor," I advised, against my better judgment. Being nice to Mark was part of what had gotten me into trouble with him in the first place. But he did sound rather awful. "Get some tests. Maybe you have mono again."

"Vi-Vi! Listen to me! You've got to—"

The phone went out, and I was grateful. Mark wasn't a bad guy, actually, but he'd always been a drama queen. Very likely he was just overreacting. He was known for not always getting along with clients and he'd probably had some sort of fallout with Mr. Rachat. Leave it to Mark to make the claim that his boss was evil rather than face the fact that he might be the one with the issue.

It's all probably nothing, and it was with that thought that I returned to my work.

☾

At about four, I headed back to the cottage, tired and out of sorts. I was also feeling a bit lonely. Actually, a *lot* lonely. Despite my earlier dismissal of what Mark had said, I was feeling a little strange about our conversation. Ryan had mentioned coming this weekend. Maybe I should call him and set up plans. At the same time I could chew him out for telling Mark where I was working.

Since my cell phone was charging I used the landline to make the call. "You're coming to see me this weekend, aren't you?" I asked when Ryan answered.

"Is that you, Vi?" he asked hesitantly, and I realized he'd only answered because my name hadn't come up on his phone. The rat was hiding out from me.

"Yes, it is. Mark James read your tweet about my new job."

"He did?" he said a little too casually. When I didn't respond, he broke, as I knew he would. "I'm so sorry, hon! I forgot he was following me. I have so many followers, it's crazy!" He did. Over 20,000 at last count. Hopefully Jason wasn't one of them. The thought made me go cold. Jason could be quite clever when he wanted to be. It was only a matter of time before he made the connection and tracked me down. "I never go anywhere, so I wanted to brag. Oh, Vi!" he gasped suddenly. "Mark called you, didn't he? Oh, dear. What did that naughty boy want now?" Even though Ryan knew Mark was after me for my connections, he wasn't about to cut him off. Mark James was Ryan's type—hot and available. Just not gay.

"What do you think?" I joked. "Actually, he wanted to warn me about the house. For some reason, he thinks something evil resides there."

"Because it probably does. That is one dark house, girl. Like the one in *Burnt Offerings*," he added with a delighted shudder. Ryan was a horror movie aficionado, but mainly because it gave him a good excuse to jump into his date's arms whenever the movie got too scary, which, for Ryan, was most of the movie.

"Well, I don't believe there's anything sinister here, but at the same time, I'm feeling a little cut off from people. I could use a friend right now. Can you come this weekend, Ryan?"

"Oh, Vi. I'm sorry!" To give Ryan credit, he did sound sorry. "I do want to see you, but I can't. I was going to call you about Mark, but I knew you'd be mad at me so I chickened out."

"I was a little mad at you," I admitted, "but not anymore."

"Oh, goodie."

"So what's your big news? New boyfriend?"

"I wish! But no. Something almost as good. I'm so excited!" He actually squealed. "Daphne wants us to go to Paris for a shopping excursion. I'm finally going to Paris, Vi! Anna's coming, too. We leave tomorrow and get to stay for eight days. Aren't you thrilled for us?"

"What?" I replied numbly. "Oh, yes. Thrilled."

"You don't sound thrilled."

"Sorry, Ryan, it's just that I didn't want to be alone this weekend." I rubbed my eyes vigorously, hoping to stem the self-pitying tears threatening to erupt.

"Oh, poor you," he cooed. "Wish I could be there for you, I really do, but it's for the best, me leaving."

"Why? Other than the obvious," I added.

"Jason won't quit calling me."

I felt a chill of fear, mixed with curiosity, go through me. "Oh?"

"You know he's been trying to get me to tell him where you are? Well, he's just so insistent and keeps leaving messages—"

The chill increased its grip. "You didn't tell him?"

"I didn't, but only because I haven't talked to him directly or seen him lately. One of these days he's just going to show up at my apartment or at work and make a big scene." Ryan sounded like he would actually relish this, which no doubt he would. "Don't you see? I *have* to leave the country!"

I did see. "Yes," I sighed, "it's probably just as well."

"He's mad, Vi. And with each phone call, he's getting madder." I heard him give a little shudder. "I've never seen him like this!"

Well, *good*. I was glad he was mad. "All right. I get it. Go to Paris, have fun. You're going to love it." I went my senior year and it was the best experience I'd ever had. "You'll see the Louvre, right?"

"Oh, sure, if I have time," he said breezily. "But really, it's all about the boutiques for me, hon."

"And the wine," I added with a laugh.

He giggled. "Of course. And all those yummy French men. Now I have to run. You'll be fine, Vi. If trouble comes up, just run to that luscious groundskeeper of yours. He'll take care of you. He certainly looks like he wants to."

"What? Corin? Are you kidding me?"

"Not in the least. Au revoir, hon! Wish me luck!"

"Good luck, Ryan. Have a great time."

"I most certainly will." He hung up, practically humming.

I ended the call and stood there with the phone in my hand, staring at the wall. The chill that had started with Ryan's news had increased and I hugged myself. I was alone now, with no friends to call if something happened. I was on my own, and that frightened me.

Though I wasn't entirely sure why.

Chapter Twenty-Six

❨

I was eating an early supper when there was a knock on the door. When I opened it, I found Corin standing stiffly outside, like a soldier at attention.

"Hey!" I greeted enthusiastically, glad to see him. His presence reminded me that I wasn't entirely alone here, even though he and I were technically only acquaintances.

He looked surprised. "Hello, Vi. I just wanted to let you know that I'm going into town to pick up some lumber."

"Oh. Do you need help with that?"

Two spots of color appeared on his cheeks. "No, thank you. Afterwards, I have to meet up with Mía. I need her to fix some structures that were damaged during the storm—a small gazebo and a little garden shed. I'll be gone for a few hours."

"Oh," I said numbly, now understanding the stiffer than usual posture and his flushed cheeks. "Of course. Sure. Well, thanks for telling me." I made to shut the door.

He stepped forward and grabbed it, stopping me. "How was the house?" he asked quickly.

I had hoped he was going to beg me to come with him and his question disappointed me. I really didn't want to be alone right now. I wasn't sure what was wrong with me, but something had changed and I felt uncomfortable, as though a storm was approaching and I couldn't find shelter. "It's in great shape. The cellar is dry as a bone, so you can tell Mía that. I found a leak in the kitchen and made note of it. We'll fix that in the renovations."

"That's good news."

"It is."

There was an awkward silence. "You'll be all right alone?" he persisted, ducking his head low to meet my eyes. He often did that, I realized, and normally I found it endearing, but right now it just made me want to cry.

I looked away. "I'm used to being alone, Corin, so yes, I'll be fine." I'm not sure why I had to add that dramatic first part, but the feeling of loneliness was becoming almost overwhelming. Ryan and Anna were leaving the country, my fiancé had canceled our wedding, my parents weren't speaking to me, and Mark had hinted about something strange going on in the house. He was likely exaggerating, but maybe not. Mark had a lot of pride, and to leave a job was tantamount to admitting failure. The guy had his bad points, but being a quitter wasn't one of them. He had never left a job, and we'd been on some pretty awful ones. Even when he had strep/mono, he'd stayed. So whatever he'd felt here had to have been pretty bad.

On the other hand, he had thought Mr. Rachat might be the source of his strange feelings, and he wasn't due back for months. I should be safe.

Corin winced a little at my response, and for some perverse reason, this pleased me. "You could come if you wanted to," he offered. "I just thought it might be a little…"

"Awkward?" I laughed and relented. "No. I'll be fine. I mean it." And I did mean it, because I just remembered something I needed to do.

"You're sure? You look tired."

"Thanks."

"I didn't mean that as an insult. You have dark circles under your eyes. I can see them."

"I'm fine, Corin. I'm just feeling a little maudlin right now. Ryan and Anna are leaving for Paris tomorrow."

"Leaving you alone?" he said, his tone thoughtful and his eyes watchful. A little breeze stirred about us and I wrapped my arms around my torso as I felt the cold slipping down to my toes.

"Not completely, of course," I said, though that wasn't exactly true. Other than Mark, who was sick and unwilling to return, no one knew I was here.

"No, because I'll be here. Well," he amended. "I will be when I get back." He gave me a strange sort of smile.

"Yes. Of course. You and me. Alone."

I might have to rethink calling Jason.

Corin gave me a considering look. "I have to get going. I'll see you tomorrow. I'd rather you didn't leave the grounds tonight. You should go to bed early, get some sleep, okay?"

"Okay. Have fun. Tell Mía I said hi."

His lips quirked a little. "I will." He paused, as though he wanted to say something more, then turned and left. I watched him go, my arms crossed in the cool wind sweeping up from the river. When he was gone, I hurried back to the table and finished my supper. Then I fetched a warm jacket, a flashlight, and a notebook.

It was time to do a little sleuthing.

☾

With the strong current, rowing across the river to the island was harder than I thought it would be, and took longer, too. Now, as I climbed out of the boat, I could see that the sun was lower in the sky than I would have liked, but it was still light enough that I was determined to keep going. I just hoped I wasn't making a big mistake.

I pulled the boat up onto shore, tying it to a post that was likely used for that very purpose, and set off up the bank at a fast pace. My foot caught a small stone and I stumbled, but caught myself before falling. Pulling in a deep breath, I told myself to take it easy, since no one knew I was out here. If I got injured I was out of luck.

There was a faint path leading from the beach into the line of trees. I followed it, past a large boulder, my eyes fastened on the trail that cut through the high grass, mindful of lurking stones trying to catch me up again. Once I made it past the tree line, the light dimmed substantially. The shadowed woods didn't stop me though. I was here, and I was going to search the island for clues. Of course, what I was really hoping to find was a cottage—a meeting place for Amenon and Camille.

A hundred yards in, give or take, I found it. My intuition had been right.

It was a fairytale cottage, tiny and cozy, and in surprisingly good shape. I approached it cautiously, as though expecting someone to be in there. The little windows were dark, the door when I tried it, locked tight. Crap. I hadn't thought about how I was going to get in. Of course Corin kept it locked. People likely came and went past the island all the time. It was too tempting not to stop, and if they stopped and found the cottage, they'd try the door.

I rubbed my temple, which was throbbing. All day I'd felt unusually tired, like I was coming down with something. The last thing I felt like doing was breaking and entering, but lucky for me, any architect worth her salt knows how to get into a locked house. Losing your key is a common occupational hazard. Well, at least for me. My father always said I'd lose my head if it weren't screwed on tight. Then he'd laugh and add that maybe my head wasn't screwed on all that tight, either, so I'd better be careful.

What an ass.

I wandered around to the other side and discovered my way in. The storm had broken a pane on the back door window and I was able to easily reach inside and unlock the door. It seemed rather serendipitous—if I'd come out here before the storm, I might not have gotten in. It was as though someone was guiding me, showing me the way. I felt a slight shiver and stepped inside, over the broken glass.

The house was very dimly lit and obviously not wired for electricity, so I flicked on the flashlight. The beam spotlighted a tiny, old-fashioned kitchen, a small round table, bistro-style, and a fireplace. Fronting the fireplace was what looked like a bearskin rug and a small couch. It was a very charming set-up, though I couldn't help feeling uneasy, almost claustrophobic, as I looked around. I was either feeling the bleak miasma of an abandoned home, or something else, something more forbidding. I rummaged around, but didn't find anything that leapt out at me and proclaimed, "This is it! The answer to all your problems!"

To my left was a low ceilinged, narrow staircase that would make anyone above average height duck as they climbed up it. I was fine. I trotted up the stairs and found two rooms—a bedroom, complete with a bed and dresser, and a rather crude bathroom. I doubted they had plumbing out here, and as there was no toilet, figured I was right. Likely there was an outhouse near the house. The cottage was not a place to live for any length of time, but it would serve for romantic trysts.

I crossed the bedroom, hoping to find something—anything—that might give me an idea of what had happened to Camille, but again no obvious clues jumped out at me. Sighing with disappointment, I went over to the small window, which had a window seat, and looked out to see only trees and more trees.

Feeling drained, I sat down and the wood below me creaked and actually moved a little. At first I thought the seat was just wobbly from old age, then a thought occurred to me. I slid off and pried at the wood. It didn't move and I shined the flashlight around. In one corner, barely visible, was a little latch. I lifted it and tried the cover again. This time it rose and I peered inside the dark space, glad I'd brought the flashlight.

At the bottom of the little nook was an old book, its leather cover worn and smudged. There were no words or pictures on the cover, yet I knew immediately what it was…a diary. Someone had left it behind, maybe purposely. I reached in and picked it up. When I opened the book, breath bated, I found what I'd been expecting: handwriting. It was a diary! I studied it closer, my forehead crinkling in consternation. It was in French.

There was no way I was going to be able to read it here, not in this poor light and with my head pounding. I needed some ibuprofen and a French/English translator. I knew a lot of French, but there was enough I didn't know. It was time to head back.

Tucking the book in my coat pocket, I left the depressing little cottage as quickly as I could. As soon as I locked the door and started back to the beach, I felt better, but not much. My feet hardly wanted to move, I was so tired. I had to be getting sick.

As I rowed, my arms increasingly began to feel like they were filled with hardening cement. Halfway across, my fingers banged against the side of the boat, loosening my grip on the oar, which dropped into the river. While scrabbling for it in the dark water, the boat wobbled perilously, threatening to tip. I pulled back, heart beating and eyes wide, and the swaying subsided, long enough for me to grab the oar with trembling fingers. If I lost it, I realized with dread, I'd drift down the river and out to the cold and unforgiving Atlantic Ocean.

What seemed like hours later, I reached the beach and tied up the rowboat with cold, stiff fingers. Then I stumbled toward the guesthouse, each step harder than the last. There was no way I was going to be able to go to Amenon tonight.

Once inside, I took the diary out of my pocket and shoved it under my pillow. After popping a couple ibuprofens and changing into my nightgown, I fell into bed. Moments later, I was fast asleep.

☾

I awoke to Amenon's voice calling to me. He sounded upset and I sat up in bed, my head pounding. I groggily rubbed my eyes. "Amenon?" Had he somehow gotten out of the house? He sounded like he was right outside my window.

"Come to me, Vianne. I need you."

My head hurt and I was still feeling exhausted, but Amenon sounded quite distressed and I *had* told him I'd visit him. I pulled back the covers, slipped on a pair of slippers and my robe, and made my way to the chateau. It was quite bright out, and looking up, I saw we were a day or two from a full moon. Wanting only to get to the house, I hoped for the best and scurried across the lawn. No one called out to me, and I figured I had gone undetected.

The climb up the stairs nearly did me in, but I finally managed to reach the tower room, breathing hard. Amenon was waiting for me. As soon as he saw me, he rushed toward me and pulled me into his arms. I practically collapsed and he sort of had to drag me to a chair. He sat down and pulled me down on top of him so that I was sitting draped across his lap like a child.

"What is it, Amenon?" I wheezed.

He pushed back the hair from my face and peered into my eyes. "I thought something was wrong with you. I could feel it."

"I'm not feeling myself."

His expression grew concerned. "I thought so. Here," he pulled me to lean against him. "Just rest. I will keep you safe."

He supported my weight, and for several minutes we sat like that, breathing in unison. He was so warm and I felt so comforted that I nearly fell asleep, until he began to speak. "Did you find anything today, Vianne?" I was about to tell him I had when he spoke again. "It's all right if you didn't. This is taking a toll on you. You must rest, regain your strength."

I sighed and relaxed, feeling better. I decided not to tell Amenon about the diary until I knew what it said. I didn't want to disappoint him. He'd had enough of that for a lifetime. Tomorrow I'd spend the day translating, and if Corin asked me why I wasn't working, I'd claim I wasn't feeling well. It wasn't a lie. I still felt off, like my head was filled with helium. Translation work would be hard, but physical work would be harder.

Amenon tilted my face up and kissed me deeply. I was so drowsy that the touch of his lips on mine made me feel as though I was drowning in liquid heat. My head stopped throbbing and I let myself dissolve into Amenon, into the sensation of his hands restlessly roaming my back, his palms tracing my curves, the pressure becoming more insistent with each pass.

"Oh, Vianne. I want you so much!" he breathed into my ear.

"I want you, too," I whispered.

He kissed me again and again, his lips on my neck, on my chest. I knew he wanted more from me, but my head was spinning and I felt a lethargy that bordered on losing consciousness. Finally I managed to push away from him.

"I'm not well," I gasped, barely able to breathe. "I-I'm just tired," I assured him. "I need rest."

"Of course you do, ma chérie." He kissed me again, long and hard, and this time, I wondered vaguely if I could even get back to the cottage. My arms and legs felt like jell-o and my head was pounding again.

"I should go." I tried to stand, but Amenon pulled me back to him.

"One more kiss," he entreated, and I didn't argue. I was too tired.

Finally he let me go, then gently pushed me to my feet. This time, unlike the others, he walked me out of the room and down the stairs, all the way to the entry door, his arm supporting my shaking frame. We stood in the foyer, moonlight creating a silvery, magical air around us. "You came downstairs."

He smiled, a tinge of triumph in it. "I am stronger now. Stronger than ever. It's my love for you, Vianne. You have given me this gift."

"I'm glad, Amenon. I'll try to come back tomorrow, but if I'm coming down with something, I might not make it."

He squeezed my arm and the sensuous vibrations returned, flooding my body, weakening me. "You will feel better in the morning. You *must*. You are my angel, my reason for living!"

"I'll try my best."

"I will be praying for your fast recovery."

"Thank you, Amenon. Goodbye," I said hollowly, and stepped away from him, already feeling bereft without his touch.

"Au revoir, Vianne."

I staggered out the door, remembering at the last second to lock it behind me, then made my way across the lawn. I was halfway to the guesthouse when my knees buckled and I fell.

"Vi!" I heard a voice call before I hit the ground with a thud and my mind blanked out.

☾

Chapter Twenty-Seven

"You're awake," *Corin said* as my eyes fluttered open. Oh, crap. Getting rescued after passing out once is embarrassing. Twice is just plain humiliating.

"I'm so sorry," I moaned, struggling to sit up. I was in my bed, under my covers, and Corin was sitting on the bed next to me.

He pushed me gently backward. "You haven't been eating again, have you?"

I stared at him. Is that what he thought? It was tempting to go along, but my pride wouldn't let me do it. "I'm eating plenty, thank you, but I think I'm coming down with something."

"Ah." He looked relieved. "That makes sense."

"What happened that first day isn't like me, Corin. I love to eat. I really, really do. I was just messed up, you know?"

"Yes," he said sympathetically. "I do know what that can do to a person."

Of course he did. He'd gone through something similar. But he wasn't the one who'd had to be rescued twice. He was as strong as the granite this state was built on. "Why were you outside? It's late."

"I might ask the same of you," he said as he tucked my covers in around me. I realized I was shaking from a chill that wouldn't let me go. Had he been watching me? Spying for Mr. Rachat?

"I think I was sleepwalking," I tried. "Do I have a fever?" I felt like I had a fever, but not because I was hot. I had the 'chilled to the bone and won't ever be warm again' part.

He squinted at me, as if gauging the truth behind my question, then pressed the back of his hand against my forehead. It felt cool and soothing. "Vi! You're burning up." He sprung up from the bed. "I'm getting you some ibuprofen."

"It's on the bathroom counter," I called weakly, insanely glad I actually did have a fever. I didn't need to add hypochondriac to his list of my weaknesses.

A minute or two later he returned with a glass of water and two pills. I downed the pills, then drank all the water. I was terribly thirsty. "You're not working tomorrow," he told me when I handed back the glass. He was standing over me, kind of hovering, actually, his expression unrelenting.

"I'm sure I'll be better in the morning," I croaked, not sure at all.

"I don't care. You're not working and that's that."

"But we're on a deadline, Corin!"

"Yes, but we can't start work until approval goes through. I gave Mía her packet of information and tomorrow she's going to order everything on the list you gave me. Cabinets, appliances, lumber…that sort of stuff."

I relaxed slightly. I had already checked and double-checked everything I was ordering and through whom, and I'd have to check it all once it arrived to give my final approval on it, of course. Still, I was glad she was taking the busywork part of the task over. I had also tracked down and ordered pretty much all the items that would make the kitchen and bathrooms unique and period authentic, so I wouldn't get behind on that if I did skip a day.

"That's good."

"So no working." He actually waggled his finger at me.

"Let's just play it by ear, okay?" I said finally, in an attempt to get him to take his scowling face and go away.

He sighed. "I guess that's the best I'm going to get from you, isn't it?"

"Oh, please," I groaned. "If someone told you not to work, you'd do it anyway, wouldn't you? We don't have much in common, but we do have that."

"You don't think we have much in common?"

I studied his face, surprised by his dismayed tone of voice, but when I looked at him, his expression was smooth and controlled, as it typically was. "I'm a moon dweller, remember? Your feet are planted firmly on the ground, Corin Groundskeeper."

"Sometimes I can be a moon dweller," he said, a bit sulkily, I thought.

"Really? That I'd like to see."

"Well, sometime I'll show you. Now," he leaned down and straightened the blankets, "you need to get some sleep. It's very late, Vi. You keep awful hours."

"So do you," I accused, wondering again what he'd been doing up so late and why he'd avoided answering me. He should have been in bed a long time ago. He could have been spying, but another, worse, thought occurred to me. Maybe he was just getting home from his tête-à-tête with Mía. The idea of it stung, though it had no right to. "All right. Go. I'm tired." I waved him away, feeling suddenly teary. I closed my eyes and tried to think of Amenon.

"I'll check on you tomorrow," Corin said, though his voice sounded far away, as I was already drifting off to sleep. "Sleep now," he said softly, so softly the words almost didn't register. "You have nothing to worry about from anybody else. It's just you and me here, Vi. Just you and me and nobody else."

☾

I awoke the next morning feeling better. The chills had gone and I didn't feel as lightheaded and out of sorts. But I still wasn't myself. I gingerly climbed out of bed and made myself some eggs and toast. Eating helped, and after a long, hot shower and two more ibuprofens, I was approaching somewhat normal. I still felt unusually tired, but I'd take it easy.

I set myself up on the couch with my laptop and settled into working on finishing up my search for the remaining items on my list. Every five or ten minutes I'd look toward the door, as if expecting someone. After doing it six or seven times, I realized I was watching for Corin. I sighed and rubbed my temples. I was such an idiot.

I went back to searching when suddenly I remembered the diary. After all that had happened, I'd forgotten about it. My whole body flushed painfully when I also remembered that Corin had been in my room, fussing with my pillows. What if he'd found it?

I set aside my laptop and rushed into the bedroom, my heart beating wildly. Crap, crap, crap! My hand slid under the pillow, groping about and finding nothing, until at last my fingertips hit up against something solid. The diary. I grabbed it and pulled it out. It was safe. Even if Corin had seen it, he hadn't taken it. Good man.

I carried the old book back with me to the couch. Pulling an afghan around my shoulders, I settled into the arduous task of translating French to English. Paging through the diary, I was both glad and disappointed to see that there weren't many pages with writing on them. It shouldn't take me too long to do the translation. I had, after all, once read Voltaire's *Candide* in French. Opening up a word document, I began to type the translation, occasionally looking up words. The process went faster than I thought it would, and finally I had it all written out. I set down the diary and began to re-read what I'd translated.

To whoever finds this, I have written down my story so that someday, if the worst were to happen, someone will know the truth. I am frightened, but I cannot lose my child. I will not. I will fight them.

My name is Camille Renard and I work for the Sowles family. I was with them for five years before they dismissed me. I had always thought they were good people, but I found out differently after what happened to Amenon, my love.

Amenon wanted to marry me, and I him. He was everything I ever wanted in a man. He had many admirers, rich women of the highest status, beautiful, accomplished women, intelligent women. But he chose me, a woman whose family had fallen on hard times. I can read and write, and I know my sums, but that is about it. For Amenon to love someone as unworthy of him as I am means it is true love.

As is the way with passion, we became lovers, and not long after our relationship became intimate I found myself with child. When Amenon's parents found out, they tried to send me away. But Amenon rescued me and set me up here, in this cottage on the island, to wait out my confinement. That time was the best of my life—Amenon took such good care of me. He was amazing, strong and clever, charming and oh, so handsome. I counted myself so lucky to have won him.

And then our son was born and everything fell to pieces. Somehow the Sowles found out that I was staying on the island—I think it was through Betsy, who'd always been jealous of me—and so they hired men to kidnap me. The brutes took me back to France and left me there, penniless, without a family to take me in, and worst of all, without my two loves. My kidnappers threatened that if I showed myself in America again, they'd kill me, and they'd kill my son, too.

It took me over a year and cost more dignity than a soul should have to part with to make my way back to my lover and our child. After sending him a letter, disguising my identity by writing as a man would and using the name of one of Amenon's friends, my love wrote me back and told me he would come for me when he could. But I knew they wouldn't let him leave.

I was his only chance for escape. I changed my name and darkened my bright hair. I disguised myself as a high society lady. I looked very different from the naïve young maid who'd left their employment. The cost of all this was terribly high, but I would pay anything to save my loves.

But my nightmare was not over. When I returned to the chateau, I discovered that Amenon was dead and my son living with the Sowles. They had dismissed all their help—to avoid the scandal, I was sure—and were raising him on their own. My poor little boy. He was being cared for by monsters. I had no proof, but I was sure they had killed Amenon. He had defied them and he paid the price for it. They had taken away my reason for living and to this day I suffer from it.

All that was keeping me going was the thought of our son, and so I schemed to get him back. I went to the house, and I confronted the Sowles. I told them I knew what they had done to their son, and judging by the look on their faces, I was right. Blackmail is an ugly word, but I wielded it like a sword and they gave in, agreeing to let me stay and look after my son. They were frightened of me, but over time, I came to see that they were frightened of something else, too. I never quite knew what it was, but if I were to guess, I would say it was their guilty conscience haunting them. That, and Amenon's ghost. I felt his presence in the big house, and there were times when he frightened even me. He so desperately wanted to come back and be with me and our son that his desire tainted everything in that horrid house. We moved to the gatehouse, and that helped, but I was also very lonely without my love.

Day by day the Sowles faded before my eyes, as though something was sucking the life right out of them. They were dying. Before all this had happened, I had been a foolish girl, but now I was a mother and for the sake of my son, I learned how to be ruthless. I made sure the Sowles took care of their grandson before they died. Monsieur Sowles wasn't keen on the idea, but Madam Sowles went ahead with my request. She made sure that after their deaths, we would be looked after. We would not be destitute.

There was not much I could do to avenge Amenon's death, but I made sure his son would have what was his right. One day, though, I know he will be avenged. One day I know he and I will be together once more.

There was a blank page, then one last entry.

The Sowles are dead, and I would like to think that at last I am free of them. But I fear I am not. A few months before he died, Monsieur Sowles came to visit us. As we drank our tea, he watched my son for a very long time, and then he said something that chilled me to my bones.

"Don't let him live. He has the taint. I can see it in his eyes."

It was the last thing any mother would want to hear about her child. Monsieur Sowles was wrong, of course, but there was nothing I could say to convince him otherwise. After that, I kept a close eye on my boy. But I couldn't watch him at all times, and one afternoon he slipped away from me, to the chateau. He loved that place, like his father did, and many were the times I had to go fetch him. On that day, though, after I brought him home, he became very ill and finally admitted that his grand-père had given him some pudding. I was truly frightened, but I managed to make him purge it, and afterward, he recovered, though slowly. There was another attempt, when a stranger tried to lure him from the grounds, but my son is clever and a survivor like me and would not go.

So yes, the Sowles are dead, but I would not put it past Monsieur Sowles to have paid someone to finish the job he'd started. I fear for my son's life, and I fear for my own.

I am leaving this diary in the one place I was ever truly happy and perhaps one day someone will read it and know our story. I do not want to go on without my Amenon, but I must, for our son's sake. He is a sturdy lad, very serious, but sometimes he does things without thought—a legacy from his grandparents, I imag-

ine. I watch him carefully, knowing he carries their evil seed within him. It is my job to be sure it does not sprout.

I dearly hope that God guides me in this endeavor.

~Camille Renard
In this year of our Lord, 1896

I fell back against the cushions as though winded. Amenon had been telling the truth. His parents had killed him. And even though there was no record of a Camille Renard, I had proof that she had survived Amenon's parents. I also had proof that Amenon had a son. I couldn't wait to tell him.

My growing excitement quickly soured, though, as I recalled something. Hadn't he denied the existence of a child? Had he forgotten about him, just as he'd forgotten about Camille? It was a puzzling phenomenon—the way his memory was fading—and a little worrisome, actually. Maybe he was in denial. He'd lost the two most important people in his life and knew his parents had killed him, so it made sense to want to forget all that. I had nearly shut down after Jason had canceled our wedding, so I knew a little bit about the strange way our minds can work.

The clock on the computer said it was after twelve, and yet still no visit from Corin. It was just as well. I didn't want him seeing the diary. Folding up the translation, I tucked it into the diary, then shoved the book under the couch. I closed the translation website and then shut the laptop and set it on the coffee table. Time to eat.

I shakily stood and headed to the kitchen, but a knock on the door stopped me halfway there and I backtracked. When I opened the door I found Corin holding two plastic bags. "I thought you might not be up to making lunch. I would've come earlier, but I discovered a tree about to fall on the gatehouse, so I had to take care of that first."

I smiled and ushered him in. "You're a godsend!" I sniffed the air. "Indian!"

"I hope you like it."

"I love it. The spicier, the better."

"How did I guess that about you?"

I grabbed one of the bags he'd set on the counter and sniffed deeply. "Chicken tikka masala?"

"Good nose." He opened the other bag. "One's mild. That's mine."

I pulled out a takeout carton and handed it to him. "This one says wimp. Must be yours." I reached in and pulled out a tinfoil package. "Aloo paratha!" I exclaimed as I opened it.

"You can't have Indian food without flatbread," Corin said. He fetched some plates from the cupboard while I grabbed a couple diet Cokes. He eyed the one I held out to him, then shrugged and accepted it. After piling food on my plate, we headed toward the couch.

"I believe you," Corin said as he sat down. Unlike our first encounter, he sat next to me on the couch. I scooted over to make room for him.

"About what?"

He nodded at my heaping plate. "That you love food."

I laughed. "Told you."

"You look much better today," he went on and I realized he was staring at me. The fork I was aiming at my mouth stopped and I turned to meet his blue-green eyes. They didn't give much away, and I found myself wondering what exactly was going on in that brain of his.

I looked away. "I feel better, thank you," I said politely, then took a bite. I didn't look to see if he was still watching me, but felt that he wasn't. Good. This wasn't going to be pretty. As I ate, a part of me began to wonder at his turnaround regarding me. Checking up on me, bringing me Indian food. Didn't it seem a bit quick? Could I really trust him? His parting words from last night returned to me and I swallowed hard. *It's just you and me here, Vi. Just you and me and nobody else.* Was that meant to be reassuring? Or was it a threat? "How's the yard work going?" I asked quickly, knowing I couldn't let myself start thinking this way. Corin was a nice guy. I couldn't let myself get paranoid.

"Slowly."

"You should hire someone to help."

"I'll be fine."

"You're kind of stubborn, you know that?"

He poked me in the side. "Well, aren't you the pot calling the kettle black?"

"Isn't that racist?" I joked.

His head snapped up. "I'm not racist."

"I was kidding, Corin. You really need to work on that sense of humor."

He paused, his fork hovering in mid-air. "Maybe I do."

We ate the rest of our meal in companionable silence and I was grateful. Despite feeling better, I was still tired out. Not only that, but reading Camille's diary and wondering about Corin's motives had added to the turmoil in my mind, making focusing harder than normal.

I noticed Corin had finished eating so I asked him a question I'd been wanting to ask for a while. "How did your family get the job of groundskeeper?"

He stiffened beside me. "The job of groundskeeper?" he repeated, as though buying time. It was a move I often used myself, so I recognized it immediately. "Oh, well, I'm not entirely sure. It was a long time ago."

"Okay, then when did they get it?"

"Some time in the late 1800s, I believe," he answered cautiously.

Camille must have hired Corin's ancestor, then, after the Sowles had died. Maybe she and the groundskeeper had even married. I froze. If they had children, then Corin and Amenon's son were related! But only through Camille, not through Amenon. If she and the groundskeeper had married, they hadn't stayed in the big house, since it had been sold to other families. I nodded, putting the pieces together. They had continued living in the gatehouse, of course. Corin was the groundkeeper's ancestor, after all, and that's where he had grown up and still lived today.

It was a bit of a tangled mess, since I wasn't absolutely sure about any of this, but it made sense. If only I could find out something more about what had happened to Camille and her son. I wished she had written down her son's name, but perhaps she'd been afraid to name him in case someone who wished them harm came across the diary.

"Are you all right?"

I glanced over at Corin to find him studying me intently. I laughed. "Sorry. I think I'm in an Indian food daze. I probably shouldn't have eaten so much."

"I think it was good for you to eat so much."

"So I don't keep passing out on you?"

"Because you look a little washed out, like you're not getting enough nutrition. A little extra weight will do you good."

I laughed harder. "Are you kidding me? Jason was always riding me to lose weight. He even gave me a one-year gym membership, 'for my health,' he said. I never went, of course. Who wants to watch this penguin body running in circles?"

Corin frowned. "Penguin body? Vi, I think you have body dysmorphia. You have a lovely figure, just as it is."

The funny thing was, I was pretty sure he meant it. "I think every woman has a bit of body dysmorphia."

"You might be right. Jessica was obsessed with her weight. Frankly, it gets a bit tiring listening to someone go on and on about how little they ate that day or that they might have gained a pound and now have to go work out. Women think men care about that sort of thing far more than we do. Really, we don't notice nearly as much as you think we do."

"Ah. That's why so many men are obsessed with models."

"I think we're told we're supposed to be attracted to them, so we think that's what we should say. Nothing against models, and there's certainly nothing wrong with being thin, but a good number of models are simply too thin for my tastes."

"Ah." Was this guy for real? Or was he just saying this for my benefit? "Well, that's refreshing to hear."

"Healthy and confident is more attractive than anything."

"I suppose you're right. My mother always told me and my sister to watch our weight or guys wouldn't find us attractive, and we'd have a hard time getting jobs, too. She never said that to my brother, though. Nice double standard, huh?"

He stood up. "I've learned that women can be their gender's own worst enemy."

True. "Well, you can rest assured that I'm a good eater. Maybe not the healthiest, but I do stay pretty active. I just don't like gyms. I prefer doing things that are fun for exercise, like boogie boarding."

"Boogie boarding?"

"Don't tell me you haven't ever gone boogie boarding?"

"Well, I, um…"

"You live right by the ocean, Corin! When I'm feeling better, I'm taking you. It'll be your chance to prove you're not such a dull guy."

"I never said I was dull."

"Good. It's a date." A date? I mentally clapped a hand to my forehead. "I mean, then it's all set. First hot day, I'm taking you boogie boarding."

He took my plate from me. "Just as long as I don't have to get wet."

"Ha. You'll be getting plenty wet." He took our dishes to the kitchen and I could hear the water running. I suddenly felt very tired. "Want any help?" I mumbled.

"You rest," he said.

My eyes closed. Some time later, I heard his footsteps near me, felt him pulling the throw up around my neck, then I thought he said something about my very possibly being the death of him.

I smiled sleepily, then dropped off.

Chapter Twenty-Eight

My phone ringing woke me from a sweaty dream where I was running from some nameless group of people. Normally I enjoyed these dreams, because I'm always pretty ninja-like in them, but not this time. This time, whatever was chasing me, couldn't be eluded. It just kept coming at me. Coming and coming...

"Hello?" I said groggily.

"Miss Alexander?"

"This is."

"Hi, it's Tom. From the library."

"Oh hey, Tom! Sorry, I'm a bit out of it. I think I have the flu, and I was napping."

"Oh, that stinks," he said sympathetically, but behind the sympathy was a curious sort of vibration. "I won't keep you long, but I thought you'd want to know this."

I gripped the phone tighter and sat up straight, suddenly wide-awake. "You found her."

"I did! It took me a while. I searched for everything you told me, but it was only when I tried different names matching her initials that I struck gold. It helped that I knew you worked at Chateau de Sowles. I searched for the name of the house and then just started reading." He paused and took a deep breath. "And you'll never guess what her name was."

"I don't think I will."

"She changed her first name to Caroline, there's the C, and the last name to Rachat, there's the R."

Rachat? "You mean, the current owner of Chateau de Sowles is descended from Camille Renard?" My mind was spinning. "But how can that be? I don't understand. Did she get married? Take his last name?"

"Not according to my sources. She lived alone with her child for her entire life."

"Do you know her son's name?"

"I didn't get that far, just thought you'd want to know about Camille right away."

I released a pent-up breath. "I did. Thank you, Tom. You're my hero."

"I'll keep looking, okay? Probably in the Special Collections Room, now that I know her name."

"Yes, do. Call me any time, day or night, and let me know what you find. And Tom, thank you so much."

"It's totally my pleasure. As you've probably guessed by now, the chateau is my obsession. Along with its owner."

"Oh? You know him?" There was a long silence. "Tom?"

"Hm? Oh, yes. No. I know *of* him."

"Good or bad?"

"Depends on who you're asking."

"And what's your opinion of Mr. Rachat?"

"I'm sure you have your own opinion," he hedged.

"I've never met him."

"Of course you—" A furious knocking at the door interrupted him.

"Sorry, Tom. Someone's here. Call me when you know more, okay?"

The pounding grew louder and more insistent. "Will do. Bye." He hung up and I did the same as I pushed myself to my feet.

The pounding had yet to stop. "Holy crap, Corin! Just hold your horses!"

I swung open the door and my mouth dropped open in shock. "Jason."

He pushed past me, into the cottage. "Who's Corin?" he demanded, rounding on me.

"He's the groundskeeper here." I tried to swallow, but fear had created a lump in my throat. It was one thing to stand up to Jason when I didn't actually have to talk to him; it was another having him in the same room with me, obviously livid. I slowly turned around to face him, purposely leaving the door gaping behind me, for a quick escape, if needed. "How'd you find me?"

His hands were on his hips and he was pacing around the living room, looking at everything with a critical eye. "Some guy called me. Said he used to work with you."

"Mark James." Damn him.

"Yeah, that's right. He told me you might be in trouble." He swung around and faced me. I vaguely noted that his blond hair was perfectly coiffed and the long drive had done nothing to wrinkle his chinos or shirt. It wouldn't have dared. "Why didn't you return my calls? How'd you end up here?"

"I'm— Well, I'm working here. It's a job."

"And you couldn't have told me? Or your parents?"

My heart was in my throat and my chest was tight, but something else was happening, something strange and wonderful. I was getting angry. "You didn't talk to me for a month, Jason!" I cried. "You have no right to me anymore. You gave that up when you canceled our wedding!"

Jason looked surprised at my vehemence, and I was glad. I wanted him to be surprised. For far too long I'd been excessively complacent with him, with all the men I'd dated, actually. I'd give in to their every whim and desire and put my own wishes on a back burner. I'd been the quintessential doormat since I'd started dating, and right now I was tired of guys wiping their feet on me.

"I was giving you space."

"No. You were pouting. I wasn't the perfect girlfriend and that annoyed you and you decided, at the cost of my parents' budget and, more importantly, my dignity and feelings, to punish me."

"I did not! I only wanted to have the perfect wedding, and I was afraid you didn't want the same."

"You know how many times I told you that I didn't want a big wedding?" I cried, shaking. "How many times I told my mother and father? Usually I just go along with what people tell me, but for once, I put my foot down. When nobody listened, I rebelled." Yes, that's exactly what had happened! I'd rebelled, and it had been so scary and out of character for me, that I'd been knocked backwards for weeks. "It wasn't my most mature moment," I admitted, "but it was all I could think of to do, since nobody was listening to me!"

He made placating gestures with his hands. "Now, now, Vianne. No need to get so upset. We had a misunderstanding. That's all. We can fix this."

I drew in a deep breath. "I don't want to fix this."

He stepped backward. "What are you talking about? No." He shook his head. "You're just mad. You don't mean it."

"See? There you go again. You don't *listen* to me! And, frankly, I'm tired of it." A shadow darkened the doorway and Jason's features hardened. I spun around. "Corin," I breathed. "Hi."

His expression was inscrutable as he took in Jason. "I came to tell you that the gate was left wide open."

"Are you sure you didn't come to scold me for leaving it open?" He had the grace to blush slightly. "Maybe at first. But then I thought someone had come in and so I came to check on you." He nodded at Jason, but his eyes never left mine. "Are you okay?"

Jason stepped forward and put his arm around me. I tried to shrug it off, but his hand gripped my shoulder tightly. "She's fine. I'm Vianne's fiancé, Jason Sanders. And you are...?"

"I live here," Corin answered shortly. He looked at me. "Do you want him here?"

I finally managed to peel Jason's fingers off my shoulder and step away from him. "Not really. But now that he is, I suppose we need to work this out. No more running," I vowed, and instead of feeling frightened at the prospect, I felt liberated. No more running. It was time to take a stand.

"Do you want me to leave?" Corin asked.

"We do," Jason answered for me.

"No, *we* don't. *I* don't."

Corin nodded. I thought he'd be uncomfortable at the thought of having to witness what was obviously not going to be a pleasant conversation, but he looked strangely pleased.

"Vianne! I'm not talking about our personal issues in front of a stranger."

"He's not a stranger, he's my friend." I wasn't so sure if that was true, but right now I needed it to be. "Now, I need you to listen to me, Jason Sanders, and listen to me good. I don't want to marry you. We had our chance, and it didn't work out." He opened his mouth to protest and I held up my hand, regally, like a queen. The gesture worked surprisingly well—he shut his mouth. "We're not good for each other, Jason. You need someone different. I'm too messy, too absentminded. I don't care about getting ahead or looking good. I have no desire to rub shoulders with the elite. Those are things you want, and I can't give them to you. So it's better that we go our separate ways."

"And then what?" he demanded angrily.

I shrugged. "I don't know. Right now I just want to do my job."

Jason's upper lip curled disdainfully. "And how are you going to do your job—*this* job—without the backing of AA&D?"

"I'm doing just fine without AA&D. Ask Corin."

Corin frowned. "You aren't with AA&D?"

"My father and mother refused to fire Jason after he canceled our wedding," I explained, watching his face carefully, "so I left the company."

"And you were going to tell me this when?" His tone was cool and I started to get nervous.

"I, well, I didn't mean to fool anyone. Mr. Rachat's letter had been addressed to me, not AA&D. He must have known that I could work alone." When Corin didn't say anything, I grew flustered. "And I'm doing the job just fine on my own! I'm fully licensed in this state, too, so I'm not violating any laws. And besides, if I worked through AA&D, my father would come in and steal my ideas and pass them off as his own, and I refuse to let him do that to me again!"

"Vianne!" Jason admonished. "Your father has never taken your ideas, much less passed them off as his own. He has told me many times that you're not ready to work alone. You're too green, he said, too naïve, and no offense, hon, but you're not nearly experienced enough."

I stared at him, too stunned to respond. My father had said all that about me? "Oh, Jason. Are you taking his side?"

He blinked, his blue eyes growing a little panicky. "No! Absolutely not. But you must admit that you're not ready to work alone."

"I've been ready for ages, Jason. But my father hasn't wanted to let me go because he knows I'm the one who makes AA&D work." I wasn't being arrogant, simply telling a truth that I was only now just realizing. For a long time now my father hasn't taken a job he couldn't at least bring me in to consult on. I was better than him and he knew it. To keep me from going, he'd always treated me like I still had so much to learn. And I'd believed him. Mostly. Some part of me must have known differently, to be able to see the truth now.

Jason gave a harsh laugh. "Well, let's see how well you do when you get fired from this job."

"I won't get fired!" I turned to Corin. "Will I?"

"I'm not sure—"

I stomped my foot angrily. "I can't believe you, Corin! There's no one else who can do this job like I can. And with all the weird stuff going on in that house, there's no one else who will do it."

"What weird stuff?"

"None of your business, Jason. Now the two of you need to leave my sight before I lose it, big time!"

"Vi—" Corin began.

"Unless Mr. Rachat tells me to go, I'm not leaving this job, Corin. Now get out, both of you, before I start screaming!"

My expression, which I'm sure resembled a cranky toddler or a demon, must have been convincing, because both of them headed for the door.

"We'll talk more later," both Jason and Corin said at the same time, then gave each other a dirty look. Well, Corin's was more of a cold stare.

"Get out!" I pointed at the door. When they didn't move, I put a hand on their backs and pushed. Once they were outside, I slammed the door and locked it.

Then I burst into tears.

Chapter Twenty-Nine

I was crying, but they weren't tears of sadness. No, I was furious! Who did Jason think he was, storming in here, threatening my job? What an ass. He and I were through. And how dare Corin get upset because he didn't do a thorough background check on me? Neither he nor Peter had asked about my current status, probably because they were desperate, so I hadn't told them. Not my fault.

My father was the worst of the three. To tell Jason that I wasn't capable of working on my own was a huge betrayal. To think, all these years, I'd been flattered by his need to have me around, to keep an eye on me, he'd said. Yet, time after time, I'd been the one to make the big discovery or keep the team from potentially destroying a major historical find. Me. Not my father.

I wiped my face angrily, sniffing. Well, no more. My blind eyes now could see. Vianne Alexander was strong enough and skilled enough to work on her own and if Mr. Rachat didn't like it, he could stuff it. I was doing a good job on a house that wasn't even his. Not by rights.

Or was it?

A chill shook me as I recalled what Tom, the one good guy in all this, had told me in our phone call. Camille Renard was actually Caroline Rachat and she'd never remarried, so she must have passed the name Rachat along to her child. She'd apparently also passed along a legacy where the offspring kept the name Rachat. She must have started the practice to protect their identity, and subsequent generations had maintained it.

So if Mr. Rachat was the true heir to Chateau de Sowles, he'd come from bad blood—Amenon's parents. Was that why Mark had felt tense whenever Mr. Rachat was around? Because of that bad blood?

The question was, could I tell Amenon this? Wouldn't knowing his son had been tainted and had spread it to his descendants destroy his world? Again?

I sighed and headed for the bathroom. Once there I splashed cold water on my face and dried it. I had to tell Amenon something. But what? Maybe I'd just tell him that I'd found proof that Camille had lived and that he'd had a son, who also had survived to produce heirs. Mr. Rachat was proof of that. I wouldn't say anything about my theories regarding their nature, because that's all they were—theories. No need to worry him about something that might not be true.

Heading out to the living room, I was surprised at how dark it was already. A glance at the clock told me it was after seven. I had slept longer than I'd thought. The sleep must have done me good because I was feeling reasonably well.

Corin had boxed up the leftover Indian food and I pulled it out of the fridge. As I heated it up, my mind refused to allow me to think about him and how he was going to betray me to Mr. Rachat. I was just going to have to jump that hurdle when the time came. How he could be so nice to me, bringing me food, checking up on me, rescuing me at the bar, and then turn around and get me fired baffled me. It was almost as though he'd been setting me up.

But for what?

The Indian food revived me and I actually felt a little energy stirring inside. Tonight I had something positive to tell Amenon, I was no longer going to be my father's minion, and Jason and I were through! Several big weights had lifted off me, and I felt like I could do anything.

I pulled Camille's diary out from under the couch cushion to re-read it. Before I spoke to Amenon, I wanted to be sure that I'd translated everything correctly. As I opened the diary, my cell phone rang. I glanced at the number, recognizing it. "Hey, Tom!" I answered enthusiastically. He must have news.

"Hey, Miss Alexander. Feeling better?"

"I am. Thanks for asking. Let me guess, you found something else."

"I did." His tone was gleeful. "Camille's son. You're never going to believe this. His name was Corin."

"Corin?" I echoed. "But that's the name of the groundskeeper here. What a coincidence."

There was a brief silence, then Tom gave a forced laugh. "Yes, what a coincidence. Listen, I have to go. We're closed, and I really should head out."

"Oh, Tom! You're closed? I'm so sorry. I'm making you work on your time off."

"Oh, believe me, Miss Alexander, it wasn't work for me. Have a good weekend, all right?"

"You too, Tom. Thanks again." We both said goodbye and I hung up, quite aware that Tom was acting strangely and that I was missing something important. I tried to concentrate, tried to elucidate whatever it was that was bothering me, but it wouldn't come.

As I washed up, I pondered the fact that Camille and Amenon's son's name had been Corin. I now had something even more concrete to tell

Amenon, plus I had a lead to follow. My cell phone rang again and I cursed it. After I answered the phone—*if* I answered it—I was shutting it down. I had no patience for humans tonight.

Anna's face appeared on the screen. Strange. She and Ryan should be on their way to France. "Anna?" I answered. "Are you all right?"

"Vi! I caught you. Thank God." There was a rumbling noise in the background, as though she was surrounded by people.

"What's wrong, Anna? Is it Ryan?"

"Ryan's fine, Vi."

"I'm fabulous!" Ryan yelled in the background.

"Oh! That's a relief."

"I'm calling from the airport bar." That explained the rumble. "Our flight's leaving soon, and we're getting ourselves good and drunk so we can sleep the whole way. It's my surefire way of handling jet lag."

I thought it was a surefire way of feeling awful, but what did I know? "So you're just calling to chat?"

The phone crackled. "Well, no. I have something to tell you. I've been feeling guilty about it for a long time and well, if something happens to me, I need your forgiveness."

I felt a queer tingling go through my body. "What is it, Anna?"

"It's about Jason."

"Oh?"

"Don't go back to him, Vi."

"Why?" I asked, deciding not to tell her just yet that Jason and I were through.

"You're too good for him."

"I'm getting the feeling that I am."

"He hit on me," she said in a rush. "When you guys were planning your wedding. He stopped by my office and asked me out. I thought he was just looking for some pre-wedding moral support, but no, he wanted more. I should've guessed, Vi, but I was PMSing like crazy and just didn't get it until it was too late."

"Ah. I see." At the bottom of my translation notes, I began to write Caroline Rachat's name over and over again.

"Please don't hate me, Vi!"

"Hate you for sleeping with my fiancé?" The writing turned to furious scribbling. "Why would I do that?"

"What? No! I didn't sleep with him. I admit he's tempting. But Vi, I know I'm not the greatest friend..."

"I am!" Ryan hollered into the phone.

"Knock it off, Ry. Vi, I know I'm not the best friend you'll ever have, but I would never do that to you."

I thought for a moment, then realized I believed her. Anna wasn't high on most of society's moral code, but she had her own set of rules that she didn't violate, and one of them was, *Don't steal another woman's man. Ever.* "Then what did you do wrong?"

"I should've told you, that's what I did wrong. But I was stupidly afraid you'd think the worst of me. Ryan told me you weren't like that, and I know that, Vi. I do. But still… I didn't want to lose you."

The claws loosened their grip and I felt my throat tighten with emotion. "Yes, I suppose you should've told me, but it doesn't matter anymore. I'm not marrying Jason."

"You're not!"

"Nope."

"But that's great news!"

"I'm glad you think so."

"I do. Because he's been trying it with me again."

"Again? I thought he was going after Ashley Winterton."

"Probably is. But…and I didn't want to be the one to tell you this… you know how it's the messenger that gets killed? Well, anyway, I'm willing to take that risk. The truth is, that boy hits on most anything with a pulse."

I stifled a crazed giggle. I hit on guys with no pulse. Did that make me worse? "Well, then it's a good thing I broke it off."

"Are you sure you're done with him? Because you know what you can be like…"

"A doormat? Spineless? A wimp?"

"Nice, Vi. I was going to say you're too *nice*."

"Oh. Well, that sounds better, but I'm kind of done with that."

"Don't be completely done with it, Vi," she begged earnestly. "I need you to be nice. You keep me on track, and well, I have good reason to want to stay on track these days."

"Oh? Do tell."

"Just keep your fingers crossed for me, Vi, and I'll let you know more soon."

"All right, Anna. I won't push you, and I'll send good vibes your way."

"There's something else, Vi. Something good that should cheer you up."

"I could use some cheering up."

"Oh, poor Vi. Ryan said we were abandoning you."

"Oh, it's not that. I'm fine now. I just had it out with Jason this afternoon, that's all." It wasn't all, but I wasn't going to spoil things for my friends. "He tracked me down, so Ryan can stop worrying about giving me away. Jason knows."

"He came to your workplace?"

"Yeah, and he let it slip that I'm not working for AA&D."

"That jerk!"

"I'll be fine. I'm not losing this job."

"Good for you, Vi! You really are changing. All right. Now for my news. This will perk you right up. You know the groundskeeper?"

"Yes?" I said cautiously. "What about him?"

"Well, I thought there was something familiar about him and when Ryan told me the name of the house you're working on, something about it bothered me. Then, just this morning, it all came together. Your groundskeeper is none other than Corin Rachat. Can you believe it?" I didn't respond because shock had stolen my voice. "Vi?"

"I-I'm here. I... Well, I didn't know."

"I didn't think you did. Not with the way you were talking to him. So relaxed and casual. I thought maybe you had no idea he was your boss."

"My boss," I croaked. "But he's in Europe. On his honeymoon." He had to be.

"He was supposed to be. But apparently he caught his girlfriend doing his best friend!"

I made a gurgling noise. Corin Groundskeeper was actually Corin Rachat. My boss. I was so getting fired.

"Are you okay, Vi?"

"He was here, Anna. When Jason said I wasn't actually working for AA&D. He was upset about it, and now I'm going to lose my job."

"Oh, bummer. I wonder why he didn't tell you who he was, though? I suppose he was trying to lay low. He's a big deal in Portsmouth. A rags to riches story, from groundskeeper to owner of Rachat Real Estate, and now, Chateau de Creepy. He does a little bit of everything, I guess. That's what the papers say, anyway."

The whole story made sense to me now...why the job was canceled on such short notice, Corin's attitude when he saw me, his reluctance to take me on. He'd been trying to hide out. Oh, crap.

"And he didn't say anything to you later?" Anna went on. "No hints?"

"No!" I cried. "Not a word."

"You know, I got the feeling that he liked you."

"He lied to me," I said aloud, suddenly realizing that he had tricked me, just as I had tricked him. But his deception was worse. It had to be. "I thought he and I could be friends."

"They're calling our flight, Vi! I have to go. Are we good?"

"We're good," I said dazedly. "Have fun. Tell Ryan to buy me something nice so I don't have to wear yoga pants anymore."

"Oh, thank God he finally told you about that. They are not your friend."

Great. "All right, just for not telling me about Jason or about the yoga pants—and I'm not sure which omission is worse at this point—you owe me something gorgeous from Paris."

"Oh, Vi. I'm going to miss you!"

"No, you're not. Now go have fun. Au revoir!"

"Au revoir, ma chérie!"

I ended the call and turned off my phone. I couldn't stand any more horrid revelations tonight.

My fiancé had very likely cheated on me, or at least, had wanted to.

My boss was Corin Groundskeeper.

He had lied to me.

I was going to get fired from the best job I'd ever had.

And it was likely that after this weekend, I'd never see Amenon again.

Chapter Thirty

☾

It didn't take me long to figure out how I felt about Corin lying to me. I was hurt, and I was furious. I was hurt because even though I'd been feeling a little strange about him lately, I had thought we were becoming friends. I was furious because he'd allowed something to happen that was going to put my entire career at risk. He'd led me on with his little ruse. When I realized that numerous people had been in on it, as well, I literally went red with embarrassment. I know this because I was staring at myself in the mirror, wondering what the heck I was going to do now.

Peter Paddington and Mía Bonita knew. George from the Athenaeum was in on it. Even Tom at the library must have known. I was the only one not in on the game. Once again a man had taken advantage of my naïveté. Damn Corin. He'd done everything he could to keep his true identity from me, and that was subterfuge, plain and simple.

This was just so embarrassing. Everyone knew who Corin Rachat was except me, the one who saw him on a daily basis. Well, it was time for that to change. I went on-line and googled his name. He came up right away, along with numerous photos of him out and about in Portsmouth. Anna was right. He did do a little bit of everything. His business, Rachat Real Estate, dealt with multi-million dollar properties on a regular basis. Recently he'd been getting into working with historical renovation, though, according to him, that was more of a hobby. Even so, it did explain how he'd found me. He'd read the article about me, had seen my picture. He knew me far better than I knew him.

Numerous articles were devoted to his impending nuptials to the gorgeous Jessica. She was perfect, as evidenced by the many photos of her, making me doubt Corin's words about models and how they weren't all that attractive to him. She truly could work as a model, but apparently was satisfied being Corin's arm candy. Surprisingly, there were very few articles about the messy affair that had ended their fairy-tale wedding plans. I was even more surprised by how little these articles revealed about what had happened. Jessica and her lover were definitely made out to be the bad guys, whereas Corin was the victim. The journalists appeared to side with him and made it clear they were circling their wagons to protect him. How unusual in these days of paparazzi and celebrity magazines.

I sighed and shut down my computer. My life was a mess and I didn't know what to do. The thought of losing my job was almost painful, but worse was the idea that Corin had lied to me about who he was. I could accept that he hadn't wanted a stranger finding out about Jessica's betrayal, but he could have come clean after getting to know me a little better.

I was restless and the hour was growing late. It was time to visit Amenon. I grabbed Camille's diary and stood up. Amenon deserved to know the truth about his love and the diary might serve as a way to help him remember her. I had been selfish, hoping to keep him to myself. I realized now that all that had been a fantasy, designed to deal with the anxiety of leaving home and becoming an adult. Other than the fantasy part, I hadn't been acting like myself at all. Normally I wouldn't have tried to insert myself into his life so aggressively, but there was just something about Amenon that made me do stupid stuff. No wonder Camille had fallen for him. He had that certain *je ne sais quoi*. In spades.

Tonight I would set things right, then let him know I would be leaving soon. Maybe knowing that he had a son would help him move on. It was worth a shot, because if he didn't move on, I didn't know what would happen to him. He seemed caught between two worlds, neither alive nor dead, and was certainly not your typical spirit, either.

I pulled on a jacket, grabbed my flashlight, stuck the diary into an inside pocket, and headed outside. A sound to my left startled me and I spun around. "Who's there?"

"It's me, Corin." He stood huddled against the wall of the cottage, hands deep in his pockets.

"I suppose you've come to fire me, Mr. Rachat."

"You figured out who I am." His tone was flat.

"With Anna's help. Otherwise your secret would've stayed safe. If she hadn't made the connection, I would've been the only one who didn't know."

"I'm sorry about that," he said stiffly. "I didn't know if I could trust you."

"The whole time?" I couldn't keep the hurt from my voice and mentally cursed myself. Silence. "Look. I'll save you the trouble of firing me. I quit."

"Now, Vi. Let's not get hasty here. Stay. Finish the job. Please." He held out his hands.

"You just don't want to have to hire someone else."

"That's not it at all. I want you to stay. Nothing has changed between us. I'm still the guy you met."

"No, you're not! You're my boss. And you made me think you were the groundskeeper!"

"I *let* you think that. I didn't make you."

"Same difference!"

He sighed and took a step toward me. "My being Corin Rachat doesn't change anything."

"It changes everything!" And then it hit me like a brick just how much it changed things. He was Corin *Rachat*. He was the man whom Mark James had said was always around whenever he felt an evil presence in the house. Corin Rachat was evil. I took a step away from him.

It's just you and me here, Vi. Just you and me and nobody else.

"I'm going for a walk," I said as forcefully as I could with a shaking voice. "Please don't follow me."

"Vi, don't do this."

He made to come after me and I skittered away. "Good night, Mr. Rachat. I hope you have a pleasant evening." Then I turned and fled toward the river's edge. A glance back over my shoulder told me he hadn't followed. I actually did go to the river and stood listening to the waves lap against the shore while I waited, listening for footsteps. Twenty minutes passed. Then thirty. I was trying to be very patient, but it wasn't easy, being that I kept imagining him coming up behind me and pushing me in.

When I deemed enough time had passed, I stealthily made my way up to the house. The moon was full tonight and it shone down on me like a spotlight. I could only hope Corin had returned to the gatehouse and wasn't lurking about, intending to convince me to stay, or looking to silence me.

After letting myself in, I hurried up the stairs, two at a time. On the second floor, I thought I heard something behind me, but when I froze and listened, the sound didn't repeat itself. I was just being paranoid.

Again I found Amenon peering out the window, the curtains parted to let the moonlight shine into the room. He must somehow have lifted the sash—I could feel a cool breeze brushing past me as soon as I stepped inside the room. Hearing me, he spun around and strode toward me, gathering me in his arms. All my good intentions went out the door and I clung to him, nearly sobbing.

"Vianne, Vianne," he murmured into my hair. "What is the matter, mon amour?" *Amour, not chérie.* I had gone from darling to love. Oh, he was not making this easy.

"Nothing, really. It's just that I haven't been feeling well and things have been going wrong all day." I felt strangely reluctant to elaborate about my everyday, real world problems. I didn't want that life touching this one.

He pulled back and looked me over. "You look tired, chérie. What can I do to make you feel better?" His tone was more than solicitous. There was an undercurrent of enticement in his voice, an invitation extended.

I felt dizzy and swayed a little. "I, well, I don't know."

"Come, sit with me." He pulled me over to the bed, lowering me to sit down next to him. Our arms and legs seemed to meld together where they touched one another, and I could feel Amenon's heat flowing through me like a seductive current.

"I found something," I said quickly, knowing that if I didn't say it now, I wouldn't. When around Amenon, I found I wasn't myself. I felt weak and ready to do his bidding. No wonder Camille had loved him so much. No wonder she felt like his passing had left a hole in her that couldn't ever be filled. At the thought of leaving him, I felt much the same way.

Before I could back out, I pulled Camille's diary out of my pocket and handed it to him.

He took it from me, a quizzical look on his face. "What's this?"

"It's Camille's diary. The woman you loved when you died. I thought that reading it, having it, would help you remember her."

Amenon's expression was hard to read, but then he smiled. "You would help me to remember another woman? You are a kind soul, Vianne. I have always thought you so."

I gave him a tight smile. He wouldn't think that if he knew what I really wanted to do…grab the diary back and chuck it in the fire. "Read it. It's not long, but it explains a few things." I pulled out my flashlight and flicked it on.

Amenon opened the diary, his movements quick and easy, and positioned it in the circle of light. I waited and watched him, his full lips moving slightly as he read. When he was done, he glanced through my translation notes, then slapped the book shut with one hand. "I knew it," he breathed.

"Yes?"

"That my bloodline continued."

That was not what I was expecting him to say, though admittedly, in the past, having a son to carry on your name was very important. "Yes. You had a son. His name was Corin."

Amenon's head swiveled toward me, almost with a snap. "Corin?"

I nodded. "I'm pretty sure that the man who owns this house is your ancestor."

"That is perfect!"

"It is!" I agreed, warming to his enthusiasm. "Now you don't have to go. Your ancestor owns this place. He'll keep you safe when I'm gone." I wasn't sure about Corin keeping Amenon safe, but then, I wasn't sure about any of this.

"When you're gone? Oh, Vianne, you can't go. I'm not through with you yet."

Not through with me yet? "Excuse me?" Was this some strange phrase Victorians used?

"I'm not finished with your services, mon amour."

"My services?"

Hearing the displeased note in my voice, Amenon flashed me a charming smile. "Sorry. Sometimes I say things badly. What I mean is, I need your help."

I studied him, feeling a slight stirring in my gut, the same stirring that warns a person when something bad is about to happen. "To do what?"

"There is a way I could stay with you, Vianne. That is what I mean."

His hand reached out to brush a curl away from my cheek. The gesture calmed me and I leaned against him, grateful he still wanted me around. Something about all this didn't make sense, but his stroking fingers made me not care.

"What do you need me to do?" I said, my voice dreamy and distant. Amenon was putting me under his spell. *Under his spell.* The meaning of these words suddenly hit my brain and I jerked upright, away from his hand. "What's going on, Amenon? This all seems very strange."

He sighed. "I was hoping to spare you this, Vianne, but it seems I must tell you everything. Is that what you want?"

I nodded, half reluctantly. I wasn't quite sure I did. What if I found out something I didn't want to know?

"Then I will start with the day I died. That day I learned something about my past that changed everything."

"Go on," I prodded when he hesitated.

"As you wish. You see, Vianne, my father wanted me to know why he had to do what he did to me, so he decided that before killing me, he'd unburden his soul. First, he told me a longwinded account of his childhood growing up in France. I'll spare you that, saving only to say that the Sowles family was quite poor, so poor that they had to beg to keep from starving. My father wanted a different life, so he ran away from home and found a ship to sail on. An unlikely friendship sprung up between my father and the ship's captain. As it turned out, the captain was a rich man, but as he had no heirs when he died, he left everything to my father. Very convenient, hm?"

I nodded slowly and, satisfied, he went on. "His future secure, my father returned to France only once. Finding his parents long since deceased and his siblings scattered, he decided not to stay. It brought back too many painful memories of the misery and humiliation he'd suffered as a child. The short time he was there, however, he met my mother and married her within months of their first encounter. They eventually settled here in Portsmouth, a port he had visited many times during his life at sea, and he built Chateau de Sowles as both a reminder of the life he once had, and of the life he wanted so dearly to have.

"He and my mother wanted nothing more than to start a family, but for some reason or another, they could not. For years they tried, and most everyone in the town knew their dilemma and either pitied them or whispered that they were cursed."

His foot started to tap, slowly, then more quickly, like a predator readying for the chase. "One night, an old woman showed up on their doorstep. She was near death, some sort of fever had caught her, and they nursed her back to health. When she recovered, she asked them that if they could have one thing as a reward for their kindness to her, what would it be? They did not want for anything that she could give them, they told her, but if the fates were willing, then they would dearly love to have a child.

"It turned out that she *could* give that to them, Vianne. According to my father, she made their wish come true. Unfortunately, she was not a creature altogether pure of heart, so her methods were not true, and they came at a cost. She took a little of my father's essence, a little of my mother's, did her dark magic, and created a son. Me. There was only one problem. This child had no soul." He turned to look directly at me, a challenge in his eyes. "That means *I* have no soul, Vianne."

I couldn't help myself. I gasped in alarm. Amenon had told me something was missing about him, but had claimed he didn't know what. But he had known. All along. My feelings that something was not quite right returned in a rush. While pretending to get more comfortable, I pushed myself a little ways away from him. His touch made it too hard to think rationally and I desperately needed to keep a clear mind right now.

"I did not tell you, Vianne," he said, as though reading my mind, "because I was afraid of how you might feel toward me. I was, and am, a freak of nature. I did everything I could to fit in, but I never felt right." He peered out the window, where the full moon was shining full and bright in the black sky. "I always felt like I was the moon itself, that I was to be forever cool and distant, never a part of all the warmth and activity going on down below. Even before my father told me, I knew I was different. I just didn't realize how different." He rubbed his face tiredly and I felt a stirring of sympathy for him. What a horrible revelation for him to have heard.

"When I reached a certain age," he went on, "my parents told me I couldn't ever have a child. They didn't tell me why, other than hinting at some sort of mutation that could be passed on. But that wasn't fair to me, was it? I deserved to carry on, just as other humans did, to take my chances just like the rest."

I reached out and squeezed his hand, and he turned to look at me. "Don't you see, Vianne? In not telling me the truth, they unleashed something terrible. They started a legacy of wickedness." His upper lip curled into an ugly sneer. "After finding out what I'd done, they killed me. They burned my body, and they put my ashes inside that wall."

I now knew what the report on the sample I'd given to Katelyn would say—that there was human DNA in it, likely bone fragments, too. Amenon's body had been burned to ashes and mixed into the plaster that made up the Ship Room's wall, supposedly Monsieur Sowles's favorite room. I wasn't sure if sentimentality or morbidness had made him choose that room in which to wall up his son.

"When you took down the wall," Amenon continued, his voice deceptively calm, "I was at last released from my prison. Soon, though, I discovered that I wasn't entirely free. I had my substance, but not my physicality. Not enough to leave this place. I was trapped inside Chateau de Sowles like a criminal, doomed to live out my days alone, and so painfully bored. Oh, Lord, I must leave this place, Vianne! And now I can, thanks to you."

"But why did your parents kill you, Amenon?" I asked, hoping to stall, hoping to understand.

"You really want to know?"

I swallowed hard. "I do."

"They thought I was a murderer, Vianne. Can you believe that? 'What did you do with her?'" he mimicked in an ugly tone. "As if they thought I'd killed Camille. I didn't kill her, Vianne. I didn't need to. I kept the child, then hired a couple thugs to dump her in France. I'm not a complete monster, like they thought. I let her live. Of course, she thought it was my parents who'd done it, and I let her think that. She wrote to me, and I wrote back that as soon as it was safe, I would send for her. But I didn't send for her. I had the child I wanted. I didn't need her anymore. I know that sounds cold, Vianne, but she was not good enough for me." It sounded more than cold, it sounded delusional. Amenon had just told me his father came from nothing, and here he was, one generation removed, and already passing judgment.

"I hate to admit it, but my parents were right," Amenon continued, thankfully oblivious to my thoughts. "I could do better than a servant. I had proven my point to them—that I could bear a child—but then I realized that my child would be tainted by Camille's inferior blood. He was worthless. Unfortunately, before I could right my wrong, my mother discovered the boy and told my father. They decided they would keep him. By that point, I'd stopped caring. Babies aren't very interesting, especially ones you have no use for. Isn't that right?"

He looked at me, as though waiting for me to agree with him. "So what ha-happened after that?" I asked instead, casually slipping my hand from his and pretending to scratch an itch on my leg.

"I overheard them, Vianne. They—my *parents*—were plotting my death."

Amenon started speaking in a heavily accented voice, as though his father was channeling through him.

We started this, Mary. We must end it. We have created an unconscionable creature.

Not entirely, Henri. Now Amenon's voice sounded eerily like a woman. *He has his good moments.*

But they are only moments, mere punctuation in a long sentence of misdemeanors.

What about the child? The tone in Amenon's voice was fretful.

It is an awful truth, but he must go, too. He is likely tainted, as is our son.

Not yet, Henri! the woman begged. *Give him time to grow. We must know for sure, or we are no better than our son.*

Time will change nothing, Henri replied, his stubbornness reflected perfectly in Amenon's voice.

It might. Just please let us try! It will make up for what we are about to do.

All right, Julietta. You win. The boy shall have that time. But if we see the signs of taint in him, we must do what we have to do. We must not hesitate.

Yes, of course, she replied, relieved.

"I could not believe how my mother fought for my child's life," Amenon said, returning to his normal voice. "But not mine. Honestly, I'd rather they had taken the little cur's life. He was more than an annoyance; he was a hindrance to the carefree life I led. I had tried more than once to rid myself of him, but my mother seemed to sense what I was about and found a way to stop me each time."

He slapped his knee in disgust, which was good timing, because otherwise he'd have seen the look of horror on my face. "But that is neither here nor there, Vianne. What is relevant is that I knew they were trying to kill me. What I didn't know was how. In the end, they surprised me, though I shouldn't have been since they took the coward's way—they poisoned me. Do you know what it's like to be poisoned, Vianne?"

I shook my head, too frightened to speak. Amenon was the mad one, not his parents. And no one knew I was here with him. Even if Corin heard my cries for help, he would have no idea how to get into the tower.

"It's horrible, the pain excruciating. I couldn't move, could barely see the hand in front of my face as the poison did its work. My father only told me about my past after he'd poisoned me. He asked me to come into the Ship Room, for a talk, you see. I was wary, knowing what they were plotting, but I had a hangover from the night before and drank the whiskey he offered. I never could resist a drink. He knew that about me." His bitterness blighted each word. "So while I lay dying, my father told me why I shouldn't have had a child, why I must die. He wept, Vianne. As my father was killing me, he was begging me for forgiveness! Can you believe the sheer gall of it?"

"No," I replied shakily, taking the opportunity to move farther away from him.

"He *burned* my body," he spewed, and I wondered if that was why he was always so hot. Or maybe it was because his soullessness had turned him into some sort of creature from hell. "But what he didn't realize is that you cannot kill a man who has no soul. My body was gone, but my essence was not. Whatever that witch woman had done to me, she'd somehow made me immortal. But not all-powerful, more's the pity, and I couldn't escape from that wall. For years and years, decade upon decade, I was trapped, only able to show myself as a mere shadow." His teeth ground together for several seconds. "But then you came, Vianne, and you released me." He lunged forward and grabbed both my arms. "You saved me!"

"I'm so glad," I managed to gurgle around the lump in my throat.

"But now I need you to take the final step."

"The final step?" I repeated, not sure how much more of this I could stand. I wanted to make a run for it now.

"To be able to leave this place, I have determined I must take over someone's body, and only you can help me do that. Before I was released from the wall, I made the attempt with the people who bought the house. They had to be a certain type: attractive, open to suggestion, a moon dweller, as my father called them."

Moon dweller. There was that dreadful phrase again. I was beginning to despise it.

"My attempts didn't work, and before long, the people stopped coming. Then, when I'd nearly given up hope, one young man came here to the house. I thought he might be the answer, but my attempts on him didn't work, either." Mark James, I suddenly realized. He was talking about Mark James. "I thought that my being trapped in that wall must be what was keeping me from succeeding," he continued. "Once I was free, I tried with you, Vianne, and after kissing you, I began to feel empowered, revived. I was hopeful that I finally had my answer. But even though I was no longer trapped in that wall, even though I was growing stronger every day, nothing has changed. I still can't leave this house." So that was why I'd been feeling so awful lately. Amenon had been trying to take my body, and not in a good way. "But now I get it." He gave me a smile, and the triumphant glee in it alarmed me. "When you first mentioned Camille, I thought of the boy, of my bloodline, and knew he was what I needed. To be free of this prison, I will need someone of my blood. And you found him for me, Vianne."

"I did?" *Oh, no.*

"You know him, of course. The owner of this house, and my ancestor, Corin Rachat. You showed me who he is, Vianne, and I have you to thank for helping me take back the life that was stolen from me!"

Chapter Thirty-One

☾

I was hoping Amenon hadn't seen Caroline Rachat's name, which I'd written over and over again on my notes, or that if he had, hadn't made the connection, but he had. I groaned inwardly, feeling horrible and frightened. This was my fault! I had to do something to save Corin.

"But how could you use Corin Rachat to leave the house?" I asked. "You already have a body. Why do you need his?"

He grinned, but it no longer looked charming, just creepy. "That shall be my little secret, Vianne."

He was right, but I had a theory. Maybe his 'essence,' or whatever it was the witch woman had created for him, needed a complete, living body to be able to leave the house. The wall, which was in pieces and likely in a dumpster somewhere, still had Amenon's remains in it. Perhaps this dispersion of his corporeal body prevented him from going beyond the chateau's boundaries. Until he could take over the living body of a blood relative, he wasn't getting out. I was just conjecturing, but it made a twisted sort of sense.

I stood up. Whatever the reasoning, I wasn't going through with it. I switched off the flashlight, knowing I had a better chance of getting away in the dark. "I'll tell you what. I'll go and get Corin right now. All right?"

Amenon clamped a hand around my wrist and squeezed, forcing me to drop the flashlight. It hit the floor with a thud and rolled a few feet away. "Not necessary. Just call to him. From the window. I know he roams the yard at night. I've seen him, been drawn to him. I must have known all along that he and I were connected, that our meeting was meant to be."

I swallowed. This had all gone so terribly wrong. What had seemed like a harmless fantasy on my part had blossomed into a nightmare. Corin was right about moon dwellers being a danger to themselves and others. Living so high above the real world, we couldn't see how foolish we were being until it was too late.

And now, it was too late.

Amenon pulled me over to the window, his fingers biting into my skin. I tried to fight him, but I felt weak and he seemed unnaturally strong. "Call to him." When I didn't say anything, he tightened his grip. "Do it, Vianne, and I might let you live." Ah. All pretense of loving me was gone. He had crossed over, and there was no turning back.

"No, Amenon," I said through chattering teeth. "I won't do it."

"You're willing to die for him?" he growled. "Why? I heard you speaking to him earlier, down on the lawn. You were quite angry with him."

"I was."

"Yet now you protect him." He leaned closer and breathed into my ear and the heat of his breath made me shiver in the cool air. "Why is that, Vianne? You aren't in love with him, are you?"

"What? No!" I gasped. "I barely know him."

"You barely know me and yet you have feelings for me, don't you? I've not lost my touch, it seems. Or is it that you are a simple-minded female, like all of them, and fall in love at the drop of a hat? Like Camille did? Like all the others I so easily seduced. Come to think of it, there's likely more than one of my children running around the city."

I shuddered at the thought. "I might be angry with Corin, but he doesn't deserve this."

"I will make him so much better, Vianne," he said. "Less boring, right? Less dull."

"He's not boring! He's just, um, upstanding and conscientious."

He laughed. "Damned with faint praise. He's like Camille that way. She was the practical one while I care little for what is good and right. To me, being good is the same as being dull."

"She never knew about that part of you," I made myself say. "How did she not see through you?"

He laughed. "I am very good at hiding my dark side, as you know. Now call him," he threatened, his voice icy, "or I'll throw you out this window."

"No!" I cried again, fighting to break free. His touch, nearly scorching, no longer felt so wonderful, more like he'd poured boiling water on my skin. "Let go of me!"

"I guess I'll have to fetch him myself." Amenon jerked me toward the opening. There was no screen in the frame, not that it would have kept me from plummeting to my death. He yanked me in front of him and pushed on my back, hard. My hands flew out and caught the sill, and I struggled and fought to hold myself back, but Amenon was too strong. He pushed harder and I felt my fingers slipping, my feet sliding.

"Vi!" a voice behind us cried. Amenon's grip lessened and I threw myself backward, knocking him away from me. As he tried to regain his balance, I frantically crawled away from the window, away from him. I looked up in time to see Corin leap across the floor and tackle Amenon, taking him down. Locked together, the two rolled across the floor.

"Run, Vi!" Corin shouted.

And leave him alone with that monster? No way. I wasn't about to sit there like a helpless female and watch them fight, either. I grabbed the chamber pot from under Amenon's bed and lifted it into the air, waiting for the opportunity to crack him over the skull.

But even with the moonlight, it was dark in the room, and the two bodies blended together like shadows. I got as close as I dared, but it wasn't close enough. "Stop it!" I screamed, hoping to distract Amenon long enough for Corin to escape. "Let go of him!"

Amenon laughed wickedly. "I have him exactly where I want him, Vianne. Only a few moments more and the deed is done." As he spoke, I saw one of the forms on the floor start to brighten, like a coal when someone blows on it. Amenon was heating up. The light spread to Corin, quick as fire, and he cried out in agony. What was Amenon doing? Trying to melt himself into Corin?

In obvious pain, Corin struggled to break free, but Amenon grabbed a fistful of his hair and slammed his head into the floor. Corin sagged weakly, but was thankfully still conscious, his hands grappling with Amenon's in an attempt to pry his fingers away.

Amenon laughed and tightened his grip. "It won't be long, my friend, and we will be one! Then nothing can stop me!"

Corin roared and struck out, but Amenon took the blows calmly. He hardly needed to fight back against Corin's weakening struggle. I had to do something, and quick.

Amenon was still the brighter of the two, so I decided now was the time to make my move against him. I lifted the chamber pot, but Amenon spotted me and lashed out, his fist cracking against my kneecap. My knee buckled and I fell backwards. As I hit the floor, the chamber pot fell from my hands. Knee throbbing, I scrambled for the pot, which had rolled under the bed.

"Almost there," I could hear Amenon whispering as I crawled after it. "Almost there."

Lying next to the bed, my short arm strained and my fingers flailed about as I attempted to reach the chamber pot. At last my fingertips brushed against the cool ceramic, but couldn't find a purchase. Sucking in my breath, I slid under the bed and at last found a handle to grab hold of. Getting back out was hard, with the pot in one hand making it awkward to maneuver.

Eventually I made it out from under the bed, and one-handed, pushed myself to my feet. When I was standing, chamber pot gripped tightly with both hands, I turned to face Amenon and Corin. Both figures were glowing as brightly as the sun now, and looked about ready to explode.

Fear rippled through me as I hobbled toward Amenon, whose face was barely recognizable in the bright glow. He was so intent on whatever it was he was doing to Corin, that this time he didn't see me. Lifting the chamber pot, I brought it down on his head with all my strength. His body jerked, then went still.

I sagged in relief and shock. I'd done it. I'd knocked him out. The danger was over. But if that was the case, why were Amenon and Corin still glowing?

"Get away from him, Corin!" I shouted, running to pull them apart. As I grabbed Corin's arms to drag him away, bolts of light leaped out of his body, knocking me across the room. "Corin!" I shouted as I struggled to sit up, my head spinning and my whole body tingling painfully.

He didn't answer, only kept growing brighter and brighter. Even unconscious, it seemed Amenon was so strong he was able to exert his power over Corin. I could only guess that Amenon meant to either absorb Corin into himself or melt into him. Either way, Corin was going to die.

I was half dragging myself, half crawling toward them, when suddenly, still locked together, the two men began to jerk and spasm, as though being electrocuted. Corin whimpered, then the sound turned into a howl that seemed to go on forever, before stopping abruptly and everything went dark.

"Corin?" I whispered into the dank atmosphere. The room was too warm, and I was sweating and shaking. "Are you okay?"

I patted around on the floor until I found my flashlight and shone it on the two men. I was shocked, then frightened, to see only one figure lying on the ground. I flashed the light around the room, but no one else was there.

My light landed on the remaining form once more, and I recognized Corin's red hair glowing brightly in the flashlight's beam. He wasn't moving. "Corin?" I called again, desperately. "Answer me!"

He didn't respond and I wondered if that was because he was no longer Corin. I crawled the rest of the way toward him, cautiously, flashlight prepared to strike and limbs ready for flight. When I reached him, I touched his shoulder. He was very warm, just like Amenon.

He stirred and I pulled back, frightened. "Vi?" he called weakly as he sat up, rubbing his temples. "Is he gone?"

"Corin! You're okay!" I scrabbled forward on my knees and hugged him hard, then pulled back, embarrassed. "Sorry. But I'm just so glad it didn't work!"

"What didn't work?" he asked muzzily.

"Hang on a second." I used the flashlight to study him, my eyes searching for any signs of Amenon. When I couldn't find any, not that I really knew what I was looking for, I moved closer. "Tell me something only Corin would know about me."

He gazed at me quizzically. "You're a very messy eater."

I laughed. "Okay. Amenon wouldn't know that about me. So you're still Corin?"

"I'm still me." He looked me in the eye, his face, shadowed by the glow from the flashlight, was grim. "I heard Amenon's story…about his parents, about what happened. He said he didn't have a soul, and he said he and I were blood related? Is that true?"

I sighed, wishing I could shelter him from the truth. "I'd better tell you everything." So I did, from discovering the tower and Amenon, to my research and finding the diary in the little cottage on the island. I, of course, left out my make-out sessions with Amenon. Corin did not need complete confirmation of how totally stupid I was. "So yes, you're related," I ended my story.

"And he was trying to use me for my body?"

"That's my line," I teased.

"You know what I mean."

"Yes, I guess so. But you stopped him. How did you do that?"

Corin shrugged uncomfortably. "I have no idea." He pulled back from me and pushed himself to his feet. "I need to leave this place."

"I'm sorry I didn't tell you about the tower," I said quickly. "I guess I was kind of under Amenon's spell." It sounded lame as I said it, placing the blame on Amenon like that when it was really my own fault all this happened. "You were right about me. I'm a moon dweller. A stupid, foolish moon dweller."

"You're being too hard on yourself," he replied brusquely. "I'm the one who didn't believe in ghosts, then had one nearly take me out. Maybe if I'd believed, this wouldn't have happened."

"I don't know about that. I believe in ghosts and all this still happened." I laughed nervously. "Actually, I'm not sure if Amenon was really a ghost, or something else."

"Whatever he was, he's gone now. Ready to go?" He indicated the way with his hand.

I went out before him, still feeling like something wasn't right. Then it hit me. "How did you even know I was here?" I asked as I pushed open the secret door leading into the conservatory.

"I followed you." So I had heard something on the stairs when I was coming up. "The door didn't quite latch, which was good since I wouldn't have been able to find the trigger in the dark. When that man, Amenon"—he said the name reluctantly—"tried to throw you out the window, I made my move."

"Well," I said breezily. "You saved my life."

"I think we saved each other's lives," he said, his voice subdued.

After that we didn't speak. I had a feeling Corin was furious with me. I'd lied about AA&D, I'd lied about the tower and Amenon, and I'd nearly gotten him killed. I deserved to lose this job. I deserved worse, actually.

When we reached the guesthouse, I turned to Corin. He stood there in the moonlight, almost glowing like a ghost. I shivered. "I'm so sorry, Corin."

"As am I." He sounded almost wistful as he said the words. Then, before I could apologize again, he turned and left.

I went inside and locked the door behind me.

Chapter Thirty-Two

☾

When I awoke early the next morning, the sun was shining brightly through my windows. Feeling heavy at heart, I went about getting ready for the day. After breakfast, I'd start packing. Then I would wait for Corin to show up and ask me firmly, but politely, to leave this place and never come back.

I was just washing up the last of the dishes when there was a knock on the door. *He must be in a hurry to get rid of me*, I thought glumly. I felt so depressed and so mad at myself for being such an idiot. Maybe my father was right about me. I wasn't ready to work on my own. I was simply too foolish, too sentimental, too impractical.

"Yoo-hoo!" someone called as I shuffled morosely toward the door. Yoo-hoo? That was not a word Corin would ever utter.

I pulled open the door. "Brittany!" She was standing on the stoop, a white paper bag in one hand and a coffee in the other.

"Hey, girl." She breezed past me and into the cottage. "Brought you some donuts."

To ease the pain of firing me, I was sure. Apparently Corin didn't have the cojones to do it himself. "Um, thanks."

"You don't sound too thrilled."

"I just ate breakfast," I replied, punishing myself. In truth, I could still eat a donut after a Thanksgiving meal. In fact, once I had. But eating a donut would be a reward and after what I'd done, I didn't deserve one.

"And that matters in what universe?" She set the bag on the breakfast bar, pushed her sunglasses up onto her head, then took a sip of coffee. "Save them for later, then," she said with a shrug. "Say, I have some news. So I heard the cat's out of the bag regarding Corin, a.k.a. Mr. Rachat, a.k.a. my boss. Sorry I had to keep that from you. He went through a lot with that, *witch,* Jessica, and he just wasn't sure you could be trusted not to tell people that he was hiding out at the chateau until everything blew over."

My shoulders sagged. "I understand. I'll pack my bags as soon as you go. I can be gone in an hour or so."

She looked at me as though I'd gone crazy. "Girl, what are you talking about?"

"He's firing me, of course. I deserve it."

She put a hand on her hip. "And why would he do that?"

"Because of the AA&D thing."

She waved that away. "He said you'd think he was mad about that. He isn't. Not at all. He knew all along they weren't a part of the package. He only wanted you."

I swallowed, suddenly remembering something he'd said before, and what about it had bothered me. *"That's why Mr. Rachat contacted AA&D, actually,"* he'd said. *"He'd read about you in an article and wanted to have all the expertise your firm has to offer for this project."* But actually, he'd contacted me directly, not AA&D, and AA&D hadn't even come up in my interview with Peter Paddington. Had Corin been testing me, saying that? Or just messing with me? Based on what Brittany was telling me, I had to guess he'd been messing with me. I recalled the glint of amusement in his eyes when he'd said that. Yes, totally messing with me.

It seems the man had a sense of humor, after all.

"So he's really not firing me?"

"That's what I'm trying to tell you! Mr. Rachat wanted me to make it clear that you are the only one for the job and that we were all to do everything in our power to keep you happy."

My mouth dropped open. "He said that?"

"Word for word, hon."

"So why did you come?"

"Oh, Mr. Rachat left on a long business trip this morning, leaving me and you in charge. He offered his apologies, but it was unavoidable."

He was gone? Corin was gone? For some strange reason, this felt worse than if he'd fired me. "Oh, I see. I think I'll have one of those donuts now."

Brittany grinned and took one when I opened the bag for her. "Smart girl."

We sat there and ate our donuts and drank our coffee while Brittany went on and on about what a good guy Corin was. He built houses for Habitat for Humanity, he volunteered at the library, reading to kids, he donated money to countless causes. The community of Portsmouth loved him.

By the time she was done and had left, promising to take me out on the town soon, I was thoroughly depressed. According to Brittany, and to an entire city, Corin Rachat was one amazing man, something I'd already sensed about him. And I'd driven him away with my lies. I'd blown it with the one guy who'd ever treated me decently.

I sighed despondently. Amenon was right. I was in love with Corin… and I had denied it, loudly and vehemently, when asked, which Corin had heard. Not that he returned my feelings, but it was just one more thing to add to the list of crimes against Corin that I'd committed.

And now he was gone.

☾

He didn't come back. Days turned into weeks, weeks turned into months, and still no sign of him. Anna and Ryan returned from Paris, giddy and with many stories to tell. They came to visit me several times, though I often had a feeling that when we were in Portsmouth Anna was looking to run into Clint, or her destiny, as she put it.

A few days after Corin left, Tom from the library called to see how I was feeling and I told him that I knew who Corin Rachat was. He said he felt horrible deceiving me, but Mr. Rachat had called ahead before my visit and asked the staff not to give him away since he was trying to remain incognito until the uproar died down. Corin must have done the same at the Athenaeum with George. I felt like a fool, but I deserved it after what I'd done with Amenon.

Anyway, when I told Tom that Corin Rachat was Amenon's ancestor, he was thrilled. "It makes total sense, Vi!" he cried, finally calling me by my first name. "The people loved Amenon, and people today love Corin Rachat!" Tom, it turned out, had a bit of hero worship when it came to Corin and Amenon.

It wasn't until late one August weekend that I realized the real reason why he liked them so much. Ryan had come to visit and we decided to go see Tom at the library. Before I knew it, those two were chatting away and making plans to attend Strawbery Banke's annual wine and food festival in September. So the hero worship of Amenon and Corin had been more like a crush. It seemed that like me, Tom was a bit of a moon dweller, so I was glad he'd found someone more realistic, and not *straight*, to fall for.

I heard back from Katelyn about the wall sample. I was right about what it contained—human DNA and bone fragments. Monsieur Sowles must have added it to the plaster when the new wall was being built, likely by his own hands, especially if he had dismissed all the servants. Burning Amenon's body and hiding his remains in the wall made no logical sense, but maybe Monsieur Sowles believed that since dark magic had created his son, he had to do something unusual and extreme to contain that magic.

I asked Katelyn to destroy the report and not share her findings with anyone, which she readily agreed to. The sample I'd sent seemed to have disappeared and she felt awful about losing it. She shredded the report as we were talking, and I felt a small relief to put that behind me. It was odd that the sample had gone missing, but probably meant nothing. Katelyn's office was very busy and sometimes things accidentally ended up in the garbage. There seemed no other good explanation.

Time passed. Anna got caught up in her relationship with Clint, which she finally felt comfortable talking about without worrying she was jinxing it, and Ryan and Tom were still together—a new record for Ryan. For my part, during the day I worked hard on the renovations, checking and double-checking to be sure everything was perfect. It was the least I could do for Corin. He probably no longer cared about making everything strictly Victorian, but unless he came back and told me differently, I was going ahead with it.

During my time off, I went for long walks or rowed out to the island. I fixed the broken window and cleaned the whole cottage, top to bottom. With each visit, the house grew less gloomy, the atmosphere less oppressive, until at last, one day, I felt it was a good place again. I avoided touring the grounds with the vain hope that Corin, when he returned, would still want to show me everything he'd done.

When it got cold outside, I watched my Jane Austen movie collection and thought about myself, my life, my relationships. It was a tough time, being that I didn't particularly like the conclusions I was coming to. I'd discovered that I was the type of person who put others' needs before my own, and not always in a good way. Worse, I thought of relationships like fairy tales, that my love should sweep me off my feet and that feeling would last forever, and we wouldn't even have to work at it. I thought I had that with Amenon, but when it came down to it, despite his charm and good looks, he wasn't very much fun. We didn't even really talk about anything other than him. Corin, the one others might find dull, actually challenged me more than anyone ever had. He looked after me and he listened. He was good for me, and I'd blown it. After acknowledging this, I spent the next week crying, beginning almost as soon as I was done working, which is why I tried to work until I was nearly dropping from exhaustion.

During the remainder of my time at the chateau, Mía and I became, if not true friends, then good colleagues. She was very professional and she was also smart—the topic of Corin Rachat never came up between us. We stuck to business and were able to finish the job—including fixing the wall in the Ship Room—ahead of schedule.

I had one last week of tying up loose ends, signing off on certain jobs, and making sure Brittany paid Mía. Then, after finding out from Brittany where the furniture was stored, I hired a crew to move it back into the chateau. Corin, conscientious as always, had drawn up a plan to follow, making it easy to know what went where. Even so, I made a few changes that he would likely change back when he returned. But I wanted to put my personal stamp on the job, even if it didn't last.

Now here I was, standing in the foyer of Chateau de Sowles and taking my last walk-through. I wanted and needed to say goodbye. To all parts of the house. Since that night with Amenon, I'd avoided the tower like the plague. I'm glad to say I didn't feel any strange vibes since then, but I wasn't taking chances. Tonight, however, my last night here, I needed to purge some ghosts.

The door to the tower opened easily and I wearily headed up the steps. For one brief moment, I paused and took a deep breath, then I entered the room. There, standing at the window, was a man. My heart nearly jumped out of my chest. *Oh, no. Not again!* Amenon was supposed to be dead. He wasn't meant to be here anymore. I didn't want him, I—

The man turned around. "Corin!" I cried, a wave of relief washing through me.

"Vi," he greeted me with a nod. He was distant, almost formal, and my joy at seeing him drained away. "I was hoping you'd come up here before you left."

"I came to say goodbye. To exorcise the ghosts, or should I say one particular ghost?" My nervous laugh sounded fake, even to my own ears. Why was he here? What did he want? To chastise me one last time for lying to him? I bit my lip and straightened my shoulders. So be it. I deserved it.

"Do you miss him?" he asked, surprising me.

I didn't bother pretending I didn't know who he was referring to. "Not in the least. I feel like I had a near miss, actually, and I'm grateful for it."

He frowned. "You are?"

"You were right about me being a moon dweller. About me being too much of a dreamer, too sentimental, too unrealistic. All those things caused me a lot of trouble, and I'm done with that person. It's time to grow up."

His eyes widened. "Don't do that! All those things—they're what I love about you!"

"What?" You could have knocked me over with a feather.

"I love that you're a dreamer, Vi! It's just that, well…" He took a hesitant step toward me. "You see, my mother warned me away from people like you. I think that's why I dated Jessica, and maybe why she cheated on me…because I never really loved her. Not truly. My mother told me I needed to stay rooted, to never let my ego get too big, to never let my anger or emotions take control." He paused and glanced at the bed. "Now I know why."

"Because you have some of Amenon in you," I said cautiously, even though a part of me was singing inside because he hadn't truly loved Jessica.

"I do, and because of that, well, I can't be with anyone, even though I desperately want to be with you, Vi. You know the stigma I carry, and you know that it shouldn't be allowed to continue on."

"What are you talking about?" I pushed out through dry lips. "Are you saying you want to be with me?"

"That's what you got out of that?" he said, one eyebrow cocked.

I laughed, then hiccupped. "Oh, Corin! Do you or don't you?"

"I do. But I can't!" He stomped the floor in frustration and his childish act gave me heart. "I can't let this madness continue."

"But Corin," I pleaded, taking a matching step toward him. "You're nothing like Amenon."

He glanced at me. "Because I'm dull and he's the life of the party?"

"You're not dull! In fact, while you were gone I realized you were the one guy who has ever truly challenged me. Amenon was charming, but charm has its limits. You're the one who gives his time and money to people. You're kind and good and decent."

"I'm not sure those are selling points for a lover."

"You know what I mean! You're the kind of person a girl would want to marry."

He glanced out the window, then back at me, unconvinced, almost bleak. "You know why I do good deeds, Vi?" he asked, his voice so low it was almost a whisper. I shook my head, not sure I wanted to know. "Because I'm afraid of becoming what my mother feared. She never said what that was, only implied what it might be, and the implication was that if I didn't control myself, I would become a monster."

Ignoring his rigid stance, I rushed to him and placed my hand on his arm. He looked down with a pained expression, but I didn't move it. "Corin, monsters don't read books to children at story time."

"They do if they're planning to eat them," he said grimly. "It's a great lure, don't you think?"

"Were you planning to eat them?" I peered up into his face, taking in his gorgeous eyes, sad now, and so weary.

A small smile tugged at his mouth. "A few of them looked rather tasty."

"Kids can look tasty," I agreed. "Especially the rounder ones. But the main thing is, you didn't eat them."

"No, I didn't."

"And sometimes the best we can ask of ourselves is to not do bad things."

"Oh, Vianne," Corin moaned and pulled me into his arms. "Say you don't hate me."

"I don't hate you, Corin!" I cried, sinking into him. His arms were strong and sure as they encircled me and held tight, his lean chest a wonderfully safe port for my head. "Just the opposite," I whispered. "I think I'm beginning to love you."

"Don't say that," he murmured against my head, his breath hot against my skin. "It's bad enough that I've fallen for you. Knowing you share my feelings only makes it harder to stay away from you."

"You don't need to stay away from me, Corin. You fought the darkness in you and you won. You're safe."

"But if we had kids…"

"They'd be absolutely gorgeous."

He relaxed in my arms and I knew he was relenting. "I'm not like Amenon, you know."

"I know. I think that's what we're establishing here."

"No. I mean I'm not exciting like him."

"But you are exciting, Corin. I can feel it. You have this passion inside you. You just keep a tight lid on it. Now that you know you're not a monster, you can let go. Oh, the things we can do!"

He chuckled. "You would be good for me."

"I would."

"So you're willing to accept me, imperfections and all?"

"As long as you're willing to accept me and mine. I did neglect to tell you I wasn't with AA&D."

"I reacted the way I did because I thought you were going to end up like Jessica, telling me lies, hiding things. Thinking more on it—I had a lot of time to think, actually—I began to understand why you did it."

"I did it to get the job, Corin," I said, almost proudly. I was finally breaking free of my parents' stultifying need to constantly present a perfect face to the world. "Let's not sugarcoat it. And I didn't tell you about the tower because I didn't want you finding out about Amenon. I wanted him to be my secret. I'm no angel."

"So I guess we're equally depraved?"

"That about sums it up."

He laughed and pulled back. Looking down into my eyes, he reached up and stroked my jaw with the back of his hand, his knuckles grazing my skin lightly, sending shivers up and down my spine. "You are the most exciting, most beautiful woman I've ever known, Vianne, and I'll do anything to keep you."

"Including dishes?" I tilted my head coquettishly.

"Does it count if I load the dishwasher?"

I laughed. "Only if you unload it, too."

He leaned forward. "I'm going to kiss you now."

"I was wondering when you were going to get around to that."

His lips touched mine and I felt a spark go through me. Throwing my arms around him, I kissed him back. His hands were everywhere, touching me in places that made me sigh with ecstasy, made me want more.

At last I pulled back. "This is a lot of fun, my love, but I haven't eaten since lunch and I'm starving. I'm feeling pretty lightheaded."

"That's my excellent kissing."

"Yes, mostly. But some of it is food deprivation. I still owe you supper. Spaghetti okay?"

"Perfect, as long as it's followed by breakfast." He raised his eyebrows devilishly.

"Why, Mr. Rachat, you surprise me!"

He grinned, a real, honest to goodness smile, not just an attempt at one. "Good."

"Come on." I took his arm and led him to the door, then paused. "Wait a second. How did you get up here this time? Did you figure out the lever?"

"I went through the library."

"The library? I thought the doors wouldn't open for you."

He shrugged. "They do now."

"Strange," I mused.

"Very," he agreed absently, winding one of my curls around his finger.

"It's like, well, it's like—" I broke off, not really wanting to voice my worries.

"It's like the house has finally accepted me completely as its owner."

"Exactly," I agreed, but that wasn't what I was going to say. I was going to say, "It's like you're Amenon."

But he wasn't. I could tell. Corin felt different from Amenon. And yet... And yet there was something about him now that reminded me of Amenon, a sort of confidence, a charm, a mischievous gleam in his eye. And he'd called me Vianne earlier, when he'd only ever called me Vi.

"Should we go have some fun, mon amour?" He peered down into my eyes, his own full of deviltry and promises of heavenly delights to come.

I looked at him for a long moment, then pulled him from the room. "Definitely."

The End... Or Is It?

☾

Two years later, after making sure Corin and I really did love each other, that we held the same beliefs on the important things (like me keeping my career and him staying home with the kids), and that we wouldn't drive each other nuts living together, we got married. My parents attended the wedding, having reinstated my Golden Child status after finding out what a big deal Corin was in the New England community.

The minute they heard Corin and I were dating, they dumped Jason like a bad habit. But he landed on his feet when he asked Ashley Winterton to marry him only a few months after we broke up for good, and she said yes. When I heard about the proposal, I was as happy for him as he was for me, which wasn't much. I certainly didn't want him back, but that didn't mean I wanted Ashley to get her way. Every time I saw her, she practically crowed with delight at her success. But when she realized I was with *the* Corin Rachat, she was the one who had to eat crow. It was lovely to see.

At any rate, Jason had it made now. Ashley was so rich he wouldn't ever have to work again. It's a year after they tied the knot now and he has yet to make an attempt to find a job.

Having to deal with my parents' hypocrisy and Ashley's latest attempts to ingratiate herself with me was all rather revolting, but having turned over a new leaf with my vow to be more mature and adult-like, I only let them bother me a little bit. Corin might beg to differ on that, so don't ask him.

We held the wedding at the chateau and it was every bit as magical and wonderful as I hoped. We hired a wedding planner, thank goodness, so all I had to do was point and she would make it happen. Ryan and Anna were my bridesmaids. Ryan looked very dapper in his Victorian suit—yes, all the members of the wedding party wore period piece outfits—and Anna was resplendent in a lavender dress. She actually wore color, which goes to show that she was a changed person. She and Clint were very much in love and I was very happy for her. Ryan and Tom are *still* dating and are perfect for each other, a sort of yin and yang match. A few months ago Ryan and Anna moved to Portsmouth and started their own design business, so I now pretty much have everything I want in the world. I'm a lucky gal.

Before the wedding, I made sure to reach out to my siblings, Nick and Kat. They were actually pretty cool about everything, and I'm thankful siblings share more genes with each other than they do with their parents. It also helped that Corin sent some accounting work Nick's way, and asked Kat to serve as legal counsel for a new non-profit project he was working on. They liked him from the beginning, actually, just for him. When he showed them around Portsmouth, introducing them to some big names, that didn't hurt, either.

Peter Paddington came to the wedding, along with his six kids and beautiful wife, but Mía opted out. She claimed a previous commitment, although we both knew the real reason, a reason I didn't share with Corin or he'd never want to work with her again, and I couldn't do that to her. I didn't blame her for staying away. I would have done the same thing.

I eventually got the conservatory I wanted, though convincing Corin to make a change wasn't easy. He liked things as they were, still stuck on keeping the chateau as it was in the 1890s. I thought he'd get over that, but apparently I was wrong. Fortunately, I found a design that was terribly Victorian and Gothic and eventually he agreed to it. The funny thing is, he now spends more time in there than I do. He's gotten into growing exotic plants, the kook.

So we are very happy.

But things aren't entirely perfect. I've noticed that Corin has become a very warm person, and by warm, I mean body temperature-wise. Could it be genetics, passed down from Amenon? Maybe. Though I didn't notice him being any warmer than the usual before Amenon disappeared.

And then there's that mischievous gleam in his eye, and the excursions we take, simply looking, as Corin puts it, "for excitement." Of course, these traits might have been in Corin all along, and it took our relationship to bring them out.

Maybe.

But I have to wonder… Did Amenon ever really, truly leave? Or is he still with us, biding his time, waiting to be freed once more?

I don't know the answer to that. All I can do is love Corin as he is, enjoy our little adventures, and wait for our child to be born. And while I wait, I will hope with all my heart and soul that he doesn't have deep brown eyes and dark, curly hair, and a penchant for getting into trouble.

☾

An Excerpt from Kristina Schram's

The Wrath

Praise for *The Wrath*...

"Loved this book."

"Satisfyingly creepy."

"I couldn't put it down."

"The story drew me in from the very first paragraph."

Chapter One

✴

The Man on the Train

The window seat called to me and I seized on it like a talisman. I wanted to believe that the little haven it created would shelter me. It was an illusion that I needed, for the simple reason that this journey I'd embarked upon was not safe. Not in the least.

Still, here I was in England, safely seated, with train schedule clutched in one slightly trembling hand, the cryptic letter that had started it all, folded and worn from many failed attempts to interpret its message, tucked in the front pocket of my new slacks. I felt nervous and a little bit frightened, but also mildly triumphant, even a bit rebellious. Instead of retreating, as was my typical response to challenges, this time I had dived forward. Of course, I'd only done so because *this time* I felt in my heart that if I didn't follow my mysterious quest through to its end, I wouldn't recover from the failure.

Besides, my mother wouldn't have let me return home. And when I thought about it, nor did I especially want to go back. I was embarking on an adventure of a lifetime. For too long I had lived at the periphery of life, hiding out in the shadows cast by the brighter and more beautiful. I'd wasted altogether too much time ducking humankind.

"Is this seat taken?"

The voice startled me, its deep resonance breaching my port as ruthlessly as a torpedo. The train, on its way to Newton Abbot, had stopped just outside London. The passengers, all of whom had been waiting impatiently on the platform, swiftly boarded the train—a rush of businessmen and women in dark suits, teenagers sporting ear buds and texting with frantic thumbs, and the requisite horde of tourists, bedecked in practical clothes and cameras.

I glanced to my left and then up, straight into the most challenging eyes I'd ever seen—eyes that dared me to say yes, to say anything at all. I hadn't the breath to speak so I shook my head. No, the seat was not taken. With a brusque nod, the man slipped into the chair opposite me, next to the window. He was six or seven inches taller than my five-foot-seven frame, his legs as long as a distance runner's. He took up a lot of room and with nowhere else to go I felt myself pushing back into my seat.

After a bit of maneuvering, we now sat knee to knee, or more accurately, knee to shin, with only an inch or two to separate us. His closeness made me feel prickly inside. Several itchy spots broke out along my back, none of which I could reach gracefully. First I tried to ignore them. When that failed, I attempted to relieve the itch without using my hands, which only made me look like a goon as I wiggled and rubbed my back against the seat as surreptitiously as I could, while hoping no one noticed.

Moments later a crowd of boisterous tourists entered our car and pushed their way into seats. Talking loudly, their presence and my itching back left me no space to study my seatmate, no time to wonder, did I register in his thoughts at all? How very aggravating, especially when all I wanted to do was look at the man who was taking up all my space, and scratch my back, of course.

A large man, uneasily dressed in a navy blue, off-the-rack, polyester business suit with shiny elbows, breathily took the seat beside me. The scent of fried fish and the salty tang of sweat engulfed me soon after he sat. His girth, like too many scoops of ice cream piled on a cone, spilled over the armrest, into my sanctum. Itches forgotten, I scooted over toward the window to avoid his hefty elbow swinging like a pendulum as he attempted to stow his battered briefcase below his seat. My knees banged against the passenger opposite me, yet he made no effort to move out of the way.

The businessman straightened up with a sigh. "Do yeh happen to know what time it is, Miss?" An innocent, entirely normal question to ask of a person, yet I avoided his eyes as though he'd just asked me for my phone number, focusing instead on a drop of sweat sliding down his ample cheek and past a mole the size of a pencil eraser on his jaw. "I lost me watch yesterday and now I don't know whether I'm coming or going."

I shook my head. "I'm in the same boat as you, I'm afraid," I told him with an apologetic shrug. "Or is it train?" My attempt at a joke appeared to fall flat and I hurried on, "I'm not sure I have the right hour. I've just come over from the States. I meant to check at Paddington, but I just made the train myself." I glanced at my new wristwatch, silver and gold, a going-away present from my father. "I think it might be around 1:00."

In unison, we looked toward our neighbor across from us, expectantly. Feeling our gaze, he reluctantly peered over his paper. His heavy lids gave an annoyed flicker, then he slipped a long-fingered hand into the pocket of his gray tweed jacket to pull out an impressive silver pocket watch. Pressing a button at the top, the face popped open.

"2:05," he corrected me, barely glancing my way. The face closed and the watch was promptly hidden away again, quick as a mouse. He was

English, then, his ethnicity coming through loud and clear in a mere three syllables.

Before I changed my watch over to the correct time, I made sure to memorize the initials I'd seen engraved on his watch…N.A.T. The letters should be easy to remember. Add a 'G' at the beginning and you'd have the tiny, flying pests that swarmed a person on humid summer days in Minnesota, and which had a surprisingly nasty bite considering their size. The man seated across from me, hidden behind his paper, was as annoying as those little bugs. Except, unlike the gnat, he didn't swarm a person, nor did he bite. At least for the moment. He was infuriating in his elusiveness—the newspaper serving as his shield against common people like myself.

"Really?" the big man wheezed good-humoredly. "Well, I'll be buggered. That's a first. I'm right on time!" He beamed, his full, red cheeks like bulbs. "I don't ride the train much, but me car's in the garage, and I hate riding the bus as much as I hate not having pudding for dinner. No room to stretch yer legs on these things."

"The chairs are very close together…" I put forth.

"Too right." He blotted at his face with a stained, vaguely pink handkerchief. "So ye're from the States, are yeh?" I bobbed my head. "Which part?"

"That depended on my parents," I told him.

"Army brat, eh?"

"Actor brat," I amended. There was a reason I knew about Minnesota summers. We once stayed in Minneapolis for five months—my parents were in a play at the Guthrie Theater— bugging out just before winter set in.

He gave a shout of laughter. "And now ye're here."

"And now I'm here."

He pushed back against his seat, chuckling. The chair tried to maintain its uprightness, then gave in, leaning backward like a sapling in the wind. "Well, be a luv and wake me at Newbury. I'm whacked." A moment later, he was snoring softly; his cavernous nostrils above a mustache the color of ginger quivering delicately.

Newbury Station didn't come quickly enough. While I liked the man, I soon tired of fighting off his elbow. The appendage took up a surprising amount of space, crowding me against the cold glass. When we finally rolled to a stop nearly half an hour later, I nudged the man. He snorted, then stared at me blankly. "This is your stop."

"Right!" he cried, moving quickly to grab his scuffed, brown briefcase. His fingernails, short and square and surrounded by doughy flesh, were buffed to a high shine. Crappy suit, lovely manicure. Go figure. "Well, goodbye to you." He nodded at our fellow passenger, who didn't look up to respond. My new friend winked at me. "Good luck with that one," it said.

Watching him squeeze his way down the narrow aisle, I was surprised to discover that the car had emptied like fish from a net. I had been abandoned. I frantically consulted my schedule. The next stop wasn't due for quite some time.

So it was just me, and the Impenetrable Wall. Super.

After ten minutes of fidgeting with the zipper on my purse and staring out the window, I finally gave in. I could no longer deny myself another peek at NAT, though I'm not sure why I felt so curious about someone so supercilious. At the moment, he was reading his paper, by all appearances thoroughly engrossed in its contents. But as my gaze slid over toward him, he shifted and my eyes dashed back toward the window, spooked like a child. I didn't want him to catch me ogling him. I had some pride, deeply buried, which resurrected now and again. Besides, I felt quite sure his big head didn't need any more flattery filling it—I imagine it was on the verge of exploding as it was.

A minute later, I tried again. I couldn't help it. Not looking at him was like trying not to goggle at a car wreck. His paper had his full attention and I thought he must be reading about a murder to warrant such scrutiny. More likely, though, it was probably only the stock report, all that talk of mergers and pork bellies making his cold, little heart go pitta-pat.

The paper drooped and dipped to neck level and my eyes zoomed back in. He was in his late-twenties, I calculated, maybe ten years older than myself. He had dark hair, freshly cut, worn close to the scalp on the sides and longer on top, and brown, deep-set eyes. Slightly curved lips, the lower a bit plumper than its mate, punctuated his pale skin. His ears were a bit on the large side, which his haircut didn't bother to hide; his long nose boasted a bump centered in the middle of its slope. All in all, his features were reasonably attractive, I conceded. He wore a dark, heather-gray blazer over a light blue oxford, the two colors bringing out the best in each other. Except for his ink-stained fingers, he looked expensive. He was someone my mother would call, 'the right sort of person.'

Naturally, I disliked him.

Without warning, the paper gave a bow. He was folding it, putting it away. My eyes quickly slid back to the window, taking refuge in the green fields.

"What are you looking at?" The words, coming a minute later, couldn't have been more unexpected. My eyes jumped back to him.

"You," I said, realizing as soon as the word leaped out of my mouth that the retort had sounded much better in my head. I cringed. Out loud it sounded purposely childish. I sighed and my fingers automatically laced together, as though seeking solace, and I felt hot and cold all at once. Sophistication has never been my forte.

A dark eyebrow rose. "I meant, before. Out there." He nodded at the window. "What do you see in all that?"

"I guess I see my future," I blurted out, once again forgetting to think before I spoke. My mother hated it when I was cryptic like this, but sometimes I couldn't help myself. My future *was* what I was seeing, or at least thinking about. Unfortunately, my honesty often came out sounding flippant, as though I were playing games with people.

"And what does your future hold?" His smile was condescending; he might just as well have inserted "my dear" at the end of the question. To him I was just a way to pass the time, like a cat toying with his four-legged—less than sublime, but it will have to do—dinner.

Knowing I was about to be dismissed, I plowed ahead anyway. "It holds grief," I replied in my best gypsy fortuneteller voice. I pointed at the raindrops starting to spot the thick windowpane and my finger absently traced one's wayward path down to the sill. Based on the fact that my past had been full of trouble, going mainly by the name Silvia Filmore, also known as my mother, it was a good answer. "But I think it also holds endless possibilities." I gestured at the broad expanse of moor that stretched on forever, into the distance. My greatest wish was to have a life of choices and paths to take, without being steered—forced—down them. So far, my wish has remained only that—a wish.

He nodded, thoughtful, his dark eyes on mine. "Pain and possibilities. That sounds like a good life to me, Madame Gypsy." He ran a finger around the back of his collar as though to loosen its hold. I had the fleeting impression that he wore formal clothes out of habit, and perhaps might have chosen something altogether more comfortable if he put any thought into it.

I laughed in surprise, the sound echoing as loudly as a crow's caw. "Pain is good?"

"Pain is growth." He stopped, his wide brow crumpling, as though warring thoughts fought beneath its thin layer of skin. "Or it can be. Some people do the wrong thing with their pain."

"Maybe they only do what they know best. It's not wrong, just all they know."

His expression was wry, almost grim. "Then they should try harder to know more."

I leaned forward. "Geniuses know a lot and look at how they suffer."

"They know facts, not necessarily themselves."

"Or maybe they know themselves too well," I answered back, enjoying this. "They know they have a dark side."

"Perhaps," he conceded. His fingers tapped a slow beat against the armrest; the sound like drums before an execution.

The rain started to pelt the glass in earnest, blurring the view. "Which one are you?" I ventured. "Self-aware, or unenlightened?"

He shrugged. "I don't know, probably somewhere in-between. You?" He leaned forward as though truly interested in what I had to say. We were very close now; I could smell his cologne and it made me think of spring and new beginnings.

I felt a tiny thrill flutter in my stomach. Could he really be interested in my opinion? How exciting and unexpected. The problem was, I wasn't sure how to answer his question. Before this conversation I would've said that I knew myself too well. My character was a topic I'd thoroughly dissected and found wanting at every inspection. The constant search exhausted me. Each time I hoped to find something redeeming—something that made me who I was, unique and worthy of notice—and each time, I failed. I could do a lot of things reasonably well—Mother had made sure of that—but nothing I did was my *own*.

"I'm starting to realize that I don't know myself at all." I frowned, wishing I could take the revealing words back. I wasn't used to sharing. On the few dates I'd been on, and with the few, temporary friends I'd had, I never spoke of myself at a depth more personal than my favorite band or what I liked on my pizza. I think I was afraid to go deeper, afraid of people's judgment—worse, afraid they would find there was nothing there.

He stared at me, studying me. He was entirely aware of my presence, I realized. I stared back at him. Typically I would have looked away, down at my feet, back out the window. But not today. There was too much at stake, though I had no idea what was at stake, or why I felt this way. Maybe it was the foreign country, maybe because I might never see him again.

"Where are you headed?" he asked, still looking at me. He leaned his aristocratic head back against the chair, away from me, his chin raised, his deep, brown eyes pensive. I pulled back, too, wishing fervently that I knew what he was thinking so I could say what he wanted to hear.

"Filmore Estate in Ellwood," I told him. "Near Dartmoor."

He sat up, his knees pulling away from mine. "Pardon?"

I frowned, pulling out the directions from my pants pocket. "Filmore Estate in Ellwood. It says right here." I held up the piece of paper for him to see. He snatched it out of my hand.

Face drawn, he handed the directions back to me after reading them, and shook his head. "You can't go there."

My heart beat a little harder. "What do you mean I can't go there? Is there something wrong?"

"There's something wrong all right." His dark eyes were wary, almost angry, the tips of his excessive ears reddening.

I waited. "Could you explain?" I asked when he said nothing more.

He shook his head, turning to look out the window at the rain. "I can't believe this. Of all the bloody rotten luck."

He was scaring me. I leaned toward him again, imploring. "Please tell me what's wrong. Are my aunts hurt? Insane? What?"

There was a groan. His profile was hard, a shadow of stubble just beginning to mark his jaw. "They're your *aunts*? Not just friends you call aunt? A quaint custom your family practices?"

"According to my mother, we are truly related. What is all this?"

"I can't say," he mumbled, searching about for his things. He grabbed his neatly folded newspaper and black leather briefcase, and stood up nearly hitting his head on the overhang. "If you'll excuse me, I cannot stay here. Not with you."

I fell back against my chair with a thump, stunned, and watched as he ducked low to exit the swaying car. After he disappeared, I wished, childishly, that on the way out he'd hit his perfect head. Then he'd have something to remember me by. Because it wouldn't be my name he'd recall.

He hadn't bothered to ask what it was.

Other Books by Kristina Schram

The Wrath: A Paranormal Gothic Romance

When a cryptic letter arrives from Evalina Filmore's two aunts, she travels to England to find out what they want, figuring this will be the chance to experience the romantic adventure she has so often read about in her beloved gothic novels. When she arrives, she finds the eerie mansion, the strange atmosphere, and the adventure, as hoped. But there are troubles. On the train, she meets a man who, upon learning her name, walks away without a word of explanation. Not long after, she passes unharmed through a wood called the Wrath, even though, as she later learns, no one ever has. While in the Wrath, she meets a tantalizing and seductive stranger, one who just might be her gothic hero. But he has a secret. It seems everyone in the village does, including her aunts, and it's up to Evie to figure out what is going on before the Wrath lures her in and never lets her go.

I Shall Return: A Paranormal Gothic Romance

Journalist, Lily MacKenzie, is off to the Highlands of Scotland on a newspaper assignment. But in reality, she has another mission in mind, one she desperately needs to keep secret. Her arrival starts off unexpectedly when she encounters Greg Huntington, a stranger who seems to know her even though they've never met. Things grow more peculiar as she gets to know the Derings of Dundeid Castle, the lodging where she's staying. Andrew Dering, the god-like laird, is welcoming enough, but appears to be hiding something. His cousin, Vivian, seems intent on sabotaging Lily's efforts, while another relation, Ophelia, sees Lily as her savior from a mysterious illness. As Lily works to unravel the mystery that set her on her journey, events grow increasingly complicated and dangerous, and she finds herself caught between two very different men. The reason behind her mission makes it difficult to trust either one, but when she finally ends up choosing, things go very wrong, and Lily ends up fighting for her sanity and her very life.

Mayhem at Nepenthe Manor: A Pandora Belfry Adventure (Book One)

 Precocious and morbidly obsessed with death, Pandora Belfry has spent her entire life at Nepenthe Manor, a dark, Gothic mansion also known as the local loony bin. Recently turned fourteen and growing exasperated with her stifling life, Pandora wants two things more than anything else in the world—to make her escape from the asylum, and to get her mom to finally act like a real mom. Until these wishes are granted, she acts as self-imposed ringleader to a wayward posse of inmates. Known amongst themselves as the Secret Six, Pandora and her friends spend their time at Nepenthe Manor stirring up trouble—holding weekly Midnight Meetings to concoct schemes, sneaking into places like the Nepenthe family cemetery and the forbidden attic, and generally doing everything they can to avoid the curse of living a mundane life. But when a mysterious new inmate arrives at the manor, things change for Pandora, and not for the better. In retaliation for a trick she plays on him, the charming and handsome Xavier connives to take over the posse, threatens to divulge one of Pandora's biggest secrets, and refuses to tell her what he did to get himself locked up. This boy is obviously hiding something, and it's up to Pandora to use whatever nefarious means necessary to find out what it is, before he destroys the only world she's ever known.

The Labyrinth of Lunacy: A Pandora Belfry Adventure (Book Two)

 Pandora Belfry, along with the eccentric members of her posse, is back, and looking for trouble. The posse's first order of business is to break into the off-limits labyrinth, even though they can't find its door. Against her mother's wishes, Pandora also works to solve the mystery of her father's identity. Perhaps he's a staff member, or maybe he's the stranger haunting the beach late at night. Topping the list of possible dad candidates is the new therapist, Dr. Steele, who keeps popping up in Pandora's life like an annoying, but handsome, nanny. To add to her problems, Pandora's date with the slimy, but oddly fascinating, Dougie Daft, is fast approaching. She isn't sure how to get out of it, or even if she dares to. Her new acquaintance, Giganticus, certainly doesn't want her to go, but if she doesn't, she'll be obligated to Dougie Daft, and that's the last thing any sane person would want… Come join the posse on their latest, a-maze-ing adventure. Just one warning: Watch out for snakes!

The Changeling's Tale: A Paranormal Fantasy
(Book One of The Forest Immortal Saga)

When sixteen-year-old Gabriel Hawthorne's dad gets sick, Gabe and his brothers are forced to move to an old family farm in Maine to make ends meet. From the moment they arrive, Gabe realizes something is not quite right about the brooding forest surrounding their new home, and does everything he can to avoid it. He soon finds out that there are good reasons to stay away from the woods. People have gone in and never returned. Pets around town are disappearing - believed to have been taken by a wild creature - and a strange woman warns Gabe to stay away from the forest or "they will get ye." But when he discovers that as a child he went missing in the forest for two days, with no memory of what had happened to him, he becomes truly frightened. When the inhabitants of the Forest Immortal come for him once more, Gabe learns what monsters lurk within the dark trees. But this time, the forest doesn't want to let him go. This time it intends to keep him - and use him for its own wicked purposes.

Oswald's Revenge: A Paranormal Fantasy
(Book Two of The Forest Immortal Saga)

When the first perplexing riddle appears on the secret door to his turret room, Gabe Hawthorne knows he's in trouble. He suspects Oswald, leader of the Rogues, a troublemaker who has claimed Gabe is trying to usurp his title, King of the Forest Immortal. But Gabe wants nothing to do with being King, or the forest itself. He just wants to solve the riddles and end this mess once and for all. Standing in his way are two local busybodies determined to take ownership of the forest and cut down all the trees to make way for malls and condos. Gabe, along with his two brothers and their friends, race to stop them, but are routed at each turn by a host of enemies. Gabe must solve the riddles and end this dangerous game before someone dies, but as the cold of winter approaches, time is running out. If Gabe cannot complete their mission soon, he could end up trapped in the Forest Immortal… Forever.

Meltdown: A Paranormal Fantasy
(Book Three of The Forest Immortal Saga)

It has been a long, cold winter, and Gabe Hawthorne is growing uneasy. Trouble is brewing. The Rogues are showing no signs of awakening from their slumber, and the threat of eviction looms over Gabe's family. And then Gabe discovers a powerful cloak that makes him hear voices and incites him to do dangerous things. To make matters worse, trouble ignites between Gabe and Jake Morrigan, son of the determined real estate agent who wants to destroy the forest and turn the land into a tourist attraction. After a fight between Jake and Gabe, Jake goes missing and Mrs. Morrigan points the finger at Gabe. Soon half the town thinks he's guilty. When the inhabitants of the Forest Immortal at last begin to awake, Gabe wishes they'd stayed asleep. A sickness has infected them, rotting their minds and weakening their bodies. As matters escalate, Gabe is forced to make a terrible choice - his life or the forest. But if the dark forces have their way, neither will escape death.

The Chronicles of Anaedor: The Prophecies (Book One)

Strange things happen to fifteen-year-old Lavida Mors. Maybe that's why her father sends her away to Portal Manor, a mysterious family estate she never knew existed. Lavida quickly discovers that not everything at Portal Manor is as it seems when she stumbles across a secret passage to a hidden world - Anaedor. Populated by strange and powerful, supposedly mythical, creatures, Anaedor has descended into a world of turmoil and anarchy. It is a realm on the verge of war, and an evil being seeks to seize control while chaos rules. To do so, the power-hungry fiend must eliminate the *One,* whom the Prophecies predict will destroy the evil of Anaedor. Unfortunately for Lavida, there are those who believe *she* is *One.* On the order of the evil creature, the enigmatic and dangerous Frio takes Lavida and her friends captive, forcing them to stand trial for crimes against the citizens of Anaedor. In attempting to escape the dark forces of this volatile world, Lavida is compelled to make a terrible choice: reveal a secret she has harbored nearly all her life or let her friends die.

The Chronicles of Anaedor: The Return to Anaedor (Book Two)

After escaping from Anaedor, fifteen-year-old Lavida Mors starts a training course with her guardian, Mrs. Keeper, in hopes of improving her magic skills before the dreaded Malvado returns. But while trying out a new spell, something awful happens, and she vows never to do magic again. When an unexpected discovery forces her to return to Anaedor, she is faced with her most terrifying challenges yet. Strife reigns in the hidden underground world as lootings and burnings break out, and numerous enemies conspire to capture Lavida, fight her, even kill her. Without magic, how can she possibly flee from dragons, escape the Goblins, outwit the ruthless Frio, and fight a duel with a young rebel intent on proving she's not the *One?* Time is running out. If Lavida doesn't learn to trust herself and her skills, a series of catastrophic events will ensure that she and her friends never make it out of Anaedor again.

The Chronicles of Anaedor: The Lost Ones (Book Three)

Sixteen-year-old Lavida Mors is in for a long, hot summer. With no way into Anaedor, the Lost Ones seeking refuge at Portal Manor are taking over the house, creating havoc and misery. Lavida is overwhelmed trying to keep up with her chores, learning magic, and fighting off the Pixies—tiny creatures who have made it their mission to harass Lavida at every turn. Meanwhile, unbeknownst to the residents of Portal Manor, the AAK is hard at work opening a Portal to the Upland. They are successful at last, and the twins, Loria and Darian, on the run from Malvado, along with the AAK leader, Trey, manage to make it through the opening only to have it collapse behind them. With no way back into Anaedor, they are forced to take refuge at Portal Manor. As they try to settle into this strange new life, tensions between the humans and the Anaedorians grow, creating rifts between Lavida and her friends. To make matters worse, Frio, Amoral Hunter Leader, is hiding out in the Upland, and when he goes after Lavida, he starts in motion a series of events that could end up costing Lavida her life.

The Chronicles of Anaedor: The Uprising (Book Four)

In this final book of the Anaedor series, sixteen-year-old Lavida Mors is placed in grave danger when a group of young Anaedorians infiltrate the Upland. Their orders are to eliminate the evil one, whom they believe is Lavida, and then launch an Uprising to take over the Upland. Disguising themselves as humans, they befriend the unwitting Lavida and her friends, allowing them easy access to Portal Manor. Darian and Loria, Blendar twins and Lavida's friends, and Trey, ex-AAK rebel leader, have come to the Upland to warn Lavida about the intruders. But before they can do so, Darian learns something about Lavida's past that turns him against her. Surrounded by betrayal and danger, and faced with an astonishing revelation that makes her question everything about her existence, Lavida feels increasingly alone and afraid. If she cannot convince Darian and the others that she is not the evil being they think she is, she will lose everything to the Uprising.

The Battle to Become an Author: When Great Expectations Go Awry

Are you looking to find an agent and/or get published? Are you a published author frustrated with the whole process? Or have you simply heard the horror stories and are looking for a ray of light before plunging into the fray? In this short booklet, author Kristina Schram discusses how one's unrealistic expectations about becoming an author can contribute to feelings of negativity and isolation. Dr. Schram offers a real-world discussion of this growing issue, humorously incorporating her own experiences throughout. She also offers insights and ways to cope with the increasingly difficult battle to become a published author. Come prepared to challenge your own expectations, to laugh and to cry, and to battle against the forces conspiring to keep you from reaching your writing potential!

About the Author

Sitting at the very edge of the Atlantic Ocean –
on the New Hampshire coastline

When author, Kristina Schram, was growing up she wanted to be a star. When that didn't turn out quite like she expected, she turned her mind to achieving other goals: Earning her Ph.D. in Counseling Psychology, working as an Artist-in-Residence at local schools, being a free-lance editor and reader, coaching parks & rec basketball, protecting the earth through recycling and using green products, and publishing her first novel, a YA fantasy called The Chronicles of Anaedor: The Prophecies.

Knowing what it's like to struggle with self-doubt and lack of confidence, her biggest dream (in addition to owning a castle) is to stamp out low self-esteem for everyone, especially young people. She lives in beautiful, wooded New Hampshire with her husband, three boys, and various pets, and can also throw a tomahawk, if need be. One of her favorite things to do is walk with her dog in the woods, where she searches for the impossible around every corner. Sometimes she finds it.

For more information on Kristina Schram, feel free to make a trip to her website: www.kristinaschram.com. She's also on Facebook, Twitter, and Pinterest.